Blood Ninja III

Also by Nick Lake

BLOOD NINJA

BLOOD NINJA II
THE REVENGE OF LORD ODA

Blood Ninja III

The Betrayal of the Living

NICK LAKE

SIMON & SCHUSTER BFYR
New York London Toronto Sydney New Delhi

SIMON & SCHUSTER BFYR
An imprint of Simon & Schuster Children's Publishing Division
1230 Avenue of the Americas, New York, New York 10020

For information about special discounts for bulk purchases, please contact
Simon & Schuster Special Sales at 1-866-506-1949 or business@simonandschuster.com.

The Simon & Schuster Speakers Bureau can bring authors to your live event. For more information or to book an event, contact the Simon & Schuster Speakers Bureau at 1-866-248-3049 or visit our website at www.simonspeakers.com.

Also available in a SIMON & SCHUSTER BFYR hardcover edition
Design and cover photograph by Krista Vossen
The text for this book is set in ITC Esprit.
Manufactured in the United States of America
First SIMON & SCHUSTER BFYR paperback edition August 2013
10 9 8 7 6 5 4 3 2 1

The Library of Congress has cataloged the hardcover edition as follows:
Lake, Nick.
Blood ninja III : the betrayal of the living / Nick Lake. — 1st ed.
p. cm.
Summary: In sixteenth-century Japan, Taro enlists his friends to help
vanquish a dragon in hopes of winning a reward that would allow him to marry Hana,
but he also faces surprisingly difficult obstacles as Kenji Kira raises the dead
against him and his own flesh and blood betrays him.
ISBN 978-1-4424-2679-5 (hardcover : alk. paper)
[1. Ninja—Fiction. 2. Vampires—Fiction. 3. Dead—Fiction. 4. Japan—History—Period of civil wars, 1480–1603—Fiction.] I. Title. II. Title: Blood ninja three. III. Title: Betrayal of the living.
PZ7.L15857Bn 2012
[Fic]—dc23
2011023891
ISBN 978-1-4424-2680-1 (pbk)
ISBN 978-1-4424-2681-8 (eBook)

This one, like everything, is for Hannah

PROLOGUE

MIYAJIMA ISLAND

THE INLAND SEA

1566

The killing part was easy, the ninja had always thought. A child could do it. There were so many ways a body could die: sword strokes, blows from heavy objects, poison. It was almost comical how simple murder was.

No—the challenge was not the killing, at least when it came to people who had taken reasonable precautions against assassination; it was the approach, the strategy of it, the cunning. It required a number of abilities, from agility and impersonation to the capacity to plan far ahead, to anticipate the other's move. Just as he was now doing, with only half his concentration on the card game taking place on the table before him.

The ninja possessed all these abilities in abundance. He was a master of disguises, and he had only one mantra: Always be one step ahead. *This was why his services were so expensive. Six hundred* koku *for a life, no negotiation. As a result, he was a very rich man, and this was one of the reasons he was not giving all his attention to the game of cards, whose stakes—while high to the other men around the rustic inn's table—were nothing to him.*

The other *reason was the fisherman sitting at the other end of the room, deep in conversation with the small town's only geisha, a woman whose time cost almost as much as that of the ninja, but—presumably—with more pleasurable results. It was odd that a woman of such cultivation and beauty, not to mention such exorbitant rates, should be speaking to a mere fisherman, in such a rude hovel as this. Not just speaking to him, but apparently flirting with him, touching him, acting for all the world like she was in love with him. It was very odd. And it was for precisely this reason that the ninja was observing them so closely.*

He had been watching them, in fact, all night. Indeed, it was the need to follow the fisherman that had placed the ninja here, in this inn on the inland sea, playing cards with household servants and the poorer kind of merchant, though in these times, when little cargo could leave or enter the port town, all merchants were more or less pitiful.

The inn was little more than a room, really, of perhaps fifteen tatami mats in size, lit by whale-blubber candles. It was so close to the rocky shore that the sea could be heard, whispering on the other side of the thin wooden walls. There was no choice of drink, only sake—a rough local variety.

He glanced down at his hand, then at the player who had just put money in the pot. He raised, then turned back to watch his target. The game continued, in a sequence of murmurs, sighs, bids, and counterbids that the small part of his mind engaged on the task could have predicted down to the tiniest gestures of the players.

Fifty heartbeats from now, the fat rice merchant would fold, nervous, even though he had a better hand. This would leave the ninja free to take the pot.

Over in the other corner, the target was leaning closer to the geisha, whispering something in her ear. She threw her head back, glossy black hair shining in the light, and laughed prettily. Then she put a hand over the fisherman's hand. With her other she took from her kimono what looked like a gold necklace. She fastened the necklace around the fisherman's neck, in the manner of a keepsake, kissed him tenderly, and got up to leave. The fisherman followed her to the door, said good night to her, then returned to his sake with a smile on his face, absent-mindedly touching the necklace.

Forty-seven heartbeats . . .

Forty-eight heartbeats . . .

"I fold," said the fat merchant, a bead of sweat running down his cheek.

"Very well," said one of the more senior household servants. He jerked his head at the ninja. "I call," he said.

The ninja smiled. "As you wish." He put his cards down on the table, then scraped the pile of money toward himself, gathering it in a fold of his cloak, not waiting to see the other's cards.

"Hey!" said the man who had called him. "You haven't seen my cards yet."

"I don't need to," said the ninja. "I already know them."

Outside, the ninja followed the geisha down a dark alleyway that gave out onto a small crescent beach. He looked down, saw her footprints lit by moonlight, heading toward rocks at the far end of the bay. He followed, one eye on the sea, which even he could appreciate was beautiful. The moon was low and fat in the sky, shining a path on the still water, perhaps a path to takama ga hara, *where the gods lived in the sky. Around the headland, he could just see one of the supporting beams of the famous torii, a shrine in the form of a great red gate, its swooping roof like a gull's wing, that stood in the shallow water of the next bay along—it was a famous pilgrimage site and one of the wonders of Japan.*

But it wasn't what had brought him to this part of the world.

No—what had brought him here was before him, perhaps two ri *from the shore. A small, steep-sided island, which the locals avoided even looking at. Not out of superstition, but out of plain self-preservation: for the island was the haunt of much-feared pirates, who in recent months had grown more and more bold, to the point of halting trade from the port. That was why the ninja had come. To kill the leader of the pirates; a job that even his employer had told him was impossible. An impossible assassination! It seemed tailor-made to whet his appetite.*

Even now that he had planned it all out, he was aware of the possibilities for failure, and he knew that even if he managed to get over to the ferociously guarded island, and past the vicious pirates who lived there, to kill their king, he would probably die immediately afterward.

But he didn't mind. If he died in the execution . . . well, it would still be his greatest coup, the crowning glory of his life as a ninja, and if no one ever heard about it, well, that didn't matter either. He'd killed very important people and made their deaths look like illness, or accident. He didn't do this for the notoriety. He did it for the pleasure of winning the game.

He didn't know who had hired him, and he didn't care. There was a system—they would leave a letter for him at a certain shrine, along with instructions for where to find the money. It was best that way: better for him and better for them that he not see their faces.

He reached the rocks, drawing into the shadows out of habit. He silent-walked on the hard-packed, wet sand, one hand ready to draw his weapon. Two heartbeats later and he was behind the geisha, who was looking out to sea. He cleared his throat.

The geisha turned, gasping. Her hands went to her mouth—a classic gesture of fear in a woman, which fools might see as weak. The ninja wasn't a fool, though—always be one step ahead—and he knew the movement for what it was: a human instinct acquired through millennia of violence, an urge to protect the neck. Not, in fact, a bad idea. Of the many comically simple ways to kill a person, punching or slitting their neck was the easiest. It was absurd, really, how close the artery was to the skin. Death was a constant companion to all people, and it was as close to them at all times as the artery in their neck.

In this case, of course, the geisha's protective response seemed especially appropriate. In other circumstances, he'd have been tempted to drink her blood right there and then, drain her dry and leave her body here to be further leeched by the sea. But he wasn't ready to drink quite yet, even though she was very attractive, and he could smell and hear her blood ticking through her veins.

Slowly, she lowered her hands. "You startled me," she said.

"Evidently."

She half smiled and dropped her eyes, eyelashes long and dewy. He had to admire her training. Every fiber of her body must be screaming for her to run—people feared vampires, could sense they were not human, even if they didn't know why—but she was still playing the geisha, still going through the routine of charm.

"You gave him the necklace, I saw," he said. "But tell me: What did you learn?"

"I learned that fishermen's mouths taste of fish," she said, crinkling her nose. Then she laughed at his expression. "Don't worry. I found out everything you need to know."

He dug his nails into his palms, not wanting to hurt her. "Then tell me," he said, with infinite patience.

"There's a small warehouse," she said. "Close to the inn, with a red lantern outside. That's where he stores the rice and so forth for the island. Every week, the fisherman rows across from here to the island, with supplies. He's due to go tonight before dawn."

"I know," said the ninja. "That's why I'm here now. What about the signal?"

"You were right," the geisha replied. "He has a lamp that he takes on the boat. Dutch design, I gather. When he comes near to the island, he does three long flashes of the lamp. That tells them it's him, so they let him land without firing on him."

"And then?"

"Then he leaves the rice on the beach and rows back to the mainland."

"Good," said the ninja. "That's good."

The geisha glanced back toward the town. "I must return. The madam will be waiting."

"We said six hundred koku, *I believe," said the ninja.*

The geisha nodded, holding out her hand.

The money he had promised her was the same as his fee—he was not motivated by money, had too much of it already, in fact. In some ways, really, his services were even something of a bargain. Six hundred koku *was a fortune if the person you wanted dead was not heavily protected. But he charged the same for any job, and the same fee was a steal for the murder of a well-guarded daimyo in a castle, or a pirate king on an inaccessible island. In this particular case, he would have been happy to do the job for free, just for the thrill of it.*

He would *have been happy to do it for free—but there was the matter of his strength, and his hunger. He would need to be in peak fighting condition before the sun rose. He opened his mouth, revealing his sharp canines.*

The geisha backed away. Her already large almond eyes went wider, and her mouth turned to an O of surprise. To her credit, she didn't scream—there wouldn't be any point, this far from town—and he admired her training once again.

"I'll be missed," she stammered. "They'll find you."

"No," he said, almost sadly. "Didn't everyone see you talking to that fisherman all night? And then, when he goes missing too . . . An open-and-shut case, I think. Elopement, or murder-suicide. It doesn't really matter which. It just depends on whether they find your bodies."

That was when the fear really entered her eyes, and she did scream then—it was quite gratifying, really.

He moved in a flicker and he was on her; he knew that for her it would seem as if he crossed the space between them at the speed of thought, and in fact that was not far from how vampires moved. His teeth found her neck, and he bit down, and then he was flooded with the heat and savor of her blood.

Afterward, he pushed her body into a crevice in the rocks, ready to take it with him later and dump at sea—just as if the fisherman had taken her out on his boat.

He smiled.

Always be one step ahead.

A couple of hours later, he shipped his oars as the little rowing boat neared the sheer-sided island. He could see the break in the cliff ahead of him, the natural haven in which supplies were landed for the pirates. He lifted the lamp he had procured—ironically, for not much less than he'd promised the geisha, but then he wasn't doing this for the money—and covered, then uncovered the flame, once, twice, three times. There was no response, but he hadn't expected any. The signal was just to make sure he would not be shot through with an arrow before he could even get near.

Bringing the boat up onto the beach in a susurration of wood against sand, he jumped nimbly over the side. As soon as he was on dry land he was running, keeping his profile low, making for the forested darkness ahead of him. He dropped behind a tree, caught his breath.

He waited for several heartbeats, watching for movement, for lanterns coming down from the heights of the island. But there was nothing, as yet.

He waited for longer. He could be patient. It was one of the abilities for which he was paid.

Sometime later the ninja saw, from the sea just beyond the little harbor, three flashes of light. The fisherman was arriving, with the real shipment for the pirates. He would have to hurry now.

He listened.

From above him, the inevitable commotion. A lantern flared into life—another, another. Voices shouting, the alarm being sounded. They would have been expecting one signal—now that there had been two, they would know that an interloper had come to the island. If he had killed the fisherman, they would never have suspected.

But he wanted them to suspect, he wanted them on guard. In fact, he was counting on it.

Drawing his short-sword, he ran up through the trees, finding a rough path that could have been an animal track, but that he hoped would lead up toward the pirate lair. He could hear bodies crashing through the foliage, could see lights dancing among the trees.

Shouts from the beach. The fisherman had been apprehended, he saw when he glanced back.

He turned back again, continued running.

He had made it maybe a quarter of a ri *up the hillside when two men, one armed with a matchlock rifle and the other with an axe, stepped out from behind the trees ahead of him, barring his way. He darted forward, sword in hand, and that was when he heard the voice from behind him.*

"Drop the weapon," it said.

The ninja glanced behind him to see more guns pointing in his direction. He was smart enough to know that all those lead balls flying through the air would tear him apart, no matter how quickly his vampire skills might allow him to move aside. He raised his hands, dropping the wakizashi.

Seizing him roughly, the men fastened his arms behind his back and dragged him uphill.

He was on his knees in a natural arena, carved from the rock by ancient seas. Ahead of him, sitting on an outcropping of stone, was a hooded figure he took to be the leader of the pirates—the man he'd been paid to kill. Around him stood dozens of men, some of them hooded too, as if they wished to conceal their identities. All were armed.

He looked to his left and saw the fisherman sneering at him. The man had been restrained, at first, but when the pirates saw that he was the same man who usually brought their food and sake, they had untied him and concentrated their anger on the ninja instead. For all that, though, they were still standing close to the fisherman, their weapons in their hands. And his goods—the barrels of rice and sake—were laid out on the floor of the cavern, held, like their carrier, in uneasy suspicion until the whole situation had been resolved.

"How did you learn the signal?" said the leader suddenly. There was something strange about his voice, the ninja thought. As if it were being made by an apparatus of wood and leaves, dry things, not living flesh. It was like the sound of the wind in the trees, only with words in it. "You'll die anyway. But I would like to know. And your death might be more . . . pleasant, if you cooperate."

The ninja raised his head. He would not be cowed by those who desired his death; otherwise he would have to be always afraid. He looked at the leader, or rather at the pool of darkness that was his hood.

"I had it from a friend of yours," he said, gambling that at least one of the mainland's merchants would have seen fit to do a deal. "One of the merchants who pays you for protection. He sent me, when he heard that this vermin"—he indicated the fisherman, his gloating expres-

sion just turning to confusion and suspicion—"planned to come here and kill the pirate king, and take the island for himself."

The fisherman stared. "I planned no such thing!" he protested. Good. The ninja liked it when they protested. It made them seem less believable, even if the opposite was the case.

"I can prove it," said the ninja. "Just untie me."

One of the pirates laughed. "You must think us fools," he said. "You'll slit our throats."

"I have no weapon. And it is this snake"—again, he nodded to the fisherman—"you should fear, not me. I was sent to warn you."

The leader, on his stone seat, inclined his head. "It is true," he said at last. "The man isn't armed. Loose his bonds."

He felt the ropes around his wrists go slack, and he stood stiffly, rubbing his arms. "Bring me those barrels," he said, gesturing to the cargo the fisherman had brought. When they were in front of him, he walked round them, the pirates watching him warily all the time, then selected one.

"Open it," he said.

One of the pirates stepped forward and pried the lid off the barrel, causing rice to leak out onto the rocky floor. The ninja thrust his hand into the rice, gripped the handle of the sword concealed inside, and pulled it out. There was a collective gasp.

"This is the sword he intended to kill you with," he said. The words were only half out of his mouth when the pirates were on him, weapons leveled, but he just flipped the sword so the handle was facing the nearest one, and handed it over. "I told you. I'm here to warn you. Not to attack you."

The pirate took the sword—the ninja noticed that one of his eyes was gray and one green—and looked at it, a frown on his face.

"I've never seen that sword in my life!" the fisherman said. "He must have put it there!"

"In your rice barrel?" said the leader, in a dangerous tone, the voice still air and ash, nothing moist or human in its sound. "When his hands were tied?"

It might as well have been a command, because right then the pirates nearest to the fisherman grabbed him and held him still. Again, it struck the ninja as odd that some of them wore such deep hoods, so that he couldn't see their faces. But he couldn't think about that. He had to concentrate on the game. He had to remain one move ahead.

The fisherman was staring at him with wide-open eyes, terrified, as if he were some species of demon. But the ninja ignored him. "There's more," he said.

"Yes?" said the leader, interested now, underneath the cold languor.

"The merchant who sent me told me the price for your life," said the ninja.

The leader inclined his hooded head. "Really? I should like to know what it costs to betray me."

The ninja knew that he could not discover the necklace for himself—he would have to direct someone else, for it to be believed. "Around his neck," he said. "It's pure gold; Chinese. There is a clasp made of two heavy balls, and on one of them is engraved the kanji for power."

The fisherman had gone white. He leaned his head back, as if he could somehow get his neck out of the cavern, and with it the incriminating necklace.

"He's lying!" he yelled. "It was a geisha! She said she loved me, and she gave it to me as a keepsake. . . ." He trailed off, as if even he recognized the absurdity of the story.

At the same time, the fat pirate behind him got his hands around his neck and unclasped the necklace. He held it up, then peered at the clasp. "I can't . . ."

"Not many of our brotherhood can read," said the leader. He held his hand out. "Bring it to me."

The hooded figure on the stone seat took the necklace when it was proffered to him, raising it to examine it by the moonlight. He sucked in a breath. "The stranger speaks the truth," he said. "The kanji is here, as he described."

The pirates around the ninja took a step back, just as the ones around the fisherman drew even closer, locking him in a circle of blades—the movements complementing one another, as if the pirates were one creature, with many bodies.

"Wait . . . wait . . . ," said the fisherman, but the leader made a brusque gesture and he was dragged away.

The leader swung the necklace in his hand, looking at the ninja, or at least that was what the ninja thought. It was hard to tell, given the hood he wore. Eventually he spoke.

"You seek a reward, I presume?"

The ninja shook his head. "Only the necklace," he said.

"The necklace?"

"Yes. It was stolen from my employer, before it was given to the traitor. His wife holds it very dear."

The leader nodded, slowly. "Very well." He beckoned the ninja closer, then threw him the necklace.

The ninja caught it, throwing his body forward at the same time. His fingers stretched the chain, which wasn't gold at all, but toughened steel with thin plate over it, the heavy ball clasps perfect weights for turning a length of metal into a tool for strangling. The necklace was a manriki*—a chain weighted at each end, designed to be flicked suddenly at a target's neck, wrapping itself around. It was in the nature of a ninja's weapons to appear to be something else.*

He was a vampire, and he moved at the speed of thought. The leader of the pirates did not even get his hands up before the ninja landed on him, flicking one end of the necklace so that it spun, weighted by the clasp, around the man's neck. He could hear men rushing toward him from behind, the hush of their weapons against the air, but they would never be fast enough. Not only was the chain strong enough to choke, but he'd had it sharpened, too, in such a way that when he stretched it—just . . . so—the links presented sharp edges. Enough to cut through a man's windpipe in seconds.

Of the many ways to kill a person, the neck really was the easiest.

The ninja squeezed, hard, and as he felt the chain dig into the man's esophagus—dig surprisingly quickly and easily, actually—he felt the pleasure of a job well done. He had gotten onto the island, and he had gotten past the pirates by ensuring that he was captured by them. In short, he had been one move ahead, all night.

He squeezed, and squeezed, and finally the pirate king stopped moving. The ninja closed his eyes and smiled, waiting for the blow from behind that would kill him.

Nothing.

He frowned, turning, and—

—he was on the cold stone floor, looking up at the pirate leader, who was, inexplicably, standing up. He was also very, very strong, the ninja realized. He must be—one moment the ninja had been crouching on his corpse, or what seemed a corpse, and the next he was lying several strides away, his whole body aching.

The man who had thrown him off so easily unpeeled the chain from around his neck, looked at it for a moment—or seemed to, for again it was hard to tell—then let it drop to the ground.

And that was when he lowered his hood from around his face.

For the first time in the ninja's life—he was normally the one doing the killing, not the one screaming—he let out a sound of terror, and he felt his heart stop for just a moment.

Under that hood, there was no face. Just the grotesque grin of a skull, hanging with tatters of skin.

The ninja scrabbled at the ground with his hands, kicking with his feet, trying to crawl backward away from the monster ahead of him, so terrified he was not even aware of the indignity of his situation. He mewed, like a kitten.

"You did not expect this," said the pirate leader. It was a statement, not a question.

The ninja babbled. He looked behind him and saw that some of the other pirates had lowered their hoods too, and they were also dead. He thought he might begin to cry, something else he had never done before. It was usually his victims who cried, if he gave them the chance. Which wasn't often.

"My name is Kenji Kira," said the dead leader. "I was the bangashira for Lord Oda no Nobunaga, the commander of his armies. Did you think that a piece of jewelry would kill me?"

The ninja said something, but it didn't come out of his throat. He had heard of Kenji Kira, and where before he had been terribly afraid, now he felt that he might just turn to liquid and melt away.

"Speechless, I see. You did well, though, I will grant you that. I pre-

sume you wanted us to catch you, so that you could get close to me?"

He nodded—it was all he could manage.

"And the necklace . . . and the sword . . . I imagine, if circumstances had allowed it, you might have used the blade instead?"

He nodded again.

Kenji Kira clapped, softly. "Really, well done. Now all that remains is for you to tell me who hired you."

The ninja shook his head. "I . . . d-d-d-don't know. I never know."

"But you receive instructions. Money. Someone must give it to you."

"Only through—"

"Letters, yes, I know." A sad shake of the head. "Yet still, you know who it was. You do. You just don't want to know it. But I have heard about how you play cards. I have heard about how you carry out your missions. You always think ahead. Just ask yourself . . . what if your opponent were thinking further ahead? Just imagine it. And then ask yourself what you know, deep down."

The ninja stared, confused. At the back of his mind, a taunting echo.

Always be one step ahead.

Well, he wasn't now. He wasn't at all. He had a feeling, like a shiver inside him, that the person, the thing, standing in front of him was more than one step ahead. Was many, many steps ahead.

The pirate leader approached. "It's really very simple," he said. "The person who hired you . . . was me." Then he drew a beautiful katana *from under his cloak, and he must have been a man who knew that a neck presented the simplest opportunity to kill someone, because he brought it crisply down and cut the ninja's throat.*

The ninja crossed the bridge over the Three Rivers, which was all spangled with jewels, and he came to the other side. To death. He was surprised to find it exactly as described, and at the same time completely different.

He walked over the gray ground, until he came to the seat where Enma would sit—he could tell, because standing to the sides were the judge's guards, Horse-head and Ox-face, huge demons with weapons longer than a man.

But Enma's chair was empty, and the ninja wondered what this meant. Enma was supposed to judge the souls of the dead, to decide where on the wheel of samsara they would end up—whether they had accrued good enough karma to go to the heaven of Amida Buddha, or whether they would be reincarnated as a horse or even a lowly dog in the realm of beasts, or condemned to eternal starvation and loneliness in the realm of hungry ghosts. Or, worst of all, tortured forever in the hell of meifumado.

Yet Enma wasn't here. Did that mean the ninja would not be judged at all? Or did it mean something worse?

The ninja didn't have the chance to think about it for long, because then there was a sound behind him, and he turned to see the pirate leader, Kira, his hood still down. Only now, his bones were clothed in flesh, and he looked much as he must have looked in life. Not exactly as in life, though, the ninja thought. There were holes in the skin, where it looked as if maggots or slugs had been feeding, tears that indicated the gnawing teeth of rats. The ninja shrank back a little. Kira ignored this. He indicated the empty chair. "I killed him," he said.

"You . . . killed . . . Enma?"

"Yes. It was easy. He's only a man, after all. I challenged him, and I won. It was perfectly legitimate."

"But Horse-head and Ox-face—"

"Accept that a stronger judge was required. One who wasn't so . . . sensitive to the rules. One who might allow them to return to earth one day. One who wasn't so particular about the dead staying dead."

The ninja cocked his head, catching something in the walking skeleton's tone.

"Yes," said Kira. "I'm bringing you back with me, to life. You're dead, of course, so you'll rot like me. But you'll get used to it. Luckily, you have not been dead long, so you will retain human language, and a semblance of your prior personality. Those who have been dead for longer are . . . different."

"I don't understand," said the ninja.

"It lessens them, the experience of being dead."

"No. I mean, I don't understand this. You. What I'm doing here."

"You don't? And yet your father said, always be one move ahead."

"How do you—"

"I am Enma, remember? I acquired his powers when I spilled his blood. I could judge you, if I wanted. But I sense that it would be painful, for both of us."

Kira was looking at him, and though the dead man's decaying face was capable of little expression, it was as if he was waiting for something. The ninja thought, harder than he ever had before, knowing that he was being offered a chance here that might never be repeated. He could see shapes moving, farther into the gray land of death, and he had a nasty feeling they were some of the people he had killed.

"You . . . hired me, to kill you. So you could see how good I was. It was a test. And now you want me to join you."

Again, that ironic, soft clapping.

"Good. Now, follow me, and let's go back to the island, shall we? Your body will feel strange to you, I know it from experience. But I find there's a cure for that, in the blood of a still-beating heart. The fisherman will still be alive. I suggest we go and eat him."

The ninja followed, but there was one more question. He asked it.

"Why?"

Kira spread his hands. "I wish to build an army," he said.

"But this . . ." The ninja gestured at the bridge they were crossing, its jewels, the figures of the demons standing guard, dwindling behind them. "Death . . . Was it necessary?" He felt upset, but in a way that was oddly distant, as if someone had offended him in a half-remembered dream, and he still felt obscurely angry. "Could you not have just paid me to join you?"

"Living things will always betray you. An army of mercenaries is good. An army of the dead is better. Fear induces betrayal. Yet what do the dead have to fear? They're already dead."

The ninja nodded. "But what do you need this army for?"

"There is a boy I would like to kill," said Kira, bitterness in his voice.

"A boy? But that should be easy."

Kira hissed. "This isn't an ordinary boy."

CHAPTER 1

THE TENDAI MONASTERY

MOUNT HIEI

TWO MONTHS LATER

Taro drew back the arrow, stretching the bow, imagining all his fury and frustration flowing down his arm and into the wood of the shaft.

Then he let it all go.

The arrow struck the fan he was using as a target, nailing its center to the tree, which was seven *tan* away. His feelings, though, returned almost immediately, creeping back into his heart and mind.

He sighed, nocking another arrow. He was using long shafts—eight-hand lengths—of pure bamboo, tipped with sharp heads of antler bone, fletched with goose feathers. Arrows built for distance. His bow was new, a gift from the abbot. He no longer used the Tokugawa weapon, because he didn't think of himself as being a Tokugawa, didn't want to see himself as having a destiny anymore. It was his destiny that had ended up with him killing Lord Oda on a mountainside, in an explosion of blood.

He knew that soon he would have to make some kind of decision.

Hiro and Hana were happy to remain here with him, of course, for as long as he wanted. Shusaku had gone . . . actually, Taro wasn't sure where Shusaku had gone. He had said he had errands to run in Edo, the capital city, and—in his usual mysterious way—had left it at that. Taro hadn't seen his mentor for a couple of months. Little Kawabata had decided to stay at the Hongan-ji, the monastery of the Ikko-ikki. He liked the attitude of the warrior monks, who trained with guns and swords, and who believed that anyone could reach enlightenment, even the lowest of peasants.

Taro suspected that wasn't the whole reason, though. On the battlefield, Taro had discovered that he could control Lord Oda's body with the Buddha ball, because it was Taro who had turned the daimyo into a vampire. Taro had *also* turned Little Kawabata. So, in theory, Taro could make Little Kawabata do what he wanted, as long as he was holding the Buddha ball. For some reason that Taro didn't fully understand, his blood in someone else's body was subject to the ball in the same way that the weather was. When Taro had seized control of Lord Oda, stopping the daimyo's sword, he'd wondered if Shusaku would be able to do the same to him, since it was Shusaku who had turned Taro into a vampire. But it seemed the power didn't work without possessing the ball.

The ball could make it rain; it could also make a vampire he had turned do whatever he wanted, including exploding in a rain of blood, as Lord Oda had. As a result of this realization, Taro had taken to hiding the ball away. He was afraid of it—it was too powerful, and he didn't want to strike anyone with lightning, or call out to his blood inside them, as he could do with Little Kawabata if he wanted. But even though Taro never took the ball out, Little Kawabata still seemed to distrust him. He seemed uncomfortable around Taro, seizing any excuse to go elsewhere. Taro understood it—but it didn't stop him from feeling hurt, especially since he'd saved Little Kawabata's life once.

But then, if he was really honest with himself, he'd have to admit that he didn't feel completely at ease with Shusaku anymore either. His mentor had turned *him*, and Taro now knew that this gave the older ninja the power to move his limbs if he ever got hold of the ball, to call on his own blood inside Taro's body.

Taro was honest enough with himself to know that this was partly why he hadn't really resisted Shusaku's only half-explained departure.

He trusted Shusaku, but there was trust and then there was *trust*. Taro was a vampire, but he wasn't immortal. A good blow to the heart, or a severing cut to the neck, and he would be dead. He knew that Shusaku would sacrifice him in a moment for what he perceived as the greater good; and he knew how loyal Shusaku was to Lord Tokugawa. He didn't want to think about what might happen if the daimyo ever found out that Taro still lived, and asked Shusaku to rectify the situation. It would be unthinkable for a daimyo to have a son who was a vampire, let alone to publicly acknowledge the fact. And Taro had learned what daimyo did about things that were unthinkable. They made them go away.

Shusaku had invited Taro to go with him, of course, had alluded to some exciting missions on the horizon—assassinations was what he meant—but Taro wasn't sure he wanted to be a ninja, any more than he wanted his destiny, whatever that was. After Lord Oda's death, all he wanted was to remain quietly in the place where his mother had been so happy, thinking, training with the abbot.

But it had already been nearly half a year since Lord Oda died, and monasteries didn't make a point of accommodating people forever unless they were to become monks—which was another thing Taro wasn't sure he wanted to do.

Then there was the tricky subject of Hana. It was obvious to the monks, Taro could tell, how he and Hana felt about each other. The two had made no great attempt to hide it, but then how could they? The monastery was on top of a mountain. It didn't offer much privacy. Still—what was he supposed to do? Clearly he couldn't stay at the monastery, with Hana, pursuing a relationship that was not sanctified by marriage. Just as clearly, he couldn't leave her in order to take monastic vows. The problem was that he couldn't marry her either. How could he? He had nothing to offer her—no land, no title, no income. She was a noble, and even if he had killed her father, which was a topic neither of them ever discussed, she was still used to a certain style of life, a certain amount of power.

After Lord Oda had died (*after I killed him*, Taro thought), they had left the battlefield quickly, before Lord Tokugawa's troops arrived to mop up the last of the Oda samurai. No one had surrendered, of course. That was not the samurai way. But the losing soldiers had been given the chance to commit seppuku on the battlefield, to join their fallen leader with dignity, and most had taken it. The register of wandering *ronin* had not been greatly expanded that day. Lord Oda was cruel, but he was proud, and his samurai were the same.

Of course, Lord Tokugawa was going to wonder who had killed his enemy Lord Oda—as well as where Oda's body might be, since Taro had reduced it to a fountain of blood. But when Taro returned to Shusaku, who was sheltering from the sun in the Ikko-ikki castle, the older ninja had known what to do. With the help of the monks, he had put about the rumor that a champion of the Ikko-ikki had done the killing—a furious fighter, who had attacked Lord Oda so vigorously that he was cut into many tiny pieces and trampled into the mud. This hero, the rumor said, had subsequently disappeared into isolation, to meditate and to repent his violence against the Buddha's creatures.

It was a preposterous story, but then it was no more preposterous than the truth, which was that Taro had spoken to the blood pounding in Lord Oda's veins, the blood of his victims, and made it leave the evil daimyo's body in one great burst. Anyway, no one could contest it. Most of Lord Oda's samurai, who had been present when he died, had later killed themselves. A few had been too cowardly to cut open their own guts, even with a second ready to behead them right away, but no one paid attention to the gossip of *ronin*, and so the real story had yet to be told.

Taro was glad. It was not in his interest that the truth

should come out. Again, what would he do? Stand before Lord Tokugawa and say, *Hello, I'm your son, I killed Lord Oda, and by the way, Shusaku lied when he said I was dead?* He might as well stab himself through the heart, and save himself a lot of time and pain.

No. Better that he should remain unknown, uncelebrated, unhated. Only then there was the problem that if he was unknown, he would also remain without land, money, or title—and then he couldn't possibly ever marry Hana. She was still the daughter of a daimyo, even if he was a dead daimyo. She carried an ancient and noble name—one to which Lord Oda no Nobunaga had attached an even greater weight of nobility, with his famous victories. A person marrying her might not gain an army, but he would gain influence, and respectability. She would be a rich prize. One Taro couldn't hope to deserve.

And then there was Hiro, too. What was he supposed to do about Hiro? He couldn't leave his best friend behind either. It was impossible to know what Hiro wanted. Hiro had no family, save for Taro. He had always been content to follow Taro wherever he went, and to begin with, Taro had justified this to himself with the knowledge that Hiro had always dreamed of adventure. But it was hollow comfort. Taro knew by now, as Hiro must know, that adventure was a poor alternative to a quiet life. Adventure involved pain, and fear, and people dying.

The kindest thing would be to let Hiro go back to Shirahama, to live in his old hut and be a fisherman there. But of course Hiro wouldn't go. Taro had saved his life when they were young boys, and Hiro saw it as his duty to follow Taro forever. If Taro tried to send him away, it would insult Hiro dreadfully.

The problem of Hana, the problem of Hiro. Both of them just went round in circles in Taro's mind.

We're trapped, thought Taro. *All of us.*

He nocked another arrow, no closer to finding a solution, and let it fly. The *thwock* as it slammed into the target gave him no satisfaction. Then he heard Hiro's voice behind him.

"We thought we'd find you here," he said.

Taro turned, groaning. "The two of you are ganging up on me now?" he asked.

Hana laughed. She had grown stronger in the months that had passed since she fell into a coma after going into the burning temple to rescue the sacred scrolls. There was a flush to her cheeks now, a light that flickered in her eyes. She was beautiful.

"We said one more chapter, and then you could practice the bow," she said mock-reprovingly.

"And then you left me alone while you went to get water, and I was so lonely I had to distract myself somehow." Taro held up the bow. "*This* doesn't abandon me with boring old books."

Hana put a hand on her hip. "Hiro, restrain him and carry him back to the hall, please," she said. Hiro stepped forward, shrugging as if to say, *Sorry, she's the boss.*

Taro made a gesture of defeat. "No need," he said. "I like my bones the way they are. Intact."

He was only half joking—Hiro had gotten even tougher since he had been training with the abbot's monks. He was learning kicks and punches to go with his wrestling holds, and Taro wouldn't want to be the one to anger him in a back alley—or refuse to accompany him back to the dreaded books, for that matter.

Shortly afterward he sat with Hana at the desk, which was situated under a large paper shoji window, to let in the maximum light. They were doing the founding stories of Japan—the Shinto tales that every child knew, but that Taro had been forced to learn, painstakingly and over the course of what felt like a very long time, how to read. It was frustrating to expend that amount of effort, and to be rewarded with a story that he had known all his life. But Hana said that the tales were one of the oldest books in the land, and an important part of his heritage, and if he wanted to learn the kanji properly, there was no better place to start.

Start!

It had been months already, and he saw characters dancing in front of his eyes when he closed them at night; meaningless, taunting scrawls in black ink. He'd mastered the simplified women's writing system long ago, before he lost his mother, before he fought Lord Oda. But now Hana wanted him to conquer the Chinese ideograms too, the kanji.

Of course, despite being a girl, she herself could read the kanji perfectly. Just as she could ride a horse into battle and defeat a samurai with a sword. If he didn't like her so much, he could really start to hate her. Bloody perfect samurai girl—

"You're daydreaming," she said, whacking his hand with a rolled-up scroll, as if she could hear his thoughts.

"Yes, yes . . . ," he said. He ran his finger along the page, looking for the place where they had left off. It was the story of Amaterasu, the Goddess of the Sun, and her brother Susanoo, the God of the Wind.

He began to read, haltingly at first, then with more confidence.

> And being brother and sister they were always competing with each other.
>
> Then, because Amaterasu was given dominion over the lands, Susanoo her brother grew wrathful. He trampled her rice fields, filled the irrigation ditches with mud, and spread dirt through her halls. But Amaterasu did not upbraid him, saying that he must have done these things inadvertently. This only made Susanoo even more violent. He broke a loom in Amaterasu's weaving hall, and while she saw to the weaving of garments for the gods, he threw into the hall a heavenly horse, from which he had flayed the skin, causing such fright among Amaterasu's attendants that one of them died on the spot.

Amaterasu, terrified, fled to the cave of heaven and shut herself in.

Then the whole plain of heaven, *tanaka ga hara,* was cast into darkness, and the world, too. Eternal night prevailed. Now the eight hundred myriad deities cried out in the darkness like crickets, and a thousand sounds of woe rose in heaven and on earth. The gods begged Amaterasu to come out, but she refused. They knew that she must be made to leave the cave, or all of creation would die in the darkness.

Then Omoikane, the God of Wisdom, conceived a plan. He assembled the long-singing birds of eternal night and made them sing outside the cave. He took iron from the heavenly mountains and called on the great smith Amatsumara to make from it a shining mirror. He also instructed Amatsumara to make a string, eight feet long, of five hundred jewels. Then he took the jewels and the mirror and he hung them on a cedar tree that was growing outside the cave in which Amaterasu was hiding.

After this, he bade Hachiman, the God of Force, stand just behind the door to the cave, where he could not be seen. And he positioned Ama no Usume, the Goddess of Levity, in front of the cave, standing on a drum. She was dressed in the moss of the heavenly mountain, fashioned into a sash, and her headdress was of pine needles from heavenly trees, and the flowers of heaven were a posy in her hands.

Then Omoikane told Ama no Usume to dance, and she began to leap and turn on the drum—but no sooner had she started dancing than the moss she was wearing fell down, and she was naked. The eight hundred myriad gods burst into laughter, and she laughed too, continuing to dance.

Now Amaterasu moved aside the door to the cave, and peered out to see what the gods were laughing at.

She said to them, "I thought that owing to my retirement the Plain of Heaven would be dark, and likewise the earth; how is it that Ama no Usume makes merry, and that likewise the eight hundred myriad gods all laugh?"

Then Ama no Usume spoke, saying, "We are glad because there is a new god more bright and illustrious than you."

Amaterasu was furious to hear this, and came out of the cave to see this god. Omoikane rushed forward and turned the mirror toward her, saying, "Here, this is the deity of which we speak."

Amaterasu gazed into the mirror, amazed at the being of light she saw reflected there. Immediately Hachiman leaped behind her and secured the chain of jewels across the cave, so that she could not return.

At first, seeing the way she had been tricked, Amaterasu was angry, but then Ama no Usume began to dance again, and all laughed, including Amaterasu. She called for Susanoo, her brother, to be forgiven for his impetuous behavior. But the other gods, and Amaterasu's father, who had made all of creation, refused, and so Susanoo was banished from heaven.

Then Susanoo descended to earth, in the form of a man, with a strong body, swift of movement, perfect for fighting. He traveled the lands for some time, until he came to the source of a great river. Here he heard, all of a sudden, a sound of weeping. He went in search of the sound, to see who was crying.

Eventually he found an old man and an old woman. Between them was sitting a young girl, and they were hugging her and lamenting over her.

"Who are you, and why are you weeping?" Susanoo asked.

"We are *kami* of the earth," said the father. "River gods, who dwell in this place. This is our daughter Kushinada-hime. The reason we weep is that formerly we had eight daughters. But they have been devoured, year after year, by a fearsome eight-headed dragon, and now our last daughter waits to be eaten."

Susanoo thought for a moment, seeing how beautiful the daughter was, the curve of her jaw and her big bright eyes. "If I kill the dragon, will you give me your daughter?" he asked.

"Yes," said the river god, without hesitation.

Susanoo immediately instructed the *kami* parents to brew strong sake and pour it into eight buckets, and then to await the arrival of the dragon.

When the time came, the dragon actually appeared. It had an eight-forked head and an eight-forked tail; its eyes were red, like the winter-cherry or like great rubies; and its teeth and claws were longer than swords. As it crawled it extended over the valley itself and also the mountains behind—it was a creature bigger than the landscape.

Susanoo positioned himself behind a fence and placed the eight tubs of sake behind it. Then he called out for the dragon to come and get him. But the dragon, as he had hoped, was distracted by the sake, for all dragons love wine. It put its eight heads through the bars of the fence and began to drink. Soon it fell into a drunken stupor, with its heads trapped by the fence.

Now Susanoo drew his ten-span sword and began to cut off the heads of the dragon. But as he reached the final head, the dragon awoke and smashed free of the fence, breathing fire toward him. Susanoo jumped aside, slashing wildly at the dragon. He struck its tail, and felt his sword resound with the impact, sending a shiver of shock up his arm. He looked down in wonder at his blade and saw that it was chipped, and so he knew there was something hard inside the dragon's tail.

Slashing again, he cut open the tail, avoiding the flames with which the dragon was trying to roast him, and pulled out from inside the most beautiful

> sword he had ever seen, the sword that became known as Kusanagi no tsuri.
>
> Throwing aside his inferior sword, he seized Kusanagi, and dancing around the dragon's remaining head, he cut it off with a single stroke, and so Kusanagi became the first and only sword to kill a dragon. Then Susanoo took Kushinada-hime as his wife and went down into the lowlands to make his home, where he and his wife . . .

Taro broke off, embarrassed. Hana leaned over his shoulder—he felt the softness of her hair on his neck—and peered at the words on the page.

"Ah, yes," she said. "The tales as they are written are not always suitable for children."

He felt blood rush to his cheeks.

"Well," she said. "Let's leave it there. You read well today, Taro. You will be the equal of any daimyo in the land soon."

He half smiled but felt irritated. Did she think he wasn't already? He knew she meant well—he thought he knew, anyway—but sometimes her interest in his improvement could be a little patronizing. Or maybe it was just his pride, wounded by having to learn how to read, at his age, from a beautiful girl.

But then she smiled back at him, and he forgot all that—he couldn't believe he had thought anything negative about her. She was the kindest person he had ever known, and he wanted her by his side always.

He just had to work out a way to make it happen.

He coughed. "Hana . . . You know Susanoo and the girl, the *kami*? They had no palace. No inherited land. But they were happy, right?"

Her lips twitched with amusement. "Are you asking me something, Taro?"

He shook his head. "I just . . ."

She put a hand on his shoulder. "I never asked to be the daughter of a lord," she said. "I never even enjoyed it, really. As long as I can read, and dance, and ride, I will be happy. Anywhere."

He narrowed his eyes, wondering if she was saying what he thought she was saying, but she turned away from him and began rearranging brushes in a pot.

He thought about the last time he had remembered the story of Susanoo and the dragon. He'd been sitting on the roof of a grain store, waiting for Little Kawabata to come back, so he could trap him and get him back for trying to kill him. Even then, when his whole world had been turned upside down, his father murdered by ninjas, his true identity as Lord Tokugawa's secret son revealed, he had not known how far he would end up from the comforts of his seaside home. He had not known that he would see his mother killed in front of him too, or that he would rescue Hana from the kind of death she had fallen into, or that he would kill a lord.

He closed his eyes and prayed, fervently, that nothing so eventful should ever befall him again. There was a time when he had enjoyed stories like that of Susanoo, had dreamed that one day he would find a legendary, magical sword and fight a dragon. Now he couldn't think of anything worse.

Please, no dragons.

No swords.

He ignored Hana when she asked him what he was doing, if his head was hurting.

He didn't know what he had been thinking. If Hana was happy to live in poverty with him, then he was happy too, it was all he wanted. Perhaps they could return to Shirahama. He knew how to fish, had learned it from his father. And his mother had been a respected ama diver. He would be welcomed there.

Yes. A peaceful life, by the sea. Hiro would come too, he knew it. Hiro would love to be back there—he could challenge passing *ronin* to wrestling matches again. The two of them could—

"Taro?" He looked up and saw Hana frowning at him, concerned.

"You look tired," she said. "Why don't we leave it there for today."

"Yes, Sensei," said Taro, with a slight smile.

Hana rolled her eyes and put away the scrolls. She straightened up. "What would you say to some sword practice?" she asked.

Taro grinned. "I'd say let's go."

"Taro, Taro, Taro." She sighed. "You do realize that you will have to be able to read, if you're to make something of yourself? People won't always be trying to kill you, you know. And you're perfectly safe here on the mountain."

"You would think so," said Taro. "But people keep abducting me and making me read things."

Hana stuck her tongue out at him. But she went to get her wooden sword, anyway.

CHAPTER 2

Taro woke.

He lay still on his side, in the room that he shared with Hiro. It was late at night; he'd sparred for a long time with Hana, then had eaten a simple meal with the monks before bed, and the muscles of his chest ached.

It was unlike him to wake suddenly in the night. He was a deep sleeper. Something must have woken him. He glanced around the room, without moving his head; instinct told him that if someone had come in, it would be better if he should appear still to be sleeping. Everything seemed as it should: Hiro's chest rising and falling, the corners of the room pooling with darkness, as if a great tide of black liquid had swept through the place, and was beginning to drain away.

A sound?

He focused on his hearing, which he knew was extraordinarily acute. From far away, a *ri* or more, he heard an owl cry. Closer by, a fox barked. He closed his eyes.

There.

In the corridor outside the room, something had creaked—so lightly as to be imperceptible to the human ear.

But Taro was not human.

The creak came again, a fraction louder this time. Someone was approaching—someone who wanted to be quiet. Taro reached under his futon and felt the smooth, round shape of the ball, which he had hidden there. As soon as he had ascertained that it was still there, he pulled his hand away, but it was too late. With that one touch, the voice of Lord Oda was in his mind, like a snake curled up in there.

You'll die soon, boy, and then you'll be like me, you'll be nothing and—

Taro winced. To begin with, the ball had seemed a blessing—a remarkable object that gave him power over the weather, over the blood in any vampire he had turned. But in the months following Lord Oda's death, he had become more and more aware of the darker side to its power: its ability to wake the voices of those he had killed.

Which, because his was the loudest and most recent voice, meant Lord Oda. Taro didn't know if it was his imagination or not, and he didn't care; he just avoided touching the ball as much as he could.

The sound of Lord Oda's voice still in his mind, like a bitter taste still on the tongue, he slid from his futon, barefoot. He walked silently to Hiro's side and put his hand on his friend's shoulder. When Hiro opened his eyes, Taro covered the other boy's mouth, darted his eyes to the door.

Hiro nodded and got up, very quietly. The futons were laid right on the floor, so there was nothing to hide beneath, but Hiro went and stood to one side of the sliding door. Quickly Taro stuffed whatever clothes and belongings he could find under Hiro's bed-cover, arranging them so that they roughly resembled a sleeping body. Then he went to stand opposite Hiro, next to the door.

Shhhhhhhh.

Someone opened the sliding door, ever so slowly. Then from the darkness outside the room came a darker shape, black-clad, padding into the room. The ninja paused before moving toward Hiro's futon, a dagger in his hand.

Curses, thought Taro. *A weapon would have been useful.*

He *was* wearing his *shobi* ring, though. Ninjas liked concealed weapons—no doubt the one creeping into the room as these thoughts flashed through Taro's mind had many of them—and this was one of the best. So good, in fact, that most of the time Taro forgot he was wearing it. To all outward appearances it was just a wooden ring—and actually it *was* just a wooden ring. But with it, someone who knew where the pressure points were located on the human body could do a lot of damage.

Someone like Taro.

He motioned for Hiro to stay still, then he flowed forward, so fast that a human observer would only have seen him disappear and then reappear behind the ninja. All in one smooth motion, he brought the *shobi* ring down on the man's neck, striking the sleep point, and the ninja sank with a rustle to the ground, like a flag when the wind drops.

Taro took a deep breath. His heart thudded in his chest. *Still alive.* He'd had the advantage of surprise, but the ninja was a vampire—all ninjas were—and Taro knew that it would be foolish to underestimate a vampire; he knew more than anyone the powers they possessed. He looked down at the unconscious intruder. Who could—

Maybe Taro heard the faintest susurration of silk clothes, maybe he felt the gentlest motion of air on his neck. Whatever it was, Taro started to turn, and that was the only thing that made the blade slide between his arm and his chest, cutting deep into the flesh and missing his heart by a finger-span.

Hesitation would have been fatal, so Taro didn't hesitate—he continued his turn, sudden and hard, twisting the sword in the ninja's hand even as it bit further into his side. He felt one of his ribs snap, felt the bitter-cold touch of steel on his muscle and sinew. Heard blood dripping—*tap tap tap*—on the wooden floor. More importantly, he heard the green-branch crack of the ninja's wrist, heard the man grunt in pain.

All of this had happened in the time it takes to send an impulse from brain to feet—Hiro would still be standing by the door, Taro knew.

By now Taro was facing his opponent, and he went for the sword that was still held limply in the ninja's hand. He couldn't see the man's face—the ninja wore a black cloth wrapped around it, as Taro had once. At the same time as Taro tried to catch hold of the sword, Hiro came up behind the ninja, snaked his forearm round his neck, and got him in a chokehold.

The ninja dropped the sword.

Yes, thought Taro, as he—

Quick as a sprung trap, the ninja struck back with the elbow of his injured arm, hitting Hiro in the chin, and Hiro was big but he was thrown back like a straw man, with a loud *crack*, sliding backward on the smooth wooden floor before coming up against the wall, head lolling on his chest. At the same time, the ninja raised his knee and drove a kick straight forward. The foot sank into Taro's stomach; he doubled up, falling back onto the futon.

So fast.

So strong.

My gods. I'm going to die in this room.

Taro was so used to fighting humans he had started to think of himself as invincible; this attack by another vampire had shown him in the space of a few heartbeats that he could still be killed.

Easily.

He'd been on the verge of death so many times, part of him was surprised that he hadn't gotten used to it; but most of him was just screaming wordlessly inside him, saying it wanted another day, even another hour, just that.

He watched, the wind knocked out of him, as the ninja leaped at him. Was Hiro alive? Taro didn't know, and the thought that he might be dead was almost as bad as the thought that Taro might be about to die himself.

The man hadn't bothered to pick up his sword—he just let a dagger drop into his good hand from his sleeve as he flew through the air, holding it point down, spearing Taro's heart as he landed on him with all his body weight behind the blade.

No.

At the last possible instant, Taro got his hands up and gripped the ninja's wrist, stopping the blade. *Oh, gods.* The man was like a being made of metal, powered by storms or the sea. Holding him back was like holding back the tide. The point of the dagger slid, slowly but surely, down toward Taro's heart. And then, to Taro's horror, the man brought up his other hand, the one whose wrist was broken, and placed it on the hilt of the dagger.

And, with both hands, he pushed even harder.

Taro couldn't even imagine the pain the ninja must be in, could see white bone sticking out from the wrist, in the gap between the man's black sleeve and his gloved hand. But still he brought the blade mercilessly, powerfully down, no sound escaping from his hidden lips.

There was only one, horrifying option, and the part of Taro's mind that was nothing but a chaotic, inarticulate cry for just one more moment of life made it without him even knowing it. Shusaku had always said, *If you can't overcome your enemy's strength, use it.*

Suddenly switching the orientation of his force, Taro pushed the blade to the right and let go.

The ninja was still exerting all his power and weight downward: The dagger hammered through Taro's chest, pinning him to the futon. Pain leaped at Taro, mouth open, and swallowed him whole. Blood flooded his lungs, gathered at the back of his throat.

He ignored it, throwing his arms around the ninja's neck, like an embrace, drawing him inexorably closer. The man struggled, but Taro held on to his own wrists, formed an unbreakable cordon of bone and muscle, hugged tighter. The ninja might be strong, but to break free he had to use his back, his stomach, whereas

Taro was using his much stronger arm muscles in a bear hug from which there was no escape.

Just as the man's face was about to touch his, Taro brought his head up, violently, and sank his teeth all the way through the black fabric of the ninja's clothes and into his neck. He held on, and he drank.

Blood filled Taro's mouth, sweet as nectar, hot as life. The ninja writhed and wriggled like a cat in a sack; Taro only tightened his hold and bit deeper. His teeth loved the feel of the flesh against them, his throat loved the blood that gushed down it, and he drank and drank, feeling life force drain from the ninja and into him; the rule of all existence.

So that one may live, others must die.

As the blood flowed into Taro, he felt his strength returning, felt the awful beast of pain that had swallowed him start to spit him slowly out. He wanted the dagger out of his body, could feel it in there, an alien presence in his chest, cold and inimical, but he couldn't let go, not yet.

Even when the ninja went slack, Taro didn't stop. He had already fallen for that trick. He had to be sure. It was only when the blood stopped coming, and he found himself sucking noisily at nothing, that he let his head drop. The ninja fell, and Taro used his new strength to inflect the momentum of gravity, twisting the man's body so that it rolled onto the futon, and from there to the floor.

Taro got up, gingerly, having to lever his body to remove the point of the dagger from the wooden slats below him. The pain retreated a little, still growling. He wasn't sure whether to take the dagger out or not. He had an idea that the blood loss might be worse if he did, that he should get someone—one of the monks, perhaps—ready to stanch it with bandages and pressure before he removed it. Right now it didn't matter. The whole of the dead ninja's supply of blood was in his body, racing through it like lightning, like pure power.

Taro walked across the room to where Hiro lay, his steps

somewhat unsteady, despite the astonishing energy he had taken on, not just the blood of a person, but the blood of a vampire—all of it. The hilt of the dagger protruded from his chest, as if it were a handle, intended to steer him.

"Are you alive?" he asked his old friend.

Hiro looked up groggily, eyes glazed. "Yes."

Taro sighed in relief. "Thank the gods."

"Um . . . ," said Hiro, hesitating as he took in Taro's appearance. "Are you?"

CHAPTER 3

It was a week before Taro was fully recovered. The abbot had downplayed his injury to the other monks—he knew that Taro was a vampire, but the fewer other people who knew, the better.

All that week, Taro lay on his bed in terror. Guards had been posted outside the door, five of the legendary swordsmen of the Tendai sect. But still he feared another attack. Worse than fear was boredom: The guards couldn't keep Hana out, and she visited him often, first to berate him, then to bring him endless reading material. He had never wanted so much to heal.

Meanwhile, the abbot and Hiro also spent much time in Taro's room. They discussed the attack endlessly—who might be behind it, what they might want. The answer to the second question seemed obvious: to kill Taro. But who would want to do that? There was Lord Oda, of course, but he was dead himself, with the exception perhaps of the voice awoken in Taro when he touched the ball.

Once, Taro took it out, to see if he might learn something. But all he heard was, *Cursed boy, you cursed boy, you will die and you will be nothing, you will die just like me*, and he wrapped the ball in cloth and hid it away.

What was obvious was that Taro couldn't stay at the monastery any longer—even if he had wanted to, it was not right to subject the monks to danger. The abbot never came out and said it, but Taro could see the thoughts behind the man's eyes, like fish in a murky pond: They said that anyone who could afford to hire a ninja was a powerful enemy, and the monks of the Tendai monastery had enough of those already.

On the seventh day, then, Taro was glad when he opened his eyes and the morning light didn't hurt them, when he took a deep breath and his lungs expanded without pain. He sat up experimentally. Felt the smooth strength in his limbs. Swung his legs off the bed and stood on the hard wood floor.

Hiro slept beside him, drool running in the crease at the side of his chin. Taro smiled. "Guards! Come quick!" he shouted.

Hiro's head snapped up. He jumped to his feet, bleary-eyed, mouth open. "Wha-wha-whass . . ." He looked at Taro, standing there. "Curse you," he mumbled.

"You have drool on your chin," said Taro.

"I know. I was saving it for later."

Taro smiled, and Hiro smiled back. Taro had been feeling guilty, before the attack, about Hiro following him through life. Now he was just glad his friend was with him. Just then there was a knock on the door.

"Yes?" said Taro.

Two guards came in, their hands on the pommels of their swords, darting their eyes around the room. Taro flushed guiltily. "Ah . . . false alarm," he said. "I thought something terrible had happened to Hiro, but it turned out to be just his snoring."

Hiro glared at him, as the guards backed out of the room.

Shortly afterward there was another knock on the door, and the abbot entered without waiting for an invitation, robes sweeping as he walked. He didn't bat an eyelid when he saw Taro standing there. Hana followed him, and she winked at Taro as she entered the room, unable to keep the happiness from her face at seeing him up and about.

"Good, you're healed," the abbot said matter-of-factly. He patted a scroll that he was carrying. "There's a message."

"For me?"

"Not as such, no." The abbot came and stood by Taro, his face set in its usual kindly expression.

"But . . . ?"

"Well, I don't quite know how to take it, actually." The old man was looking at the scroll as if its existence somehow confused him, as if it might have appeared suddenly in his hand, out of thin air, when he was outside Taro's room.

"Yet you brought it to me." Taro spoke slowly, noting the distance in the abbot's eyes, almost as if the man had been sleeping, and was only slowly waking up.

"The message is from the boy in Edo," the abbot said. The boy in Edo was the shogun—a child a few years younger than Taro, theoretically protected by lords like Lord Tokugawa and Lord Oda. But Lord Oda was dead now, and Lord Tokugawa had taken Oda's considerable lands and numerous allies, making him in practice the ruler of Japan.

And, if rumors were to be believed—and Taro had learned enough to know that they should be—Lord Tokugawa was plotting to one day overthrow the boy he apparently served, and become shogun himself.

For now, though, the boy shogun still ruled, at least in theory.

"What does the message say?" asked Taro.

"It is a call for champions," said the abbot. "Edo is beset by a dragon, and the shogun is promising the title of daimyo, and a territory of twenty thousand *koku*, to anyone who can kill it. I had heard murmurs of it from passing *ronin*, but this official message appears to confirm that—"

"A *dragon*?" said Hiro.

The abbot sat down on the bed with a sigh. "Apparently. There's a rumor that it's burning villages near Edo, getting closer and closer to the capital."

Taro's thoughts echoed in his head, mocking.

Please, no dragons.

Every child in Japan grew up hearing about dragons. Where Taro had grown up, the risk had come mostly from the sea dragon, which was known to create great storms when it wished to punish people for forgetting its power, sending enormous waves called tsunami to crash onto the coast, sweeping away houses. But Taro knew that dragons also lived under the earth, sleeping mostly. Only sometimes they got angry and came to life, breathing fire that rained down from mountains and destroyed everything in its path.

Yes—Taro knew about dragons. But it was in the same way that he had known about *kyuuketsuki*, before he became one himself. In a distant, safe way. He had never contemplated the idea of *seeing* a dragon, much less fighting one.

Still, Taro felt his pulse quickening. Twenty thousand *koku*! The number indicated the amount of rice the territory could produce, and by direct extension, its worth. One *koku* was the measure of rice required to feed a single samurai for a year. Twenty thousand was an unimaginable sum. It was in taxes on rice production that a daimyo made his fortune—it would be no great exaggeration to say that Lord Tokugawa's war against Lord Oda, and the wars of both against the warrior monks, had been funded by rice.

Hana turned to him, holding out a hand. She looked sad. "Taro . . ."

He ignored her. She thought she wanted a quiet life now; she had never been a peasant. She didn't know the misery of going hungry. He would not take her to Shirahama, to be the wife of a fisherman, living in a rude hut such as the one he had grown up in. She might be angry with him at first, if he decided to battle the dragon. She might think he was placing the lure of adventure above the prospect of a quiet life with her. But she didn't understand what it meant to be poor, not really. If he did this, and if he won the reward the shogun was offering, she would be grateful. She would understand.

One day.

"Why do you bring me the message?" said Taro, though he knew perfectly well why.

"I thought . . . you might be interested," said the abbot.

"In the dragon? Or in the reward?"

"Both. I know you have been growing restless here."

Taro nodded slowly. It was true that he couldn't remain at the monastery any longer.

"I wish you could stay," said the abbot. "I wish I could make you a monk, and teach you. I think you would make a good addition to the order. But it's not safe. And really . . . I don't know if it's what you want."

Taro glanced at Hana, who had a strange expression on her face. "I don't know what I want," he said. "But a dragon? It just seems ridiculous. I mean, they don't exist, do they?" Some thought the dragon in the mountain, and the great fish under the earth whose twitching caused earthquakes, were merely stories told to explain the unexplainable.

The abbot smiled. "You're a vampire," he said. "You traveled into the realm of hungry ghosts and spoke to your mother; you rescued Hana from death. Tell me. Do *you* think the dragon is real?"

Taro thought for a moment. "Perhaps. But I don't know if I could fight one."

"Of course you could. The more important question is whether you could *win*," said the abbot. "Dragons are much more powerful than ninjas," he added significantly.

Taro thought back to the attack in his room. "Then . . . I could die."

"You could," said the abbot. His expression was inscrutable. He handed the scroll to Taro. "I must send my rice taxes to the shogun this month," he said. "A full cartload. You could take them for me. See Edo. Decide what you would like to do. No one is going to judge you if you are not interested in facing a dragon. They are terrifying creatures." A shadow passed across the old man's eyes. "Take the rice for me. The rest is up to you."

"All right," said Taro. "I've never been to Edo before."

The abbot nodded, then swept out of the room again.

He felt Hana flinch beside him, but he ignored her disapproval. In his mind, he had already made the decision to face the dragon. Of course he had: He'd never faced a dragon before, and he would have wanted to do it even just to see if he would win. The reward, though, was what made it impossible to refuse. With the money, the prestige . . . he would finally be worth something as a husband. He would be a worthy match for Hana. And maybe . . . just maybe . . . he would be one step closer to fulfilling his destiny. The prophetess had told him he would be shogun one day. It seemed to Taro that killing the dragon, ridding the country of a monster, might be a good first step.

He knew it would hurt Hana, but he had no choice.

One day it would all be clear to her, the reason why he needed the land and the title, and they would be married and stand on the ramparts of a castle together—he smiled even more at the thought. He was still staring at her when Hiro, who never seemed to feel the tension in any situation, put a hand on Taro's shoulder.

"So," he said, pointing to the scroll in Taro's hand. "Are you going to do it? Because Taro, my friend, I've got to say, a dragon . . ."

Hana sighed. "Of course he is," she said. She turned her back on him, but not before he saw that there was a tear on her cheek.

It struck him like a physical blow.

CHAPTER 4

NEAR THE CAPITAL CITY OF EDO

The man—though boy might have been more accurate a term—was scaling the lower slopes of Mount Fuji. He turned and looked back on the city, so small below him. He had not left Edo often, and he was surprised to find how much world there was outside it. He'd thought its streets, rivers, and alleys contained everything there was to see, from prostitutes to children's entertainers, from samurai to noodle makers. He'd thought it all went on forever, a giant construction of bricks, roof slates, cartwheels, endless streets; made by people, moved by people. Yet here he was, not two days' walk away, and the place seemed miniature, a toy.

He paused, feeling a telltale contraction in his chest. He pressed his hands to his sides, closed his eyes, and concentrated on his breathing. It had plagued him since childhood, this affliction. He would be running or walking—or sometimes just sitting still—and his lungs would close, as if operating of their own volition, leaving him gasping for air. Sometimes, though, if he caught the signs in time he could stop it, by focusing.

There was the terror, though, that was the problem. Once air became something he had to fight for, he was seized by a fear that nearly immobilized him, a conviction that this time, *this time he was going to die. He wasn't afraid of being hit or hurt, which was lucky given his upbringing, but he was so frightened of the tightness in his chest that he almost wanted to die, to make it stop.*

He thought there was nothing more terrifying in this entire world than the idea of running out of air.

One breath . . .

Two . . .

He straightened up. There was no one to laugh here. No one to call him slow-coach, pigeon-chest, rattle-breath. All his life, the boy had suffered such insults, as he trained to be a low-ranking samurai in the household his father worked for. Often, it had been his father doing the insulting.

Now, though, he would show them.

He turned his gaze toward the high places, the mountain peaks above him. The closest one was his destination. From the top spewed fire—diffuse, almost droplets, like burning sea foam. He could barely make out two places where the fire ran down the mountainside, finding crevasses, reaching ever farther downhill, like flickering red fingers. Already one village had been destroyed, the boy had heard, and the scouts for the shogun said the molten flames must soon reach Edo.

It was for the purpose of stopping them that the boy had been sent.

No.

No—he could not claim that to himself, even with no one else around. He had not been sent; he had volunteered for it, wishing to prove to all those who had called him pigeon-chest that he could do great things, wishing to obtain from the shogun the land and title promised to the one who would defeat the dragon.

Thinking of the dragon, his chest again threatened to close in on itself. He allowed his eyes to travel up from the path he walked—carpeted with pine needles—to the wooded slopes, cedar and ash, and then the rocky mountainside and then the fire, a continual bursting into the air as of sea spray from heavy waves hitting shore.

There was a dragon up there. There was a dragon up there, and he was going to try to kill it.

One breath . . .

Two breaths . . .

He touched the sword at his side, blinking away the sweat that had trickled into his eyes. Was it his imagination, or was the air growing warmer, the closer to the mountaintop he drew? He cursed this country, with its thin skin, and the monsters that lived underneath.

There was a giant fish that lived under Honshu island, the whole of Japan carried on its back through the sea. A carp. And when the carp had an itch, it would buck and twitch and the earth would shake, causing houses to collapse and trees to fall. There was a dragon, the dragon of fire, and when it awoke from slumbering in some high-up cave, it would spit flames and burn villages and towns until it was stopped. These things were known.

Only, at least in the boy's lifetime, neither fish nor dragon had moved or been seen, and other than the war between Lord Oda, now dead, and the Ikko-ikki monks, there had been no disruptions to the peace of the islands. It was for this reason that the shogun was so angered by the dragon—and frightened, the boy thought, he had seen it in his eyes—and had requested that it be killed. The reward was a plot of land of twenty thousand koku, *and a position as daimyo.*

But then the shogun, too, was only a boy. And not in the sense that he was not yet a man—in the simple sense that he had seen only twelve summers. It was natural that he should be afraid.

The boy on the mountainside found, to his great pleasure, that thinking of the shogun's fear cheered him up. Yes. If the shogun himself was frightened, then who could blame him, Kazue, for trembling a little whenever his eyes strayed to the mountaintop and the fire?

His breathing eased, and he continued to climb.

The eyes in the darkness told him to stop. They were red and bright, shining in the depths of the cave like enormous rubies.

"Who are you?" they said. The boy couldn't be sure, but he thought

the voice might be in his head, not echoing in the cave like a real sound.

"M-m-my name is Kazue," he said. "Of the household of—"

"Your household is nothing to me. I have lived since the birth of the world. You are mortal? That is my question."

"Ah . . . yes."

"That is a pity for you."

Kazue was shaking all over, only half from fatigue. Sweat was leaking from his every pore now, as if in the face of this flaming beast the very water in his body were abandoning him in fear, running down his face so that he tasted it when he spoke. The heat was terrible, a solid thing pressing against him, like a wall that ran all around him. The only mercy was that the fire had stopped. As he had neared the summit, it had simply trickled to a halt, as if the dragon knew he was coming, had heard his approach from far off, and was sitting like a cat waiting for a mouse.

As, indeed, appeared to be the case.

Hardly believing he was doing it, Kazue slowly drew his sword. If his tormentors from the training yard had seen him at that moment, they would have been amazed—they would have seen true courage, which cares nothing for traitorous lungs or shallow, unmuscled chests. They would have known in that moment that bravery has nothing to do with strength.

Sadly, though, they were not there—and neither, in any meaningful sense, was Kazue. Those eyes in the darkness had robbed his power of thought.

"Did you come to kill me?" said the eyes.

"Y-yes."

"And who sent you?"

"The . . . the shogun. He promised—"

"I do not care what he promised. He does not rule this land."

Kazue blinked. He had come here expecting a fight with a creature from legend, and instead he was being interrogated by something he couldn't see. "I'm—I don't understand," he said.

"You wouldn't," came the voice that seemed to be only in his head. "The emperors descend from Amaterasu. This is how it was, and how

it should be. Only he who holds the sword, the jewel, and the staff may rule."

"The shogun has those," said Kazue. It was known: He had seen the ceremonial artifacts himself, when they were displayed on feast days.

"No," said the dragon. "He doesn't. He has two treasures and a worthless trinket. The shogun is nothing."

Was this a riddle? Kazue was trying to think, but his mind didn't want to obey; it was a familiar feeling to him, since he had trouble controlling his lungs. Strangely, maybe because of the heat, his lungs themselves were working fine. He racked his brain. This was not how he had imagined his encounter with the dragon; he had seen himself destroying it in noble—if not very clearly pictured—combat, cutting off its head and bringing it back to Edo, to lay before the shogun as pretty young girls watched.

"What do you want?" he asked the dragon. "Why are you burning everything?" He had a dim thought that if the dragon wanted to talk, maybe he could talk it out of its destruction.

"I want our mother's descendant on the throne; I want the world to be as it should. I want the usurpers dead. I want justice. *Tell me: Would you go down this mountainside and kill the shogun?"*

Ten years of samurai training spoke for Kazue, in his own voice. He had been so inculcated with obedience that he could no more kill the shogun than he could cut off his own hand, unless the shogun asked him to, and then he would have to. "No."

"I thought not. Yet the one who woke me will. With my help, he will destroy the shogun and he will claim the artifacts, and at last an heir of Amaterasu will rule this country again. Unless you stop me, that is."

"Unless I . . . ?"

"You brought that sword for a reason, I presume? So wield it, if you can."

Kazue felt a rush of hot wind, as the eyes came toward him. The cave, which was a high, wide cavern, suddenly seemed small and well lit. Uncoiling in front of Kazue was a creature from legend, impossibly vast, the size of its eyes no preparation at all for the enormity of its sinuous body, its bearded and horned head. The dragon was exactly as drawn in the pictures Kazue had seen, a winged serpent with feet and claws, a bearded head like that of a dog, bristling with teeth. Its dimensions, though, were beyond anything painted by man; its head alone was the size of a horse.

If there had been a tiny part of Kazue's mind that did not accept the reality of dragons, or giant fish under the skin of the earth, it fell silent at that moment.

Suddenly the scene was more what Kazue had imagined on his way up the mountainside—yet now he knew that he would be cutting off no heads and impressing no pretty young girls. He raised his sword uselessly.

The dragon opened its mouth, and Kazue saw a flame spark behind the gate of teeth, as the creature bore down upon him. In the last moment before his mind was wiped blank by fear, and his body wiped from the earth by fire, he was capable of one final thought.

He had been wrong.

Running out of air was not, by a very long way, the most terrifying thing in the world.

CHAPTER 5

In the time that followed, Taro became less sure about his decision. For sure, it did seem like the perfect opportunity to leave the mountain behind, follow his destiny. Even if he didn't become shogun, the reward from killing the dragon would be enough.

And it wasn't as though he could have stayed on the mountain, was it? He had known that the situation was untenable, that he couldn't remain with the monks forever. He just wished Shusaku was here, so he could ask the ninja for guidance.

But he would have to try to get by without his mentor's advice, at least for now. Taro had killed Lord Oda on his own, hadn't he? Anyway, Shusaku was in Edo, or so he had said, and that was where Taro would be taking the rice taxes. At the back of his mind was a hope that he could find the older ninja, ask him what to do.

Before he committed himself to anything, though, Taro wanted to see the abbot on his own. Shusaku wasn't here; the abbot was the next best thing. A couple of days later, when he could walk easily without support, he rose early and dressed without waking Hiro. This was the first time he was going to leave his room since the attack. He reached under his futon, to check that the ball was safely hidden. He was sure it was the Buddha ball the assassins had come for—not just to kill him, but to take the ball, and with it power over the elements.

As he reached under his futon, he braced himself for Lord Oda's voice.

Then he touched the smoothness of the ball, confirmed that it was there, and—

He was Sato.

He was tall thin fast agile strong clever half-noble mountain-born, the greatest of the samurai in his father's honor guard—

For one moment, Taro resisted the ball. He remained conscious of his own skin, around his own body, in the still cool air of the monastery. But at the same time he was in another's skin, Sato's skin, and he was looking down at . . . at Taro.

The boy he'd been sent to kill.

He was in Taro's dark room, pouring all his force into his arms, pushing the dagger slowly, irresistibly down toward the boy's chest. They had said, the anonymous men who had paid him so handsomely, that the boy was to be feared, but Sato had seen little evidence to support this.

Yes, Taro had hurt him, twisted the sword from his grasp, broken his wrist. But a little struggle was to be expected. Now that Sato had Taro on his back, had the dagger pressing down, the boy's lack of strength was obvious. He felt a small smile twitch the corners of his mouth. Sato was being paid for this job, of course. But now his wrist had been broken. The boy's death was going to be a pleasure to be savored.

The dagger carried on downward, unstoppable.

Then—

A crunch, and he was hardly aware of what was happening, but suddenly the dagger was *in* the boy's chest, but not in the heart, no, not in the heart, and he pulled desperately to free it, but there were steel bands behind his neck, he couldn't move. He bucked and arched like a fish out of water—

—his mind flashed to an image of a trout, caught by one of the laborers on their way downstream, the logs rolling and creaking below them as the fish flipped silver on the wet wood—

And then needles sank into his neck, the agony, the agony, and he felt a sucking commence, greedy.

No, no, pull away, pull away—but he couldn't. He was pushing down on the boy's chest, lifting his head, panic fueling his nerves, his muscles, but Taro had the advantage, had him held tight, was draining him. He could feel his blood flowing out, hotly, out of his body and into Taro. . . .

I've already died once, Sato thought, remembering the day he was murdered, only to be saved by the ninjas. *Don't let me die again, oh please don't*—

Taro pulled himself out of Sato's mind violently, letting go of the ball as if it were a hissing snake.

Sato. The name of the man who tried to kill me was Sato.

Taking a deep breath, he straightened up.

"Taro? Are you all right?" Hiro was sitting up, looking at him with grave concern in his eyes.

"Fine," said Taro. "Just stiff, that's all."

"Hmm," said Hiro. "Where are you going?"

"To see the abbot. I want to talk more about this dragon."

Hiro nodded, and was that a trace of sadness in the cast of his face? "Of course," he said.

Half an incense stick later, Taro knocked on the old monk's study door, waiting to be invited to enter.

"Come," said the familiar voice.

When Taro approached, the abbot was using a small rake to tend his Zen garden. He greeted Taro with a warm smile. "You are thinking about the shogun's challenge," he said. It wasn't a question.

"Actually . . . ," said Taro. "I was thinking about something you said. About the dragon. You said they are terrifying creatures. It sounded almost as if you had seen one."

The abbot spread his hands. "I'm old. I've forgotten more things than you can imagine."

"But you wouldn't forget a dragon."

"No," said the abbot. "No, I wouldn't." He walked over to a paper window, through which Taro could see the shape of a tree. "We have heard rumors about this dragon for some time," he said eventually. "They say it burned a whole village last month. Several men who tried to claim the shogun's reward have been killed."

"You think I would be killed?"

"I don't know. But I know that dragons are real. I . . . I heard about one, from a friend."

Taro gave the man a hard look. He knew the abbot was lying, but he could also see pain in the old monk's eyes. He knew not to push further. It was enough for him that the abbot was taking the idea of the dragon so seriously. "And what would you do, if you were me?"

The abbot steepled his hands. "Life is more difficult for you than for me," he said. "You're not a samurai, but you're not a peasant, either. You're of low birth, yet you killed a daimyo and were trained as a ninja by Shusaku, one of the best men I have known, but a creature of the night nevertheless. You know nothing of the sutras, are condemned to feed on blood, but you have been to death and seen more of the great wheel of *dharma* than I have. You're in love with a high-born girl, and you have nothing to offer her. But this! It could give you land and a title. No one could question you then."

Taro was a little stunned. He had thought all these things himself, but he hadn't expected that others would have seen the same things. He was touched, in a way, that the abbot should understand his problems so well. Though of course the abbot didn't know the half of it—he had no idea that Taro was really Lord Tokugawa's son. "So I go, then," he said.

The abbot looked at him long and hard. "Yes, I suppose you do," he said. Then he held up a finger, as if just remembering something. "I asked if you would deliver our rice taxes," he said.

"You did."

"Good. And you will guard them with your life, I'm sure. But there's also . . ." The abbot searched among the papers on his desk, clicking his tongue on the roof of his mouth, then stabbed a short scroll with his finger. "Ah. Here we are." Taking a stick of wax, he bent over a candle, then sealed the scroll. "Would you deliver this to the shogun, when you get there? It's . . . it's a private message."

"I understand," said Taro. He took the scroll and slid it into his cloak. At the door, he turned. "One more thing," he said. "You *have* seen a dragon. I can tell from your eyes."

The abbot winced.

"It's important," said Taro. "I need to know if I have any chance. If you think I might survive."

"I think . . . I don't know."

"But you've seen one," said Taro gently, taking the risk of irritating the abbot. "I can hear it in your voice."

"All right, all right . . ." The abbot sat down heavily. "There was so much snow," he said, his voice drifting away in thought. "It was snow country, that place. And the snow erased them, afterward. Erased all trace of them . . ."

"Erased who?"

"My men."

Taro shivered; it was as if snow had whirled into the room, soft flurries of it. "Did a dragon kill your men?" he asked.

"Yes."

"Then tell me. Tell me what you saw."

CHAPTER 6

TWENTY YEARS EARLIER

This was snow country.

Kakizaki no Kendo halted his horse in the gateway and gazed out from the seaside fort over the land. To the east and west, the sea stretched out, dark and cold as night. But before him was a vastness of snow, burying the rice fields, reaching up to high mountains, shimmering with the light of a pale winter sun.

Kendo shielded his eyes from the glare. The cruel light, reflecting off the snow so that it seemed to surround him, hammered nails through his eyes. He wrapped his cloak tighter around his body, shivering.

He wished he had not drunk so much sake the previous night.

The horse he rode was experienced, proven in battle, with a nimble step. Nevertheless, the ground was rough, the snow covering holes and mounds alike, and every step sent painful jolts through Kendo's head. *Curse those Ainu*, he thought.

"Wretched Ainu," said Lord Ando, echoing Kendo's thoughts.

"Gah," said Kendo, who couldn't manage much more than that.

Lord Ando rode just behind him—he was Kendo's age, only more handsome and more confident, more everything, really. Despite that, the two had always been best friends. Now that Kendo was responsible for keeping Lord Ando alive, a certain stiffness had crept in between them, but not much.

"I did tell you to get more sleep," said the young lord, amused.

Kendo shrugged, and even that hurt. Actually, he *had* gone to bed. Just not on his own, and not to sleep. Not for the first time, he cursed his own stupidity.

Behind him, the gates to the Ando settlement closed. His men had already gone ahead, two hundred of them, all mounted. Kendo was *hatamoto* to his old friend Lord Ando, commander of the settlement's small samurai force. He had asked Lord Ando to stay at home, had told him he would be safer there—and that had turned out to be a mistake, because Lord Ando didn't want to be safe, and never had.

Now they were Outside, in a broad valley that tapered to mountains, the sea behind them.

In the cold.

In the snow.

For Kendo, there was Inside, which was within the settlement ground, and Outside, which was everything else, the whole of the rest of the island.

Hokkaido.

Kendo had spent his whole life here, been born here—was a peripheral member of a prominent family. And yet, like everyone else he knew, he was an Outsider, one of only a few hundred Japanese who had maintained a toehold on Hokkaido. They had clung to this settlement, on the tip of the Oshima Peninsula, for two hundred years, a tiny island of Japanese in a sea of Ainu. They had arrived by accident, or so the story went. A ship leaving Honshu island, blown off course to land on the southern coast of Hokkaido. The captain went to drink from a stream and found a nugget of gold in his hands as he cupped the water. He was the first Ando: He stayed to dig up the rest of his gold, and his ancestors stayed too. Many times they had been attacked, decimated even. Once their entire settlement was destroyed, and they had to rebuild again farther north. But they clung on.

Kendo was a cousin of sorts to the present Lord Ando. He would never be lord, was too far from the succession. Yet he could live a noble life here, as a valued samurai.

He could lead a proud existence—if it wasn't for the twice-cursed Ainu.

Kendo's horse threaded its way through the gravestones, which appeared as smooth hillocks in the snow. Here on Hokkaido, his people put their dead outside the settlement gates—not because they failed to honor them sufficiently, but for protection. The Ainu would not go into a place of the dead, so the cemetery was a kind of moat. A moat of corpses.

Most things about the Ainu were different. They were hairy, where the Japanese were smooth. It was said that their people were descended from bears. The men wore full beards; the women tattooed their faces with dark ink, making them difficult to tell apart from the men. They lived not in wooden houses but in huts of woven reed and thatch, and they farmed little, but hunted instead.

One of Kendo's men held up a hand. They had come to the end of the graves, and now they really were Outside. Nothing to hold the Ainu back. Kendo drew level, scanned the valley ahead. He couldn't see anything but snow, and steel-gray sky. He motioned for the two hundred riders to spread out, to minimize the risk of ambush. Not that he thought there was much risk.

They don't have a chance, he thought.

The last couple of decades, a sort of truce had developed between the Japanese and the Ainu. The Japanese gave the island's original inhabitants sake and tobacco, for the most part, as well as the lacquerware dishes that the Ainu prized so much—Kendo wasn't sure why; he had a dim notion that they used the bowls for some kind of ritual. Even the beliefs of the Ainu were different: they had never learned the ways of Buddha, believing instead that they were surrounded by spirits—the spirit of the mountain, the spirit of the sea. Of streams. Of trees.

In return for the gifts the Japanese gave them, the Ainu gave the settlers animal skins—deer and salmon—finely carved wooden items, and sea-eagle feathers which Japanese women loved to wear.

In this way—deer skins for sake—a precarious peace had developed.

Yet now a new leader had emerged among the Ainu. He called himself Koshaiman, and he had no interest in truces. He wanted the Japanese gone from the island, said they were an offense to all the spirits of the land. Just in the last month he and his raiding parties had killed twenty Japanese—some of them from a trading party that had gone far up-island, some who had been fishing or mining for gold farther up the peninsula. The Japanese had retreated behind the walls of the settlement.

Until now.

Kendo spurred his horse, pressing forward into the valley. He felt, heard, and saw his men do the same. For the first time, Kendo's hangover lifted a little, blown away by the cold air streaming past him as his horse accelerated. They followed the river, a direct line from the sea to the high places. In summer it ran with water so transparent it was as if it wasn't there; nothing but smooth stones, shifting as if lit by an invisible fire. But now it was winter, and the river was a road of ice.

Lord Ando rode behind him. The snow-covered ground, iron-hard, resounded under the hooves of the two hundred horses. Kendo could almost feel sorry for the Ainu. With their bows and their knives, they were horribly unprepared for a full assault by a samurai army.

The Japanese rode to the pass, seeing no one and nothing. Kendo signaled for the raiding party to stop. From here, he could look back to the settlement, so small from up here. And for a moment he had a glimpse of how the Ainu saw it: a little blemish, down there by the sea, surrounded by ocean and snow. He shivered.

Down-valley, the Ainu village huddled against the mountainside, as if sheltering from the elements. A dozen huts, maybe less but not much more, next to the rock on one side and a stream on the other, still flowing, the water too fast-moving to freeze. The Ainu always built by streams—they needed the water, of course, but salmon were just as important to them, for their food and for their spirits.

"Any movement?" said Lord Ando.

"No."

Mist wreathed the pine trees on the mountainsides, smoke rose from the Ainu huts. Silence reigned, until the horses came. There were no war cries, no speeches. The idea was to be quick, and brutal. Kendo pushed his horse forward, taking the lead.

"Go in through the east doors," he shouted, before beginning the charge on the village. He hoped this might give them the additional advantage of surprise. The Ainu believed that the east door of a hut was for gods to enter and leave by—they never used it themselves, would never even look through it, for fear of bad luck. So it was likely that they would never expect anyone else to go in that way.

There were many who didn't care how the Ainu lived, for the Ainu were barbarians and obviously stupid, too. They didn't even have the sense to shave. But *Understand your enemy* was a thing Kendo's father had said, and Kendo's father had kept the settlement safe for thirty years.

Kendo drew his sword, pulling his helmet farther down on his head. The steel, scoured by the winter wind, was ice-cold against his skin. The first hut was pounding toward him, and in the corner of his eye he saw just one old man emerge from behind it. Kendo didn't slow down as the hut approached—he was mounted on a battle-horse, fully armored. A hut door—even the hut itself—was a bundle of twigs in his path.

He did close his eyes, though.

Crash.

Something scraped his shoulder, as he smashed into the hut through the east wall. Another old man was inside; he looked up in surprise from the cooking fire as Kendo swept down with his sword, the blade cutting clean through the man's chest. Blood sprayed, spattered Kendo's helmet and face, startlingly hot. There was a woman, too, white-haired and slow—she was trying to run when his sword crushed the back of her skull. He didn't stop; just kept riding, bursting out through the west wall and back into the whiteness and the cold.

From all around came the sounds of . . . screaming. That was right. But not as *much* screaming as he had been expecting. As he gathered his bearings, he saw a horse stumble to his left, then go down hard, in a tangle of legs, sliding heavily to a stop. The samurai rider, feet caught in the stirrups, was thrown down like a doll, crushed and trapped beneath the horse's twitching body. Kendo took in this scene in an instant, already aware of the two Ainu who had stretched out the wire, who already were moving on the downed rider, daggers in their hands. The Japanese didn't trade swords with the Ainu, for obvious reasons, and the native tribe lacked the skills to make swords themselves—hadn't even known about metal, when the Japanese first arrived on the island.

As the Ainu approached the downed man, three of Kendo's samurai rode past, without so much as a backward glance for their fallen comrade. Kendo swore. Sensible of them, of course. But Kendo had never been sensible. The steady beat of the headache behind his eyes was testament to that.

For the second time that day, he cursed his stupidity, then rode. The two Ainu looked up, startled. He expected at least one to whirl out of the way, strike his horse with the dagger, but to his surprise he saw that both were white of beard, hobbled by age—and neither of them got out of the path of his horse quick enough.

Good.

Smoothly, he decapitated the first, then ran the other through. He leaned down from his saddle, to check the man on the ground. Alive—but only just. Blood trickled from his mouth as he looked up at Kendo with wide, blinking eyes, and Kendo knew that wasn't a good sign, but he refused to leave a man behind. Even if he couldn't risk moving the fallen horse right now, with the battle still going on. Not that he thought he could move the horse on his own: His flaw was stupidity, not arrogance.

"Play dead," he said. "We'll collect you after."

He turned the horse, getting his bearings. Flames flickered over the huts in front of him; a cooking fire had been disturbed in the raid, no doubt. Samurai on horseback hacked and slashed at Ainu on the ground—though again, not as *many* Ainu as he had expected. Not as much screaming.

There was something else, too.

He glanced down at the two men he had just killed, before riding on.

Old. Both old. And the man and woman in the hut . . .

Kendo was beginning to have a bad feeling. "My lord!" he called. He didn't know where Lord Ando had gone; the moment he had crashed through that first hut the bloodlust had been on him, the *sakki*, and the world had shrunk to a point, to a sharp edge.

He could hear fighting to his left, toward where the stream was—clashes of metal on metal, cries and grunts. Every sinew and nerve in his body told him to ride away from it, an instinct as strong as that to breathe. He ignored it, turning his horse to go to where the fight was—

Flowers bloomed in black night, the earth spun—

And then hit him, hard as a charging horse.

Kendo lay on his back, the scene before him resolving into gray sky, an Ainu man looking down. A scraggly beard, flecked with gray. The man raised the club he had struck Kendo from the horse with, long and heavy, and there was only blankness in his eyes. The look of a man concentrated on a task, the look of a man chopping wood.

Kendo closed his eyes. It would look like he had given up, and he didn't need them open, now that he had fixed the man's position in his mind. He felt the down-rush of air, rolled to the side. The club struck his shoulder, and a new flower of pain bloomed, sickly red. A glancing blow, but the crunch and the looseness told him his shoulder was dislocated.

I wish I had drunk even more, thought Kendo. *Maybe then it wouldn't hurt so much.* His head felt as though it might collapse in on itself, shattering like a clay jug.

Carelessly, the Ainu hadn't taken the sword from his hand. Kendo sat up, and swung it in a low arc. It was cold-forged steel, a family weapon, some said a Masamune. It went through the Ainu's shins like a scythe through grass, and the man fell, screaming. Kendo struggled to his feet, left arm hanging by his side. He stepped past the Ainu's severed feet and raised his sword, to put the writhing man out of his misery.

The old man looked up at him. "Prepare to meet . . . the spirit of the mountain," he said, and to Kendo's amazement he was smiling.

Just then the hut behind Kendo exploded in flame, the heat striking him like a wall, enveloping his flesh. He put up his hand to shield his eyes, bashed the pommel of his sword into his forehead.

Agh.

He staggered away from the flames, continuing toward the stream. There were fewer sounds of battle now. His horse—where was his horse? He heard a frightened whinny, then saw a horse—he thought it was his—galloping away. He turned on the spot, took in the fire all around him.

What in meifumado had happened?

Every hut was on fire now, the flames licking at the snow, causing rivulets of water to run down the slight slope toward the stream.

The stream. Have to get to the stream.

Kendo stumbled on, the heat of the fire roasting his skin. Out of the huts, and into the open valley, he felt a surge of gratitude when he saw the sparkle of the stream, a shimmering ribbon before him.

Some of his men were here, he saw. A couple of them kneeled in the snow, looking down at something on the ground. Most were still mounted—as he watched, one of them ran down an Ainu who was trying to escape toward the water. He didn't see many of the samurai, though. Why not? The Ainu should have presented no real threat.

Well, there would be time to do a head count. He plowed on toward the stream, head ringing.

And then he became aware of two things.

The first was that the object on the ground, the one the two samurai were kneeling by, was Lord Ando. The duck-feather fletching of an arrow protruded from his chest. As Kendo drew nearer, he could hear the bubbling of his daimyo's breath.

No, this was not happening.

But then he saw the second thing. Curling up into the air from the huts of the village, up and up and up into the air without stopping, was a—

—was a—

"Dragon!" shouted one of the samurai, before his horse panicked, threw him down into the snow, and bolted. Kendo just stared up into the sky. The dragon was white, shaped like a snake with wings, only a snake that was as long as the stream itself, its body an arm-span wide. Smoke curled from the nostrils of its bearded head.

The spirit of the mountain.

He sensed something break in his men, almost as if a bond that tied them together had snapped, and they began to run. The two samurai who had been tending to Lord Ando were on their feet, moving to the water, babbling.

He bellowed. "Stand and—"

No. It was too late. The rout was on. Kendo stood in front of Lord Ando, held his sword up in front of him. His arm was shaking. He watched as three samurai, who had pressed their horses back up-valley, were caught in a casual breath of fire from the dragon. Armor and flesh alike melted, the momentum of the horses carrying them forward even as the muscle dripped from their skeletons like tallow candles in a furnace, the three riders ending in a jumble of misshapen metal and bones.

Now Kendo understood why the people he had killed had

all been old—Koshaiman had pulled back the young and the strong, before invoking the dragon's assistance. Those who remained would have been volunteers, prepared to sacrifice themselves for the sake of drawing in Kendo's samurai, for the sake of the trap.

Even now, Koshaiman would be strengthening his position, higher up in the mountains.

We're going to lose this island, thought Kendo.

To his left, another fleeing soldier caught fire, burning bright for a moment, then splashing into the stream, a blackened mess. The two samurai who had abandoned Lord Ando made it as far as the water, were diving in when the dragon flew over Kendo, impossibly fast, and caught them in its jaws, and if there was a mercy in being torn apart by enormous teeth rather than burning, then their deaths were merciful.

Ducking as the dragon fluttered over him like a flag in the wind, Kendo was trying to breathe, but the air was so hot, his diaphragm refused to draw it into him, and he was suffocating in the open air of the valley, drowning in no water.

He rose again and steeled himself, expecting at any moment the torrent of fire that would strip him clean, melt the body from his bones. But it didn't come. Instead he watched as all his remaining men were burned, the dragon turning and flitting in the air as it hunted them down, roasted them in jets of fire.

All around him, the crackle and the roar.

In his nostrils, the stench of burning meat.

On his skin, the searing, unbearable heat.

He would have screamed, if he had possessed the breath to do it.

Eventually he closed his eyes, unable to watch anymore. It didn't help. The sight of his melting men was on the backs of his eyelids, refusing to leave him, showing him the horror again and again, the waxy flesh dripping.

A cool breeze, suddenly. He drew in air.

He opened his eyes.

In front of him, the dragon had settled on the ground. There was no snow anymore, just dead, brown grass. Lumps and pools that had been his men dotted the ground. The village was a grid of dark patches, round, where the huts had been. A voice sounded in his head.

"You did not run."

Kendo glanced back at Lord Ando. The man's chest still rose and fell, only shallow now, the bubbling sound weaker than before. But still alive.

"Ah," said the dragon, nodding its giant head. "Your lord."

"Yes," said Kendo. The word hurt his throat, and he realized he must have breathed in the air of the furnace, burned himself inside.

"You realize you could not have protected him?" said the dragon. It turned its head and spat fire at one of the dead men, and then there was nothing there but blackened ground, even the bones and metal evaporated into stinking smoke.

Kendo shrugged. He wanted to say, *My flaw is stupidity*. But his throat hurt too much.

"Koshaiman said you were monsters," said the dragon. "Inhuman. Ignorant of the old ways." For a moment, it looked as if it were frowning, then it rose gently into the air. It looked for a long time at Kendo, its eyes ancient, large as rock pools.

"We . . . are just . . . different," said Kendo. Every word was a sea urchin in his throat, spiked and hard.

The dragon hovered, contemplating him. "You will live together," it said at last. "Everything is one."

Then it flicked its enormous tail and leaped into the sky, and in a blink of an eye it was indistinguishable from the whiteness of the high mountains.

Kendo's body slumped, as if his tendons had been cut. He breathed in deep, marveling at the crispness and clean taste of the air. He was alive. Alive, alive, alive.

Stupid, but alive.

He looked once at his sword, which some said was a Masamune, though somehow, strangely, that detail seemed unimportant now, where before it had been such a source of pride.

Pride. What a peculiar idea.

There was blood on the sword, an abomination. Kendo stuck it point down into the ground, the last time he would strike with it. He let go.

He would never pick it up again.

CHAPTER 7

Even the abbot's story couldn't deter Taro.

Yes, it scared him. He had seen the terror in the man's face, all these years later, had felt the horror when the dragon breathed fire and burned those men up, armor and all. The abbot really had seen a dragon, and it had been more powerful than anything Taro could imagine. Powerful enough that the abbot had given up the life of a samurai forever, had left for Mount Hiei as soon as the next trading ship came to Hokkaido from the mainland. Could Taro stand against such a creature?

But there was the reward. It was too much—too much not to try. And there was his destiny, too. The prophetess had said he would be shogun one day, that because he was descended from the ama who had rescued the Buddha ball from the sea many centuries ago, he would be the one to find it again, and rule the country. Well, Taro had already found the ball. He could face the dragon, and as long as he wasn't yet shogun, he surely would not die. Not without fulfilling what fate had set aside for him. Perhaps, even, killing the dragon was a step on the way to the shogunate. . . .

Taro stopped that line of thought. He knew it was dangerous to focus too much on the prophecy—that he risked thinking of himself as invincible, which seemed like a sure way to get himself killed.

There was a feast the night before they left—a feast of such epic proportions that Hiro was nursing a sore head as they carried their few belongings to the stables in the morning mist. There, they found the abbot's last three gifts—horses, to go with the bow he had already given Taro, and the easily concealable short-swords he had presented to the three friends the previous night.

Also going with them was Jun, the boy who had helped Shusaku climb up to the fortress-monastery of the Ikko-ikki the previous year, for Shusaku had been blinded by the sun during the attack on Lord Oda's castle, two years ago now. The abbot had asked Taro to take Jun—apparently Jun had some additional message to deliver in Edo, on behalf of the monastery, over and above the delivery of rice that they would be minding. Taro didn't mind. Jun was a serious, quiet boy, who made for easy enough company.

Taro packed the Buddha ball first, wrapping it in layer after layer of cloaks and blankets. Even so he couldn't help touching it, to begin with, and when he did so he felt Sato's voice, drowning out even Lord Oda's, whispering to him about the life he had led, and it was like a dagger turning in his heart.

What good is an object of power if it speaks to you in the voices of those you've killed?

He wished he could talk to someone about it, but he didn't know how. Hiro had come in while he was wrapping the ball, had seen the expression on his face and had asked if everything was all right. Taro knew his friend suspected something, but he didn't know how to describe what was happening, how it felt when the ball spoke to him.

He pushed the ball to the bottom of his mind, just as he had pushed it to the bottom of his traveling bag. He touched the flank of the stallion he had been provided with, felt the warmth and quiver of its muscle through its skin. Last year he had walked from this mountain to Shirahama, to look for the Buddha ball. This time he would leave the monastery on more comfortable, swifter transport. He was grateful to the abbot for that.

Hiro stood next to him, looking cross. He wasn't annoyed about Taro's quest, obviously. Taro knew his friend would follow him anywhere, no matter what the reason—and in this case, Hiro was more than happy with the idea of securing a grant of land, and retiring with Hana and Taro to the country.

What he wasn't happy with was his mount, which was a shorter, stronger beast, intended to pull the cart containing the rice taxes of the monastery. "They've given me a pony," he said.

Taro turned to look. "It's a perfectly good horse." It wasn't. It was comically small, given Hiro's bulk.

"It's smaller than yours."

"Well, yes," said Taro. "But you shouldn't talk about such things in front of ladies."

Hana laughed; Hiro flushed red and turned on his heel, stuffing his cloak into his bag, then untying his horse to lead her outside. Jun stared at both of them as if they were mad.

Taro met Hana's eye, smiling. He would have liked to freeze this moment, and briefly he recalled his fantasy; the three of them living together in Shirahama, a simple life of poverty.

No.

There was nothing simple about poverty: that was something he had learned when he was a peasant. He had to kill this dragon, and accept the mantle of his destiny, since he couldn't possibly claim his inheritance from Lord Tokugawa.

Hana returned Taro's smile, but there was something missing from it. He knew that she was angry with him for putting himself in danger, that he ought to have talked to her more, about this quest, about the dragon.

He opened his mouth to say something, about his destiny, about how with the title and money that he would obtain when the dragon was dead, he could give her a better life.

But then Hana turned away and busied herself with the saddle of her horse, and the moment was past, anyway. He was doing the right thing. He would earn his reward, and he would marry her. Then she would smile for real.

He led his horse outside, his eyes on the distant lowlands, the small settlements and fields, stretching away till they dissolved into haze, into sky, or ended at the sea.

CHAPTER 8

Inside the monastery, the abbot kneeled at his writing desk. This was the only piece of furniture in his room—the abbot slept on the hard floor. The Buddha taught that stoicism was the proper response to the temptations of the flesh.

Even the desk was sparse: aside from the piece of paper the abbot was writing on, the only other object was a tray of sand, which the abbot had shaped with a miniature rake into swirls and circles. A small stone, partly covered with moss, sat in the middle of the tray. It was imperfect in shape, and if you looked at it closely, making the rest of the world disappear, you could imagine it was a large rock, standing on a beach.

This was rather the point: a daily reminder that all is one, from large to small, and the stone is to the rock as to an insect is to a man, all extensions of the totality of dharma.

Also, the abbot liked rocks.

In the abbot's hand was a writing brush, of bamboo with bristles of fox hair. He put the finishing stroke to the final kanji on the page in front of him, and appraised the quality of his calligraphy for a moment, before calling for an acolyte to take his message to the pigeon house at the rear of the monastery. Before he had become a monk, he had been a hatamoto, *more skilled with a sword than a brush, but a lifetime had passed since then, and he was pleased with the form and flow of his characters.*

The kanji were simple enough. Had Taro been there, he would have been able to read them quite easily.

They said:

> *The boy has left for Edo, to kill the dragon, as you thought he would. Lord Oda's daughter Hana goes with him, and his friend Hiro.*
>
> *I have provided Taro and his companions with horses, and sent the boy, Jun, with them. They will arrive within days.*

Next to this letter on the desk was another, its contents much the same. The abbot folded both over. Everything was set in motion. It was a case now only of waiting.

Closing his eyes, he rocked back on his heels. Taro was clever, there was no denying that. The boy had seen, from the inflection in the abbot's voice, that he spoke of dragons from personal experience.

He had tried to erase that experience, of course. There were things the baser part of his being envied Taro for—his youth, his strength, his speed. But he didn't envy him the journey he was setting off on, and he couldn't suppress a certain amount of guilt at passing on the shogun's message.

Still, there was a chance, wasn't there? The boy was a vampire, after all.

A chance?

The abbot snorted.

He had seen a dragon.

He had seen a dragon, and he wished he could go back in time and erase the memory, as the snow had erased all trace of his companions afterward.

CHAPTER 9

"No, Taro."

Hana pushed him gently away. They were standing under the last, fading glory of the *sakura*—the pink blossom that spread every spring from the south to the north of Japan, like a delicate fire. Farther south, it would already be gone, making way for the rice-planting season; here it still clung to the trees, including this natural avenue in which they found themselves, just off the main Hokkaido road.

They had stopped at a *ryokan* inn for lunch—or rather for Hana and Hiro to have lunch. Taro had caught a young roe deer the previous night, draining its blood before its heart had fully stopped beating. Back on the cobbled avenue, Hiro had walked off to a discreet distance, pretending to admire the flowers up close. Their horses were tethered to a tree a little way back.

Now Taro bit his lip, and the taste of blood was on his tongue again. He tended to forget the sharpness of his fangs. It was like carrying knives in his mouth. He had tried to kiss Hana, thinking that under the beauty of the blossom, she would be receptive to him. But she was looking at him with a strange expression, half disappointment and half pain.

"I don't understand," said Taro.

"Of course you don't."

"Is it because of the dragon?" He wondered if she was afraid he would die. Yes. That might be it.

"Is it because of the dragon?" Her voice had taken on a mocking quality he had never heard before. Her soft eyebrows were set in a hard line.

"I have to try," said Taro. "The reward is—"

"Oh, the reward. Are you telling me you're doing this for the reward?"

"Of course." She didn't seem able to grasp that the reward was a necessary first step—that the danger was in the short term, and the benefits for both of them were in the long term. The problem was that he couldn't explain it without referring to marriage, which was an unspoken word between them, always hovering in the air, but never given sound.

"I don't believe you. I think you're doing it because you were bored at Mount Hiei."

"Well . . ."

Her eyes flashed dangerously. "Yes, you were bored. And I thought you enjoyed it, spending time with me. Reading. Walking. Just . . . being."

"But it couldn't last!" said Taro. For all the reasons he had gone over in his mind—he couldn't be a monk, he couldn't marry her, they couldn't stay if they were not married . . . It was impossible. "We couldn't have stayed there forever."

"Evidently," said Hana coldly. She started walking back toward the road, but then she turned round. "You try to kill the dragon," she said. "And if it kills you, don't come crying to me."

"That doesn't make any sense!" he shouted after her, but she was gone.

All that day, she walked far ahead of him, never looking back at him. Hiro asked what was wrong, and Taro shrugged. He wasn't sure he could explain it without opening a door he couldn't afterward close. His desire to marry Hana was a private thing. If he spoke it, he might break whatever magic there was in it, and prevent it from ever happening.

Gradually the air grew warmer, which was strange, because they were not heading south. Then they began to reach the lower slopes of Mount Fuji, the foothills and valleys that spilled out from it, like the creases formed when a silk sheet is pulled up into a point. It was easy now to see the creeping tendrils of fire in the high places, the roofs of villages that had already been consumed by it.

The dragon.

The road they followed, the Hokkaido, did not go any higher, but in its skirting of the hills it did take them past one village that had succumbed. A passing merchant told them that the dragon had struck here, then retreated back to the mountaintop—there was no sign of any fresh fire.

But the village was ashes.

Taro stepped off the cobbled road and into what remained of the place. No one said anything, but Hiro and Hana followed. There was an eerie quiet, in fact—no birds singing, no frogs croaking. What was left was like the map of a village; two-dimensional. There were no walls and no roofs, only squares where houses had been, charred posts and ash marking them out. Taro nudged a blackened cooking pot with his foot. He had never seen such destruction. A bad rainy season, and any trace of the village would be wiped from the earth.

"Taro," said Hana softly. He went over to where she crouched, within one of the burned-out houses.

He looked down, saw the object she had fixated on. It was the skeleton, badly charred, of a child. Taro blinked back tears. Hana brushed her eye with her sleeve.

"There's nothing," said Hiro, who had come up behind them. "A knife. A pot. Other than that, everything is gone." He saw what they were looking at and was suddenly quiet.

“You really think you can kill this dragon?” asked Hana.

“It’s possible,” Taro said. Though looking around at the ash-drawn lines of the village, the shadows on the ground that he thought might mark the remains of people, caught in the hottest part of the fire, he was not so sure.

“Good,” said Hana. She kissed him on the cheek, then left him there, as the fine gray powder swirled around him.

CHAPTER 10

They saw no more sign of the dragon, but that didn't mean they were safe.

It seemed to Hiro that Taro and Hana needed some time to talk, so he was hanging back with Jun, letting the others ride on ahead with the cart. Taro had taken the stockier, shorter horse, the better to pull the cart with, and Hiro was enjoying riding the big stallion.

He was a little anxious, though, his feelings giving a yellow tinge to the countryside through which they passed. There was the cart, with all that rice in it—enough to tempt nearly anyone who saw it. And there was the dragon, of course. Hiro couldn't blame Taro for leaving the monastery, not after what had happened, but he wished it didn't have to be for this.

Taro could really die this time, *he thought. There were instances—not often, definitely not often—when he felt real anger toward his oldest friend, usually when Taro was taking unnecessary risks. Yes, Taro had saved his life, when they were children, and Hiro had promised to follow him. He loved Taro—considered him his only family. But did that mean he had to support every dangerous idea his friend got into his head? There had been a time, back in Shirahama, when Hiro couldn't wait to get out, to go on adventures. Now, looking back, he couldn't even recognize the person he had been then. What kind of idiot wants to leave a place of safety? To fill his life with swords and blood?*

Well, Hiro, it seemed, was that kind of idiot. And it was too late now, too late to return to the village, to un-know the things he knew, to un-see the violence he had seen. But did that mean that he should not want a future with a measure of peace in it?

Then there was the ball.

Hiro knew that something about the Buddha ball was wrong—he wasn't stupid. Troubled looks crossed Taro's face like wind over water every time he was near it, and Hiro had seen his downright agony when Taro actually touched the thing. Hiro knew how power could corrupt—he'd witnessed Lord Oda threaten his own daughter to try to get the ball. Was it possible that something similar was happening to Taro?

No—he didn't think it was that. He thought the ball might be hurting Taro, and that was something Hiro couldn't stand.

Crossing a wooden bridge over a shallow stream, he glanced around. They were passing through a narrow valley, the rice paddies sloping steeply on either side. Gulls circled above—they were drawing near to Edo, near to the sea.

"Hiro?"

He realized from Jun's tone that the other boy had said something, which he had missed as he gazed around at the scenery.

"Sorry, Jun. What is it?"

"I asked what you thought about this quest," said Jun. "The dragon. Do you think Taro can do it?"

"We don't even know if the dragon is real."

"If it is. What then?"

Hiro shrugged. "Taro's a vampire." They had hardly been able to hide this fact from Jun, since they were traveling together. "He's stronger than you or me."

"He still got a dagger through the chest," said Jun.

"Yes. But you know, he wants to do this. He hates to be still. He has . . ."

"Courage?"

Hiro adjusted the reins, to lead the horse around a large rock in the path. "I was going to say he has a destiny. He feels it, and anyone can see it. So he's not afraid of things like we are. He doesn't think about what he wants. *He thinks about what he's* meant *to do. If he didn't, he'd just marry Hana and live quietly. But that's not how Taro thinks."*

"Interesting," said Jun. "And what about you? What do you want?"

Hiro looked at him, startled. "No one . . ." It wasn't a question anyone ever asked him. "I don't know," he finished lamely.

"Not at all? I mean, if you could have anything, if you could be . . . free."

"Free of Taro, you mean?"

Jun shook his head. "Not necessarily. But you know, you don't have to do everything he does."

"That's where you're wrong. He saved my life. So I do have to."

Jun raised his hands. "All right. But just saying you didn't. What would you want to do? If it was just you?"

Hiro thought for a moment. "I'd go back to Shirahama. I'd be a fisherman, and I'd live in my little hut, take a wife."

"The quiet life," said Jun.

"Yes."

Hiro watched as Taro and Hana rounded a bend ahead of them, the path dissolving in the dappled light from a grove of trees. "What about you?" he asked. "What would you do, if you weren't . . . Actually, what are you? I know you helped Shusaku, and then you were working with the abbot. . . ."

"I'm not anything," said Jun. "I go here and there. I was with Shusaku, then he asked me to stay with the Ikko-ikki, to help them with their guns. After Lord Oda died, he suggested I stay with you and the abbot at Mount Hiei. I just try to be useful."

"Worse things to be," said Hiro. "But you haven't answered my question."

“Question?”

“What you would do. If it was up to you.”

Jun scratched his chin. “I would be a daimyo, *and have a big castle,” he said. “And lots of concubines.” He gave Hiro a grin, and the two of them laughed. “I’d have lots of intrigues and wars with the other daimyo. I wouldn’t want a quiet life.” He shivered, as if at some horror only he could see.*

“Well,” said Hiro. “We shall have to agree to differ.”

“Yes. Because I’m sure it will be no time before you’re a fisherman and I’m a daimyo. Just the small matter of a dragon to kill first.”

“Yes,” said Hiro, as they entered the grove and he felt the particular coolness of air on his skin that is only found beneath trees. “Nothing’s ever easy, is it?”

As if to illustrate his point, a scythe appeared, rusty but sharp, out of the gloom and stopped, its point quivering in front of Hiro’s once fat belly. He wasn’t so fat anymore, and right then he wished he was. At least fat gave some cushioning against stab wounds.

Hiro got his bearings: Jun was looking at him with wide eyes, a dagger held to his neck. He was no longer on his horse; the horse was grazing absentmindedly at the moss on the floor of the grove, as Jun dangled from the arms of a massive bandit.

The man at the other end of the scythe aimed at Hiro’s stomach leered at him.

“Off the horse.”

Hiro dismounted slowly. He sized up his opponent. The man was thin and dirty. Taro and Hana were standing very still ahead, the cart beside them, their horses grazing nearby. Taro, or someone else, had removed the cart horse from its harness, and the bars were lying on the ground, the cart leaning as if prostrating itself to some deity, the god of wooden wheeled implements or some such—

Stop.

Hiro was babbling in his mind; he had to learn to stay in the moment, like Taro did. He continued his sweep. There were two more bandits standing up ahead, one of them pointing some kind of spiked field implement at Hana, like a rake but with straight tines. Hiro knew nets and rods; he didn't know anything about farming. He did know, however, that tools of quality did not tend to be rusted and pitted, like the scythe in front of him.

That makes the blade weak, which means—

No. It makes them poor and desperate.

Still. The man with the dagger to Jun's neck was standing way *too close—he wouldn't be able to keep his balance if Jun should stamp on his foot or lean back into him, it would knock him over. He'd had to let Jun down, presumably unable to hold him up, despite his huge bulk. And that scythe really was very rusty. . . .*

"Let us go," Hiro was surprised to find himself saying.

Scythe-man laughed. "Might be we will. But we'll help ourselves to that rice first."

"If it was mine, I'd give it to you," said Taro. "I can see you're hungry." The man pointing the rake at Hana was definitely emaciated. "But it's not mine to give."

"Don't care. Give it, or die. Those are your choices." It was always the man with the scythe who spoke. Hiro saw a scar on his cheek, but he thought perhaps it came from a farming accident. The man was not holding the scythe like a warrior.

"I'll give you a cupful each, to take to your families. And you'll say thank you."

Another laugh. "We'll take the lot. And we won't say nothing."

Taro sighed. "Accept my offer. Please."

Hiro knew the tone behind that "please." It wasn't fear. It was weariness. Sometimes, when two people have spent nearly their whole lives together, they can read each other's minds, or at least anticipate exactly how the other person will think, which amounts to the same thing. Hiro knew, in that moment, what Taro was thinking. He doesn't want to hurt them. He knows he can win, but he doesn't want to hurt them. *For one tiny moment Hiro had a glimpse of what it must be to be Taro—to be able to inflict such damage on people; to be afraid, though, of doing it. He'd seen the expression on Taro's face when he touched the ball.*

Hiro had occasionally wondered what it would be like if he was a vampire too. Right now, he was happy not to be.

"What a shame," said the bandit. "Guess we'll have to take it then."

"You don't want to do that," said Hiro's mouth, again to his surprise. It seemed that he didn't want anyone to get hurt either.

"Does that ever work?" asked the bandit. "You just tell people not to rob you and they agree?"

"Yes," said Taro.

"Amazing. Must be some stupid thieves about."

"You'd be astounded," said Taro. "Some of them—if you can believe this—don't listen when they're told to leave people alone."

"Wha—"

Taro hardly seemed to move, but Hiro saw his sleeve flutter. The bandit holding the rake suddenly had his hand nailed to it by a shining shuriken. *In front of Hiro, the man holding the scythe dropped his weapon, cursing. He clutched his hand, from which protruded another of the five-pointed throwing stars.*

Quickly Hiro picked up the scythe, bringing it round smoothly till the point was a fraction away from the man holding the dagger to Jun's neck. "Drop it," he said.

The dagger fell to the floor of the glade—thick with pine needles, it received the blade with a dull, soft sound. Meanwhile Hana had drawn a short-sword—with it, she pressed the man who had been threatening her backward, and he tried to drop the weapon, except the throwing star was still in his hand.

"Over here," said Taro. He pointed to the cart.

Hiro indicated with the scythe, telling the man who had dropped the dagger to move. He gave a light kick to the leader, herding both of them toward where Taro stood. From the corner of his eye he noticed that Jun was shaking.

When the three peasants were together, Taro looked them up and down. "The stars are clean," he said. "Take them out, and the wounds should heal well. Keep them wrapped—don't let infection get in."

The leader looked at him in confusion. His scar twitched. Hiro realized that he wasn't much older than they were, though his lank, greasy hair and gray complexion made him look older. "But . . . You're not going to kill us?"

Taro stared at him. "No. I told you what I was going to do." He unlaced the leather coverings over the rice, exposing the great pile of it. Then he rummaged in his bag until he found a cloak. He filled the cloak with rice, tied it in a bundle. "I make that about three cupfuls," he said. He handed the bag to the unwounded bandit, the one who had held the dagger to Jun's throat. Then Hana slowly lowered her sword.

Eyes on them the whole time, the three bandits began to shuffle away, wary, like hunted animals.

"Aren't you forgetting something?" Hiro called after them.

The leader stared, startled, then his shoulders slumped. "Thank you," he said.

"See?" said Taro. "I told you so."

And then he tied up the rice again, and went to the cart horse, clicking his tongue to calm it as he approached.

CHAPTER 11

They came into Edo on an unassuming wooden bridge. They had followed the Hokkaido road for the last several *ri*, blending in with the hundreds, thousands of other travelers on Japan's most important highway. The first thing that Taro noticed was that Edo was a city of water—a floating city, built on bridges and stilts, its streets lying on thin islands in the marsh, surrounded by rivers and canals.

But whenever they turned, they saw the mountain of Fuji behind them, its famously smooth, conical shape obscured by dark clouds of smoke at its top, the rivulets of red fire running from it visible even from here. It was impossible not to turn all the time—to remind oneself that back there, on that mountaintop, was a dragon, and it was sending fire farther and farther down the mountainside, closer and closer to Edo. Others, too, were unable to tear their eyes from the mountain, and made gestures to ward off evil as they hurried on their way down the cobbled road. Even from here, Taro thought he could just make out the silhouettes of burning trees.

Those in the valleys were terrified—they knew it was only a matter of time before the molten rock reached them, and many had already fled. In fact, a lot of the other travelers on the Hokkaido were refugees from the fire. As they passed through those scorched lands, Hana had wept; Taro had come close too. The sight was one of hell on earth. Taro still wanted the twenty-thousand-*koku* territory, of course, but another motive had taken hold in him.

He wanted to put out that fire.

As they walked through the outer streets of Edo, Taro noticed that everyone in this enormous city was either earning money or spending it. On street corners, troupes of wandering actors performed Kabuki plays, while people sat on benches to watch them. Sleight-of-hands pulled doves from their cloaks; men sold fish and rice from stalls. Preachers, contortionists, acrobats, and the sellers of miracle cures all jostled for attention from the crowds.

Taro felt overwhelmed. He had thought he could find Shusaku here—the older man would know where to go, who to speak to, and perhaps more important, who not to speak to. But Taro had not counted on the sheer size of the city and had no address with which to start looking. He cursed his own naïveté.

No sooner had they entered the city than Jun slowed his horse and turned to them.

"I will leave you here," he said. It was the most he had spoken to Taro in the last few days. Even when they had stayed in a travelers' inn, at a fork in the road, he had only nodded, shyly, when offered a sleeping mat by the window.

Taro bowed to the other boy. "It has been a pleasure to travel with you," he said, a little untruthfully.

Jun took their horses, too—saying that he knew a place they could be stabled, until such time as monks might come from the Tendai monastery to collect them. He left them with the cart horse only, so that they could pull the rice cart through the cobbled streets. Jun offered to take that, too, but Taro had promised the abbot he would deliver the taxes in person—even if he personally would have liked to turn around, take the rice to the peasants, and distribute the lot of it, not just the cupfuls he had given away. There were people starving, people dying out there, and the shogun was taking cartloads of rice from the monks. It wasn't right.

Yet Taro had made a promise. He'd sworn to the abbot he would bring the rice to the shogun's palace, and that was what he intended to do. There was the message, too, of course. It still lay snug inside his cloak, unopened. The abbot had said it was private, had made him promise not to read it, and Taro intended to honor that promise.

They crossed a bridge over a canal and entered a poorer district. It was already late, the moon a thin silver sliver in the dark blue sky. The cart horse's breath wreathed in the night air.

Here beggars worked the street corners. One of them, Taro saw, had a monkey on a chain—he was poking the monkey with a stick, making it dance. The sight was less amusing than saddening. There was a smell everywhere of cramped humanity—its sweat and its refuse. Piles of rotting vegetables and other unmentionables rose up in odd places, like pustules on the skin of the city.

At each side alley they passed, or so it seemed, there was a girl kneeling on the ground, a single tatami mat in front of her. These girls would look up when the group passed, gazing at Taro and Hiro with beseeching eyes, quoting small amounts of money, rice, or—on a couple of occasions—sake.

"What are those girls doing?" asked Taro.

"They are *tsujigimi*," said Hana. "Mistresses of the Street Corner. The lowest class of prostitute. The mats are for . . . well, you know."

Taro stopped, looking at the nearest girl. She was younger than Hana, by a couple of years, but less pretty. Taro wasn't sure how much of that was accident of birth, and how much was the harsh life of the street, which had leeched the color from her skin and sketched shadows under her eyes. Her threadbare mat was laid out on the mud in front of her, for any passerby to see. "What . . . right here? In the street?"

Hana shrugged. "They don't have anywhere else to go. The

yakuza control the brothels, most of which are located in their own district, on a private island. Only the rich can gain access. And only the prettiest girls are taken in—and they're worth most when they're virgins. After that they have to learn some accomplishments, if they want to remain geisha. Musical instruments, massage, wit."

"You seem knowledgeable on the subject," said Hiro, a little teasing, but mostly genuinely curious.

"My father," said Hana simply.

Taro saw the girl in the side alley look up at him, and began to walk again, so as not to feel her eyes on him. "But what about their parents?" he asked. "Why don't they do something to stop it?"

"It's their parents who sell them," said Hana. "In the case of the brothels, anyway. I suspect many of these *tsujigimi* have no parents. They would have died, of starvation or war."

Taro felt a little ill. They were in the capital city, the seat of the shogun, and people were living like this! They had come into the city through the Gate of Eternal Youth, walked through streets lined with the prosperous houses Taro had expected, and teeming with merchants, yet here were young girls prostituting themselves on the streets.

They were looking for somewhere to stay, so when an attractive woman stepped out into the street and said, "Rooms, five yen a night," he turned to Hana inquiringly.

"No," said Hana. "Remember what I said about the prettier girls?"

Taro stared at the innocuous, ordinary-seeming house the woman had come out of. "That's a brothel?"

"You didn't think you'd pay five yen for just a bed, did you?"

Hiro was looking at Hana admiringly. "How did you learn all this?" he asked. "This isn't exactly your kind of area. You're highborn."

"Yes," said Hana with a shrug. "But you hear a lot, when your father has his own army."

Crossing another canal, and choosing a street turning at

random, they began to enter a gradually more respectable part of town. Hana didn't know Edo very well, and so they were having to wander a little in order to find a place to stay.

Hana had laughed at Taro's suggestion that they ask someone for directions. "If you want your throat slit, be my guest," she'd said.

They walked down a street of small houses where red lanterns hung from the eaves, illuminating the doors. But there was something odd. Everywhere else in the city, even more so than in the country, the houses had been protected by charms—*majiwari-zawa* monkey carvings, hanging from the eaves to protect the occupants from disease and misfortune, *o-fuda* tablets hanging from every door to ward off malign spirits. Here, though, in *this* street, Taro could see none. He thought that was strange. Even in the poorest parts of town, the little tablets had been hanging, protecting the inhabitants of even the rudest huts from attack by things of the night.

Just then a woman opened a door to their left. "You are looking for rooms?" she asked. Taro was surprised when he saw her face—her voice had sounded old, but her appearance was youthful.

"Yes," he replied tentatively.

"I'll give you twenty yen for the night," the woman said. "And your friends can stay for free."

"Twenty is too much," said Hana automatically. "We can't pay more than two."

The woman laughed, a throaty laugh that seemed to come from somewhere deep inside her. "No, my dear," she said. "I will pay *him* twenty yen." She cocked her head at Taro.

Taro frowned, bewildered. "You'd pay me to stay in your inn?" he asked.

Now it was the woman's turn to look confused. "That isn't why you're here?"

"We just want rooms," said Hiro. He sounded weary, and nervous.

The woman stepped closer to Taro, avoiding the muddy places

in the street. She wore an expensive silk kimono. "But you *are* a *kyuuketsuki*, aren't you? I could smell you from two streets away."

Taro took a step back.

"It's all right!" The woman laughed again. "You're welcome here." She backed away from Taro and opened the sliding door to the house she had come from. "Come, look."

Taro turned to Hiro, who shrugged.

He went over to the door and peered inside into the gloom. Lying on cushions on the floor, separated by shoji screens that flickered with candlelit shadows, were sleeping bodies—young and old, male and female. Without thinking, he stepped into the room, following a sort of corridor between the screens, to get a better look at them. He was half-conscious of Hiro telling him to be careful.

No—not sleeping. Taro saw their dull eyes turn to him languidly. Were these opium addicts? They seemed drugged, that was for sure. Small smiles played on their lips. His eyes growing accustomed to the gloom, he noticed that not all the people were lying down; some were sitting, gazing at him hungrily. The very faint music of a *biwa* reached his ears; somewhere, at the rear of the room, someone was playing an old song.

Something brushed his arm; he turned, startled, to see the woman standing next to him. Hana and Hiro were behind them, looking tense, as if they expected a fight at any moment. In this light, Taro could see that the woman wasn't young, as he'd thought. She was beautiful, though, with elegantly arched eyebrows and bow lips.

"What's wrong with them?" he asked.

That laugh again. "Nothing. They are in a state of bliss."

Taro crouched down. There was a man at his feet, a portly man of middle age, lying senseless on a mat. His eyes stared up at the ceiling. There was a mild smile on his face. Taro examined him carefully. Then he gasped: On the man's neck, two small droplets of blood shimmered in the candlelight.

"Yes," said the woman. "I drank from him myself."

Taro could feel his feet backing him away, though he hadn't thought consciously about moving. "You . . ."

"I drank. You could too. In fact, I would pay you. And your friends could stay too. It would—"

"Wait," said Hiro, putting a hand on Taro's shoulder, stopping him as he walked backward into his bulky friend. "They *want* you to feed on them?"

The woman looked genuinely embarrassed, and a little confused. "I thought you knew!" she said. "I thought you came to this street for a reason. You know, the lack of *o-fuda* hanging outside is the signal."

"I did wonder about that," said Taro.

"Explain, then," said Hana to the woman, a little abruptly.

The woman—vampire, evidently—led them back to the street. Once outside in the moonlight, she gave Taro an apologetic smile. "It's something in our saliva, or in our teeth, or something," she said. "Apparently it's better than opium. Someone discovered it by accident—a vampire was careless and left his prey alive. But that person spoke to others about the feeling of it, the paralysis, the hallucinations, the meditative calm . . . and after that, people began to seek us out. To pay us."

Taro was still amazed—not least because Shusaku had never mentioned that his bite might have an effect on the victim other than their loss of blood. Maybe he didn't know. Shusaku was an oddly innocent person in some ways, Taro thought, despite all the men he had killed. Or perhaps it was because Shusaku had always fed on animals, when he could—it was true that he was rare among ninjas for his reluctance to drink human blood. And on those few occasions when he did, Taro supposed that Shusaku had usually escaped long before his prey regained consciousness. "They *pay* you to bite them," he said slowly.

"Yes. And we get sustenance. Everyone wins."

Hiro pointed to the door. "The people in there, they didn't look well. I mean, apart from lying there like that. They looked pale. Thin. Do they really win, in the end?"

The woman gave a small, strange smile. "Well, no. They die, usually. But they die happy." She turned to Taro. "Thirty yen?"

she asked, but even in her voice he could hear that she didn't expect him to accept.

Taro shivered. "No, thank you. But if you could direct us to an inn, we'd be very grateful."

The woman—Taro never did learn her name—nodded, disappointed but still friendly. "If you ever find yourself in need of money, or shelter, you know where I am," she said. Then she described how to walk to a good, reasonably priced place to stay.

As they left the street and followed the woman's directions, Hiro turned to Hana.

"I guess there are some things even the worldly daughter of a daimyo doesn't know, huh?" he said.

Hana hit him playfully on the arm. "Keep walking," she said. "You could do with the exercise." This was no longer true—any fat Hiro had once carried had been left behind, on the walks to and from Mount Hiei, and on the training ground. But Hiro looked at Taro anyway, mock-wounded.

"Can't you control your girlfriend?" he asked.

Taro shook his head. "I'd have to turn her first."

"No way," said Hana. She glanced back toward the strange house they'd just come from, part warped brothel, part drug den. "You vampires are revolting."

Taro put his hands up. "Right now, I'm not going to deny that." So far, Edo had not turned out to be at all what he had expected.

But the biggest surprise was still to come.

CHAPTER 12

The next day came on them like a bad mood, muggy and overcast. The guards at the Palace of Long Life gave them some trouble at first, their eyes hard and unfriendly.

"What's in the cart?" one of them asked.

"Rice," said Taro. He lifted the cover, showed them the pile of gray grain.

The guard poked his sword halfheartedly into the rice a couple of times, then nodded to them. "I saw the sword you've got hidden under that cloak," he said, "and thought you might have decided to take up the shogun's challenge."

"What, this little shrimp?" said another, fatter guard. He pushed Taro hard in the chest with a chubby finger. "This stripling? He'd be no more than a tasty morsel for the dragon. We've seen men twice your size go up that mountain and never come back."

Taro smiled thinly. He would have liked to break the man's finger, but he restrained himself, barely. Anger swirled in him—and something else, too. A chill of premonition. Maybe it was crazy to go after the dragon? But he thought of the prize and knew he couldn't turn back. He had no choice. There were no futures open to him, other than the one that led to the dragon, and the prize.

"Hand over the sword," said the first guard, in a sort of spoken sigh. Taro was actually impressed that he had seen it so easily. Of course, the guard didn't know about the throwing stars up his sleeves, or the dagger in his boot, and Taro wasn't about to tell him. He drew the hidden short-sword and handed it over.

"Rice store's in the east quadrant," said the fat guard. "Hand it over, then get home."

Taro tapped his chest, where the scroll was. "Actually, I have a message for the shogun too."

The big guard sighed, stepping aside. He gestured vaguely to the buildings of the palace. Taro had never seen anything so grand—the roofs higher and more delicate than those of the Tendai monastery on Mount Hiei, and tiled with brilliant red. He felt small and insignificant, which he supposed was the point.

"The shogun is practicing his *inu-oi*," said the guard. "You'll find him at the back."

Taro wanted to ask at the back of what, but the guard had turned to his friends, making it clear the interview was over. Taro shrugged and walked through the covered archway into the palace that was almost a city itself, within the city.

"What's *inu-oi*?" he asked Hana. *Inu* meant "dog," but that didn't help Taro to work out what the word signified, what it was the shogun was practicing.

"It's a samurai game," she replied. "I don't think you'll like it." She had decided to come with Taro and Hiro into the palace, despite the risk that she might be recognized as Lord Oda's daughter. As she pointed out, it had been nearly two years since any samurai had seen her in her true guise, and she had changed much since then. Anyway, who would expect the daughter of a fallen daimyo to turn up at the shogun's court, in the company of two lowborn adventurers?

First they went to the east quadrant. When they got there, Taro stood openmouthed. The grain store was not a store but a warehouse, a palace of rice. It stood the height of three men, and was as long as the great hall at the monastery on Mount Hiei. Inside, sunlight fell in sharp shafts through the gloom, cutting through it, illuminating miniature mountains of rice.

What does the shogun need with all that rice? thought Taro.

"Taxes?" asked a burly man who had been raking rice into one of the bigger piles.

Taro nodded. "From the Tendai monastery on Mount Hiei."

The man went to a side wall and took down a scroll. He ran his finger down it, then made a mark with a grubby fingernail. "Five hundred *koku*, right?"

"Give or take three cupfuls," said Taro.

"What?"

"Oh, nothing." Taro began to remove the harness from the horse. "There'll be a boy named Jun along soon, to collect the beast," he said.

The burly man shrugged. "Long as he don't eat the rice," he said.

"Jun doesn't eat raw rice," said Hiro. "It gives him wind."

The man gave him a withering look. "Funny," he said. "But you won't be laughing if your horse eats any of this rice, I promise you."

Hiro nodded, mock gravely.

"Get out, all of you," said the man, turning to his rake.

They left the rice store and began looking for the shogun. So far the grounds had been easy to navigate, but Taro guessed that was because the shogun *wanted* people to bring rice—whereas it seemed he didn't want people finding his own court too easily. Twice they got lost and had to ask for directions from passing servants, such was the scale and complexity of the palace. Doors gave onto doors, which gave onto passageways and courtyards, all bustling with people, busy about their tasks. It made Taro think of an anthill, and the way that the ants scurry around it, carrying out their incomprehensible duties.

Eventually they reached a much wider courtyard, whose floor was bare earth instead of stone. There were a great many people here, most pressed around a large circle. Shouts of encouragement and exasperation resounded off the walls of the surrounding buildings. There was a smell of cooking in the air—rice cakes—and a festival atmosphere reigned.

Hana led the way toward the front of the crowd. To those who turned, irritated, when she eased past them, she smiled a demure smile, casually melting their hearts. Taro and Hiro followed, Taro noticing that he received more sharp elbows in the side than Hana did.

Before long, they were able to create some space around themselves, and Taro could see what was happening in the center. A circular enclosure had been staked out, similar in size to the main hall of the ninja mountain. Within this was another, smaller circle—the two circles divided by a fence, and another, taller fence on the outside.

There was a loud bark, then something flew past, within the confines of the larger circle. Taro realized it was a dog, running fast. Then there was the *zzzip* of an arrow, and a shaft stuck from the ground where the dog had just been.

A groan from the crowd.

Taro narrowed his eyes. In the smaller, inner circle, a young man sat astride a horse, a bow in his hand. He wore the *mon* of the shogunate on his light armor, but no helmet. From his face, Taro would judge him to be no more than twelve years old—his features refined, set in an expression of disappointment, mixed with amusement.

The shogun.

As Taro watched, the boy ruler of the country pulled another arrow from the quiver at his back, urged his horse into a canter with the pressure of his legs, and nocked the arrow—riding with no hands—as the horse gained speed, turning the circle defined by the inner fence. This time the horse was running counter to the dog, and as the terrified dog streaked round, the shogun rose from his saddle, paused a moment with the arrow drawn back, and let fly.

The arrow met the dog on one of its bounds, its force so great that the dog was driven straight down to the ground, nailed to it, with shocking suddenness. The shogun raised his bow, easily grasping the reins with his left hand, and brought the horse back to a trot.

Cheers from the crowd.

Taro looked at Hana, who seemed stricken, embarrassed, as if because she was a member of the samurai class from which the shogun also came, she was somehow responsible for its excesses. Taro's heart was pounding in his chest. The boy had shown astonishing skill, that was for certain. But to what end? A dog was dead, for no other reason than entertainment. Taro was reminded of Shusaku's assertion—which had appalled him two years ago—that while samurai may prize honor above all things, very rarely do they show anything other than cruelty, and mindless obedience.

Taro had seen enough, the last two years, to know that Shusaku was right.

"Now what?" he said, as the shogun inspected his bow, turning it in his delicate hands.

"Now they bring out another dog," said Hana.

When the game finally came to an end—with five dogs dead or dying in the dust—the crowd began to disperse. Even so there was a cordon of attendants around the shogun, stepping forward to take his bow, or his quiver, to lead away his horse, to congratulate him on his marksmanship. Taro began to despair of ever reaching the shogun, but Hana seemed to know instinctively who to talk to, and she led the way to a tall, harassed-looking man in gray clothes.

"My friend here has come with a message from the abbot of Tendai monastery," she said.

The man glanced at the shogun, who was pointing to one of the dead dogs, acting out with boyish enthusiasm the arrow shot that had brought it down. "Come to the throne room at dusk," he said. "We won't get him inside until the sun has come down."

CHAPTER 13

It was the dog that warned him.

Most dogs had been taken already, by the collectors who worked for the shogun in Edo. It was said that he played a game with them, shooting them with arrows, but this was commonly held to be a tall tale, something not to be credited. Enki thought that the shogun—who was a boy like him—probably loved dogs as much as he did.

If I were shogun, I would make every dog in the land my pet, *he thought.*

This particular dog—a lowly mongrel, its parentage unfathomable—had never been taken, though the officials had seen him on their travels. The reason was that he had only three legs. Enki understood that, too. If he were shogun, he wouldn't want a crippled dog.

But he was glad that the dog had been left behind, because he—like the shogun—loved dogs. He loved to pet them, feel the rumble of their breathing through their chests. He loved to bury his face in their fur, feel the comfort of their warmth and softness. He loved to throw sticks for them to fetch—even a dog with three legs would try to catch them in the air, and more likely than not he would fail, but he would always bring the stick back eventually. Enki admired that kind of determination.

Anyway, on that day the dog—Enki just thought of it as the Three-Legged Dog; it would never have occurred to him to name it—was limping up the hillside for its stick when it stopped suddenly, sniffing the air. It began to tremble, then urinated—but not with its leg cocked, to mark its territory, more as if it had no choice.

Enki was suddenly afraid. Many of the other families had already left the little village, terrified of the smoke that was on the horizon, farther uphill. But Enki's parents, and others, had scoffed at this.

"Fire doesn't run," they'd said. "We'll have plenty of time to move, if we need to." Not that they could afford to, of course: All their wealth was in the rice that grew around the village, on flooded terraces. This was what they used to pay their taxes. Enki had been young when his parents explained that the wealth of lords was measured in koku *because one* koku *was the measure of rice a samurai required to live for a year, and the lords were allowed to claim this rice from their peasants.*

Their parcel of land was one koku*—a small amount to live on, when a third of it had to go to the daimyo, who in these parts was none other than the shogun himself.*

Enki approached the dog, which was whining, turning around and around. He bent to pet it, feeling the trembling of its muscles through its fur. The dog snapped at his hand with its teeth. With a cry, Enki pulled his hand back; quick, but not quick enough—blood ran from his fingers. He backed away from the dog.

His first thought was of the dead. There was a rumor, from the next village, that a couple of the people who had died in the last month had come back, the flesh rotting from their bones. These revenants staggered to their homes in straight lines, for the dead cannot turn corners. The people in the next village, so they said, had been forced to rearrange the stone paths between their homes, to make them twist and turn, and so keep the dead out, though Enki didn't understand why the dead couldn't simply take a straight way over grass, or rice fields.

So Enki's first thought was that he would look up and see a man with the skin and muscle falling off, lumbering toward him.

He looked up.

That was when he saw liquid fire, bright red, rolling like a wave down the hillside. Above it, like dark clouds, coiled the body of the dragon, its head wreathed in steam.

When the fire touched rice plants, trees, birds, and huts, they burst into flames, only to be consumed by the redness. Enki was amazed—he had never seen something like a tree burning, would not have expected even that they could. His mouth dropped open as he saw the speed with which the fire ate the world. It flowed redly toward him, and when it touched the dog the rear half of the animal simply disappeared, smoking, and Enki learned that dogs can scream, before the rest of it vanished into ashes.

It was true, Enki saw. Fire didn't run. But it did flow, and it flowed very, very fast.

He turned, screaming a warning.

The words were not even out of his mouth, his other foot not even on the ground, when the fire caught him.

He wasn't able to witness it, but had he seen himself die he would have learned that a person, just like a tree, can burst into flames.

CHAPTER 14

"Do you see them?" whispered Hana.

Taro nodded. He and his friends were standing at the rear of the throne room, and Hana was talking about the objects that hung on the wall at the far end, behind the shogun's chair.

A mirror, a chain of jewels, and a sword.

Each of the items looked simple enough, but Taro was still awe-struck to see them, something he had never thought he would do in all his lifetime. These were objects from legend, not things you could just *see*, hanging on a wall. These were the Three Treasures, the possession of which gave the right to rule over Japan.

The mirror and the jewels were the very ones that had been used to lure Amaterasu from her cave, in the story that Taro had been reading back at the monastery. And the sword? That was Kusanagi, the legendary sword taken by Susanoo from the tail of a dragon. Later he had given it to his sister Amaterasu, the Goddess of the Sun, a gift of apology for ruining her crops and killing her attendant.

Each of these objects was priceless, and the three of them

combined were a treasure of unimaginable value. They had been given by Amaterasu to her son, who was half god and half human, and who had become the first emperor. And from that day, they had remained with the imperial family of Japan, until the last of the god-emperors was drowned in the famous battle between the Heike—the protectors of the emperor, who was only a boy at the time—and the ambitious Genji, when the Genji stole the throne.

It was a story Taro knew well, since he had grown up in the place where the final battle between Genji and Heike had taken place, where the Heike had perished, their ships burned and sunk—his fishing village of Shirahama. On the beaches of his home, it was said that the giant crabs that appeared in summer, bearing crosses on their backs, were the spirits of the Heike returned for *obon*, since the *mon* of the Heike was a cross.

In Shirahama there were many who still mourned the Heike and prayed for the true emperor to return.

But when they slaughtered the Heike, the Genji had taken the Three Treasures, and so they had claimed rightful rule over the country. And so, for the generations and generations afterward, as the Genji gave way to other families, and the whole imperial power base gradually slipped, the Three Treasures had hung on that wall, behind the ruler. And when Hideyoshi, the father of the boy who sat on the throne, had defeated all the other daimyo and named himself imperial regent, protector of the land, the first thing he had done was to parade down the streets of Edo, showing the Three Treasures to the populace, to tell them he was anointed by the gods. Taro hadn't even been born when it had happened, but he'd heard about it all his life, even after Hideyoshi died young, leaving his son to rule.

Right now, looking at the Three Treasures, Taro had an odd feeling of fate, and connection. All three objects had been seized by the Genji off the shore of Shirahama, his own village, five hundred years before. He remembered seeing the crabs, the ghosts of the Heike, when he had returned to Shirahama the previous year, remembered how he had seen his mother's ghost at the same time.

He wondered now if the wreck he had dived to, trying to find the Buddha ball, could be one of the Heike's ships—he thought it was likely. It would certainly explain why the people of his village had a superstition against diving or swimming there.

The bad karma from such a slaughter, even one that took place so long ago, would pulse down the centuries like blood through veins.

He remembered how Heiko had talked of the famous Hoichi, who had been haunted by the ghosts of the Heike, made to sing the ballad of their destruction over and over again, until a monk painted the Heart Sutra all over his body—emptiness is form, and form is emptiness—to hide him from the sight of the dead and from evil spirits. Which was exactly what Shusaku had done, with his tattoos, to make himself invisible to other ninjas.

The treasures, Shirahama, the Heike, the Heart Sutra.

Connections—but what did they mean? It seemed to Taro that he would understand something, if he only stretched his mind.

The room began to spin, as a feeling overtook him that he had come to this room not to see the shogun but to see the Three Treasures, which seemed to throb on the wall.

"Whoa," said Hiro, as he caught Taro under the arms, propping him up.

"Do you need blood?" asked Hana, concerned. Taro didn't know what she planned to do if he said yes. Offer him her neck, maybe.

He thrust away the thought, concentrating on the shogun instead of the treasures. "I'm all right," he said. "Honestly." He wondered how much longer they would have to wait. Two men were standing in front of the shogun, arguing. Taro assumed they had brought some kind of dispute before him. The boy looked bored, more than anything—though the man who they had talked to outside, the chamberlain, Hana said, would occasionally lean in from behind the boy and whisper something in his ear.

Taro sighed, leaning against Hiro even though he didn't really need to.

But just then something happened that snapped Taro abruptly back to full alertness.

His father walked into the room.

The real one.

His real, true father. Taro suddenly found it a little difficult to breathe.

Lord Tokugawa, the most powerful daimyo in Japan, had entered the hall through a partially hidden doorway behind the shogun. Now he came to stand next to the chamberlain. Taro would have known the Tokugawa *mon* anywhere—it had been carved into his own bow, the one he had grown up with—but it was the face that told him for sure, the face that was more like Taro's than that of the gentle fisherman who had brought him up. Taro had only seen that face once before, on a ship off the coat of Shirahama, and then he hadn't known it was Lord Tokugawa, so it was as if he was seeing his father for the first time.

The shogun turned in his chair, acknowledging the man who must be Lord Tokugawa with a curt nod. Lord Tokugawa bowed, an icy smile on his lips.

The daimyo protect the shogun, thought Taro. *But Shusaku says Lord Tokugawa wants to be shogun himself.* He wondered what was going through his father's mind; what it cost him to smile at the boy shogun like that, all the time nursing his ambitions. With Lord Oda dead, there was little to stand in his way, if he wanted the shogunate to himself. Taro half wondered why he didn't just seize it, killing the boy and claiming the throne.

My gods, he thought. *I'm starting to think like him.*

Again, Taro wished he had Shusaku with him, to advise him. Part of him was worried that Lord Tokugawa would know him as soon as he was called forward. That he would recognize his features, mirrored in Taro's face, and know he was his son.

He can't possibly, he told himself. *He thinks you're dead.*

He turned to Hiro. "Do you think he'll know who I am?" he whispered.

"Why would he?" said Hiro. "He's never seen you before. Not since you were born."

Taro nodded. Still, his hands trembled when he was finally called forward. He was uncomfortably aware of the Buddha ball, which he had hidden in a fold of his cloak. He was sure the shogun would want it as much as Lord Oda had, if he knew the power it contained—and that made his hands shake all the more. But the shogun took his trembling for nervousness in the face of power, Taro could tell from the faintly patronizing cast of the boy's eyebrows.

"So," said the boy. He had pretty, feminine features. "You have a message for me?" His high voice was still that of a child.

"Yes, my lord," Taro said. He looked at the shogun's entourage, to check what he was supposed to do. Then he approached slowly. He took out the scroll from his cloak, and a young boy almost ran forward to take it from him. The boy returned to the shogun and handed over the message.

The shogun casually broke the seal, unrolled the scroll, and read it. He frowned, sighed, then handed the scroll to Lord Tokugawa.

"The abbot will not refuse me again," he said darkly. Then he turned to Taro. "But enough of that. The abbot also says that you are considering my challenge. To kill the dragon and claim the reward I am offering. Do you intend to take it up?"

Hana glared at Taro. He ignored her and bowed. "Yes, my lord."

"And these are your companions?"

"Yes."

The boy peered at Hana. Taro felt a fist clench in his stomach, as Hana stiffened. She'd cut her hair short and was wearing simple clothes. Surely the shogun wouldn't recognize Lord Oda's daughter?

"You look . . . familiar," the shogun said to her. "But also different. I wonder . . ."

Taro pressed his nails into his palms.

Behind the shogun, Lord Tokugawa leaned forward, staring intently at Hana—too intently.

Time seemed to bend, and stretch.

Hiro, at least, was thinking. "My sister works . . . on a certain island," he said. "She is a very accomplished girl. When she asked for permission to visit the shogun today, with her brother and her friend, who is going to kill the dragon, why, of course they were happy to grant her request."

The shogun straightened his back, coughing. "Ah," he said, and Taro saw that Hiro's gamble had paid off. The shogun was only twelve, at most, but that was old enough to visit pleasure houses, it seemed, if you were the leader of the country.

Lord Tokugawa leaned back into a standing position, disinterested again, or seeming so.

The shogun steepled his fingers. "You say you wish to claim my reward," he said.

Taro nodded.

"So what are you doing here? Come back when you have killed the dragon." He turned, dismissing them.

Taro stood up. The shogun was not looking at him but his anger had been building up in him since the first dog was pinned to the ground, and he couldn't stop it coming out now any more than he could stop himself from breathing. "In that case," he said loudly, "I will see you again soon."

They were following one of the many corridors, disheartened, when there was the sound of a throat being cleared behind them. Taro turned, and couldn't stifle a gasp when he saw Lord Tokugawa standing there, hands clasped in front of him.

"I— My apologies, my lord," said Taro, bowing low, as one should to a superior. Beside him, Hana and Hiro did the same. "I was not expecting—"

Again, his heart was beating a rapid tattoo in his chest. This was his father. He was addressing words to his father. Surely the man would hear himself in his voice, see his eyes in Taro's face.

"It is I who should apologize," said Lord Tokugawa. "I startled you. It was not my intention."

"My lord is most gracious," said Hana, her head still low.

Panic raced through Taro's mind like a trapped rat. Had Lord Tokugawa recognized Hana, even if the shogun hadn't, and come to confront them, to take her into custody? Taro wasn't sure what the daimyo would want to do with the daughter of his fallen enemy. Kill her, probably, so that she could never have any claim to her father's land and troops.

He glanced out of the open window beside them, saw the infinite rooftops of Edo, stretching to the horizon. Wood and tile and mud, crazily packed together, sliced in every direction by gleaming rivers like blades. A crane flew overhead, calling. A stork settled on a nest. He wished he were a bird like them and could fly away.

Lord Tokugawa didn't lay a hand on Hana, though, or seem interested in her in any way. It was Taro he was looking at. "You're going to try to kill the dragon," he said.

"Yes," said Taro.

"You will fail."

Taro's mouth flapped uselessly. Hiro answered for him. "He looks like a boy, but he's stronger than you think," he said.

"It doesn't matter," Lord Tokugawa replied. "It's a question of the weapon."

"Weapon?"

Lord Tokugawa smiled—Taro thought it looked like the smile of a wolf. For a moment he had considered asking the daimyo if he knew where Shusaku might be, since Lord Tokugawa had employed the ninja in the past. But seeing that smile, he thought it might be a very poor idea. "The only weapon that has ever killed a dragon is Kusanagi," said Lord Tokugawa. "True or false?"

"True," said Hana softly.

"Indeed so," said Lord Tokugawa. *My father, my father, my father*, thought Taro. He was standing right next to his true father, and yet he could be miles away, for all the good that it did him. Part of him wanted to embrace the man, but it would be madness. He'd be run through in seconds, or worse. He could see the *katana* at the lord's waist. "Does it not strike you as strange, therefore," continued Lord Tokugawa, "that the shogun does not simply take down Kusanagi from the wall and present it to his strongest samurai, so that they may kill the dragon?"

Taro thought about this. Actually, it did seem a little strange. But he wasn't concentrating—he was looking at Lord Tokugawa's face, wondering if this was what he would look like when he was older.

"To date," said Lord Tokugawa, snapping Taro back to the corridor, "eleven men have gone up that mountainside, mostly *ronin* desperate to regain some measure of honor. None of them have come back. Tell me: Why would the shogun offer such an extraordinary prize to strangers, when he has men he could order to go, and a magical sword in his possession, one which—it is known by all—once killed a dragon?"

It was Hana who spoke. "Because the sword is not Kusanagi."

Lord Tokugawa clapped softly. "Very good, girl," he said.

"But—" stammered Taro. "The Three Treasures—"

"Are a lie. To some extent. The mirror and the jewels, as far as I know, are real. The sword is a fake."

Taro felt that dizziness again. This was like saying that the Buddha had never existed.

"Oh, there *is* a Kusanagi," said Lord Tokugawa, apparently seeing Taro's disbelief. "But the Genji never recovered it, after their sea battle with the Heike."

"So all these years, the sword was lost?" said Hiro.

"Not lost. *Taken.*"

"Taken?"

Lord Tokugawa leaned in close, as if what he was about to say was dangerous—which, Taro reflected, it probably was. "The boy emperor who drowned with the Heike fleet—Antoku—was a direct descendant of the Sun Goddess. When he died, it's said that all the *kami* and spirits wept, and the dragons wreathed themselves in black mourning smoke. The dragons especially were furious: They were Amaterasu's children too. So the dragon of the sea took Kusanagi and hid it away—until a true emperor, of pure heart, should appear."

"Why are you telling me this?" said Taro.

Lord Tokugawa spread his hands. "I would not like to see another young man die needlessly. You impressed me in there, when you stood up to the shogun. I thought it only fair to warn you. Go up that mountainside and you will die, like all the others. *Unless* you can find Kusanagi."

"I wouldn't have any idea where to look," said Taro.

"The dragon of the sea took it, or so it's said," said Lord Tokugawa. "I would start by searching his house."

"His house?"

"Miyajima," said Hana slowly. Lord Tokugawa was nodding encouragement. "It's a shrine to the sea dragon, on the inland sea."

Lord Tokugawa smiled that ghastly smile again. "And suspiciously well guarded, for a shrine. It's Buddhist now, of course, even though it's still a place of worship to the sea dragon—and has a large monastery attached to it." It was not surprising that the place should have become a Buddhist temple. Buddhism had absorbed Shinto; it hadn't replaced it. "But not so large that it should need three hundred armed samurai around it, at any one time."

"Three hundred?" said Taro. "And how are we meant to get past those, to secure the sword?"

"We don't have to," said Hana, "if we go as pilgrims."

Lord Tokugawa turned to Taro. "You should keep her," he said, gesturing to Hana. "With her brains and your valor, you'll go far." He peered at Hiro. "What does this one do?"

Taro put a restraining hand on Hiro's shoulder. "Oh, he has his uses."

Lord Tokugawa bowed a very shallow bow, as befitted their lowly status. "I certainly hope so. And I hope you will heed my warning." With that, he turned on his heel and strode off, disappearing almost immediately around a corner.

His footsteps echoed to silence.

CHAPTER 15

Lord Tokugawa waited in his favorite teahouse, which was a boat floating on his favorite river in Edo. Lanterns hung from the eaves, and from the side of the boat, which was open to the elements. In this way the teahouse was illuminated by the flicker of light on water. An enamel cup—worn and chipped just so, in such a way that the shadows caught it, giving it texture and meaning—sat steaming on the low table in front of him.

There was no one else there—he had asked them all to leave, and they had complied, because he was a daimyo. The most powerful daimyo, now that Taro had killed that despicable pig Oda.

Ah, Taro!

He had stood before his son that day, watching the boy shiver with anxiety. He'd seen Taro's eyes dart to Hana, over and over, as if he were worried she might be discovered as Lord Oda's daughter—something that seemed to worry him more than his own safety in the shogun's court. That was good: It suggested a certain nobility in the boy, a certain desire to put others above himself.

It might be that he would even manage to find Kusanagi. Lord Tokugawa certainly hoped so.

He called for Jun. The boy had arrived earlier that day, letting Lord Tokugawa know the moment that Taro reached Edo, so that he could prepare to bump into him after his audience with the shogun. If Taro were to confront the dragon without Kusanagi, he would be burned like a kernel of rice in the furnace, and if there was one thing Lord Tokugawa was not going to tolerate at this moment in time, it was the death of another son. It was bad enough that Lord Oda had held his youngest son captive and allowed him to die of neglect, after forcing Lord Tokugawa to sacrifice his eldest son. This was why he had wanted an audience with Taro as soon as possible, even if he could not reveal that he knew who Taro was.

Now, though, there was a chance Taro, his brave son, would be armed with Kusanagi. A weapon with which he might—just might—kill the dragon. The knowledge filled Lord Tokugawa with relief. He had envisaged the boy roasted by the monster, bringing all that Lord Tokugawa had planned to a premature and hideous end.

Jun entered, bowing. He still bore the mud of the road on his cloak.

"Dear me," said Lord Tokugawa. "Were you raised by monkeys on Mount Takao, boy?"

"I . . ." Jun looked down at his muddy clothes. "Sorry, my lord," he said. "I will commit seppuku, if that please you."

"Of course it wouldn't please me, you imbecile," said Lord Tokugawa. "Just try to remain presentable."

Jun bowed. "Yes, my lord. Was there anything else?"

"Indeed. Your companions from Mount Hiei. I want you to watch them," Lord Tokugawa said. "When they leave, follow them. I hope they will go to the inland sea, but follow them anyway. And don't let them see you. Can you do that?"

Jun laughed. "Taro and Hana just gaze into each other's eyes. And Hiro is a simpleton. It will be easy."

Lord Tokugawa's movement was almost languid, but it was also terribly fast. Before Jun could even raise his hands, the daimyo's hidden short-sword was pressed against the soft flesh of his neck.

"Never dismiss a task before you fully understand it. There's more," he said icily.

"Y-yes, my lord?"

"Once he has been to the inland sea, it is possible that Taro will go to face the dragon that has been terrorizing the mountains north of here. If he does so, you will help him. My son must survive the encounter. He has great things ahead of him, and he must be alive to see them out. If necessary, you will die to protect him. Can you do that? Think more carefully about your answer this time."

Jun swallowed. "Yes."

"Good," said Lord Tokugawa, withdrawing the sword. "Now go."

CHAPTER 16

For two days Taro, Hana, and Hiro had walked through a burned, arid landscape, their tongues and throats on fire, their feet blistered and sore.

It wasn't the dragon that had burned the land. They were far south of Edo now, on a plateau, heading for the temple at Miyajima. It was a drought. The land beside the narrow road was cracked as dead skin, the rivers dry. Starving beggars supplicated them as they passed. Taro had the impression that they had died without realizing it, and found themselves now in the realm of hungry ghosts. It was a high land here, but it was flat, and for as far as the eye could see Taro could perceive only dryness—bleached earth, dead trees.

The first Taro knew of how bad it was came when their horses were stolen. They had not been in the province long—just enough to see the lay of the land, and the way the drought had bitten into the hope and happiness of the people here. They were rounding a bend when at least twenty peasants stepped out from behind some trees, makeshift weapons in their hands.

"Hand over the horses," they said.

"Wait," said Taro. "We have money. More than you can sell the horses for." His hand went to his coin purse. He wasn't especially afraid—these people would be no match for a samurai woman, a ninja, and a wrestler, all armed with swords that no peasant could afford to buy, even with a lifetime's wages. But he didn't want anyone to die unnecessarily, least of all himself. Fights were unpredictable things: He could slice open eight of these men with his sword, only to have his head cut off from behind with a scythe.

The biggest peasant made a spitting gesture but didn't actually spit. That was how thirsty people were. "We don't want your money," he said. "We want the horses."

"Why?" said Hana.

"Because we want to eat them."

Taro had hesitated, thinking about fighting for them. But they had already passed people who said that the drought had affected the whole province. Would they make it many more *ri* with the horses anyway? A tear had been in Hana's eye when they dismounted, handing over the reins, and he had noticed Hiro brushing his eyes when he thought no one was looking too.

But what were they to do? They had to reach the inland sea, and this was the only passable route.

The second indication of how bad things were came when they passed some women, on their knees in drying mud that had once been a rice paddy, scouring the dirt with their fingers. Occasionally one would exclaim in triumph and lift something to her mouth.

"What are they doing?" asked Hana.

Taro had grown up a peasant, so he knew. "They're looking for snails," he said. "They live around the roots of the rice."

"Gods," said Hana. "They must be starving."

Hiro shook his head, and Taro felt a pang of sadness. There were some things Hana didn't understand at all. "Usually they'd cook them," said Hiro. "But they always eat the snails."

"Why?" said Hana. "They're growing rice."

"Yes. And a third of it goes to the daimyo. That doesn't leave much to live on."

Hana didn't say anything after that. Her father had been a daimyo—she had eaten the rice that belonged to people like this, people reduced to sucking the flesh of dead snails.

Just outside the next small village, they came across a group of emaciated peasants, halfheartedly carrying out a rice-planting ritual. They stood in a thin layer of mud, planting seeds that could not possibly grow and singing in reedy, dry voices.

Plant the young seedlings,
Plant the young sprouts,
Plant them far and wide,
Let women's hands spread them out.
Yare, yare.

O mighty deity,
God of rice and home,
Were it not for him,
We'd be planting little stones.
Yare, yare.

The rice-planting god,
He ties his kimono with a bright red cord,
But then he sits on his throne
And he looks mighty bored!
Come up and stay,
He likes to say,
Come up to heaven when the rice is gone!
Yare, yare.

With the end line of each verse, they bent forward and pushed their seeds into the mud, the song giving their work rhythm. It was a measure of the misery that had befallen this part of the country that an old man was planting with them, even though planting was traditionally women's work. Looking at the few women working alongside him, Taro assumed that many had already died. Nor were there many seeds—after only two repetitions of the song, all the rice was planted. It would not take, either, Taro thought. Not enough water. He was uncomfortably aware of the words of the final verse, how the planters wished to join the rice-planting god—a god adored by all peasants, for he provided the food that nourished them—in heaven when the rice ran out, and they died.

Taro was afraid that time would come soon, for these people. He wondered about using the Buddha ball to make it rain, but dismissed the thought guiltily. The ball was too powerful. No good could come from employing it. His hand brushing the roundness of it under his cloak, he went over to the planters.

"Why are you planting?" he asked. He hadn't drunk—water or blood—for the two days they had been in this shallow valley, and his voice came out croaky and cracked. "With no water, they won't grow."

An old man straightened his back with an audible crackle. He seemed to be the leader of this little band. "We've always done it," he said simply.

Taro regarded their emaciated frames. "Do you not have grain stores?" he asked the peasant.

"Our taxes go up every year," the old man replied. "We give more than half to the shogun now."

"The shogun?"

"Yes. He's the daimyo of this province, and the next." The peasant indicated the women and children working with him, their bony frames. "Do you have any food?" he asked. "Water?"

Taro shook his head. "We didn't know," he said. "About the drought. We didn't bring anything." This was mostly true—actually, Hana had a water skin in her pack that was for emergencies. What they were going to eat he had no idea. He wished he hadn't given the cartload of rice to the shogun's rice store now; he wished he had it here, with him, and could distribute it to the peasants.

If I was shogun, I would not steal the people's food, he thought.

"Here," said Hana, throwing the skin to the old man. He caught it deftly enough, then kneeled down in the mud.

"Thank you, thank you, lady," he said.

Taro turned to Hana. She shrugged. "They need it more than we do," she said. Taro and Hiro exchanged a look. There was no use arguing with Hana—she was a *betsushikime*, a female warrior, and she was fiercer than her beauty suggested.

"My lady . . . ," said the peasant tentatively, from his kneeling position on the ground. Hana turned to him.

"Yes?"

"Please . . . a blessing, if you would? We are simple people. A blessing from a beautiful woman, a samurai, too . . . it could change our luck. Just a touch, that's all I ask."

Hana looked embarrassed, but she took a step toward him and bent down. At that moment the peasant, surprisingly lithe and quick, reared up. He caught her by the hair, and suddenly a knife was in his hand. He pressed it to her neck. "We'll take your money, too," he said to Taro.

Taro trembled, with anger and fear. "Let her go," he said.

"Your money. Your food. Your weapons. Everything."

"Taro," said Hiro. "We can't give him everything." He glanced meaningfully at Taro's cloak. The Buddha ball. Taro thought desperately.

He was still thinking when Hana kicked the peasant's foot out from under him, caught his knife arm as he fell, and twisted it behind his back. Wrenching hard, she made the knife fall from his hand, then pushed him facedown into the mud. She left him there for a moment, struggling, then let him up. His face came out of the mud with a sucking sound, and he gasped for breath.

Hana picked up the knife and threw it away. She spoke to the women. "This is what happens when you pick on a samurai," she said. She reached for the water skin and picked it up. The man looked up at her from the mud with empty terror in his eyes.

Hana met his eyes, hesitated for a moment, then threw the water skin down again by his side. "Share it with the others," she said.

Taro smiled, shaking his head. In that one gesture were half the things he loved about her. She was walking toward him then, tucking a strand of her disarrayed hair behind her ear, and he couldn't help smiling.

"What?" she asked.

"Nothing. Just . . ." He couldn't tell her he loved her, the words would not form in his mouth. "I think you're amazing."

She pulled a face. "Enough," she said, but her tone was gentle, playful. "Or I'll drop you in the mud too." She could, too—at least, if his guard was down. That was another thing he loved about her.

He performed an elaborate bow, as was appropriate for a peasant greeting a samurai. She raised her eyebrows. "Very funny."

With the effusive gratitude of the peasant women ringing in their ears—something which, oddly, made Taro feel ashamed rather than pleased—they carried on down the road. Taro muttered a prayer to Kannon, the bodhisattva of Mercy, to take pity on these peasants and give them rain, give them food to eat. Even the man who had pulled the knife—Taro understood why he had done it. It was thirst and starvation that had forced him. He prayed also to the rice-planting god, who seemed to have abandoned this place.

It didn't seem that Taro's prayer was answered—at the next crossroads, they saw a mother holding a baby. Both were dead.

Everywhere they passed they saw the same thing: inns and houses abandoned, beggars lining the road, corpses waiting to be buried. People were emaciated, hollow-eyed. The drought had robbed them of food as well as water. A couple of times Taro was afraid that they would be attacked again, their paltry supplies stolen—but when he twitched his robe to show the hilt of the sword underneath, the peasants backed off.

It was several *ri* after the third village they passed that morning that they saw the dead being burned. They watched as a shallow grave was dug and lined with trimmed branches and straw. Then the terribly thin, pathetic-looking bodies were placed gently inside it. Finally more wood was piled on top. A peasant dressed in torn rags crouched over a pair of sticks, calling up a spark to set the wood alight. Soon it was burning fiercely. Taro, Hiro, and Hana waited as the pyre burned, paying their respects to the unknown dead.

Strangely, though, it didn't stop there. Taro was surprised to see two men go over to a pile of large stones and begin to roll them, together, toward what were now the smoldering embers of the fire. Between them, they hefted up a rock nearly as big as a man and threw it onto what was left of the bodies. More stones followed, until there was a huge pile of rocks where the ashes had been.

This time they didn't have to question the peasants—one of them came over to where they stood, bowing in greeting. He looked ashamed at being caught in this act of desecration. "We mean no disrespect," he said. "But they come back otherwise."

"They come back?"

"The dead," said the peasant.

Taro and his friends shifted, uncomfortable. "What are you talking about, the dead come back?" said Hiro.

"We bury them; they dig themselves out. Come walking home, looking for food. Sometimes they decide the living look good to eat. The dead are always hungry."

"No!" said Hana, shocked.

"Yes, lady. So we burn them—that usually works. And we put the rocks, in case some of the bones haven't turned to ash. They get up, if there are bones."

Taro could see madness in this man's eyes, perhaps stemming from hunger and thirst. He nodded encouragingly, as he backed away toward the road. Hana and Hiro followed.

"You watch out!" the man called after them. "Don't sleep outdoors." Taro couldn't stop a shiver from running down his skin at that, even though the story was plainly ridiculous. They did nothing but sleep outdoors—they had no other choice.

CHAPTER 17

They were sleeping when the dead found them.

Taro was woken by a scream. He rolled over onto his feet, eyes scanning the shadowy scene. It was Hana. She was on the ground, grappling with a figure that had her by the hair.

They were in a shallow depression in the ground, a natural campsite protected from view by those passing on the road. Between them, the remains of their fire glowed dimly. Nearby, the darkness of a forest loomed. And over Hana was this bent and angular intruder, seeming more animal than human, though it was standing on two legs.

Hiro got to Hana first. He kicked at the figure, his foot connecting with its head. It fell backward onto the ground, and Taro saw for the first time that it was a woman. The lower jaw had fallen or rotted off, revealing a row of black and crooked teeth. The eyes were bloodshot and staring, the skin bluish, and not just from the moonlight.

A dead woman.

Taro spun as a shuffling sound came from behind him. From the corner of his eye, he saw Hana get to her feet, leaping backward so that she, Hiro, and Taro formed a tight circle, facing outward. On his side, Taro saw a pair of men, one missing an arm, stumbling toward him. They were mumbling, and he remembered the sounds from when he had been haunted by his mother. It was the tongue of the dead, incomprehensible to living ears. Taro's eyes were not totally accustomed to the darkness yet, but he thought there might be more behind them, if it wasn't the shadows of trees, moving in the wind. There was a smell of rot, all-surrounding, all-enveloping.

"How many?" he asked.

"I've got three," said Hiro.

"Two," said Hana, a little breathless.

That made seven, at least.

"My gods," said Taro. "What is happening here?"

No one answered—there wasn't time, because just then Hiro broke away, drawing his short-sword and slashing in one fluid motion. Taro saw the attacker's legs cut off at the knees, and before the body hit the ground he was turning back to his own two ghosts. The first was nearly on him.

His mind was spinning like autumn leaves, caught in a violent wind. What were these dead people doing, attacking them? It seemed the peasant had not lied.

He whipped out his own sword, leaped forward. The dead were not armed, there was that to be grateful for. But they were strong. He cut the first one open from shoulder to side, so that now both ghosts had only one arm. And yet this one kept coming, reaching out for him with the arm that remained. The arm he had chopped off lay twitching on the gray ground, he noticed. His nostrils were full of the smell of decay, like rich ground full of mold and mushrooms—and under it, the metal smell of ash, from their fire. He hoped Hana was all right. He could hear her cries behind him, but they were cries of battle, not of pain.

He hoped.

He spun, cutting at the legs of the other one, as Hiro had done. It crashed to the ground like a felled tree, and he turned to the other, which was a mistake.

As he thrust his sword into its stomach, the corpse whose legs he had severed grabbed hold of his ankle with its one arm. Taro let out a scream as the bony fingers dug into his flesh. He slashed at the body on the ground, which was groaning all the time, he realized, a low sound like the rumbling breathing of cattle. Its head lifted up, like a snake's, and came down hard on his leg—he felt the teeth break through the skin of his leg before the pain hit him.

Screaming, he stabbed down desperately at the creature's neck. The thing was tearing at his leg, not biting and holding on with its teeth but ripping strips of flesh, feeding. He had opened up four or five slashes in its back, but it didn't stop, and the feeling was of his leg catching fire.

Where was the other ghost? He turned just in time to strike it in the face with the end of his sword, the arc uninterrupted, the blade taking off the lower jaw to make this one a match to the woman that had grabbed Hana. It staggered backward, giving him a moment's respite to look down again, at the one eating his leg. Making an effort to pause, despite the agony, he aimed and cut, removing the hand that was still attached viselike to his ankle.

The hand remained there, fingers closed around his flesh, as the arm oozed black blood. The dead man seemed untroubled by the loss. Desperate, Taro began to hack without focus, just thrashing away with his sword, no elegance at all in it. He assumed his friends were too busy to help him

(*Let them be busy, let them not be dead*)

and the world seemed to have shrunk to just him and this dead man gnawing at his leg. It seemed appropriate: It was the dead man who stood between him and staying alive. He was struck by the awful realization that this might finally be the time his luck ran out, this might be the night he died.

Suddenly the biting stopped, the pressure on his leg eased, and both the dead man's head and hand fell away. He realized that he had cut right through the neck with one of his wild threshing slashes.

"Take off their heads!" he called out. "It stops them!"

"Thanks," said Hana. Taro was glad in that moment that she was a *betsushikime*—if she hadn't been a warrior, she'd be gone by now.

He wasn't able to be pleased for long that she was alive, though, because then the one whose jaw he had separated was on him, clutching at his cloak. He got his sword up and against its throat, then pushed. The blade went through easily, and of course the dead man continued to claw at him, but that was before he wrenched the sword to the left and right, sawing through the neck as through a slab of meat.

Head and body fell, the body toppling away from the head, which dropped straight down.

Taro peered into the gloom, saw more bodies coming. He turned to Hana. She had just been seized from behind, by a child that was clinging to her legs. The gesture seemed so innocent, so playful, that for a moment he hesitated, but then he heard Hana scream as the child's teeth sank into her back.

Taro jumped, sword flashing in a vertical arc. It hit the child's head at the apogee of the curve, when all his weight was behind it, and the blade drove all the way down to the waist—Taro was afraid that he would cut Hana, too, but he had judged right; she lurched away, unharmed. The body of the child split like a pea pod, stinking.

"There are too many," said Hana. Taro looked up and saw it was true. Hiro caught an old woman—or what had been an old woman—on the backstroke, lopping off her head. He sidestepped the falling body.

"Too many," he said.

Taro just nodded. He glanced around, sizing up the corpses that staggered toward them. They must have come from all around—had they even been following, and if so, for how long? They didn't seem capable of thought, or planning, but that didn't mean they weren't.

Suddenly Taro remembered something the peasant had said, the one who had explained the stones. *We burn them—that usually works*. He reached into his cloak, taking out the Buddha ball. "Cover me," he said, crouching down in the mud and blood.

It was the first time in many weeks that he had held the ball, afraid as he was of the voices that were awakened when he did so—Lord Oda's, mocking and cruel; Sato's, confused and regretful.

But now he had a good reason: They were surrounded, and losing.

Inside the glass of the ball, he saw dark clouds covering the Earth. A tiny full moon hung above the clouds, like a silver bauble. He allowed himself to flow down his arms, then his hands and fingertips, until he crossed over the glass and was falling through the dark mists of night toward the Earth.

Then he stepped out again, into the ordinary world, and held himself in both places. He closed his eyes, reaching with his mind, and gathered the force that lives in the air, unseen. Catching it, he rolled it, like a skein of wool, holding it together. Then he pushed it to where he wanted it to go, and released it.

Lightning didn't so much shoot down from the sky as simply appear, a crackling bridge between earth and sky—it was so fast that it could as well have come from the earth as from above. The dead person immediately in its path was incinerated, collapsing in a heap of dust, and those around it burst into flames, like wax candles, stumbling into one another, spreading the conflagration.

Taro pointed to the place where they burned. "That way," he said. "Head for the flames, it's where we're safest."

"Then the trees," said Hiro, panting as he caught up. Hana had caught hold of Taro's hand as they ran.

"Trees?"

"The dead can only move in a straight line," said Hiro.

Taro could have hugged him, if they weren't rushing through a terrain of burning, bubbling bodies, those who had still not been reduced to ash clutching at their clothes as they passed. It was true—the tales said that the dead could not turn corners, and what was a forest if not a place of corners? It was impossible to walk in a straight line through a wood. The trees would get in the way.

A hand reaching out—

He ducked, letting go of Hana's hand, rolling. He slashed with his sword, severing another neck.

Two in front—

He was still inside the ball, as well as in this world, and he struck, sending the unimaginable power of the lightning straight into the left one's head, which exploded. The other whirled away, on fire, screeching—or perhaps that was just the noise of its flesh burning. Taro noticed that he no longer had full control of the weather—he had collected all this energy, in the air, but it seemed he had brought clouds with it, or perhaps it was the rubbing together of the clouds that made the energy. At any rate, the sky was now filled with black, boiling, roiling thunderclouds, obscuring the light of the moon. Rain began to fall, so torrential and hard that it stung the skin.

At the edge of the trees, he pushed Hana ahead.

"Guard her!" he shouted unnecessarily to Hiro. He knew his friend would lay down his life for Hana simply because Taro loved her. That was how good a friend he was.

Taro turned, to stop any dead getting too close, and that was when a dirt-covered hand closed over his mouth, twisting viciously, and everything went black.

CHAPTER 18

Shusaku usually perceived his enemies as red diagrams, traceries of blood against the blackness, pulsing in the eternal night of his blindness. The heart, pumping. The tubes receiving; so many of them, it had surprised him when he first lost his sight, and learned to hear the blood instead, and so see it in his mind.

But these enemies, he couldn't see.

He could sense Taro, running ahead of him—also Hana, and Hiro. He would know the rhythm of their heartbeats anywhere, Taro's especially. The boy was like a son to him. And he could tell that they were fighting, that Taro was using the Buddha ball. He felt the heat and the charge in the air when the lightning hit the ground.

But as for the things they were fighting, he couldn't see those.

You can't see them because they're dead, *he thought. It was a thought to paralyze him. He had a particular terror of the dead, often imagining that the many people he had killed in his life were crowding around him, using up his air, threatening to submerge him. Taro had told him to let it go—had told him that he had looked inside Shusaku when he held the Buddha ball, and seen no ghosts consuming him. But Shusaku didn't think it mattered whether ghosts were real or not.*

The guilt was real. That was all that mattered.

With a force of will, he got a grip on himself. As soon as he'd heard from the abbot that Taro was going to Edo, to confront this dragon everyone was talking about, he had left the little village in Monto territory where he had been questioning old soldiers in the hope of finding—after all these years—who had killed his Mara. He hadn't told Taro of this mission, of course, had said instead that he was going to Edo, which was sufficiently large that no one would ever find him there.

He hadn't told anyone where he was really going, in fact.

And now, because Taro had decided to take up a ridiculous quest, he had to let it go. Not that his questions had been getting him anywhere—everyone just repeated the same old story, that Mara had evidently come across someone looking to kill Lord Tokugawa, and they had killed her to get her out of the way. It left too many questions unanswered, though. Chief among them: If an assassin had been frustrated in an attempt on Lord Tokugawa's life, wouldn't he have tried again?

These questions would remain, for the time being, unanswered. And thus Mara's killer still walked the earth, unavenged. Shusaku couldn't bear it. But Taro was like his son, and Taro was alive, where Mara was not. Taro had to come first.

Cursing his surrogate son's stupid bravery, Shusaku had traveled to the capital himself. On arriving, he had seen no trace of Taro, but he had spoken to inn owners, prostitutes, and street vendors, and eventually he had come across a rumor that Taro had gone to Miyajima, to try to find Kusanagi. It had always been whispered, Shusaku knew, that the sword hanging in the shogun's palace was a fake; to hear it repeated so idly, though, by a seller of hot pies, was shocking. Almost like being told that the earth beneath your feet was really air, and you were living in the clouds. It strongly suggested that support for the shogun was waning, and that troubled him more than anything.

Still, Taro's quest made sense to Shusaku. No one could kill a dragon without the legendary sword. But it was dangerous, too. Anyone who possessed the sword—if they could only get hold of the mirror and the jewels, too—could claim the country. Taro would have the key to the shogunate, and more, once he laid hands on it. Many were those who would wish to take that key from him.

Was this what Lord Tokugawa was after? Or did he simply want Taro to take the throne that he himself could not, to secure it for his bloodline if not his own person?

It had been a long time since Shusaku had heard from Lord Tokugawa—he had expected to, after the battle and Lord Oda's death. He had thought every day that a pigeon must soon arrive at the abbot's coop, bringing a summons. But there had been nothing.

It made him a little nervous. With Lord Tokugawa, the things you knew about were always less worrying than the things you didn't know.

Well, it didn't matter. Lord Tokugawa was always scheming, and there was no point trying to anticipate him. It was said he thought in years, where others thought in days and weeks. Anyway, there was no time, because Shusaku was still surrounded by the dead. Could they see him? He wasn't sure. Things of the spirit world generally couldn't, because of his tattoos, but did the dead count as spirits?

It wasn't the time for reflecting on the matter.

Luckily, whether they could see him or not, he at least knew where most of them were. They moved clumsily and loudly, and the ones on fire were hot enough to feel, although he wasn't especially worried about them. He concentrated, drawing in his qi. *Then he began to move, in a run that was more like a dance. Leaping, ducking, pirouetting, he placed the dead by their footfalls, and decapitated them as he passed. He felt the fingers of one brush his hair, even as he rolled on the ground and came up, his sword snapping round behind him.*

He heard the head hit the ground at his rear.

One of them was lying on the ground in front of him, obstructing his path, and he tripped on it—but he didn't fall, just stumbled. Coming out of the unsteadiness, he struck out at what he assumed was the neck of the one in front of him; his assumption was confirmed by the thud of the head on the grass. Now he knew that the dead could not see him—because, as talented as he was, he would not be alive if they could. There were so many of them, they would just overwhelm him. No, the sutra that was burned and tattooed onto his body must be making him invisible, he thought.

You can't see me and I can't see you, *he thought.* But luckily, you are ever so noisy, and I am not.

Taro was just ahead of him now. The boy had stopped, abruptly, as if caught by one of the corpses.

Then, to Shusaku's horror, Taro's heart stopped beating.

The thin tree of blood that was Taro's body, at least as far as Shusaku perceived it, went limp. Still upright, though—Shusaku guessed that a corpse was holding him up.

Shusaku almost went down on his knees.

No.

Taro could not die.

But then, to his amazement, the blood began to flow through Taro's body again; he could hear it, and it was glorious. But Taro still wasn't moving, and Shusaku knew if he didn't act quickly the boy would be overcome, and die.

Stranglehold? Twist hold? He guessed that the corpse that had grabbed Taro had deliberately or accidentally performed one of the throat moves that cuts off the blood supply momentarily, knocking a person out.

He could sense Hiro and Hana moving toward Taro, but they would not be as quick as him. He prayed as he moved, prayed that his strike would be true, would not go too far and cut Taro's neck too. He hoped his years of training with the sword would not let him down.

Coming up behind Taro, he brought his sword round in a tight circle, hoping too that the enemy was where he assumed it to be. An error as small as the width of a silk scarf, and he would kill Taro in an instant.

He felt the blade cut through flesh, but he could not tell whose.

His sword's path ended, and he allowed himself to stand still, feeling everything that was going on around him.

A moment later he heard the dead person's head hit the ground.
Then he heard Taro fall too.
He held his breath.
He sent up a prayer.
And then he heard it—
Taro's blood, singing in the eternal darkness.

CHAPTER 19

Taro was making it rain.

On Shusaku's suggestion, they had climbed trees to wait out the rest of the night, then had forged ahead in the pale dawn light to the next reasonably sized village, where Shusaku had paid for shelter from the sun in a peasant's hut. It was unfortunate that the older ninja couldn't go out in bright sunlight—it meant they would have to travel at night, which was when the dead appeared to walk the earth, but it was a relatively small price to pay for having Shusaku back.

Shusaku knew about the quest to find Kusanagi, and said he had come to help. He was worried, he said, that Taro would be in terrible danger if he did find the sword. Many were the minor lords and samurai who would be tempted to kill him for it, to use it to bolster a claim to the throne.

Taro hadn't even thought of that. In truth, he was extraordinarily grateful to Shusaku, for realizing the danger as much as for coming to his side. He'd known he missed his mentor, but he hadn't realized quite how much. Indeed, it was a measure of how much he needed Shusaku, how foolish he still could be, that it had not even occurred to him that the quest might put him in danger, other than in putting him up against a dragon.

He and Shusaku had spent the whole night talking, catching each other up on everything that had happened since Shusaku left the monastery. And Shusaku had blood, too, in a water skin. He gave it all to Taro to drink, saying that Taro needed his strength back. Taro had drunk deep, relishing the iron taste of it, not asking where the ninja had gotten it from. He didn't want to know.

Shusaku had no more idea that they did of why the dead were walking the earth. "These are troubled times," he had said casually. As if the waking of a dragon and the waking of the dead were minor inconveniences. Still, with him by their side, they would have a better chance against the reanimated bodies, and that was a good thing.

"But the dead don't just walk the earth," said Taro.

Shusaku had shrugged. "Perhaps something has happened to Enma," he said. Enma was the guardian of the underworld, the man who judged you when you died, decided which realm you would be sent to. Taro would have thought he was an invention, if he hadn't seen him with his own eyes, sitting at his chair with his demon attendants.

"You think that could happen?"

Another shrug from Shusaku. "Enma's meant to be human, isn't he? Only he lives for a longer time than any normal human. And he dies, eventually, to be replaced by another. Maybe one Enma has died and another has not yet been found to take on the job."

"You're saying the dead are getting out of death because of a problem of *inheritance*?" said Hiro.

"Problems of inheritance are serious things," said Shusaku. "I've assassinated a lot of people because of them."

And that, it seemed, was about as much as they were going to understand about the dead walking the earth.

For now, though, Shusaku was safely inside, and Taro sat with

Hiro and Hana in a shady courtyard between several huts. The village was protected by a stockade of stakes, and a ditch. Besides, Taro knew how to deal with the dead now.

He would simply use the Buddha ball and burn them.

All night it had rained over the forest, following Taro's calling of the lightning, but now the storm clouds had passed, taking with them the rain. In this village, they hadn't even seen it, though some said they had heard the sound of thunder. But the companions had seen, again, the damage done by the drought. Fresh graves, outside the village. Starving people, begging them for water and rice.

Well, Taro couldn't give them rice. But he could give them water.

Looking down at the wrapped Buddha ball, he reflected that he should have done this earlier. So much suffering could have been allayed, if not prevented. He glanced at Hana, who was leaning up against the wall of a hut, eyes closed, resting. She looked so serene and so beautiful—it was hard to imagine that only hours before she had been decapitating the dead.

Slowly, gingerly, Taro removed the layers of cloth covering the ball. He was always amazed, every time he saw it, by how beautiful it was. The delicate glass, the tiny world inside, interlocking green and blue. He steeled himself, then seized the ball in his hands.

He was gliding along a river, it seemed, as night fell. He could smell pine trees, could feel the motion of the river, hear its softly whispered song. He tried to stop it, tried to remain Taro, the rain pattering on his head. *I'm in a village, I've just made it rain. I'm Taro.* But the pine trees and the river were strong, they were unstoppable, and they pushed the present out of his head.

And then he wasn't Taro at all anymore.

He was Sato.

He stood in a forest glade, moss underfoot. Samurai surrounded him—his enemies, come to finish him off. He had hoped to outpace them, to follow the river to safety, but it was impossible. He had already lost too much strength, since the attack on his father's men, since he was forced to start running. He spun, countering their blows as best he could, but there were too many of them—a dozen, perhaps, and he was on his own.

Then the nearest samurai was on him, burying a sword in his stomach.

Sato stared down at the horrifying wound.

He choked, gasped, cried . . . he felt his blood pooling at his waist, soaking his silk trousers, something no man should ever have to feel. The samurai held the sword there, face close, looking into Sato's eyes. There was a cruel light in the other man's eyes. *He wants to see me die*, thought Sato. *He enjoys it.*

A sudden desire washed over him, to not give this man what he wanted. Stupid of the samurai, also, to come this close to a downed animal. A downed *predator*, because what was man but the greatest predator?

Sato was strong, nimble. He raised his hands, grabbed the man's face. He put all his remaining strength into a single twist, heard the samurai's neck break. Then he let the body slump to the ground as he pulled the sword out of himself, a long sigh of pain escaping him. He could hear someone approaching from behind and to the right—he swung the sword, a scything motion, low.

A scream, so satisfying. He craned his head and could just see the foot, severed at the ankle. The form of the samurai he had mutilated lay writhing on the ground.

Something exploded in his head, throwing up sparks in front of his eyes.

And then, mercifully, he blacked out.

When he opened his eyes again, there was a face in front of him—actually just eyes, really. The rest of the face was covered by black cloth.

"You're strong," said the eyes. They were huge, black. Sato didn't know how much time had passed, but it must be midnight or beyond. There was hardly any light. "You fought."

Sato couldn't manage to say anything; his tongue felt like a foreign body in his mouth, big and clumsy as a slab of hanging meat.

Other figures emerged from the gloom behind the man, also

dressed in black, also masked. *Is this a dream? Is this death?*

No. He knew what this was, if he was honest with himself. He knew what these men were, though he had only ever half believed in their existence.

Ninjas.

The closest one put out a hand and touched Sato's arm, very gentle, very compassionate. Sato almost wept. "Join us," he said, "and you have a chance to survive."

Sato opened his mouth, let out a croaking imitation of speech. "I . . . am . . . samurai."

"Not anymore," said the ninja. Then he pounced, a blur, and sank his teeth into Sato's neck—

"Taro!"

"Taro!"

Taro opened his eyes slowly. Hiro and Hana crouched in front of him, brows furrowed.

"Are you all right? Your eyes rolled up in your head. We thought you were having some kind of fit. . . ."

Taro looked down at the ball in his hands, bracing himself for Sato's voice, for Lord Oda's voice, for more scenes from Sato's past. But there was nothing. It sat there, inert, just a glass ball with the world in it. But he had *lived* Sato's death. He had been there, he had been Sato for that moment, which was the same thing as being Sato forever.

"It's . . . the ball," he said eventually. "It's so powerful."

Hiro crouched down farther. "You don't have to use it," he said. "You don't have to, if you don't want to."

Taro shook his head. "I *do*. People are dying."

"Just . . . look after yourself," said Hana. "I don't know what happened there, but it was terrifying. One moment you were sitting there perfectly normally, the next your eyes went strange, and you were gone. . . ."

"It's all right now," said Taro. "I can feel it." He wasn't lying—he couldn't sense anything from the ball now, no insistent voices of the dead. The only thing that was good about Sato's death was that at least he had replaced Lord Oda, for the moment. The bad thing was that it wasn't just a voice—it was a whole being, it was a kind of possession that took hold of Taro as soon as he touched the ball. *It's because I drained him*, he thought. *It's because I have so much of his blood inside me.* He wished he hadn't killed Sato, but what could he have done? The man had been trying to kill him.

It's whoever sent him, Taro thought. *Whoever sent him is to blame.*

But he didn't entirely believe it.

Now, though, was not the time to think about it. Now was the time to make it rain. Closing his hands tight around it, he dropped into the ball, and his awareness shrank and expanded at the same time, till he was moisture suspended in air, high above the ground.

The clouds began to mass soon afterward, drawing in from all over the country to gather over this province. Dimly Taro heard people exclaiming, from all over the village.

"Come and look!" they said. "Clouds!"

For a moment, Taro remained diffuse, spread out over many *ri*; he was a constellation—a thousand constellations—of droplets of water, hanging in the gray sky, separate. Then he contracted, pressing all that water together, tightening it, until it could no longer occupy the same air.

Rain poured down.

When Taro came back fully into the ordinary world, he found that he was soaked through. Hana and Hiro were holding out their water skins, and the rain was coming down so fiercely that they were filling quickly.

"That rice might grow now," said Hiro.

Taro hoped so.

Just then, someone came running toward them. A woman, grinning from ear to ear. "We're saved!" she called out as she passed. "The gods have saved us."

Taro looked down at the ball, feeling ashamed again. He should have used it earlier, but he had been afraid. In his mind had been the picture of Lord Oda bursting open, blood spraying everywhere.

"Did you hear that?" said Hiro, distracting him. "You've been promoted again. Already the son of a daimyo and now a god. Should I address you differently?"

"Don't give him ideas," said Hana. "He can barely read, and his manners are appalling. I only put up with him because he makes quite a good sparring partner."

Taro smiled. He might be a killer, and he might be afraid much of the time, but he couldn't be all bad. Otherwise he wouldn't have friends like these.

Taro and Hana walked hand in hand, Hiro and Shusaku somewhere behind. Ever since Taro had decided to take up the shogun's challenge, a distance had grown between him and Hana, a discomfiture. Hana hadn't spoken about it again after that day under the *sakura* blossoms—indeed, she was friendly to him now, affectionate, even. But the accusation she had made, that he found a quiet life with her boring, hung between them. It made it impossible for them to be natural with each other. They slept conspicuously far from each other at night.

Now, though, with the world fresh and dewy around them, their embarrassment was starting to lift. When they had woken, Shusaku shaking them into wakefulness before dusk, she had walked over to him and kissed him.

"That's for the rain," she had said.

Now they walked through a sparkling land, surrounded by full rice paddies, the croaking of frogs. How the frogs had survived the drought Taro didn't know. Perhaps they had buried themselves in the mud. He suspected they had been luckier than the snails. Everywhere they passed smiling peasants—still thin, but hopeful now, their eyes no longer haunted. In most places could be heard the rhyming refrains of rice-planting songs, as the seeds—useless without water—were laid out in the paddies.

"Have you ever—" began Hana, then broke off.

"What?"

She brushed hair back from her forehead, tucking it behind a perfect ear. It was in small gestures like these that her beauty hit him like a punch. "I wondered . . . if you had given any thought to the prophecy lately."

"The one about being shogun one day?"

"Yes. It must have occurred to you that if we find Kusanagi, you could keep it for yourself. Even if you don't want to think about that, other people will, believe me. As soon as you have that sword, and others know about it, it will be like having a warrant out on your life."

Shusaku had said much the same thing. Taro scratched his head. "You think it's that dangerous?"

"I think it's more dangerous than you can imagine."

"Well, I mean, it's a great sword, but . . ."

"But nothing. It's not the sword—it's what it *means*. Listen: Imagine you are a noble, or Lord Tokugawa even. Would you go and kill the shogun right now, assuming the opportunity arose? Would you remove him and take the throne?"

"Of course not," said Taro.

"Why not?"

"Because the shogun is the shogun. It's a birthright. The country would rise up in arms."

Hana raised her eyebrows. "Perhaps there is something inside your head after all," she said breezily. "No one can challenge the shogun's right to rule. *Unless* they can prove that the shogun has been using a fake sword, pretending to possess the three sacred objects, when really he has only two."

"But if someone had the real sword . . ."

"That would be more than enough proof, yes."

Taro's head reeled. He'd been thinking of the sword only as a tool with which to kill the dragon, despite Shusaku's warning. But it was so much more than that, of course it was. There was someone else who would kill him for it too, for quite the opposite motive—and that was—

"The shogun," said Hana. "He'd assassinate you and take the sword in a heartbeat also. Better that than risk the truth coming out."

"Gods," said Taro. "I don't know if I want it anymore."

Hana shook her head. "I didn't say that. You just need to be careful, and you need to be absolutely sure what you're doing. Don't take the sword if you're not prepared to take the consequences."

"You mean . . . becoming shogun, or getting killed?"

"I would prefer the former," she said with a smile.

Strangely, he found that the idea of being shogun frightened him more than the idea of being killed. He'd been to death itself, after all, he knew what it was like. And if anyone chose to attack him for the sword, well, he could deal with that when it came.

But the shogunate.

It had occurred to him, of course it had. With the sword, the true sword, he wouldn't just be a dragon-slayer. He would be a person in possession of one of the most important and powerful objects in the land, the birthright of the first emperors. Of course it had crossed his mind that there might be too much coincidence here: The prophetess had told him he would be shogun, and now here he was searching for a sword that might just help him to do it.

The question was—did he want to be shogun? He knew it was his destiny, but destiny and what he wanted were different things.

Hana peered at him. "The thought of being shogun frightens you?"

He could feel the tension in her hand, feel that she was nervous. "I suppose so," he said. "It just seems so . . . unlikely. I don't know the first thing about ruling a country."

"But look what you've done. This entire land is supported by rice. It pays the daimyo. It feeds the troops. It keeps the peasants alive. With the Buddha ball, you could ensure that the rice crops never fail. It would be the greatest gift a shogun could give."

He hadn't thought of it that way. He watched a heron land in a rice paddy close to them, raising one leg to peer down into the water. It darted its beak like a spear and came up with a frog.

"Is this why you want me to be able to read so badly?" he asked, raising his eyebrows.

He was joking, but she nodded. "A shogun has to be able to

read," she said. "Even if the people are more impressed by famous swords."

He closed his mouth, surprised.

"You must understand me," said Hana. "I don't like you because I think you're going to be important. I like you because you're kind, and thoughtful, and brave. But I think you'd be a good shogun, too."

They didn't speak much after that; Taro was too busy thinking, questioning his motives. Hana had spoken with the best of intentions, but her line of thought worried him. He wondered now if he was impelled by ambition or instinct, if deep down he wanted Kusanagi because he wanted to be shogun, and having the legendary sword would strengthen his claim. He didn't think so—as far as he was aware, he was doing it because he wanted to kill the dragon, claim a territory, and marry Hana. But what if there was a part of his mind that operated without his knowledge or consent, and it had another idea?

Hana could tell that she had troubled him, he knew, and so she kept quiet. But she left her hand in his too. He liked its smoothness and warmth. It was a contrast to the ache in his legs, the pain from his blistered feet.

He missed his horse.

It wasn't long before they had to find shelter, the sun having grown too bright for Shusaku. Really they could cover only a couple of *ri* each morning and evening, and in this way several days passed as they crossed the province. A couple of times they saw dead people, but never in the numbers that had attacked them that first night, and they were able to avoid them by keeping to villages or forests that were all angles.

As to what had brought them out, the companions had no idea. Even Shusaku was at a loss.

"I've never seen anything like it," he said. "In my experience the dead stay dead. Except for vampires, of course."

"It's an omen," said Hana. "The country is in trouble. Dragons are waking. The dead are walking. It's because of the shogun, hunting dogs in a palisade when he should be looking after his people. The dead are rising up against him."

Taro glanced at her when she said this. She seemed to be talking to him again, even though she was addressing Shusaku. But she didn't meet Taro's eye.

"It's annoying," said Hiro. "They stink and they just mumble nonsense."

"That's what annoys you about them?" said Taro. "Not the fact that they try to eat you?"

"I don't like people who smell," said Hiro, shrugging. "It's why I've always had a problem with you."

It was when they came down from the plateau to the next province, which lay by the sea, that Taro saw the terrible evil he had done.

There was a hint of it, even, on the way down, though he hadn't wanted to recognize it. They had descended a wide gorge, which Shusaku said was the quickest route down from the highlands, a good, clear path. But in places there was no path. Instead the stream at the bottom of the gorge had swollen, breaking its banks, sweeping away the rocks of the path when it got too close to the white, raging water.

None of them spoke of it, but when they left the gorge and saw the first of the villages, its wooden huts swept away, reduced to a few spars and a bell tower sticking up from the shallow water, none of them were surprised. Taro gazed around him in devastation and horror. He could see no one—until a miserable-looking man appeared, riding a buffalo.

"What happened?" asked Taro, though it was obvious. He did most of the speaking for them these days. The appearance of Shusaku's face was so terrifying that he kept himself hidden behind a deep hood, talking to strangers only when absolutely necessary.

"The water came all at once," said the peasant. "We had no warning. The stream was dried up; had been for weeks. We were so thirsty, and our crops were failing. We prayed for water. Then, when it came, we prayed for it to stop."

Taro could see where the houses had stood, some of them, anyway. There were broken wooden supports where walls should have been. "Did anyone . . . ," he began.

The peasant, who wore a wide-brimmed hat, tipped it back so that Taro could see the dark circles under his eyes. "Most were sleeping," he said. "The water was too fast. Some clung to trees, or the roofs of their huts. But water . . . it's stronger than you think."

Taro didn't need to be told that. He'd grown up by the sea, where there were tsunamis. He felt his legs buckling with the awful realization of what he had accomplished.

"They may be all right," said Hana. "They may have come to dry ground." It wasn't clear whether she was addressing the peasant or Taro.

The peasant shook his head. "It's been days since they were swept away. No one is coming back." He patted the flank of his buffalo, and began to ride slowly off across the shallow, still water. Then he turned to look at them. "But maybe that's a mercy," he called out over his shoulder. "Before the flood, we learned what it's like, when the dead come back."

CHAPTER 20

Taro trailed his fingers in the water of the inland sea, as the shore—and the people he had drowned—receded behind them. There was only a thin moon in the dark sky, but enough to sail by. It was not large, the inland sea. Already Taro could see the outline of the island they were heading to. He wrapped his cloak around him, against the chill that came from the sea, even this near to summer. He could feel the Buddha ball pressing into his side. He would never use it again.

Behind him, Shusaku was talking to the fisherman whose boat they had hired. The man was nervous. He'd spoken of pirates, when they first approached him, and increasingly violent attacks. He'd also mentioned something about ships crewed by the dead, which Taro would have dismissed as a tall tale until a few days ago, but now it seemed all too possible. In the end, it had taken all of Taro's money, combined with all of Shusaku's, to convince the fisherman to set sail with them, even for the short journey to Miyajima.

Taro wasn't interested in talking, though. Both Hana and Hiro had tried, and Shusaku had offered him blood. He had ignored them. Once again he'd tried to help, and he had ended up killing. He felt as though the weight of the people he had brought to an end was pressing on his chest, stopping him from breathing. His mother, Heiko, even Yukiko, who wouldn't have turned into a murderer if Taro hadn't gotten her sister killed.

The moon was nearing its highest point as they drew close to the temple. Taro couldn't help a gasp, even though he'd heard stories of how beautiful the place was. Before them, rising from the sea itself, was a torii gate, a sweeping gull wing of a structure. Its posts stood in what seemed from this distance deep water, but revealed itself moments later as a shallow bay, walkable even. The water around the posts of the gate shivered and shimmered, creating a huge, moving reflection that stretched all the way toward them.

The fisherman brought the boat about, having gone as far as he could. Shusaku handed over half the money, as had been agreed on the mainland. Then he, Taro, Hiro, and Hana disembarked, jumping down from the side into the knee-deep water of the bay. The torii rose above them, something delicate and miraculous. Taro could not understand how it had been built; the posts must have been sunk in the bottom of the sea, at low tide. No one knew how, of course. The temple had been old when the boy emperor Antoku was killed in the last battle of the Heike.

"Come on," said Shusaku. "We should go to the temple monastery before the sun rises."

"Will they let us in?" said Hana.

"We'll be pilgrims," said Shusaku. "At first, anyway. They'll have to."

Taro turned to them. "I'll catch you up," he said. As they headed toward the long, gently sloping beach, he moved instead toward the torii. When he came to the base of it, he looked up at the arc of red above him, like a wooden rainbow. The water gleamed silvery all around him.

Reaching into his cloak, he took out the Buddha ball. Without meaning to, he glanced at it, and for a moment was almost pulled into the moonlit sky of the little world in his hand. He wrenched his eyes away from the magical glass globe.

Then he hefted it in his hand and drew back his arm to—

No.

A thought struck him.

He remembered Lord Tokugawa saying that Miyajima was a Buddhist temple now, with a monastery attached. Of course it was; there were no purely Shinto shrines anymore. Everything was Buddhist, because all the local *kami* and spirits had simply become part of the Buddhist pantheon—heavenly beings, in service of *dharma*. Buddhist monks believed in dragons as much as peasants did.

What it meant, though, was something important. Taro hadn't really given any thought to how he was going to *get* Kusanagi. Neither had Hana or Hiro, he realized. They'd heard that it might be here, and they'd come looking for it, as if the monks would just hand it over. But if they *did* have the legendary sword, it was hardly likely they would simply give it to him, was it? Even if he said he wanted it to kill a dragon.

But they were Buddhists.

They might give it to him in return for something else.

Something more valuable.

Something once owned by the Buddha himself. Only . . . might they abuse it? No. They were monks; it wouldn't be in their nature. Better it should be with monks, who served Buddha, than with a boy who used it to drown innocent people.

Yes. It would be safer all round. The right thing to do.

Taro lowered his arm and tucked the ball once again into the folds of his cloak. He had been about to throw it away, but now he needed it again. If he could use it to get the sword . . . Well, it would never bring back the people he'd drowned. But it might help him to save those whose villages were being burned by the dragon. And it might help him to marry Hana.

CHAPTER 21

Kenji Kira was glad he had recruited the ninja. It had been an inspired idea, he thought, not being one for false modesty. Hiring an assassin to kill himself! The attempt itself was a kind of audition, and a test of his island's defenses at the same time. Actually, he had been a little upset when the ninja got close enough to wrap that chain around his neck—it had been nicely done, but what it said about his security was not flattering.

A few of his crew had died after that—and those ones he hadn't brought back.

But the important thing was that the ninja was talented. It was a burning ambition of Kenji Kira's to kill the boy Taro—especially after the news reached him that Taro had destroyed Lord Oda. Yet it wasn't the only thing that drove him, and there were things that needed to be done first. He wanted power, too. Land. Influence. Wealth.

A woman to stand by his side.

Hana.

He had nothing to fear, not anymore. He was already dead, and he couldn't rot, because he was made of bone. It was everything he had dreamed of. Now he was free to build his empire, little by little.

He already had the inland sea in his pocket. The merchants paid him taxes now, in return for not capturing their vessels—imagine it! They actually paid him for his piracy. The province's daimyo knew about it too, but what could he do? There was no way his troops could challenge the pirate island. Anyway, Kira had heard rumors that the man was a secret Christian. He would not be hard to push out of the way, once Kira began to consolidate his territory.

There was, however, one merchant who apparently didn't know about Kira's grip on the inland sea—the one on the heavily laden ship just ahead.

Kira was looking through a Portuguese spyglass he had taken in a haul of booty soon after he'd arrived at the inland sea—a place conveniently far from the shogun's influence or control—and began to build his little army. He could see that the ship had raised all its sails, trying to outrun him, heading for the natural harbor just ahead.

They would fail.

He waited until his own ship had gained a little more, and the prey had drawn closer to the rocky arms of the bay. Then, raising the matchlock rifle at his side, he fired a shot over their bows. It wasn't meant to scare them. It was meant to give the ninja his signal.

The newest member of Kenji Kira's private army did not hesitate. Even without the spyglass, Kira saw the chain go up, snapping taut just in front of the fleeing ship. There was a crash as it cut into the bow, a splintering sound as the rear of the ship rushed to fill space still occupied by the front.

A movement from the rocks—the ninja was on the chain, running on all fours like a monkey toward the stricken merchant vessel.

Extraordinary.

Kenji Kira congratulated himself once more on his choice.

"Prepare to board," he said to the men beside him—at least, some of them were still men.

There was a ram on the front of their ship, a big fist of iron. It slammed into the other ship, forcing it even farther onto the chain, wood crying out as it bent and broke. A couple of the merchant crew fell into the water, screaming. Kenji Kira ignored them, because they wouldn't be a threat anymore. Sailors didn't learn to swim; it was one of their many stupidities. Along with greasy hair and poor hygiene. Kenji Kira had been trapped on a field of the dead once, held immobile beneath a dead horse. That had been a more unpleasant experience than being in close proximity to sailors—but not by much.

The ninja was on the other ship already. Kira saw his shadow flit behind the mast, then heard a cry from one of the sailors—a cry that was quickly cut off.

But even the ninja couldn't kill them all.

The ram had brought the decks of the two ships together. Kira was on the merchant vessel with the first wave, as was his rule, seeing the stinking long-haired defenders staring at him and his crew with abject terror. He had a club in his hand; He'd discovered a liking for the way that it crushed and shattered, something more satisfying than the slicing of a sword. A man stood before him, defending his own life and his cargo. He had a short blade in his hand.

He decided to let the man stab him—it was a good strategy, intended to wrong-foot the enemy. It also amused him. The short-sword grated between the bones of his empty rib cage, a sound like a ship's hull on rocks. Kira twisted his torso, trapping the sword, pulling it from the man's hand. An image: staring, fearful eyes in front of him. He struck up and outward with his club, and the sailor somersaulted backward, landing on his face with a final-sounding crunch.

Beside him, his men dispatched other defenders just as quickly. The ninja killed one of them ruthlessly from behind. One of the less bright among Kenji Kira's crew, one of the still living, had been fighting the sailor from the front, and was too slow to stop his sword from swinging at the ninja. The ninja turned his body, let the blade pass harmlessly by him. In a continuation of the same movement he swung his own sword; the pirate's head hit the deck, rolled, and fell into the sea with a *plop*.

The ninja turned to Kira, shrugging an apology, when he realized what his instincts had done. Kira shrugged back. It wasn't important. He had no room for idiots.

A gun went off; shards of deck flew up as a hole gouged itself into the wood at Kira's feet. He pointed up at the rigging, saw the ninja jump for the mast, begin shimmying up.

A moment later, a diminishing cry—then a splash.

Kenji Kira surveyed the ship. Everyone who had been on it was either dead or in the water, which meant they would soon be dead. He gestured toward the hold. "Take everything," he said.

Then he bent down to the body at his feet, the one he'd struck with his club. He picked it up in one hand, grabbed an arm, tore it off. He prized open the chest, snapping the ribs. Tore out the heart.

Raised it to his fleshless lips.

When he had fed, he took in the ship again. He was a little shocked, despite himself, at how many pieces the dead man was now in. Had he really ripped his legs out of their sockets?

Well, the hunger had been on him. He had discovered early on, when he ate Yukiko's heart, that the dead needed to ingest the flesh of the living if they were to remain in this realm of existence.

He saw that some of his crew, the dead ones, were eating too. Good. They would need their strength, for the coming battles. He was disturbed to see that a couple of the living ones were also gnawing on bones, but he supposed it showed ambition, at least. He held the prospect of eternal life over some of the men, leaving them mortal for the moment—it wouldn't do if he had an army with no fear at all.

It would mean they wouldn't be sufficiently afraid of him.

When he looked to the north, he saw something on the horizon. A ship. As far as he could tell, it had not noticed him and his men, hidden as they were by the embrace of the bay. It was still sailing straight for Miyajima. He raised the spyglass to his eye socket.

The torii gate dedicated to the sea dragon swam into view, an elegant brushstroke in red. He swung the eyeglass, keeping it level with the sea. He passed the ship, moving too quickly, then turned the spyglass back, more slowly this time.

It was a fishing vessel, no more. Perhaps taking pilgrims to the temple; it was common for fishermen from the mainland to do so for a price, though he had noted with some satisfaction that the price had gone up since he had been operating in these waters.

He was about to lower the spyglass again when he saw something that shocked him. Sitting at the prow, was that . . .

No. It couldn't be.

He examined the other figures—a large young man, a beautiful woman, another figure in a hood that covered his face.

A beautiful woman.

Hana.

And the one sitting in the prow—that was Taro. Kenji Kira had been sent to kill the boy two years ago, and the closest he'd gotten was to face him in the monastery on Mount Hiei. He would have killed him too, if the traitor-girl Yukiko had not stabbed him from behind, bringing to an end his mortal life.

Well, he'd killed Yukiko, tearing out her heart and devouring it. Now he had only to kill Taro, the boy who had defied him, who had made him look a fool, who had stolen the girl he loved, the beautiful Hana, who should have been Kenji Kira's wife. The boy who—if the rumors Kira had heard on his way from Mount Hiei were to be believed—possessed the Buddha ball.

Lord Oda believed the Buddha ball would give him control over all creation, over the five realms of samsara. Lord Oda had failed to find it. But imagine if Kenji Kira were to take it! Imagine if he were to kill Taro, and claim his treasure. Oh, it would be beautiful, it would be perfect. It was something beyond his wildest dreams of power.

And Taro had just sailed into his little patch of the world.

His kingdom.

This, thought Kira as he absentmindedly licked the blood from around his mouth, was something of a mistake.

CHAPTER 22

MIYAJIMA

THE INLAND SEA

Taro could see from some way off that there was something strange about the island. The color of the hillside, as it drew near, was not green but a sort of dull brown, and it seemed smoother than it should be.

He had an idea what it was.

He had an idea what it was, but he pushed it down, buried it. Buried it as—

No. He would not allow it to be true.

When they drew into the shallow bay, though, he could no longer deny the evidence of his eyes.

They tied the boat to a spar and got out, feet splashing in the cold, clear water. Taro hugged himself, looking up at the hillside. The temple complex was untouched, it seemed, but the nearby villages had not been so lucky.

There was a fisherman nearby, mending creels on the beach. "What happened?" asked Taro.

The fisherman looked up. "The rain, that's what happened."

He gestured behind him to the hillside. Smooth brown mud ran from high up all the way down to the sea. At places, from out of the choking morass, the ribs of roofs protruded, the odd treetop, startling green.

"Were many people . . . ," Taro trailed off, tongue stilled by horror.

"Some," said the fisherman. "One thing for it, there's no need for burial." He spat. Then he sighed. "But most were at the temple for prayers. We were fortunate."

Taro wasn't sure he would put it like that. He knew this was his fault. That the rain he had created had fallen here, too, more of it than the place was used to, for the season, and that had made the mud give way.

He felt heartsick.

"And you?" he asked. "Did any of your . . ."

"Oh no," said the fisherman. "I ain't got family. I had a hut, but now the hut is gone, I sleep in my fishing boat."

"What is it?" said Shusaku. "What happened to the hut? I don't understand."

Taro sometimes forgot that his mentor was blind, such was his skill at sensing the presence of people, hearing the beating of their blood. But the mud slide was cold, Taro realized, and there was no blood beating in it. Those who had been caught in it were dead.

"It's a mud slide," said Hana. "The village has been destroyed."

"Oh, Taro," said Shusaku, voice filled with pity. "This is not your fault."

The fisherman looked up sharply. "Why would it be his fault?"

Shusaku straightened. "He . . . ah . . . prayed for rain, when we were on the mainland. There was a terrible drought. Now he feels guilty because the rainfall has caused so much damage. He thinks . . . he thinks he made it happen."

"Oh," said the fisherman. "Well, I don't think the gods listen to those kinds of prayers."

You'd be surprised, thought Taro.

"Was there drought here, too?" asked Hiro. "Before the mud slide, I mean."

The fisherman nodded. "Terrible, it was. I saw one man pour seawater on his rice fields. The plants will die, o' course. Desperate times."

"And now?"

Taro understood what Hiro was doing, understood too that it was useless, it was not enough, it would never absolve him.

"Now we have water," said the fisherman, nodding. "But that's no consolation to those as are under the mud, is it?"

No. No it isn't.

Hiro bowed, his expression pained. "You're right, of course."

Now the fisherman examined his creel, appeared to judge it satisfactory, and put it down on the sand. "But you didn't come for this, did you? I imagine you want the temple."

"Yes," said Hana.

The fisherman pointed up the hillside. "Well, you can't miss it. It's the only thing that ain't covered in mud."

CHAPTER 23

It seemed that the monks of Miyajima were less familiar than those of Mount Hiei with creatures of darkness, because none of them questioned Shusaku's story that he was sick, and needed to rest in the shade of the inner courtyards. The shallow waters of the bay were known for their healing properties—it wasn't unusual, Shusaku had told them on their way over, for pilgrims to come seeking a cure.

What *was* unusual was the number of guards on the outskirts of the complex. Lord Tokugawa had been right—there were far too many armed men here, most of them samurai. They wore a *mon* Taro didn't recognize, and they all had *katanas* at their waists. The cost of the swords alone, let alone the men wielding them, would be astronomical.

It must be here, Taro thought. *It has to be.*

When they entered the temple proper, though, the atmosphere shifted. Samurai gave way to plainly dressed monks, most of them absorbed in meditation, or moving off in purposeful ways, holding spades and other implements. *Going to try to dig out the homes buried by the mud.* Some of the people were obviously refugees from the village, staying here until their houses could be recovered from the mud or rebuilt. There were sleeping mats, cooking utensils. Whole families sitting against the low walls, children playing in the courtyards.

Despite this, there was a general air of sobriety and calm. An older monk greeted them warmly and listened sympathetically as Taro explained Shusaku's illness, adding that he and Hana sought an audience with the abbot, to talk to him about the possibility of their granting some money to the temple. The old monk showed them where Shusaku could sit in the shadows, and explained to Taro and Hana where they could find the abbot.

While Shusaku sheltered from the sun with Hiro, Taro went with Hana deeper into the temple complex, following the directions they had been given.

The buildings stood on the sloping hillside above the famous torii gate, practically a small town, with dormitories, shrines, courtyards, and a library. Nature, though, had been allowed to continue between the walls, so that there were gnarled trees and bushes everywhere. As they passed the library, they caught a glimpse of the many scrolls inside.

"At Miyajima," said Hana, "they hold the originals of some of the oldest works of literature in Japanese."

Taro glanced momentarily at the scrolls. "Oh, right," he said. He could still feel the ball against his side, and overlaid on the corridors and gardens of the temple complex were images that his imagination created for him, of floating bodies, drowned, bloated.

I did that, he thought. It was an idea he couldn't get used to.

"Philistine," said Hana, and he grunted. Then she stopped, taking his hands. "Sorry," she said. "I know your mind is occupied with other things. But Taro—it wasn't your fault."

"It *was* my fault," he said. They were standing underneath a pine tree that was growing in the center of a courtyard. "I made it rain, and the rain caused the flood. I made the mud slides. I killed all those people."

"You couldn't have known. You were trying to help. To do the right thing."

"So?" said Taro. "That's how I got Heiko killed. My mother. Even your father. If I wasn't trying to do the right thing, they would all be alive."

Hana closed her eyes. "My father deserved to die," she said. "And the others . . . the fault lies with him, and Kenji Kira. Not with you."

Taro sighed. He didn't believe her, not entirely, but of course he wanted to. He was a little worried about Kenji Kira, in truth. The cruel general's body had disappeared from Mount Hiei before the final battle with Lord Oda. One of the monks claimed to have seen it get up and walk away, but that was just overactive imagination, or hysteria about the threat from Lord Oda's forces, Taro was sure of it. The dead didn't walk.

At least, they hadn't until recently.

Taro frowned. He had the feeling that some profound realization was just eluding him. Then he pushed away thoughts of the past, and of his guilt.

"Come on," he said. "Let's try to find the sword. The monks believe that Shusaku is sick, but it will get harder to explain the longer he doesn't go out in the light."

They passed through a hall in which they had to skirt round an enormous sand mandala, showing the five realms of existence, and then through another in which stood a tall gold Buddha, the roof open to allow its head through. They were no longer sure they were going the right way, so when they came across a young acolyte sweeping the floor, they asked him. He pointed to a door just behind him, then turned back to his sweeping.

Taro opened the door, letting Hana through first. They found themselves in a small room, lit by candles. An old man sat on the bare floor. Taro cast his eyes about but could see no sword—in fact, he could see very little at all. The walls were unadorned wood, and there was no furniture. As Taro's eyes grew accustomed to the gloom, he saw that the man on the floor was not just old—he was ancient. As wrinkled as a tortoise, he had fine, pure white hair that flowed over his shoulders, and a beard that reached almost to the ground. He had his eyes closed, and Taro wondered for a moment if he was dead.

"You wish to make a donation, I hear," said the old man suddenly, without opening his eyes. His voice was like the breeze in dry leaves. "And yet, as you can see, we lead a simple existence."

"Your gold Buddha could buy rice for the entire country," said Hana.

The abbot opened his eyes, smiling. "That is true," he said. "But I tend to find that the hungrier people are, the more superstitious they become. Do you think the people would accept food, if they knew the Buddha had been melted down to pay for it?"

Hana let out a breath. "No," she said.

"So," said the abbot, unclasping his hands, which had been held together in the mudra of meditation. "Why are you *really* here? From what I have been told, your older companion's skin is marked with the Heart Sutra—which suggests to me that he fears evil spirits, and more than that, knows them to be real. The other boy has the muscle and stance of a wrestler. You"—he turned to Taro—"carry a hidden sword under your cloak, and you, girl, speak like a noblewoman. I don't think I have ever heard of stranger travel companions. Have you come to kill me?"

"No," said Taro. "We really have come to talk about a donation. Or . . . an exchange."

The abbot stood—or rather, he was standing. There was no transition between the sitting and the standing up, no motion that Taro could see. He was just cross-legged, and then he was on his feet. "And what is it you think I can offer you?" he said. "Forgiveness?"

Taro flinched. Could the abbot see into his soul, see his pain over the drowned village?

"Kusanagi," said Hana, bold as always. "We want Kusanagi."

The abbot's eyes flickered; the closest, Taro assumed, he came to showing surprise. "Well, well," he said. "How do you know we have it?"

Taro shrugged. "We were told that the sea dragon took it, after the last Heike emperor drowned with his fleet. This is the shrine to the sea dragon. And you have so many samurai on guard. More than a temple needs."

"Ah," said the abbot, nodding. "A clever deduction. So. You have come seeking the most famous sword in Japan. The sword that belonged to Susanoo, and that Amaterasu his sister granted to the emperors of her line. Perhaps the most priceless treasure in this entire land, the possession of which could swing the balance of power at the very highest level. What on earth do you propose to exchange for it?"

Taro stepped forward. "What if I told you I had something that belonged to the Buddha himself?" he asked. "Something magical?"

"I would say that you were mistaken," said the abbot. "None of the original treasures—the Book of the Dead, the Eye of the Tiger jewel—ended up in Japan. They all went to Tibet, and to China."

"And one was sent from China to Japan," said Taro.

The abbot blinked. "The ball?"

"Yes."

"But . . . it's a legend. It doesn't—it cannot—"

Taro reached into his cloak and drew out the ball. It sat thrumming in his hand, alive with power. The abbot came closer, to look at it. When he saw the clouds floating under the glass, the sphere of the Earth beneath them, he took a long, deep breath. "What does it *do*?" he asked.

"I'm not sure," said Taro. "But it can control the weather. It won't control people. I think it won't allow you to do bad things. It belonged to the Buddha, after all." He didn't say that it *would* allow its bearer to control a vampire, as long as that vampire had been turned by the person holding the ball, and thus had the other's blood in their veins.

It would have led to too many awkward questions.

"And you would offer me this—one of the world's greatest treasures—in return for Kusanagi?"

Taro nodded.

"Why? What does the sword mean to you?"

"There's a dragon, near Edo."

"I've heard of it."

"It's killing people, burning villages . . . The shogun wants it killed, and I said I would try. Kusanagi is the only sword that has ever killed a dragon."

"Taro is very brave," said Hana, and was that a tiny note of bitterness in her voice? "I believe he can do it. With the right weapon."

The abbot nodded. "I see." He peered at Taro. "Yet you do not want to kill the dragon because of the burned villages, or because you are brave. You are not so selfless." Taro opened his mouth to protest, but the abbot raised his hand to cut him off. "I am sure that is *part* of your motivation," he said. "But it's not all of it. There's something else, isn't there?"

"Taro?" said Hana. She was looking at him thoughtfully.

"It's true," said Taro. He rubbed his eyes. "I want the reward, so that I can marry Hana." He turned to her. "I love her, but she deserves a husband with land. And money."

"But I don't need those—"

"That's what you think," said Taro. "But you've never been hungry, not really. You've never been poor."

The abbot was nodding; Hana was staring at Taro with a strange mixture of tenderness and anger. "I understand," said the abbot. "You feel you must deserve her."

"Yes!" said Taro. "Yes, that's it."

Hana shook her head. "But Taro, you already deserve me, you—"

"No, I don't."

The abbot raised his hand again. "Let us leave that question aside for the moment." He reached out and touched the ball, just once, very softly. "I thank you for showing me this," he said. "It is difficult to surprise a man of my age, but I certainly didn't think I would ever see an object that belonged to the Buddha himself. Unfortunately, however, I cannot help you."

"You won't exchange the sword for it?" said Taro.

"No," said the abbot. "You don't understand. The problem is that we don't *have* the sword. We never have."

"So then where is it?" asked Shusaku.

They were sitting on the headland, looking out to sea. The sun had set a while ago, dragging the light from the world, like an outgoing tide. Now the torii gate in the bay below them rose from gray mist, and the hillside spilled into the sea on either side like black lava, cooling to solidity as it hit the water.

"The abbot doesn't know," said Taro. "He understood why we came here—he had also heard the story that the sea dragon took Kusanagi when the Heike and their emperor drowned."

"Then why all the samurai?" asked Shusaku.

"Apparently, as the fisherman said who brought us here, there is a terrible pirate crew operating from near here. The abbot said there were stories of a ship of dead men."

"The dead again," said Shusaku. "Something is happening, and I don't like it." He paused. "Did the abbot say if the sword had *ever* been here?"

"He says no. As far as he knew it was with the shogun at Edo, no matter what the rumors may say."

"It is true," said Shusaku, "that it may all be a malicious rumor, spread by those who wish to see the shogun dethroned."

"You believe that?" said Hiro, surprised.

"No," said Shusaku. "But anything is possible."

Hiro was looking at Taro. "If it's not here, and assuming that *is* a fake in Edo, then where is it?"

"The abbot thinks it must still be where it fell into the sea. Where the Heike were defeated."

"Shirahama?" said Hiro.

Shusaku might have been shocked—it was difficult to tell, given that he had no eyes. But he leaned back on his hands. "You're telling me that the key to claiming the throne of Japan has been in

Shirahama bay all this time—the very place we escaped from two years ago, to save your life?"

"It's possible," admitted Taro.

"My gods," said Shusaku. "It all connects. The prophecy, the sword . . . Didn't you say, too, that there's a wreck in the bay where no one will dive?"

Taro stared at him. "Of course. You think it's one of the Heike ships?"

"I think it may be," said Shusaku. "It would explain a lot, no? What if it was the boy emperor's ship? Such a wreck might well be cursed—and certainly it's feasible that people would *believe* it to be. Even if the reasons were lost in time."

"Gods," said Hana. "So we have to go to Shirahama?"

"Again," said Taro. He'd been back the previous year, looking for the Buddha ball, finding only his mother's ghost. He felt dizzy at the idea of how close he might have been to the legendary sword Kusanagi, how much time he could have saved if he had looked for it. He had even dived the cursed wreck!

"Good," said Hana. "I would like to see where Taro was born." She smiled at him—he thought it might be the first time she had really smiled since they left the monastery at Mount Hiei.

"I feel," said Hiro, "that I should mention one small problem."

They all turned to look at him—even Shusaku, who could hear where Hiro was sitting.

"What?" said Taro.

"Lord Tokugawa said that the dragon of the sea took Kusanagi, after the boy emperor was killed. Maybe that was at Shirahama or it wasn't, but if it was, then there could be a dragon guarding the sword."

Taro nodded slowly. "So . . . I need Kusanagi to kill the dragon of the mountain, because no other weapon can prevail. But to get to Kusanagi I have to get past *another* dragon."

"If we believe Lord Tokugawa," said Hiro.

"Well," said Taro, fear coiling in his belly at the idea of facing a dragon, and underwater, too. "That's just wonderful."

CHAPTER 24

The plan was to rest for a few hours, and then leave at the Hour of the Tiger, well before dawn, giving them time to sail back to the mainland without burning Shusaku. The monks had given them rooms in the complex, and Taro waited till the others were heading for theirs before saying that he was going to go for a walk alone, to clear his head. Hiro and Hana looked at him strangely, but Shusaku waved him off.

Leaving the buildings behind, he followed the hillside down toward the sea. The tide was in—less of the torii gate was visible above water now. There was a smell of salt and burning driftwood on the air, which reminded Taro of home. As he walked, he startled a rabbit—and remembered when he had shot one, with his bow, on the day that ninjas came to his little village and his life changed forever.

This one he didn't shoot. Instead he leaped forward, moving more quickly than any human ever could. He cleared a dune, two dunes, and launched himself into the air, landing on the rabbit as it tried to dive into its hole. He lifted it to his mouth and bit into it, going for the jugular so that it slackened immediately, as the lifeblood pumped into him. It didn't taste as good as human blood—it was marred by the flavor of grass—but it was nourishing, it made the night sizzle with clarity.

Coming to the sea, he let his cloak fall to the ground, then waded out. The water was cool and slippery against his skin, the moon making shifting skeins of light on its surface, a gleaming tapestry. A couple of small fishing boats were tied up at anchor.

He walked, slowed by the resistance of the water, to the torii.

Then, taking the Buddha ball in his hand, he pitched it into the water. He was glad to see it go as it sank. With the exception of allowing him to save Hana, the ball had brought nothing but bad luck and misery into his life. Lord Oda's voice, Sato's past, the flooding . . . It was bad enough that Taro was someone who spread death everywhere he went. The last thing he needed was an object that would not let the dead stay dead. Little Kawabata had been right to put as much distance as he could between him and it.

He stood for a moment, listening to the soft clapping of the water against the legs of the gate.

Was that another sound? He turned, looking around him. It seemed to him that he had heard a movement, somewhere out there in the darkness. He closed his eyes, listening. It had sounded like movement in the scrub that covered the dunes—he was three *tan* from the shore here, but his vampire hearing was sharp as a *katana*'s edge.

Nothing.

Dismissing it as another rabbit, or something in the water or the wind, he turned back to land, then waded to the shore. Wrapping his cloak around him—the night air chilled him—he took the path back up toward the temple complex. He was about to slide open the shoji door that led to his room when he stopped, going dead still.

There was someone in there. He could hear them breathing. Shallow breaths, frequent. As of someone nervous—an assassin, maybe, waiting for his victim. He leaned back, studying the paper. Yes—a shadow, person-shaped, just behind the door.

Slowly, slowly drawing his concealed sword, he put a hand on the frame of the paper screen. Then he drew it open left-handed, spinning into the room with the blade out in front of him.

"Taro!"

Hana stood in front of him, hands on her mouth. Gradually he took in the scene. She had pinned up her hair and done something to the exquisite bow of her lips—something that added gloss, and color. She wore the same kimono she had been traveling in, but it was tied loosely, her throat and the swell of her chest visible.

"I—sorry," he said. "I thought you were an intruder."

"I suppose I am," she said. She smiled slightly, lowering her hands. He was punched, hard, with the realization of how beautiful she was. It was something he tended to forget when he wasn't with her. Her face would dissolve, grow vague and ghostlike in his memory. Then he would stand in front of her and he would see the curve of her cheekbones, the perfect brushstrokes of her eyes, and it would stop his breath in his chest.

"I forgot about your vampire senses," she said. "How on earth did you know there was someone in here?"

"Your breathing," he said. "It's . . . louder than usual. Even now. Like you're scared, or something."

"Not scared," she said.

He looked at her, felt himself flush. "Then . . ."

She didn't answer that. "When we saw the abbot, did you mean what you said?"

"About giving him the Buddha ball?" He kept his face straight for a moment as she glared. Then he laughed. "Yes, I meant what I said."

"You know I don't need money, don't you? Or land."

"I know you think so."

She rolled her eyes. "I am not so sheltered as you think."

He raised an eyebrow. "No?"

She laughed and beckoned him forward.

Their lips met, and the world fell away from around them, as in a moment of enlightenment. She touched his cheek. He gazed into her bottomless eyes, feeling that there was nowhere he would rather be.

"You're beautiful," he said.

She shook her head matter-of-factly. "No. My nose is crooked, and my teeth are too small."

He laughed, and she frowned at him—as far as she was concerned, he knew, this was the simple truth. She was not playing at false modesty; in fact, there was nothing false about her, and never had been. She didn't *know* she was beautiful—that was one more thing he loved about her, along with her ability to fight, her sense of humor, her humility. She had no vanity whatsoever.

"You never wanted what your father wanted, did you?" he asked. "To marry some daimyo. To be a lady."

"Never."

He smiled. How could he be this lucky? How could there be a woman in the world so amazing as she, and not only that but interested in him—a peasant, and a vampire?

Hana was looking at him with a curious expression, however. She glanced from him to the door, then back again. "What were you doing out there?" she asked.

"Something I should have done long ago."

Understanding lit her eyes—he thought she had understood a while ago, actually. "You threw it away, didn't you? The ball?"

"Yes."

"But what if you need it? I don't like to think of you unprotected."

He laughed. "I'm a vampire. My best friend is the strongest person I know. Shusaku has killed more people since he became blind than most Sword Saints manage when they can see. You"—he tapped the hidden sword strapped to her leg—"are a little more than you appear. I don't think I need any more protection."

"You would never be protected enough, if it was up to me."

"Wait," he said. "Are you telling me you like me?"

She pushed his chest. "Idiot," she said. "I can go if you like."

"Never."

He leaned forward to kiss her again. As he did so, she caught his hands and put them on her waist. "I was thinking . . . ," she said. She cut her eyes over to the bed on the floor.

"Really?"

"Yes."

An eternity later, he traced his finger along her collarbone. He was moving slowly, awash in a warm sea of pleasure. Her breathing was even quicker now, and there was a low sound in her throat; he thought it was the best sound in the world. A light was building up behind his eyes, which were closed—it was like there was a sun rising in his head, or stars, thousands of stars.

Darkness outside him, stars inside him.

Then a flash—a moment of nothingness, followed by a rocking explosion of red behind his eyelids, and suddenly he could see every vein and capillary in them, was conscious of the blood everywhere inside him, pushing and receding like a tide, filling every part of his skin and body.

A scent filled his nostrils, an irresistible scent, the iron of weapons mixed with a note that was like nothing so much as life itself, warm and vital. His teeth were long and sharp in his mouth.

It took him a moment to realize that his eyes were open now, because the same redness that had flooded his mind had filled the room, too, so that it seemed it was an underwater hall, he and Hana floating in crimson liquid. She was looking up at him through it, mouthing something, but it was impossible to hear her underwater, in his ears was nothing but the pound and rush of his blood-tide. Her eyes were wide open, terrified. He was paying no attention, though, because that scent, so delicious, so unbelievably delicious, was coming from her—

No, it *was* her, it was flowing through her; what he was smelling was her very essence, the ebb and flow that kept her alive. He could see the artery fluttering in her neck, blue below the alabaster of her bare skin, and it struck him how *close* that artery was, all the time, to the outside wall, how it cried out to be punctured, how a person was made so vulnerable by the presentation of their neck to the world.

Not that he *thought* any of this, in any real sense. He was lost—he was a hawk, diving on a mouse, he was a shark in a sea of red.

He leaned down—she struggled, trying to push him away, but he was stronger than her, oh so very much stronger. He opened his mouth, and when it touched her warm neck he bit down, hard.

Her blood burst into him, and now the red sea was not just in the room, it was inside him, the feeling one of total ecstasy. He had the sensation of drinking life itself. He had thought that he would marry Hana, but that idea—which came to him as a wordless picture, of two people standing on the ramparts of a castle—seemed ludicrous now. So much better to draw her into him, to absorb her, to have her always in his blood, the pulse of his heart speaking in her voice.

Somewhere far away, someone screamed.

CHAPTER 25

EARLIER THE SAME NIGHT

Hiro followed at a safe distance, as Taro made his way down to the sea. Hiro had a good idea what his friend was going to do—he had observed the heartsickness in Taro ever since they saw the damage the floods had done. He knew Taro. He knew how the guilt of a thing like that would gnaw at him, drive him mad, even if he understood perfectly well that he had only done what seemed right, to try to bring water to those who were thirsty.

That was Taro—always his own worst enemy. What Lord Oda had done to him—almost killing him, murdering his father, sending Kenji Kira to destroy the prophetess and then Heiko—would never compare to what he did to himself, by refusing to forgive himself for killing the daimyo.

If Hiro had killed Lord Oda, he would be glad, and proud. Taro, on the other hand, saw it as something to be ashamed of.

So Hiro was sure that Taro would rid himself of the ball, especially now that it seemed the monks did not have Kusanagi, and so Taro could not possibly swap the ball for the sword. The thing was that Hiro was convinced Taro might need it again someday—hadn't it been passed down to him, by the ama who first recovered it from the sea? Wasn't it part of his birthright—of his prophecy, of his destiny?

Yes. Hiro was not prepared for his friend, in his constant guilt, to cast away something that might save him in the future.

And so he crept through the bracken and grass on the high dunes, ducking down low when Taro loosed his cloak and waded into the sea. When Taro reached the torii, Hiro edged farther round the bay to get a good look. Sure enough, Taro took out the ball and threw it out to sea.

At one point, Taro stiffened and began to look all around him, suspicious.

Hiro dropped to the sand, feeling it working its way into his clothes. The smell of it was of sunshine and salt. He stayed there for a moment, and when he raised his head again Taro was coming back to shore.

When he was sure Taro was gone, he stood and went down to the beach. The coldness of the water, which quickly gave way to a wonderful, smooth sensation, was like a slap followed by a kiss. He felt that he was melting into the world, as he walked out into the black bay, toward the gated shrine that rose from the water.

Reaching the gate, he measured five paces from it, going out to sea. The sand dipped here; the water deepened quickly as he went, till it lapped at his chest. His chest wasn't used to it—this water, unlike that which surrounded his legs, was cold. It was if the sea had welcomed him, but only up to a point. It was not his friend, this deeper water.

Suddenly Hiro was aware of how dark it was, and how he was out in the sea, all alone.

The moon gazed down at him dispassionately.

He dug his fingernails into his palms and cursed. Then he took a deep breath, before diving into the dark water.

It closed over his head as if he had never been there.

Hiro opened his eyes, but it made little difference. Even at this depth, no more than the height of a man, he could see almost nothing. The sea rumbled in his ears, a constant sucking noise. He ran his hands along the bottom as he kicked with his legs. What was he doing? Taro was the diver. Not him.

His hand brushed something rubbery and soft, which skittered away—he almost screamed, his mouth filling with water. He was on the surface again in moments, lying on his back, coughing. He wished, fervently, that he were back in his bed, on dry land.

He lay there a moment, then he rolled over and dived again. This time he had not been scouring the bottom long when his hand touched something hard and round. He clutched at it—almost lost it, as the smooth glass shot from his fingers—then grasped it with both hands. He kicked up to the surface and thrashed inelegantly until he could stand again.

He looked down at the Buddha ball—he could almost have kissed it.

Arriving back at the beach, he was suddenly conscious of a presence beside him.

"Yes," said Shusaku. "I thought he would throw it away too. But it seems you were quicker than me."

"I lived in a hut with him and his mother," said Hiro. "I know when he is really going for a walk and when he isn't."

Shusaku nodded, handing Hiro a dry cloak. "Or maybe I just waited, because I didn't want to get wet," he said.

Hiro sighed. "Cursed ninjas," he said. He handed the ball to Shusaku. "Here," he said. "You look after it. I don't trust myself with it." Then he paused. "But don't go controlling Taro with it."

Shusaku looked as wounded as was possible for a man with no skin worth mentioning. "I wouldn't dream of it," he said.

At that moment, the night was rent by a woman's scream.

"That's coming from the monastery," said Hiro, goose bumps on his flesh.

"Yes," said Shusaku. "And the only woman there tonight is Hana."

They ran.

CHAPTER 26

Taro flew through the air backward, hitting the wall hard with his back. He slumped to the ground, winded. He had bitten his lip when his head struck, and now his mouth was full of the taste of his own blood, as well as . . .

Hana's.

Oh, gods.

He could see her lying on the futon bed, very still. Blood covered her chest and neck, a black stain in the half-light. Shusaku stood over her—it must have been he who threw Taro across the room. Suddenly the blood in his mouth was slick and revolting, rotten. With a bang, Hiro crashed through the shoji screen, his hands balled into fists. He gaped openmouthed at Hana on the bed, then staggered back when he saw Taro against the wall, lips stained with blood. Taro wanted to say something to him, but found himself incapable. He addressed himself to Shusaku instead.

"Is she . . . ?" he asked.

Shusaku touched Hana's wrist. "No."

Just then Hana's eyelids flickered open, and there was an answering movement in Taro's chest, as if his heart had stopped beating when he saw her lying there. *He* had done that—he had lost control of himself, fed on her. He was shaking, he realized.

He was a monster, and getting rid of the Buddha ball was not going to change that.

"If she was injured, I would give her some of my blood," said Shusaku. "But seeing as you have bitten her, it would only turn her if I did." He looked at her. "You wouldn't want that?" Taro cursed himself. A vampire could feed without making his victim into a vampire—but if a person who had been fed on were to drink any vampire blood, they would turn. Taro had effectively closed to Hana the only avenue that might quickly save her.

Hana shook her head. She didn't seem able to speak.

Shusaku got an arm under her neck and another under her legs. "Come," he said to Taro. "Others will have heard that scream." He still hadn't met Taro's eyes, and Taro was afraid of what would happen when he did. Hiro had gone, Taro didn't know where. He must have stepped outside into the cool night air, to clear his head; either that or he had decided he could no longer be friends with a monster.

Taro would understand that.

Shusaku led the way out of the room, beckoning for Taro to follow him, still without looking at his young companion. Taro levered himself dumbly to his feet, mind blank with shock. He had nearly killed Hana. He kept saying it to himself, over and over, in the hope he would believe, or understand it. She might even—he realized with horror—still die.

Outside he saw torchlight, before he heard the shouts. A handful of monks, accompanied by more samurai, were spreading out before the house. Taro was immediately conscious of how this looked. Hana, draped over Shusaku's back, bleeding. The blood around his mouth.

"Kyuuketsuki!" said one of the monks, pointing at Taro.

That was the only word that was spoken—Buddhist monks

were ever warriors. The monks held heavy staffs; the samurai, swords. They charged forward together, for the moment concentrating on Taro, though a couple hesitated, staring at Shusaku—trying to work out if he was an evil spirit too.

One of the samurai was very close to Taro already. His blade was out; he would have speared Taro through the heart, ending him at that moment, but there was a snapping twitch of movement from Taro's left, and the samurai tripped, went flying. Hiro—who had stuck his leg out at the right moment—gave Taro an inscrutable look, then turned to face the other samurai. Taro leaped over the downed man, stealing his sword simultaneously, suddenly ready to fight. For himself, he didn't care if he lived or died. But he would not see Hiro killed.

He felt the weight and balance of the sword in his hand. It was good.

Turning to deflect a classic strike from the man closest to him, he felt a thrill rush through him, like water through a pipe, when he saw how slowly everything was moving. He was aware of the very particles of the air as they struck his skin; he could watch dispassionately as the useless sword of his enemy pushed slowly through those particles, sluggish as a heavy ship through water. But he was not subject to the same laws. Still-warm human blood raced through his body, making it more than human. He was conscious of the thicknesses and thin patches of the air, its eddies, swirls, and currents, as if it were an old and familiar cloak, many times repaired. He could move in the in-between, in the spaces—the vast, vast spaces—where there wasn't any air.

Stepping into the samurai's reach, he brought his sword up in a diagonal backhand strike, the blade ripping through the other man's chest, slashing his throat. Blood sprayed up to hover in the air, suspended in the thickness of the medium. The man laid himself down on the ground gently, as if it were a bed to sleep on.

As Taro flitted past him, he upturned his mouth, and blood pattered on his tongue like rain. He checked over both shoulders—saw Hiro grappling with a monk before throwing him over his hip. Saw Shusaku holding off a group of two samurai and a monk, fighting like a demon with a sword in his hand, even with Hana on his back. Taro quickly counted—seven men left to kill.

"Get to the sea," shouted Shusaku. "Leave them."

As the ninja said it, he struck aside the sword of the man directly in front of him, then ran past him, heading downhill to the beach. Hiro, too, began to run. Taro saw a monk cut toward his friend from behind, raising a staff. Hiro would never even feel it—his head would be split open and that would be it.

Rapidly calculating the distances, Taro flipped his sword so that the blade end was in his hand. It bit into his palm and fingers, but he ignored the pain. He threw the sword. It spun end over end through the air, past Hiro's head, and buried itself in the monk's chest, with such force that the monk was thrown backward to land hard on the ground.

Taro turned, to see two men blocking his way. There was fear in their eyes, but there were swords in their hands, held steadily. True samurai. Taro no longer had a sword. His eyes flicked from side to side, then he feinted to the right, before turning left. Both men followed his feint—one with a shoulder strike, one with a direct thrust that would have run through his stomach if he had gone that way. He launched himself into the air, mouth open, sharp teeth extended, almost lying down on the softness of the atmosphere, horizontal to the ground.

The only part of him to connect with the left-most samurai was his mouth; his teeth sank into the flesh of the neck, tearing through it like razor-sharp blades. The artery, severed, spewed blood. Taro could not help swallowing some of it, as he landed hard on his side, rolled, and was on his feet again running—though he spat out the skin and muscle.

He glanced back. The samurai, a bite taken out of his throat, toppled and fell. The other turned to follow him, but would never be fast enough. As Taro watched, Hiro skirted round him, running hard.

They reached the dunes, the sounds of their pursuers, their

shouts and footfalls, behind them. In the moonlight, on the sand, Taro was reminded of the night he'd met Shusaku, when they escaped from Shirahama by making for the beach, stealing a boat. It was as if that night had come around again, but this time a dark version, as the dead moon is a counterpoint to the full. This time, it was Taro who was the killer; Taro who was the intruder and the monster.

He almost wished that he had the Buddha ball, so that he could call down lightning, to incinerate himself. No. No—he didn't want the ball. He could open Hana's throat without it, suck down the blood of the person he loved most in the world. Imagine what he could do if he had the ball, too.

Shusaku came up behind him, breathing heavily—he had not had any blood, Taro remembered, and he was carrying Hana, too.

"I can take her," he said.

"No," said Shusaku, and that hurt more than anything.

Hiro went past them, then put his hands on his knees, gasping. He straightened up, pointed to the nearest boat. It was a small one, powered by oars only. It would have to do. Shusaku went over to Hiro. "Keep moving," he said. "You help me to support her in the water."

They went into the sea. The only difference between this night and the first was that there was no need to swim, they were in such shallow water. The men were just behind them—as Hiro and Shusaku waded out with Hana, Taro turned to face the quickest one. He knew the water would slow the man even more, and he was right—the strike, when it came, was something to be indulged, in a kinder world. Taro did not indulge it. He caught the man's arm, snapping it, and heard the sword splash into the water.

The last times he had truly fought had been with vampires and dead people. He had not understood, not really, what being a *kyuketsuki* meant, what the blood that coursed through him allowed him to do. He was so much more powerful than these people that it was sickening.

But there was no time to think about that. He turned and ran, or as close as he could manage, in the thigh-deep sea. Shusaku and Hiro were already lifting Hana's limp body into the boat when he caught up with them. Taro cut the anchor rope with his teeth, then vaulted over the side, picking up the oars. He needed something to distract him.

As Taro rowed, Shusaku tore strips off his cloak, using them to bandage Hana's neck tightly.

"Will she live?" asked Taro.

"I think so," said Shusaku, and Taro supposed that would have to be good enough.

He concentrated on the rhythm of the oars, focused on it entirely. The shouts of the samurai and monks faded, and the sea grew wider, until it filled the world. The black arms of the bay receded, like a person reaching out for an embrace, always denied.

It was when he touched his hand to his cheek, thinking it had perhaps begun to rain, that he realized he was weeping.

CHAPTER 27

"Why didn't you *tell* me?" said Taro, as he rowed.

Shusaku, who seemed wearier than Taro had ever known him, had explained that he thought perhaps the pleasures of the flesh (that had been Shusaku's phrase) might have precipitated Taro's loss of control, causing him to bite Hana. She, for her part, had regained consciousness and was huddled against the side of the boat. So far she hadn't said anything, and hadn't looked at Taro, either. Taro didn't care. He was just relieved that she was alive.

"I didn't know," said Shusaku. "I've never . . . I mean to say, the married vampires I know have all been married *to* vampires. I have known ninjas to prey on humans of the opposite sex. I have not known them to . . . well, you know."

"But what about you?" said Taro. "Are you saying you've never . . . with a woman? A human woman? You told me once there was a ninja you loved."

Shusaku tensed. "There was," he said. "But she was a vampire. And she died soon after she turned me. Since then, there has been no one."

Taro had stopped crying, but the world still seemed black, and unlikely to grow less so when the sun rose. Shusaku couldn't help him. No one could. "I can never be with Hana. I am a danger to her. It would be better if I were dead."

"No," said Hana softly. Taro was startled to hear her speak. "It was not Taro's fault. I was touched by something he said yesterday. I seduced him." She closed her eyes, exhausted by the effort of speaking.

Taro, who could still taste her blood on his tongue, shook his head, disconsolate. "It *was* my fault," he said to her. "It was my fault for being a vampire. When I have killed the dragon, I will give you the land and title. I will find my own path. I will atone."

"There are things we must all atone for," said Shusaku. "There is no need to do it alone."

"There is," said Taro. "If Hana does not want to be . . . like me . . . then there is no other solution but for me to leave."

She opened her eyes and looked at him. "I . . ." She looked pained. He understood—she was the daughter of a daimyo, and he was offering her the chance to be a creature of the night, an evil spirit, filled with bloodlust. It was no offer at all, and no chance.

"There is my answer," said Taro. "So. When we land, you are all free to go anywhere you like. I will go to Shirahama. I will find Kusanagi. I will kill this dragon. Then I will be alone."

"Not completely alone," said Hiro. He gave Taro a weak smile. Taro felt, despite everything, a lightening in his heart. He could rely on Hiro. His best friend would always be with him, would always take his side. It was a comfort.

Hana cleared her throat. "I'll come to Shirahama, and to Mount Fuji if you find the sword. I don't want to find out, afterward, that the cursed dragon killed you. After that, I'll decide."

Taro, his heart breaking, nodded.

They fell silent. There seemed very little to be said. Taro continued to row—Hiro offered to take over, but Taro needed it, the repetitive motion, the penance of it. He dissolved into the task so much, its mantra, that it took him a while to realize that the others were speaking, in anxious voices.

"What is it?" he asked.

"Hiro and Hana tell me there's a ship behind us," said Shusaku. Taro looked up—he would have seen it if he had not been concentrating so much on the rowing; he was facing in the right direction, after all. Following them, at a fair distance but closing, was a black-sailed ship, heavy in the water. Taro could see no movement on deck, which seemed like a sinister omen. He remembered the fisherman, and the abbot, talking about pirates.

"It's following us," said Hiro, a little redundantly. The sea was vast, and infinite in its crossings; that the ship behind them was pursuing exactly the same course as they were was more than cause for concern.

"Pirates, you think?" said Hana.

Shusaku nodded.

"What would they want with a rowing boat?"

"I don't know," said the ninja. "But it can't be anything good." He got up and stepped over to where Taro sat. "You take one oar," he said. "I'll take the other."

It was a silent chase, but no less tense for it. The black ship drew ever nearer, looming—the process so gradual that it seemed the ship was expanding in size, rather than moving. The land, which Taro occasionally turned to glance at, also rose and spread. It was impossible to tell which would happen first; whether they would reach the land or the pursuing ship would reach them.

They were heading toward a bay, though, and as its encircling outcroppings drew level, Taro allowed himself to think that they might win, that they might pull through. He glanced at Hiro, who was anxiously watching the ship.

That was when there was a crash, and the little boat slammed to a halt. For a moment, the world was turned upside down—Taro was aware only of a jarring pain in his back, the blackness of the sky, filled with the white light of stars, the shrieking of shattered wood. His head smashed, hard, into the gunwale, then he was catapulted forward; he ended up on his face, his vision filled with knots and grains of wood.

He crawled to his knees, saw Shusaku do the same. Hana was lying in the bottom of the boat, her eyes closed. He touched her; blood pulsed under her skin, but she did not wake. He cursed, casting around for Hiro. He couldn't see him. Could his friend have been thrown into the water?

Finally he turned, to see that the prow of the little boat had gone. It simply wasn't there. In its place was a heavy metal chain, festooned with slivers and shards of wood. It stretched from one end of the bay to the other, a trap they had run into.

He sensed movement out of the corner of his eye, turned, and gasped.

He was suddenly and very acutely aware of two things, both very bad indeed.

The black ship was nearly on them.

And the boat was sinking.

CHAPTER 28

A moment later, there was another shocking crash, the impact jarring Taro bone deep. He was knocked from his feet once more, and as he picked himself up he took in something incomprehensible—jutting from the splintered devastation of their boat some kind of sharpened ram. Taro bent down to check Hana. The ram had missed her, thank the gods.

There was no time to be glad of it for long, though, because already men were firing down from the ship. An arrow lodged itself in Taro's hip; he let out a cry, and snapped it off at the shaft. He would get the point out later. Shusaku leaped in front of Hana, as did Taro. From somewhere was coming a stench of decay.

Just then a hand appeared over the broken side of the boat, and Taro drew his sword. But when a head followed it, he saw that it was only Hiro. He sent up a silent prayer of thanks. He reached out his hand to give it his friend, to help him onto the boat—not that it would do much good, for the water was threatening to overwhelm them at any moment; the wooden planks seemed to be holding together more out of stubborn habit than anything else.

His hand shrank back, though, when an arrow buried itself in the wood of the gunwale, right between Hiro's fingers. Both friends froze.

"My accomplice here is a very good shot." It was a voice Taro knew well, only altered, and strange. "The next will take your mortal friend in the neck."

Taro turned slowly. For the moment no arrows came from the black ship. Shusaku stood beside him, silent. He, too, must have recognized the voice.

"Good," said Kenji Kira. He was standing in the prow of the ship, his face covered with a black cloth, as if he were a ninja. Taro could see other men, standing beside him, training bows on him and Shusaku.

"You're—you're dead," said Taro. "I saw your body."

Kira shrugged, as if death were a small thing. "I came back," he said. "Didn't you do the same?"

"I didn't die."

"True. But you *did* go into death. And you brought me out with you." He grinned, and Taro saw dried blood on the cloth around his ghastly mouth. "Almost as soon as I had left the mountain, I came across Yukiko. I ate her heart when it was still beating. I can leave death, as long as I have the living to feed on. You know what that feels like, of course." He leaned forward. "Which one of you shall I eat first?"

Taro swallowed. Was that the truth, that he had led Kenji Kira out of death? Could it be? He thought of the dead they had fought on their way to the inland sea. Perhaps the gates to the other world *had* been left open; perhaps he had made a terrible mistake.

Kira stepped forward. He reached up and began to unwind the cloths wrapped around his face. When, finally, they fell away, Taro gaped in horror. Kira had no skin anymore, no flesh, either. He was a skeleton, standing in clothes. His tooth-filled jaw opened, and he laughed. Then he beckoned for his men to step forward too. Taro saw that some of them were dead also, their flesh in several cases hanging from the bone. This was the source of the stink, Taro realized.

Behind him, Taro heard a scream. He turned to see Hana cowering against the side of the boat, her hand over her mouth. She must have woken up. Hiro was still clinging on, his body in the water.

"The dead again?" said Hana, in a low, frightened voice.

"Again?" asked Kenji Kira.

"We were attacked," said Taro. "On the way here to the inland sea. By corpses that walked the earth."

Kira cocked his head to one side. "Interesting," he said.

"They were not yours?" asked Shusaku, surprised.

"No. But let us say that the borders of death are no longer as secure as they were."

"Enma will not stand for this," said Shusaku.

"Enma is dead. I am Enma," said Kenji Kira. "Now, Taro. Hand over the Buddha ball before you die."

Taro stared at the hideous figure before him. His mind was reeling; it seemed that whatever he did and wherever he went, Kenji Kira would always be looking for him, always tormenting him. And now Kira claimed he was death itself. It was too much.

"I don't have it," he said. "I threw it away."

"You . . . *threw it away*?" The voice was rasping, full of smoke and ash. It was also incredulous.

"Yes. It did nothing but harm."

Kenji Kira drew a sword. "You lie," he said.

"No," said Hana. "No, Kenji, it's true. He made it rain, because people were thirsty. But then other people drowned. He thinks the ball is cursed. I believe him."

"You didn't see him dispose of it?"

"No . . . but—"

"Then he lies." Kira gestured to the men beside him. "Kill them, and recover the ball."

In a fraction of an instant, time shifted from one form to another, like ice melting to water, and they were all in the fight-time, the kill-time. Shusaku picked up Hana and jumped from the ship. Taro dived forward, to knock Hiro into the water, covering him. He felt an arrow drive into his back. An instant later he was in the water, wrapped in the appalling cold of it, clinging to Hiro, who was swimming already. They dived, arrows sizzling through the water around them, plunging like seabirds.

Taro reached behind his back to snap off the arrow lodged there. It was hampering him as he swam. Now he had two arrow heads buried in his flesh, both throbbing with a dull ache. Underwater it was dark, shadowy—a world of twilight. He headed toward what he thought was the shore, Hiro beside him. Soon he became aware of Shusaku, struggling in the water ahead of them. Taro surfaced, sucking down air. The ninja had Hana under one arm, swimming sideways, pulling her through the water clumsily. The only mercy was that none of the men on Kira's ship had followed; couldn't swim, most likely. And Kira would never have learned, being samurai and so having people to do such things for him.

Unfortunately, of course, Hana was also samurai.

Swimming up to them, Taro got his arm under Hana too, on the other side, and between them he and the older man were able to pick up speed, despite her weight. Hiro was a strong swimmer; he was already well in front of them, almost at the head of the bay. Ahead, hills rose above the moonlit gleam of the sand, dark with trees. Taro glanced back. The ship's sails were up, and it was coming after them, the wreck of their little boat no longer visible. He cursed, spitting out salt water as he funneled all his strength into his free arm and legs, pushing the sea behind him.

What felt like an eternity later, he kicked out with his leg and felt sand brush against it. The sea floor was shelving up to the beach. Shouting to Shusaku, he threw his last reserves of blood-power

(*Hana's blood*, a cruel voice reminded him)

into his stroke, hand knifing through the water and scooping it behind him, as if the sea were a vast dark grave and he were digging himself out of it. Then his knees were on the sand, and he glanced ahead to see Hiro stumbling up onto the beach. Getting to his feet, he caught his hands together, levering Hana up as Shusaku did the same thing. She was conscious, and coughing, as they hauled her up toward the hills. Behind them, Taro heard the ship grate into shallow water, a noise like the screeching of ghosts. Then there were splashing sounds: men jumping down.

The beach, it seemed, was a vast funnel. They were hemmed in by rocks on both sides, forced toward a fissure in the hillside, a crack of pale light in the blackness. But they had no choice but to follow, or return to the sea. Taro turned and saw that the larger ship had reached the shore. Figures leaped down from the sides into the shallow water, then started coming up through the foam, weapons in their hands.

"They're giving chase," he said.

"I know," said Shusaku.

Then they were off the sand and in the throat of the fissure, a path that was more like a passageway, walled on either side by rock. It got narrower and narrower, dimmer, too. Taro couldn't see whether it led anywhere, or whether after a while the rock would simply close up again. They had to trust that it would have some issue, though, that it would lead them through this hill and to the other side—otherwise they were dead. Vines and stunted trees clung to the cliff faces beside them. Moonlight filtered down, blue and strange, casting shifting, worrying shadows. The smell of the sea gave way to another scent, of cool earth and dampness.

Deeper and deeper they went into the passage. There were turns, but these were not sharp, and Taro didn't think they would stop the dead—it was true corners that baffled them. Hana, increasingly, was running for herself, her steps unsure but her eyes wide open and her breathing coming hard. Taro felt relief embrace him, as the cold water had earlier, only the relief was a warm sea to fall into.

Ahead, the passageway constricted—a throat, swallowing—before opening again on a vista of rolling countryside, fields and terraces stretching away to infinity, thin plumes of smoke rising from small villages, up into heaven.

They pushed on, heading for the narrowest part. Hiro sucked in breath, wincing as the many-pointed rock pressed into him, but a moment later he had dragged himself through. He turned, helping Shusaku and Taro with Hana, who was barely needing support now. She followed Hiro through the gap.

That was when Shusaku pushed Taro through, to join his friends, and wedged himself into the narrow opening.

"Go," he said to Taro. "Run. Get Kusanagi—use it to claim the shogunate. Don't give it to anyone else, no matter who—no matter what happens."

Taro stared at him. "You're joking."

"Oh, yes. It seems the time for it." Sarcasm dripped from the ninja's voice.

"No," said Taro. "No, you're coming with us."

"Don't be ridiculous," said the ninja. "This is the only way. They'll catch us otherwise." He turned to Hiro. "Make sure he goes with you," he said.

Taro shook his head. He drew his own sword, stepping up behind Shusaku. "I'm staying," he said.

Shusaku shook his head slowly, sadly. "You're not."

Reaching into his wet cloak, the ninja drew out an object, something that Taro had not thought he would see again. Something round, and shining in the moonlight.

The Buddha ball.

CHAPTER 29

Shusaku closed his hands on the ball, feeling its smoothness and hardness. He concentrated. Taro had an advantage over him when wielding it—the boy could see, where Shusaku could not. But perhaps if he focused, if he meditated, he, too, could use its power. He could feel Taro behind him, the enraged pounding of his pulse in his veins. He ignored it.

Work, ball, work, *he implored it.*

He was no longer ever really conscious of when his eyes were open and when they were closed. It was not important; he couldn't see anyway. He closed them for sleep, he thought, out of habit more than anything else. But apart from that he was not concerned with what they did. So when a thin bluish line appeared out of the darkness, stretching horizontally, he was thrown at first. It was only when he blinked that he realized it was moonlight, glowing through a crack in his eyelids.

He opened his eyes fully.

He could see.

Oh, my dear gods, *he thought.* How could Taro have thrown it away? *His eyes had been burned out of his head by the sun, but now he was holding a thing owned by the Buddha, and his injuries were meaningless. The ball in his hand was clear, crisp. Every contour and imperfection of the rock face beside him buzzed in the sharpness of his vision. He gazed around, stunned, only half hearing the shouts of Taro and his friends behind him. He looked down at the object in his hands that had done this, that had wrought this miracle.*

Beneath the glass of the ball hung a tiny round moon, suspended in space, and beneath that the sphere of the Earth, shadowed on one side, light on the other. He turned it—sure enough, on the other side was a little sun, burning down. He turned it back to the moon-side, where he presumed Japan lay, and peered down into it. Taro lunged for the ball, but he turned, his sides protected by the rock. He had seen the boy do it; surely it could not be too hard?

He stared down at the miniature Earth in his hand, saw small clouds scudding across its surface. He glanced up; clouds, racing overhead. He understood that what he was seeing was not a representation of the world—it was *the world, in miniature. He was holding the world in his hands.*

How did you get that? said his charge, his protégé, his son.

"I followed you," said Hiro. "I recovered it from the sea."

Now Taro turned to Hiro, and if Shusaku could have taken away the pain and betrayal on Taro's face, he would have done it in a heartbeat.

"No . . . ," said Taro.

"I'm sorry," said his friend.

Taro looked away from Hiro, as if his friend no longer existed. "Give it to me, Shusaku," he said. "He's Enma! You can't defeat him."

"I won't give it to you," Shusaku replied. "And Enma can *be defeated. It has been done before. Even death has to die."*

Then he blocked out the sounds from outside himself, the calling of the crickets, the cries of night birds, the hooting of owls, the steel and bone sounds of the men coming after them, approaching through the passageway. Not too close, though. There was time for this last task.

He gathered his qi, *and instead of using it to harden his muscles, to hone his bloodlust and his fight stance, he used it to cancel all other things but the ball.*

Then he gazed down into it.

A catching sensation, and he was in free fall, plummeting. He felt his stomach rush to occupy the space previously employed for his lungs, felt the air battering against him, suddenly turned into something much more viscous, much more solid. There was a cloud below him—he half feared its impact, but then he was in it, falling through dense whiteness, damp and cold.

He broke through the cloud, and now below him was the Earth, growing bigger at an alarming rate. Fields and villages were sketches drawn with a stick on sand; then they were only the view from a mountaintop, and getting closer. His heart stuttered. Would he simply crash into the ground, to be obliterated?

He closed his eyes, braced for the impact, and—

He was standing in the path that ran through the hill, Taro, Hiro, and Hana behind him. He could feel them, their anxiety speaking through their rapidly beating hearts. He turned to them. The men coming up behind were close, but there was a moment still, a moment of time.

Taro stood before him; he was struck by how strong, by how handsome, the boy had become. He was more a man, now, than a boy. Inside Taro, Shusaku noticed for the first time, was something familiar, something that perhaps accounted in some small measure for his love for the boy. It was a rhythm, a sort of voice inside Taro's flesh, a call like that of home, or a child born of your own loins.

It was Shusaku's own blood, he realized, flowing in Taro's body, always a part of it now. It meant that in a sense, Taro truly was his son, and it meant that Taro was his to control.

Hana, beside him, was unspeakably beautiful, even pale and wounded as she was. And Hiro. The overweight boy Shusaku had met that night in Shirahama, two years ago, had turned into a muscled ox of a young man.

"I see you," he said to Taro. "I see you, and I'm proud."

Taro frowned. "You can see*?"*

"Yes. It's the ball, I think." Reminded of his purpose, he concentrated on the feel of it in his hands, recapturing by instinct the feeling of falling through thin air. He made himself somehow inside it and outside it at the same time. He was already conscious of his own essence in Taro's bloodflow, was already aware that he had left a part of his heart in the boy.

Now he reached out to it.

Speaking without words, he called on his own being, his own blood, and asked it to do his bidding. He didn't know how he knew to do this; it just came naturally, with the ball in his hand. Taro had been right. It was dangerous, the ball. It was not right that a person should have this power over another, because of having turned them. He knew that if he wanted it, he could kill Taro right now, without even lifting a finger. But he wasn't interested in killing Taro. He was interested in saving him, so he could follow his mission through to the end.

Holding Taro's blood in his mind, a pulsing web, he told it what to do.

"No," said Taro, as he began to walk backward, then turned to head up into the infinite countryside, to disappear into safety. He was screaming then, screaming that word, no*, over and over as he walked away against his will. His body trembled; Shusaku was impressed by the strength even this must have taken.*

"Yes," said Shusaku softly. He fixed Hiro, then Hana, with a look. "Follow him," he said. "Protect him." He couldn't command their blood; but he could ask them, as a friend. As a mentor.

Hiro had tears on his cheeks, Shusaku saw. The sight of it drove a weight into his stomach, but he held firm, knowing that if he succumbed to his feelings now he would bring Taro back, tell him never to leave, and if Taro stayed he would die. "Now," he said. "Run."

He poured his life force into Taro, through the agency of the ball, focusing all his qi*. Taro, who had been walking shakily, picked up to a sprint, and then he passed into a copse of trees and was gone. Hiro and Hana, with one last pained look back at Shusaku, followed him.*

Good.

He turned, and saw that he had acted just in time. The first of the men were approaching the narrowest part of the passage now, bringing the scents of death and the sea with them, which two smells were, in the end, much the same thing. Their armor and their weapons scraped on the rock, a hissing sound of threat. Shusaku transferred the ball to one hand, drawing his short-sword. He had pushed most of his power into Taro; now he pulled back a little of it, letting some of his qi *flow into his sword arm. These people were pirates,* ronin, *men without honor. Even if some of them were dead, they were unworthy adversaries; on a good day he would make a pile of their bodies without even trying. Only this wasn't a good day. This was a time when his strength was at its lowest ebb, slowly abandoning him, as the sea on the beach below was drawing away from the sand, pulled by the moon.*

Taro was his moon, and he was running, far away already, compelled by the ball. And a part of Shusaku was gone with him, never to return.

The men stopped in the passageway, then stepped to one side. Kenji Kira pushed through, coming to a halt when he saw the ball in Shusaku's hand.

"Taro?" he said.

"Gone."

Kira nodded. "You always were a man of honor," he said. "It's what makes you so predictable." He pointed to the ball. "Hand it over."

"No. Prize it from my dead hand."

"Very well," said Kira. He began to move forward, motioning his men to do the same.

"You should know," said Shusaku, "that I can see again. The ball has given me my sight. Many of you will not leave this place."

A hesitation from the men—even the dead ones.

Kira laughed, the sound hollow, like the creaking of an old bellows. "This was rather foolish of you, old fellow," he said. "Even with the ball, you cannot hope to win."

"I didn't hope to win. Just to slow you down."

"I see," said Kira. "To save Taro, no doubt. Noble of you. But stupid. You will die, and I will condemn you to the worst ravages of hell. And after I am done with you, I will hunt down your little friend Taro."

Shusaku didn't bother speaking, just leaped forward. Kira, simultaneously, stepped back, waving his men past him. They came at Shusaku like a wave. He tucked the ball into his cloak, sword already swinging in the confined space. The first man to come near him received its point in a sweeping blow to the chin, splitting his head open to the top of the skull; he fell backward, his head unfolding like the wings of a butterfly. Shusaku's blade was a blur. The next man—dead already, Shusaku thought—was separated at the waist, his body hitting the ground before his legs.

A strike got inside his blade, slashing his cheek; he felt the searing pain of it, but it went no more than bone deep. He adjusted his grip on his pommel, got his sword up, and knocked the other man's weapon aside. Then he took a dagger from his belt and buried it in the man's stomach. Shusaku didn't wait for him to die, just turned past him, already meeting the sword of the next man, turning it out of his hand, and taking out his throat with a hard sideswipe.

There was no room for skill, or maneuver. Only i-aido, *the principle of the fastest strike. Luckily, there was no one faster than Shusaku—no one alive at any rate, now that Lord Oda was dead. He cut through the sea of men like a shark, his sword swinging and thrusting in brutal, inelegant, but shockingly fast strikes. Bodies formed a carpet on the ground.*

He stepped over those he had killed, trod on them, as he fought his way toward Kira. Shusaku's foot squished into the stomach wound of a man whose belly he had opened, and he stumbled. He could see Kira, laughing behind his men, who just kept coming, unstoppable.

Then he heard something—something from deep within him, voices that were not his own. It took him a moment to realize that these were the other voices that the ball had awoken in him, the pulses of those he had killed inside him, those whose blood he had taken. Just as he could reach out to his own blood in Taro, so his victims could now reach out to him, could touch him. He was conscious of them, whirling inside him. He had feared them for so long, had imagined himself surrounded by the spirits of those he had murdered, but now he found that he had been wrong—they were inside him, they were part of him, and they were not to be feared. He had never killed without honor, without a reason.

He asked the voices inside him if they would stand with him, and they answered.

They answered yes.

He spun and cut, a dance of death that strewed the passageway with body parts, sprayed it with blood. He was the sword, and the sword was him, and everything was slow because this was the kill-time. He could laugh at their clumsy attempts to reach him, to get inside his sword arm, to deflect his blade. He did laugh, then, and once he started laughing he found he couldn't stop.

At that moment, one of the dead, perhaps dead already when Shusaku had decapitated him, caught hold of his ankle. Bony fingers dug into his flesh; he went down on one knee.

He swung, cutting off the hand, but another was on him, and another. And then his sword snagged on something. He saw that one of the bodies on the ground was holding it by the blade—two fingers fell, severed, but the grip did not loosen, and a moment later Shusaku was unarmed.

He looked up and saw Kenji Kira standing smugly, his arms crossed, the moonlight glinting on his bare skull. So unfair, he told himself. So unjust that he should die here, alone. But at least Taro was safe, at least he was far from here already. He would hate Shusaku, of course, but Shusaku was not worried about that. Let him hate. Hatred at least was a property of the living.

Hands seized him, so many hands. Teeth found him, biting down. Blades cut into him.

"Take the ball," said a faraway voice.

Then the many-handed creature that was all around him pulled him in every direction, tearing him into pieces. For just one, single, shining moment before the end he was conscious of another voice inside him, or rather a presence—it was the part of Mara that was always in his blood, he knew, because she had turned him. It gave a sort of sigh, of relief, he thought, and he felt that in a moment he would see her again after all those years, holding out her arms, waiting for him, and soon after that he died for the second and final time.

CHAPTER 30

Taro, Hiro, and Hana had traveled some twenty *ri* already. The scent of the sea was a dim memory now, replaced by the eternal green dampness of the rice fields.

In the fields, women were singing rice-planting songs. Taro barely listened, though the melodies got into his head, wrapping themselves around and through him like vines, whispering to him of a time before he bit Hana, before Shusaku took the ball and made him run away, made him abandon his mentor to die.

A time before Hiro betrayed him.

Gods, but he could almost miss that time when they were fighting off dead people, and it was all they had to worry about. Now he walked in silence, his companions behind him. He and Hiro had reached an uneasy truce. Taro didn't speak, and Hiro didn't speak. Taro didn't look at Hiro, and Hiro didn't look at Taro.

It had been a long walk to Shirahama, punctuated by several uncomfortable nights in ditches and trees, the three of them reluctant to stay anywhere too long, for fear of being caught by Kenji

Kira and his men. Along the way there was also the occasional skirmish with the wandering dead—though many of these seemed to have already been burned by the peasants. Certainly there were fewer than there had been before. There was, though, the constant threat of Kenji Kira. And all through the walk, all through the eating and sleeping and defending themselves, Taro and Hiro spoke not one word to each other. Taro still couldn't believe that his friend had done this to him, had taken the ball when he threw it away—and now Shusaku was dead as a result.

Then there was Hana. She spoke to both of them, but with Taro she was often halting, unsure. She didn't hold his hand now, and he didn't expect her to. They never talked about what he had done, but sometimes, when she looked at him, he saw her touch the scars on her neck, not realizing she was doing it.

She's afraid of me, he would think, when he saw that. It was something he could never undo. Even if she wanted to be a vampire, which she didn't, she had said so—even if they could be together that way, she would always remember when he lost control of himself, and nearly killed her.

And, at the same time as all this, there was the fear.

Taro couldn't get the dragon of the sea out of his mind—the one that Lord Tokugawa had said would be guarding Kusanagi. To claim the sword, he would have to somehow defeat it, or outsmart it. He was confident of neither. *Could* he defeat a dragon? He had never seen one. Humans presented little challenge to him now, with his vampire abilities. They were weak and slow. He had a feeling dragons were not.

Nor could he forget the abbot's story of the dragon he had faced in Hokkaido. The image of the men melting, like candles. The sound of the screams, which the abbot had so vividly described. The sheer size and power of the beast. Taro had sparred with the abbot. Anything that could make that man afraid must be very terrifying indeed.

I can't beat a dragon, was the refrain that went through his head. *I may be a ninja, but I can't beat a dragon.*

He'd be under the sea, too, out of his element. And the dragon . . . well, it wasn't called the dragon of the sea for nothing. *This is madness*, he thought.

And yet he didn't stop.

All in all, then, it wasn't an enjoyable trip. They'd agreed, the three of them, that they would stay together until Shirahama. Taro would go on to Edo with Kusanagi, if he could find it. Hana would go with him—she was still insisting on accompanying him until the dragon was dead, or he was. Hiro would stay in Shirahama. Taro wanted his old friend out of his sight, and he told him so. After all, their only recent conversation had been uncomfortable, to say the least.

It happened when Taro was lighting a fire to keep them warm at night, when he saw Hiro's shoulders were shaking. He went over to his friend, hesitated. Part of him wanted to reach out, to put a hand on Hiro's back, but he didn't dare.

"Are you . . . all right?" he had asked. He kept his voice neutral. He didn't want Hiro to think that he was forgiving him.

Hiro looked flatly at him. "Fine."

"What is it?"

"Yukiko."

"Yukiko? What about Yukiko?"

Hiro stared at him. "Kenji Kira *killed* her. Didn't you hear?"

"Oh. Yes. But . . . we knew something must have happened to her, after she left that clearing. And anyway, she was a traitor. She killed my mother. Why shed a tear for her?"

"She was my friend," said Hiro. "Do you remember that?" Taro flinched. Actually, he hadn't really thought about it—all those times when Hiro and Yukiko had sparred together, laughed together. "You hate her because she betrayed you, but it never seems to occur to you that she betrayed *me*, too."

"Then you should be glad she's dead."

Hiro shook his head. "You understand nothing." He turned to the fire, and his gaze was lost in its heat and swirl.

That was the longest conversation they had, and Taro wished

the journey could just end. Spending this time with Hiro was like a long-drawn-out torture.

Eventually, though, they rounded a bend on a path that Taro knew well, and Shirahama was laid out before them, the village nestled against the hillside, smoke pluming from the houses, all exactly as Taro had left it, not once but twice. He glanced at Hiro. Back then, he had trusted his friend completely. Their lives had changed in one night—ninjas had murdered Taro's father, and Shusaku had rescued him, had led him and Hiro to the safety of a boat.

Now Shusaku was dead, and Hiro was a traitor. At least, Taro thought Shusaku was dead. There was still that glimmer of hope, mostly because of what the ninja had said in that passageway. *Even death must die*. He'd been referring to the Tibetan story of Enma and Enma-taka, the Death-of-Enma—every child in Japan knew it. Taro had even thought about it the previous year, when he had ventured into Enma's realm himself, looking for his mother.

In the story, Enma went mad and began slaughtering innocent people in a Tibetan valley. In response to this, the abbot of the nearby monastery felt himself changing, until he was enormous and his stride encompassed mountains—he realized then that he had become the Death-of-Enma, and he made the mad Enma die, and then he became the new Enma, because Enma was always a man before he was the judge of death. In this way, no man could be Enma forever.

But was the story even real? Certainly many things Taro had assumed to be fiction were real, but that was no guarantee.

And even if it was real, could Shusaku become the death of death? Would he even be able to take that form?

No. Taro thought Shusaku was probably dead back there, torn to pieces in the passageway.

"You would have regretted it," said Hiro, suddenly and softly, as they looked down at the bay. "You would have regretted throwing it away."

“No, I wouldn’t,” said Taro. He didn’t look at Hiro, just started walking again, following the path down to the village. Hana, who hadn’t been here before, was murmuring to one or both of them, in a low voice, about how beautiful it was. Taro ignored her.

Beyond the houses, beyond the beach where the fires burned salt from seaweed, stretched the gunmetal sea. He could make out the west side of the bay, where the old wreck was to be found, the wreck everyone said was cursed. He couldn’t stop a shiver at the thought of diving that water again, teeming as it was with *Kappa* demons. And then there was the dragon.

In his mind, a single, searing image: the village the dragon of the earth had burned, those marks where the people had been.

He gritted his teeth. He had to acknowledge the possibility that the dragon might kill him. He was a vampire, he was stronger and faster than any human. He could kill with ease. But if the attack by Sato had shown him anything, it was that even against another vampire he was not guaranteed success. And a dragon would be much, much stronger than a vampire.

Most likely, he would die.

But he’d do it. If there was one thing he had learned about himself, it was that he was not afraid to die. He was more afraid of others dying, and now he had lost someone else. He didn’t even know why he was going to try to get Kusanagi. Maybe because Shusaku had told him to, before he sent him on his way. Maybe because there didn’t seem anything else to do, now that he couldn’t marry Hana. Now that Shusaku was dead.

Or maybe, if he was honest with himself, it was because Kusanagi was one of the three divine objects. It would give him a claim to the shogunate, if he could recover it. And wasn’t that the point of all this, really? To follow his destiny? To become shogun? Taro wasn’t interested in the power—well, he told himself he wasn’t interested in the power. But to take control of the country for himself . . . to lower the rice taxes, to try to minimize the destructive force of conflict . . . that was tempting.

And the power. That too.

Well, did it really matter why he did it? He gazed at that shimmering patch of sea, so innocent-looking from above. The scent of pine needles was in his nostrils.

He'd dive the wreck for the second time. If he found the legendary sword, so be it.

And if he died, he died.

CHAPTER 31

Kenji Kira stood at the prow of his ship as it knifed through the waves. The Buddha ball was in his hand, humming with contained life. A fine salt spray, like rain, settled on his skin and clothes. Fluttering in the stiff breeze above him, nailed to the mast, was his new flag.

He couldn't smell the sea—he couldn't precisely smell anything, apart from blood—but he could feel it, rocking the very wood on which he stood, soaking into his bones. He liked it. He was a little disappointed that he had never known, before, how good it felt to cut through water like this. He wouldn't have wasted his time fighting battles for Lord Oda. He would have turned pirate when he still lived.

Kenji Kira, pirate!

It had a ring to it.

And then there was the salutary nature of the sea itself, the way it cradled and protected, instead of allowing decay. Throw a branch in a ditch on land and it would sprout mushrooms and lichen, grow moss like a beard, eventually dissolve into nothingness, eaten by wasps, absorbed by the ground. Throw that same branch in the sea, and it would simply wash up one day, years later maybe, pale and hard and smooth to the touch. Nor was it just the water, but what was in the water too. Say one thing for salt, Kira thought. Say that it preserves things, makes them last. For so many years he had sucked pebbles, drunk only water, eaten only rice, trying to make his flesh hard and incorruptible.

He could have simply gone to sea and bathed himself in salt water. Pickled himself. Look at what happened to fish when you salted it. The flesh never rotted. He knew this, intimately, because it was what the still-living members of his crew ate. Revolting, really, but imagine what that salt was doing to their insides! Preserving them, no doubt. Making them proof against rot, against the worms and other unspeakable beasts that invaded a person's body after death.

Yes. If he was not already a skeleton, he would like to live at sea.

He saw smoke rising beyond the headland ahead. "Is that it?" he called.

"Aye," said the navigator. "That's Shirahama."

Kenji Kira felt joy course through him, where blood could not. He had arrived at the boy's home. Did Taro already have Kusanagi? It didn't matter. If he did, Kira would simply take it from him. If he didn't, he would force Taro to find it first. It was, like the best of things, simple. And once he held Kusanagi, as well as the ball that was filling his sails, driving him at this astonishing speed toward Shirahama? Well, then he would rule all of Japan, and maybe more.

Ruler of Japan. That had a ring to it too.

He was looking forward to killing Taro. It would be even better than Shusaku's death, and that had been quite something. In the end, Shusaku had taken some time to die. His limbs severed, his head separated from his body, he had still been murmuring Mara's name, even to the very last. The fool. He had seemed to smile, right at the end, though it was difficult to tell with the ghastly horror that was his skin, all burns and strange black characters.

That had tickled Kenji Kira more than anything else. That smile. Because it wasn't over, not by a long way. Death was not the end. He had followed Shusaku into it, caught up with the ninja as he crossed the bridge over the Three Rivers. In death, Shusaku's skin was clean, not a single mark on him. He had the presence of mind to look surprised when Kira seized him, before dragging him—with the assistance of Horse-head and Ox-face—deeper into death, and through the door that led to hell. Of course, the surprise was misplaced too. Hadn't Kira told them that he was Enma, that death was his to rule? None could resist Enma. Especially not the dead.

Entering the hell realm, he had taken Shusaku to the worst tortures, skipping the knives and bees and pokers to go straight for the tree where the flaying was done. The skin grew back; that was the beauty of it. Still, he was impressed despite himself in the end—it was five times the ninja's skin had been stripped from his body, top to toe, before he told them where Taro was going, and what he hoped to do there.

It was another three times after that, before he told them about Hana, and how Taro had bitten her.

After that, Kenji Kira had left the ninja with the demons, for all of eternity.

Oh, he would have grinned, from ear to ear, if he wasn't missing all his flesh, and so grinning all the time. Hana could never love Taro now, it was impossible. He had attacked her, betrayed his demonic nature. And then along would come an old retainer of her father's, a man who had proven himself over and over again to be strong, to be ruthless. Lord Oda was dead, but he, Kenji Kira, was alive!

But soon she would be his. He would kill Taro before her very eyes, show her what happened to evil creatures that dared to hurt her.

She would be grateful—he pictured her weeping her thanks, whimpering her admiration for his resolve and his fierceness, his desire to protect her. His chest swelled with pride, and sea air.

He glanced back and up, at his ship's new standard. He had taken it from Shusaku's body, after leaving his spirit in hell. He had knelt in that scene of butchery in the rock passage, sawing with his knife, until he had the skin from Shusaku's back in his hands, bloody and fatty on one side, etched with scar tissue and tattoos on the other. Now it snapped and raced in the strong wind from the Buddha ball.

He had the ball. He had Shusaku, flying from his mast, screaming in hell forever.

Soon Taro's skin would fly below it.

Kusanagi would be in his hand.

And Hana would be by his side. Lady Kenji no Hana.

It had a ring to it.

CHAPTER 32

"You didn't find what you were looking for last time?" the priest asked.

"Well, no." Taro remembered the fake ball he had recovered from the wreck, the one his mother had put there as a false trail. He remembered removing the true ball from her chest, where she had sewn it into herself, years before. "This is something different," he said.

"Your destiny seems tied to that wreck," said the priest. He, Taro, and Hana were standing by his boat, which was tied up at the shore. The priest, whom Taro had last seen the previous year, when he helped Taro to dive the wreck, had merely nodded in greeting when he saw Taro coming down the hill, as if his comings and goings were no longer to be remarked on. Nor was he surprised when Taro asked to borrow the boat again.

"I suppose so," said Taro. He'd thought the same thing himself—how strange it was that Kusanagi might have been under Shirahama bay all that time, that he might have been so close to it when he was looking for the ball.

"Well," said the priest. "At least someone will be using my boat."

"Sorry?" said Taro. The priest of Shirahama, like everyone in Shirahama, was a fisherman first and foremost.

"Since Lord Tokugawa took Lord Oda's land, and Shirahama with it, our rice taxes have gone up," said the priest. "We spend most of our time in the fields now. There is little time for fishing."

Taro shook his head in irritation. It seemed that the daimyo, including his own father, were determined to break the peasants with their taxes. "I'll be doing a different kind of fishing, though," he said.

"And afterward," said the priest. "You will be leaving again?"

Taro nodded.

"A shame," said the priest. "But the world is vast—you must explore it. Perhaps one day, when you have seen enough, you will return."

"Perhaps," said Taro. He glanced up at the village, to find Hiro, but couldn't see his old friend. He imagined Hiro was in his hut, though there was no smoke coming from the chimney. No matter where he was, though, his presence poisoned the village. It was Hiro's fault that Shusaku was dead. If Hiro had never recovered the ball, if he'd just left it where Taro had thrown it, then Shusaku wouldn't have been able to use it to make his stupid, noble stand. Taro knew he could not stay in Shirahama so long as his old friend was there.

Hana, meanwhile, was with Taro and the priest, looking out to sea. She had insisted on coming with him on the boat, saying that someone should be on lookout while he dived. He'd explained about the curse, but she wouldn't listen. Suddenly she gasped.

"The Heike," she said. At her feet, one of the large crabs particular to Shirahama had crawled up out of the sea. It scuttled up to her, then sidled off down the beach. On its back was the white cross that made people believe the crabs were the spirits of the Heike. They were, in fact—Taro knew it, because he'd seen them change from ghostly men back to crabs, when the feast of souls, *obon*, was over.

Taro watched the crab go. Again he felt the connections resonating. The Heike, who had perished in this bay. The boy emperor they protected, who had drowned right here, in the blue-gray water Taro was gazing out at, and the sword that had been lost with him. All along, the secret to Japan's rule had been concealed beneath the smooth surface of this very bay, the one he'd seen every day of his young life, whipped up by storms, calm and translucent in summer sunshine, flooded with the fire of the rising sun. He saw a seagull dive, far out to sea, listened to the constant murmur of the waves on the sand. He tried to concentrate on surface appearance, disturbed by the picture that kept entering his mind of all the ships that must be under that calm, glassy bay, all the dead samurai whose armor and weapons littered the seafloor, who scuttled around its depths as crabs.

Repressing a shiver, Taro began to untie the boat. If he didn't go soon, he would lose his nerve. The sun was high in the sky—and he'd already wasted the previous day speaking to people he knew and catching the priest up on what he had been doing, or at least what he could say of it.

"Well," said the priest. "Good luck. May the goddess be with you."

Taro wondered if he should say that he had seen the goddess to whom Shirahama's shrine was dedicated, last time he dived. That he had been rescued by the Princess of the Hidden Waters herself. But it would lead to a long conversation, and he didn't have time for that. He contented himself with saying, "Praise the Princess of the Hidden Waters."

Actually, the Princess was part of his plan, such as he had one. He very much hoped she *would* be taking an interest in what he was doing.

The priest nodded solemnly, then helped to push the boat out. Hana and Taro jumped in, and Taro took the oars, after clearing some of the fishing paraphernalia that littered the boat—nets, buoys, a couple of weighted lobster creels.

As always, Taro could feel when they were over the wreck. The water took on an unpleasant quality, oily and slick. The birds no longer called and wheeled overhead; only silence hung over this part of the bay. Even the sun no longer seemed so warm, and he saw Hana hug herself as a thin breeze blew.

"It's too deep for an anchor," said Taro. "So you'll have to hold the boat in place with the oars." He pointed to a gnarled tree that clung to the northward cliff. "Keep it in line with that tree. I shouldn't be long."

"Taro, I . . ." She trailed off. "I hope you find it," she said, though he had the impression it hadn't been what she first intended to say. "Keep safe."

"You too," he said. What he meant was *I love you, forgive me*, but it didn't come out that way. He felt a pressure on his heart, and before his heart could have a chance to burst, he rolled backward over the side of the boat, and then he was in the water.

He took a deep breath and dived down. This time he knew where he was going—he found the spars of the ship easily, sticking up as he remembered them, like the rib cage of a great whale. The water was murky at this depth, and his ears roared with pain. He gripped one of the spars—it was slimy in his hand—and clung to it, fighting the urge of his body to rise to the surface.

Below him, a small octopus shot away, running along the sand to disappear into some hidden hole. The sand was covering so much of the ship, and the shifting sea had broken it into such small pieces, that he couldn't possibly hope to find the sword on his own, even if it was still here. He closed his eyes for a moment, hoping that this wouldn't be a wasted trip. When he opened them again, a school of small, gray fish shimmered past him, then flicked into nothingness, silver flashes disappearing into the gloom.

When the first Kappa came toward him, he was ready for it. The turtle-demon, its red eyes full of anger, swam for his legs. He pulled them up just in time and let the demon go past. But there were more of them—two seized him by the arm, pulling him down toward the sand, and his death. Others clung to his body, like malignant and enormous limpets.

He resisted only partially. His lungs began to scream at him, telling him to go back to the surface, to breathe in the cool, life-giving air. He ignored them. His vision began to go dark at the edges.

Finally, when he thought that he must drown, there was an impression of suddenly brightening light, and the Kappa began to fall away. Again, the Princess of the Hidden Waters whirled around him, her dress flowing in the water like seaweed. She was beautiful. More beautiful than he remembered. She was the spirit of the amas, their protector, and the guardian of the bay. She was a goddess.

None of which stopped him from reaching out and grabbing her. He held to her as tightly as the Kappa had clung to him.

She didn't speak, exactly, but he became aware of a questioning presence in his mind. She had turned to look at him. He felt that if he looked into her eyes too long, he would be lost. They were the exact blue of the sea, as if the water had seeped into her, filling her head.

He didn't dare open his mouth—his traitor lungs would fill themselves with water if he did. So he put all his effort into shouting, in his mind, the same words over and over. More of his vision was falling to the blackness now, and the Princess was in a diminishing circle of light, as he slowly lost consciousness.

Take me to the dragon, he thought. *Take me to the dragon, take me to the dragon, so I can find Kusanagi.*

There was a feeling in his head like a pitying sigh, and then the Princess was swimming, or gliding, and he was gliding with her. They went deep and far, hurtling out to sea; he had a moment to wish that he was not leaving Hana behind, and then all the light went from his surroundings. He thought for a moment he might have passed out, or died, but then a strange glow as of phosphorescence illuminated the seabed.

Uncurling itself before him, stretching out its endless coils, was a dragon so big that even as Taro looked at it he felt as if he were imagining things. Its ship-size head was bearded and horned. It kicked off from the seafloor with taloned feet, snaking sinuously toward him. As it breathed, fire spewed from its nostrils, boiling the sea—he had never seen fire underwater before. The fire was, oddly, blue, as were the terrifying creature's eyes. The effect was of heat haze, when it made the air bend and shimmer, and Taro understood that it was the source of the otherworldly glow. The dragon must have been as long as a valley, as tall as a mountain. Its skin, which was made up of diamonds of hard armor, was green and blue, such that if you were not looking carefully, it might blend away into the sea. He knew suddenly that he had never really experienced fear until this moment.

Then two things happened, in quick succession.

First, he felt the Princess gently remove herself from his embrace, understanding as she did it that she could have extricated herself at any time, had she wanted to, and then she was gone—he felt her departure as a lessening of warmth, a growing of fear.

Second, the dragon reared its head back, then launched itself at him, opening its mouth. The heat of a furnace enveloped him, a blue like sapphires. He had a brief image of teeth like swords, set in a wide-open jaw, and then the mouth closed over him and everything was blackness.

CHAPTER 33

THE SAME PLACE

FIVE HUNDRED YEARS EARLIER

Chikakiyo looked out across the flat, gray bay of Shirahama toward his death. Five hundred ships were anchored there, just out of bow-shot. The full might of the Genji force, arrayed against the hundred or so ships on his own side.

Today the proud family of the Heike, for whom he was a samurai, would be destroyed utterly, would be made as dust in the wind.

Chikakiyo, along with the other Heike, had hoped even as late as last night that Lord Tanso would join them, with his two hundred ships, for his family owed the Heike a great debt. But as the sun set on the straits of Shirahama, they had watched ships without end, flying the *mon* of house Tanso, as they drew alongside the traitorous Genji. It had been a shock that had rippled through the Heike, like an earthquake, when the great fish underneath Japan twists and twitches.

The rumor, just as damaging as the blow to morale, was that Tanso had consulted the gods on which side to take. He had gone to the shrine at Tanabe and spent seven days meditating there. As a result of this, however, he had received an intimation from the deity that he should pledge his allegiance to the Genji. Still doubtful, though, given his family's gratitude to the Heike, he had taken seven white cocks and seven red cocks, and held a cockfight. All seven of the red cocks were defeated and ran away, and as the *mon* of the Heike was red and the *mon* of the Genji was white, finally he had decided to side with the Genji.

Truly, thought Chikakiyo, *it seems the gods are against us.*

The gods should be on the side of the Heike, of course. They had the young emperor, possessed of the Ten Divine Virtues and the Three Imperial Treasures. He was the rightful ruler of Japan, a direct descendant of the Goddess Amaterasu, heir to the legendary objects she had passed down: the mirror and jewels that had lured her from her cave and then trapped her outside it, to make the world light again; and the sword her brother Susanoo had used to kill the eight-headed dragon, and later given to her as a gift of reconciliation.

These objects were close at hand. Very close.

Belowdecks, on the very ship on which Chikakiyo stood, were the legendary sword Kusanagi, the mirror, and the jewel. The boy emperor, too—though his mother was keeping him down there, so he would not see the Genji ships and be frightened.

Chikakiyo thought this was a good idea. He was older than the emperor, but he was looking at the Genji ships, and he was very frightened. He did not believe the gods could be on their side. Otherwise why would they have been running from the Genji pretenders for so long, why would they be so outnumbered now?

It was only the Hour of the Hare, but it was summer, and the sun was already rising slowly in the east, beginning to stain the waves with red. Chikakiyo chose to see this as an omen. Before the day was out, the water would turn to blood. Still, he knew that he would lay down his life to protect the emperor. He was a samurai: It was what he was for. He glanced to his sides and saw the other men, grimly testing their own weapons. He knew they were thinking the same thing, and that was a good thing about being a samurai—there is a companionship in duty, because you are all trained to have the same reactions, the same feelings.

Chikakiyo ran his finger along the string of his Shigeto bow, testing its tautness for the thousandth time. Then he took his quiver from his back and examined the arrows—thirty in all, feathered with the black-and-white feathers of hawks. Chikakiyo was not yet twenty, but he was the best shot in the Heike's rapidly dwindling army, and so he had been posted here, on the imperial ship.

Not that the ship was especially imperial in appearance. It was a small sloop, not even flying the imperial *mon*. Instead the symbol of a lesser lord fluttered on its mast. It sat low in the water, its paint peeling. In part this was due to the steady decline in the Heike fortunes. From the most powerful dynasty in Japan, protectors of the emperor, they had—through a succession of misfortunes, battles, and ill-judged acts of arrogance—ended up a people of fugitives, harassed and harried through the entire land and then the sea, to end up here, at their last stand, a collection of vagrant lords.

It was years since any of them had seen their ancestral lands, years since any of them had slept a full night, without being woken for the watch. And now, finally, the Genji had run them to ground, or rather run them to sea. They had nowhere farther to run. They must face their enemies now—the Genji, the proud western clan who wished to take the empire for themselves. But though the Heike had fallen, they were still samurai. They would not allow the emperor to be killed, and the Three Treasures to be taken, without a fight.

Nor were their straitened circumstances the only reason for the crudeness of the ship on which Chikakiyo awaited the attack of the Genji. This was the strategy of Lord Tometomo, the leader of the Heike forces. He had placed the fiercest warriors in the smallest ships, leaving the huge Chinese war galleons at the center of the fleet more or less undefended. The idea was that the Genji would attack the strongest ships, and the cream of the fighters could then attack them from the rear.

It was a good idea. Chikakiyo just wasn't sure if it would make up for their being outnumbered five to one.

As he thought this, Lord Tometomo himself appeared outside the deckhouse of the ship. He, too, would remain on this imperial vessel, apparently a weaker ship hanging at the back of the conflict, to help protect the emperor.

"They are too many!" he shouted. There was no need for him to keep his voice down—the ships of the Genji were still too far away for them to see him, or hear him. "It seems, if we consider numbers of warriors and ships the deciding factor, that we must die today!"

Silence.

Lord Tometomo drew his sword.

"But I say no!" he continued. "I say that fate and the gods are on our side. Warriors are flesh; ships are wood. We have the finest samurai in the land, the finest archers. They are westerners, unused to the sea. They will be like fish climbing a tree! We have only to pluck them and throw them into the waves, where they belong. They have numbers. We have the emperor, true heir of the sun goddess, and the Three Treasures!" At this, he thrust his sword into the air, and whether by plan or by accident the sun caught its blade, and Chikakiyo—along with everyone else—gasped.

Tometomo's was a simple sword, ostensibly at least. Straight, made of a steel so black it seemed to absorb the light. No decoration on its pommel, which was simply wood wrapped with leather. But Chikakiyo could feel it, even from here—it was humming in the light. It looked like a sword that could cut through the world.

"This is Kusanagi!" said Tometomo, which was of course perfectly obvious to everyone. "As long as we have this sword, and the mirror and the jewels, we cannot lose! We are the protectors of a living god, and we will not be allowed to fall. Look at the men beside you. Look at them, now."

Chikakiyo turned to the archer at his side. They were a row of archers, at the front of the ship. The first cordon against attack by the Genji, if the enemy should realize where the emperor was and come for him. The archer next to Chikakiyo was middle-aged, at least twenty-five years old. His name was Yoshimoto, and he had once gotten so drunk with Chikakiyo that they'd fallen into one of Edo's rivers and had to be pulled out by a passing fisherman. Chikakiyo knew that he had a son and daughter at home, in some small province in the mountains. Chikakiyo saw fear in the man's eyes—but he also saw pride, and hope.

"Those men who stand beside you will fight with you to the death. You know this," continued Tometomo. "But remember this! It is not just men who stand beside you. The gods stand with you too."

With that, he sheathed the famous sword and returned into the deckhouse.

At first Tometomo's strategy worked: The Genji focused their attentions on the heavy ships-of-war, ignoring the smaller boats on which were stationed the best archers and fiercest fighters of the Heike. Soon, many of the Genji ships had been surrounded by nimbler vessels and boarded. Blood ran from their decks into the sea.

The sun was higher in the sky now. Chikakiyo watched as the Heike *mon* was raised on a great ship—he thought it might have been one belonging to the turncoat Tanso. He allowed himself, for a moment, to believe that they might win this battle and cause their names to be spoken in hushed tones of reverence forevermore.

Tometomo stood on the deck near him, covering his eyes to watch the action. Often, it was hard to tell who was carrying the fight. Ships would clash, arrows would fly into the air like whining insects. Men would fall from the side, and into the waves, dragged under by their heavy armor. But they were not close enough for Chikakiyo to make out their *mons*.

It happened very suddenly, when it happened—certainly there was nothing Chikakiyo could have done about it. First the emperor asked to come up on deck, so that he could see the battle. Judging that the real heart of the fight was still far enough away, Tometomo assented, and soon the young boy stood with his mother on the deck, looking out over the shifting sea to the men dying on the other side of the bay.

"They are like toys," said the boy. "And yet they are suffering. Maybe this is how the gods see us. As things whose feelings are not to be credited or pitied too much, because they are so small and insignificant."

Chikakiyo stared at him. He had spent a little time in the company of the emperor, and he was always struck by how the boy could say things that sounded so old. It was as if he had lived before, many times.

"No," said Tometomo. "The gods are your ancestors. They will protect you."

The boy emperor's expression was half-sad, half-amused.

There was a very soft sound, something like *shhhhh*, and then there was the shaft of a long arrow sticking out from Tometomo's chest. The great general of the Heike looked down, stunned. He was wearing only the lightest leather armor, appropriate to a battle at sea. Chikakiyo heard the slapping of the waves against the deck, smelled the salt of the sea and the iron of Tometomo's blood, as time seemed to stop.

Tometomo touched the shaft. Blood ran from the wound—Chikakiyo noticed, suddenly, that the point was protruding from the older man's back. Samurai rushed forward, but Tometomo waved them back. He pointed to the arrow. Down its length something had been written. Chikakiyo saw the second half of a name—Yoichi, he thought—and then a message. *Send this back if you can.*

Chikakiyo looked over to the Genji ships, amazed. They must be seven *tan* away, a distance over which a man would be hard-pressed to fire an arrow, let alone hit his target. It was pure luck that Tometomo had been hit, he assumed. The Genji did not know about this ship and the important cargo it carried. The person who fired this arrow had simply wanted to strike a blow from afar, to show their skill.

Chikakiyo felt anger flood his body, but also admiration.

At that moment, Tometomo pulled out the arrow. He beckoned to Chikakiyo, as blood poured from the open wound. "Send it back," he said, handing it over. Then he sank to his knees, his eyes closing. Guards moved forward and caught him, taking him back to the deckhouse. The emperor, who had seemed so composed a moment ago, screamed. His mother caught him up and held him tight, then carried him toward the gangway that led down into the ship.

Chikakiyo weighed the arrow in his hand. He took his bow and nocked it, drawing it a couple of times without firing, to feel its balance. It was longer than he would like, for himself, and it was fletched with white feathers of the crane, and black feathers of the goose. A length of unadulterated bamboo. Showy, and light. Built for distance, not accuracy. Nothing like his own arrows, which were as the hawk—made to take down birds as they flew and prey as it leaped. It was said of Chikakiyo that he could kill a fleeing deer from five *tan* away, and when it was said, he never denied it, because it was true.

Fixing the nearest Genji ship—and even that was too far away—he closed down the world around him, making silence of the words of encouragement that were coming his way from the other archers. He drew the rocking of the ship into himself, so that the waves were one with his being.

He prayed. "*Namu Amida Butsu*, and especially the deities of my homeland, the *gongen* of Nikko, and *yuzen* of Nasu, please, grant that I may strike that daimyo on his horse."

There was a cough from behind him. He turned and was surprised to see the emperor, who had escaped, it seemed, from his mother. There were tears on the boy's cheeks. "I never saw a man die before," he said. Another tear rolled. Tometomo had been like an uncle to the boy, Chikakiyo knew.

"Then you are lucky," he said.

The emperor touched his arm. "Make them pay," he said. And then he turned and ran back to his mother, who appeared at that moment, searching for him.

Chikakiyo scanned the deck of the far-off ship. He couldn't make out details, but he could see a man on a horse, firing off arrows at close range into the Heike ships nearby—as if this were a land battle, and being mounted could possibly do any good. In this instance, it only made the man stand out more as a target. He wore an elaborate helmet, and Chikakiyo could see from this—as well as from the obvious fact that he was mounted on a horse worth a rice farmer's lifetime earnings—that he was an important Genji lord.

Chikakiyo pulled back the arrow, felt the tension across his chest, then let it fly—and it was precisely a case of letting it, for he felt always in these moments that the arrow wanted this, to meet its target, and he was only helping it along.

A long time passed—what felt like too long—and then, to his amazement, the man on the horse fell suddenly off it, clutching at his body.

Around Chikakiyo, men cheered and laughed, and he smiled at them weakly. It was the first time he had shot a man, though he had killed many a target and many a pretty lady's fan in his time, winning many a bet.

He felt sick.

The turning point of the battle came not with Tometomo's death but with the turning of Shigeyoshi, one of the minor lords who had always supported the Heike. Seeing the advantage slowly ebb away toward the Genji, through sheer force of numbers, he defected to their side. And bringing his ship alongside theirs, he told them of the ruse—informed them of where the best fighters were stationed, and where the emperor was being guarded.

Chikakiyo, of course, knew nothing of this. He only knew that Shigeyoshi's ship was suddenly flying the Genji *mon*, and that shortly afterward the Genji ships that were not immediately engaged in battle were plying the waves toward them.

The battle, which had been a faraway thing, became close very quickly. There were archers on the Genji ships, and soon the water was hissing with falling arrows. A moment after that they were striking the wood of the deck.

"Fire at will!" said Munemori, one of the samurai lords on the ship.

Chikakiyo subtracted himself from the world.

He took an arrow from his quiver, nocked it, sent it flying at the closest ship, and saw a man go overboard, screaming. He fired again and saw the arrow lodge in a man's arm, saw him drop his sword.

Then the ships were on them, and there was no time for seeing—he was just feeding arrows into his bow, letting them go again, freeing them into the world. He felt rather than saw the men beside him fall, noticed absently that the deck had grown slippery with blood.

He was woken from his trance only by the shudder as the two ships met—a sensation that went through his whole body, as if he were inside a vast, ringing bell. The other ship was bigger—a man jumped down, *katana* drawn. Chikakiyo's arrow seemed to jump out of his quiver of its own accord, fit itself into the drawn-back belly of the bow, then fly straight forward. It buried itself so far in the man's face that the feathers made him a new, comical nose.

Chikakiyo got the next Genji boarder through the shoulder, knocking him into the sea. He was dimly aware of people to the side of him grappling, the clang of metal on metal. He supposed that he was going to die quite soon, but they would never get to the emperor with him still living.

He had his arrow nocked to take the next one, but the man was too quick. Chikakiyo dropped the bow, drew his short-sword as he ducked, felt the other man's blade kiss the hairs on the back of his neck. He stabbed upward, hard. His sword sank into something soft, and he had to shrug off the man, who'd fallen across his shoulders as if in an embrace.

Arrow. Fire. Kill.

He slipped on the deck—he had been sure he would. He slashed to the left and to the right, thought at one moment he might have hurt one of the men on his own side, knocked aside an axe that was aimed at his legs, slit a man's throat with his blade, then managed to get one more arrow into his bow and shot a Genji samurai through the back of the neck as he ran toward the deckhouse, looking for the emperor. He did all that, and still he was surprised when he felt a coldness in his guts and looked down to see the hilt of a sword sticking out of his stomach.

He opened and closed his mouth, stupid as a fish.

He put his hands to his belly, felt the hot wetness spreading.

He did not feel the deck when it hit him.

Chikakiyo opened his eyes. By the position of the sun in the sky, he guessed it was the Hour of the Dragon, perhaps a little later. He was surprised that so little time appeared to have passed—he had little experience of death, but from what he had heard about it he expected it to last longer.

The blade in his stomach reminded him of its presence, and as the pain expanded like an opening fist, he knew he was not dead and wished he was.

He heard a woman's voice, and turned his head toward it.

The dowager empress, the mother of the emperor, stood with him at the prow of the small vessel. A band of Genji stood all around her, but at a respectful distance, clearly nervous about attacking the descendants of a god. The emperor's mother wore a double silk dress of dark gray mourning color, and under her arm was the sacred jewel, one of the strand that had held Amaterasu out of her cave, and tucked into her girdle was the mirror that had reflected the goddess's own light and beauty back at her.

The boy emperor, standing beside his mother, clutched the Sacred Sword Kusanagi. It seemed to be this, Chikakiyo noticed now, that had so transfixed the Genji soldiers.

"Hand over the boy," one of them said. "We will not harm him."

The woman laughed. Inside, Chikakiyo laughed with her—he could not manage to do it out loud, with the agony in his stomach. The Genji would never let the emperor live—it was known that they had already asked their priests and monks to find them a new emperor, someone who had practiced the Ten Virtues in their previous lives, someone born under the right stars.

“I am samurai, and the blood of gods runs in my veins,” said the boy’s mother. “You think I would surrender?” She moved farther back, to the gunwale running along the side of the vessel. “Let those of you who dare, follow me.”

Chikakiyo understood that she was going to drown herself, with her son.

The emperor was six years old.

Chikakiyo stared at him, his heart breaking, as the boy moved back with his mother, holding the sword out before him. The boy was so beautiful that it seemed there was a brilliant radiance about him, and Chikakiyo could believe in that moment that he was descended from Amaterasu.

The boy turned to his mother. “Where are you taking me?” he asked.

She bent down to look at him, tears streaming down her cheeks. Chikakiyo had the feeling that he had been returned from death only to witness this moment, so that one of the Heike should see it, and feel the pride that was required. “Some evil karma claims us, my son,” she said. “So turn to the west and say the *nenbutsu*, so that Amida Buddha and the Holy Ones may come to welcome you in the Pure Land.”

“But I don’t want to die, Mother,” said the boy, crying. There were times when he sounded very old, and there were times when he did not. Chikakiyo could still feel the shards of his broken heart in his chest.

“I know,” said the dowager. “But this world is nothing. The Buddha tells us it is small as a grain of millet, in the totality of things. There is a Pure Land of happiness beneath the waves, another capital where no sorrow can come. That is where I am taking you.”

She held him, as he whispered the words of the *nenbutsu*. Then she turned to the men who had her at bay, like a doe hunted by dogs. “At the bottom of the ocean we have a capital,” she said, perhaps to them, perhaps to her son. Then she jumped with him into the sea.

The samurai hesitated, then one of them dived in after her. There was a confusion of noises, then he shouted out, "I have the mirror!"

Suddenly Chikakiyo understood why he had been kept alive. The Genji didn't need the emperor. But they did need the Three Treasures. Anyone possessing them could legitimately claim rule over Japan, even without the blessing of the temples. Who could contest that a person owning the Three Treasures was ordained by Amaterasu, the goddess of the sun that was Japan's symbol, to have that honor?

Screaming under his breath, he crawled toward the gunwale. He could feel his blood smearing on the deck. It was not a pleasant feeling. He could also feel something trailing behind him—he feared it was a part of him. He realized suddenly that he needed something heavy. He saw that one of the dead men beside him was dressed, stupidly for this battle, in steel armor. Groping with the bindings, he took off the breast plate and helmet and arranged them as best he could on his own body.

When he reached the railing, someone shouted out. He didn't turn—just hauled himself over, the pain exquisite as the soft things that should have been inside him caught on the wood. He held on to his short-sword, or perhaps it was someone else's. He had picked it up from the deck beside him. Then he was falling, crashing into the water as if it were something solid. The steel he wore took him down quickly, into the water that grew colder as he descended, as if it were a passageway into death.

Which was what it was, of course.

He kept his eyes open, the stinging of the salt water nothing to the fire in his belly.

His blood ribboned out around him, almost beautiful, like delicate silk creatures.

Chikakiyo could see two samurai, weighed down by their armor, struggling to hold on to the emperor's mother. One of them was tugging the string of jewels, and she was rolling to try to pull them from him. He couldn't see the boy, until he turned his body and perceived—through the gloom—a slender body, drifting downward, a samurai swimming purposefully toward it.

Gritting his teeth, he forced himself down after the samurai, stretching his sword out before him, as if the sword were pulling him through the water. He could hear a thin crackling in his ears, a noise his mother—who was an ama—said was the movements of the tiny creatures that lived in the sea. The weight of water pressed on his ears. He tried to swallow, to relieve it.

Already his lungs were swollen, bursting. He almost took in a breath, but when he opened his mouth, involuntarily, the harshly salty water rushed in and shocked him into closing it again.

If the samurai had been prepared for Chikakiyo, it might have gone differently. Chikakiyo had lost a lot of blood, and strength with it. But the man didn't see him coming. The Genji had just seized the emperor's sleeve, halting his descent to the depths, when Chikakiyo mustered all his force and thrust the blade of his short-sword through the man's neck.

There was no scream under the water. The Genji samurai just went limp and floated away. Chikakiyo saw that the emperor's eyes were open, but were seeing nothing. The boy was dead. He was six years old, and he had grown up in the Palace of Long Life in Edo, which was accessed through the Gate of Eternal Youth, and now he was dead in the cold sea.

Chikakiyo held on to the frail body and would have wept, if he hadn't already been immersed in the tears of the sea. The emperor was still holding Kusanagi, and that was a mercy, at least.

Gently Chikakiyo arranged the sword so that it was between the two of them, and turned to make sure that no one else was following them. In fact, it was already difficult to see—as the water grew colder, so it was leached of light, such that they drifted down now through near blackness. His weight and the boy's, combined with the armor he wore, made them sink rapidly.

He felt something in his ears burst, and water come in—feeling with its cold little fingers. He had heard from his mother that this happened, that amas who were overambitious in their diving could have their bodies invaded by the sea, their ears broken.

They never heard again, not properly, but that wasn't important to Chikakiyo right now. There was nothing he needed to hear.

Slowly he felt his life force slip away into the embracing sea. He sent up a silent prayer to Amida Buddha, asking the enlightened one to welcome him, if it was his desire, into the Pure Land. He thanked the gods for allowing him this one final act, the saving of Kusanagi from the Genji. They might claim the throne now—probably they would have a replica made, it was the obvious thing to do—but they would never truly own it, not while Kusanagi lay at the bottom of Shirahama bay.

Just then there was a sudden lightening of the water, as if a cold blue fire were burning, and he wondered if this was death coming.

But it wasn't death. It was a dragon.

The serpent was perhaps three ship-lengths in size, and it curled itself around Chikakiyo and the emperor. Its eyes burned blue in its bearded, horned head, like sapphires. Chikakiyo was so afraid he forgot that he was dying.

Chikakiyo felt, rather than heard, the words of the dragon in his head.

"You are safe," it said.

Chikakiyo's mind spun. How could he be safe? He was dying, in the embrace of a dragon whose teeth—he could see—were longer than his *wakizashi*.

"We dragons serve Amaterasu," the dragon said. "You and the boy will be buried in my palace under the sea. I will hold Kusanagi there, and keep it safe from all traitors."

Chikakiyo smiled. He was glad. But he was worried, too, that the Genji would never stop trying to recover the real sword—and others aside from the Genji too, if it was discovered that only two of the Three Treasures had been recovered from the sea. Anyone possessing those three treasures could claim with them the right to rule Japan.

"Don't fear," said the dragon, as if it had read his thoughts. "The sword will be safe with me. If anyone comes to claim it, they will pay with all they hold dear. So it has always been."

Chikakiyo nodded slowly, pleased that he had done his duty by his emperor, as the light leaked from the world—and this time it wasn't the depth, it was his dying.

CHAPTER 34

Darkness, all around him.

Then a feeling of expulsion, violent and painful, and he was on his face on a hard floor, coughing hard. The water was gone; he was in the air again. Was he dead?

Taro levered himself onto his knees, his lungs tearing. He looked around, failing to understand. He was in some kind of cave, its walls glistening with moisture. Somewhere far away, he could hear the sea roaring. Was he *under* it? The cavern was large—as big as a palace—and stretching above was a high ceiling of rock. In the whole echoing vastness of the place, there were only three objects to be seen. One, propped against a large stone in the center of the hall, was the skeleton of a dead man, dressed in old-fashioned armor, wearing the Heike *mon* on his helmet.

The second, heartbreaking, was the much smaller skeleton of a boy, cradled in the man's arms.

And the third, laid on the stone against which the skeleton sat, was a sword so beautiful, and yet so ordinary, it took his breath away. It wasn't ornate; it was simple, actually, with a leather-bound pommel and a straight, double-edged blade. But it had a quality of ultimate swordness he couldn't remember ever having seen before. It was as if this were the original sword, and all other swords were descended from it, pale imitations of it.

Kusanagi.

A shifting noise from behind him, and then the air was filled with the swish of fast movement, as the dragon unraveled itself into the emptiness of the cavern, filling it with its unimaginable bulk. The dragon reared above him like a snake looking down on its prey. Smoke drifted from its nostrils and mouth. Its eyes glowed blue. Taro suddenly noticed that he wasn't breathing; with a conscious effort, he expanded his diaphragm and filled his lungs.

A voice spoke inside his head.

"You are the first to come seeking the sword," it said. "In five hundred years, I thought there would be more."

Taro blinked and got to his feet. The dragon did not sound angry, not particularly. Surprised, perhaps, but not angry. "They made a replica," Taro said. "I thought it was real. Most people did."

The dragon breathed fire, and Taro flinched. "Predictable," said the dragon. "But a replica cannot rule a country, not forever."

Taro patted his side, looking for the short-sword that was usually there. It wasn't. It would have hampered him when diving, of course. He glanced toward the stone where Kusanagi lay, judging the distance. Could he get there before the dragon burned him off the face of . . . wherever this place was?

"If you are thinking of trying to reach the sword," said the dragon, "I wouldn't advise it." Stretching itself out to full height, it flashed toward Taro, unbelievably fast, then cascaded down in rings around the stone, encircling it, blocking it with its massive, scaly body. It breathed fire onto the stone before Taro's feet, melting it, and Taro jumped backward.

Steeling his nerve, he went down on his knees. "Come, then," he said. "Kill me." He was ready for it. He was ready to join Shusaku.

A pause.

"Why do you want the sword?"

Taro's mind raced. He couldn't say he wanted it to kill a dragon, not if he wanted to live. Though he thought his chances of surviving this encounter were slim at best. He said the next thing that came into his mind. "I want to claim the throne."

A sensation of warm air on his face as the dragon brought its head closer to him.

"So. At last one of the Heike has come to claim Kusanagi. You are Heike, are you not? I smell it in your blood."

Taro stared. The ground in front of him had been bubbling; now it had cooled to a glassy texture, an awesome testimony to the fire's heat. The dragon was fixing him with an unreadable expression. "I'm . . ." Taro stopped. It was said that some of the Heike had escaped the general slaughter, the drowning of their entire clan. Might they not have settled in Shirahama, where their family died? It was possible, he supposed, that he might be descended from them. "I don't know," he said, in the end.

"I do," said the dragon. "Be grateful you are not Genji. Those of the Genji clan are cursed by the dragons and by Amaterasu. They drowned the youngest of her line." The dragon's tail curled, almost tenderly, around the skeleton of the boy.

Taro's confusion was deepening by the moment. "What happens now?" he asked. "Will you kill me?" The idea didn't scare him. Instead it filled him with frustration, thinking of all the things he still hadn't done. For some reason, one of the images that came to his mind was that of the boy shogun, who shouldn't be sitting on that throne. *It should be me*, he thought. *I wouldn't starve the people with rice taxes and feed their young men to the monster of war*.

"Not for the moment. Though I presume you wish to use it to kill my cousin of the earth."

Taro opened and closed his mouth.

"Don't be afraid. I have no love for my cousin. The truth is that the dragon in question is mad. Long ago a magician imprisoned him up there on Mount Fuji, which was better for everyone. Now someone has set him free. Someone dangerous, I think."

"You're saying . . . someone deliberately woke the dragon?" Taro had assumed that it had begun to plague the region above Edo on a whim, or because of some grudge against the shogun.

"Oh, very definitely. It would not be accidental. That dragon is a killer, pure and simple, mad with rage against humanity. The bonds that were on it were more powerful than you can imagine."

"And now?"

"Now the only thing that can kill it is Kusanagi, as you know, or you would not be here."

"I don't understand," said Taro. "Will you give me the sword, or not?"

"I guard Kusanagi on behalf of Amaterasu, the kindly one," said the dragon. "You would not be here if you were not pure of heart; the Princess would not have brought you. I would give it to you, if I could, if it was mine to do so. But even the pure of heart are corrupted by power, and there is an old curse on this sword. To claim it, there is a sacrifice that has to be made."

"A curse?"

"Yes. Anyone who claims the sword pays with the thing they love. You have heard of Susanoo, who took it from the tail of the dragon he slew?"

Taro nodded.

"And his wife, the *kami* girl he married afterward? I see you do. But did you also know that she died, sometime afterward, while bearing Susanoo his first and only son? The son died too."

"No," said Taro. "No, I didn't know." It was something that was never told in the tale of Susanoo.

"And the Heike, of course. Susanoo broke the curse by giving the sword to his sister Amaterasu, and she in turn gifted it to the emperors of her line. But the Heike seized all power in the capital, made the boy emperor nothing but a figurehead. They sought to own the sword. It destroyed them, in the end. So you see, even if you are Heike, which is better than being Genji, it does not give you the power to hold the sword without paying."

Taro looked at the sword. "So in order to claim it, I must make a sacrifice."

"Yes. You can have Kusanagi. But in return, you must give up the thing you hold most dear."

Taro thought for a moment. "And what is that?"

He had the impression it was approval that he was feeling from the dragon. "A good question. It is I who choose. I can look into your mind." Taro felt a prickly, cold sensation inside his head and understood that the dragon had reached in there, with invisible tendrils. The coldness wrapped itself around a single idea in Taro's mind, a single name. The dragon spoke again. "And I will remain in your mind forever, once you take the sword. I am well placed to know what you love the most."

Taro shrank back, hating the idea that the dragon was inside his head, listening to his thoughts, as well as speaking. "Hana?" he said softly. It was the thought that the dragon had coiled itself around inside his mind, the core of his being.

The dragon rested its head on its scaled body, closed its eyes. "Yes."

Taro shook his head. "No. I won't let anyone else die. No. I refuse. You can keep the sword."

"Oh," said the dragon languidly. "She wouldn't die."

"She . . . wouldn't?"

"No. She would live. She would be happy even, at least a little. And you would continue to love her. But from the moment you claimed the sword, she would never love you in return."

Taro swallowed, his throat dry. He tried to remember why he wanted the sword in the first place. To kill the dragon at Edo and claim the reward. To be a daimyo and be able to marry Hana. If he accepted the sea dragon's bargain, that would never happen; Hana would never love him. But was that the *only* reason? He searched his soul, knowing the answer already: It wasn't.

No. The other reason lay in the sight of the shogun firing arrows into running dogs; it lay in the starvation of peasants giving over more than half their rice to the country's ruler. It even lay in the sight of a drowned village; the understanding that all actions have consequences. He had known it, deep down, but had not admitted it to himself until this moment: He *did* want the throne. He would be better, he thought, than the shogun.

He would be just, he would be fair.

He would accept his destiny.

Then, too, there was the fact that Hana was lost to him anyway. He had bitten her; he would surely do so again, if they lay together. He could never marry her, even if he didn't bargain away her heart. So what would be different?

He fixed the dragon's blue eyes with his and stepped forward, in the direction of the sword on the stone.

"I accept," he said.

CHAPTER 35

It was raining lightly when Taro broke the surface.

The sword, his destiny, was in his hand.

The sun was lower in the sky, approaching the tops of the mountains to the west, and the whole bay was bathed in mist. Only the glowing contours of the land were visible, in the pale grayness. He treaded water, the sword held above the surface of the sea, looking for the boat. He saw, at last, that it had drifted a little way off, and he swam awkwardly toward it. It was hard, with the sword in the air—his shoulder muscles burned.

When he pulled himself up on the wooden side of the boat, he saw that Hana was huddled in the bottom of the boat, weeping. She looked so miserable, so vulnerable, that all he wanted was to take her in his arms, but he reminded himself that she was lost to him. She looked up, as he dropped the sword into the boat, and screamed.

"Taro!" She threw herself forward, seized his arms, and pulled him into the boat, all the time saying his name, over and over. Now that he was out of the sea he could smell the land on her, the scent of pine and earth. Her big eyes were wet with tears. "Oh, gods, I thought you were dead," she said. "You were gone so long, and then when the boat kept drifting I just stopped caring. I couldn't live without you."

"You couldn't . . ." He glanced at the sword, not understanding. Had the dragon lied?

"No," said Hana. "I love you, Taro. I'm sorry I've been so cold with you."

Taro felt a warmth expanding in his chest, like the rising sun. "I love you, too," he said. He was amazed—it seemed the curse was broken. He remembered again the meeting with the prophetess, the foster mother of Heiko and Yukiko. She had told him he would be shogun, that he had a destiny. For the first time he allowed himself to believe, really believe, that it might be true. If the prophecy was enough to break a curse so old, it must be powerful indeed.

Gently brushing one of Hana's tears from her cheek with his thumb, he stroked the curve of her jaw. Her hair was in disarray; he took a stray strand and tucked it behind her perfect ear. At the back of his mind was a worry—what would happen if they tried to go further? But he pushed that worry down. Then he leaned toward her and kissed her, and the world disappeared for an unmeasurable period of time.

Eventually he broke away, feeling the chill in the sea air. They should get back to land. He still had the throne to claim, and after that, who knew? There were other vampires, like the woman who owned the strange brothel, where ordinary people paid to have their blood sucked. Maybe he could find someone to help him; maybe there was a way of controlling his urges when . . . when in bed with the woman he loved. Shusaku had been unable to help. But Shusaku had loved only one woman, and that was before he was a vampire. It was not surprising that he should not know the answer.

Feeling reinvigorated and hopeful, Taro picked up the oars and began to row toward shore. That was when he saw, looming out of the mist and gaining on them quickly, a black ship.

He rowed desperately, feverishly, but the ship was on them, and there was no escaping it.

He could see its flag now, a shapeless thing of black and red.

Then, with a strangled cry, he recognized it. With it came the loss of all hope, the end of his stupid idea that Shusaku might have found a way to be the Death-of-Enma, to kill Kenji Kira finally and for the last time.

It was Shusaku's skin.

CHAPTER 36

"Keep rowing," said Taro. "It's me they want."

He handed the oars to Hana, squeezing past her in the boat. Kusanagi he left in the bottom. He didn't want Kenji Kira getting his hands on that, too; he already suspected that the mist in the air came from the Buddha ball. Kira would have taken it from Shusaku, of course he would.

This is bad, thought Taro. He put his short-sword in its sheath on his hip. Hana tried to stop him as he went, clutching at his cloak.

He shrugged it off and dived into the water, even colder this time. He swam quickly, in a crawl, heading for the fast-moving ship. With the ship moving toward him as he swam, they met quickly, but Taro was low in the water—it seemed they hadn't seen him dive, because no arrows came sizzling down at him. The mist worked both ways.

Skirting the ship's prow, he let its broad side slice through the water beside him, looking for a handhold. Barnacles scraped his skin, slime oozed under his fingers. The wooden hull was going by too quickly; he wouldn't find a way up. But then he saw a mooring rope, hanging down just out of reach. His nails had grown long since they had left the monastery. Gritting his teeth, he dug his fingers into the side of the ship and hauled his weight up; instantly several of his nails broke and he choked off a scream, but managed to cling on. He brought all his *qi* into a ball in his stomach, as Shusaku had taught him, then threw himself upward, stretching out his right hand.

The rope slipped through his fingers, just out of—

His hand clamped down on it, and he struck the hull, dangling. He got his other hand on the rope and pulled himself up, arm over arm. There was no time to waste. As soon as he reached the top he vaulted over, drawing his short-sword in the same movement. He could see that Kenji Kira's men were used to attacking, not being attacked. They stood around in disorganized groups, looking toward the front of the ship. He impaled one through the heart before any of them even turned, the body striking the deck as its nearest companion rounded on Taro, shouting a warning.

The warning was cut off—literally. The head rolled along the deck, and off it into the sea.

Another of them came at Taro with a club. Swords were expensive; looking around, Taro could see more sticks, chains, clubs, and spears. He sidestepped a down-sweep from the club, noting with a kind of distant horror the moldering flesh of the man wielding it, the pungent stink that rose from him. This was one of the dead ones. He blocked another strike and was shocked by the impact that echoed through him—he was used to blocking swords, not heavy bludgeoning weapons. At the same time someone struck his knee from behind—he went down hard, and the club, at least he thought it was a club, hit him in the head. Night sky exploded in his head.

Blindly, he swept his sword at ankle level, felt it bite through flesh and bone. A body joined him on the deck, wide-open eyes staring at him in agony, thrashing. A live one, then. Taro jumped to his feet, just as the club struck him in the left arm, numbing it. He let it dangle useless at his side, stumbled a little for effect. The dead man wielding the club swung it at Taro's head—Taro ducked, suddenly moving at full speed, never taking his eyes off the man, and struck. Taro's first blow bit deep into the man's shoulder and neck, and the man staggered, but kept coming. His club was rising up again when Taro struck from the other side, as if felling a tree, and the man's head lolled back, attached now only by skin.

He wasn't sure if that would be the end for an already dead man, but he thought it was probably good enough, so he turned his attention to the other—

An arrow embedded itself in his chest, just below the heart. Then a sword or something sharp slashed his back; he staggered, reeling. The world began to fade and fray at the edges. They were all around him now, leering, gnashing their teeth. He thrust his sword through the belly of one, but it only grinned harder, and he concluded from this that it was one of the dead. The putrefaction was unequal; some of them appeared almost like living people, and some of them obviously were. He could smell blood, could hear it beating. Unlike Shusaku, he could not *see* people with his vampire senses, but he was aware of them, of their heat and life.

Wait.

One of those he had hurt was a living man, wasn't he? He glanced at the ground, saw the severed feet. Repressing his revulsion, he snapped the arrow at his chest, then threw himself at the ground, just as a spear that would have pierced his heart passed over him. The deck was slick with blood. He put his mouth to it, licking it. Already his back and chest were burning, fiercely hot as they healed.

He rolled, clutching his sword tight, and came up with a diagonal slash, cutting through the thigh of one of the men and the torso of his neighbor. They both fell back, and he went for the opening, following them, parrying and swinging. One of them went down; he aimed a final thrust at the heart. Another man jumped over the one on the ground, a nailed stick of some kind in his hand.

He swung it at Taro's head, and Taro only just moved aside in time—a nail tore through his ear, and he felt it throb with pain. He whipped his sword back and then forward, heard a strangled scream from behind him as the blade came round again, biting into the throat of the one who had hit him. He had been stupid, climbing onto the ship, he realized. He hadn't even seen Kenji Kira yet; he was just focusing on each man in turn, his world reduced to a series of images and sounds; rage-filled faces, weapons arcing through the air; clashes and screams.

Someone grabbed his arms from behind. He twisted, got a glimpse of a black-clad figure and—

Too late.

A sharp, hard point pressed into his neck. A *shobi* ring, he realized. It was a ninja weapon, meant to strike a pressure point and cut off blood flow to the heart.

It worked.

Some time later he blinked up from the deck, where he was lying on his back. He flexed his hand automatically—no sword. He was looking up into the skull-face of Kenji Kira, who was standing next to a man in black. A ninja. His face was wrapped in black cloth, and Taro could see that it wasn't just for anonymity. Greenish, rotting flesh showed through the gaps in the folds.

Kira clapped his hands, and Hana was dragged into Taro's field of view. She looked furious. Kira turned to the ninja, who handed him a knife. He touched it to Hana's throat.

"I was going to marry her," he said conversationally. "But since she won't tell me where the sword is, I thought I could use her to make you tell me. We searched your little peasant boat, to no avail."

Taro frowned at Hana. He'd left the sword in the boat, with her. What had happened to it? Why hadn't Kira found it when he seized her? She shook her head, very slightly.

"I don't know," said Taro. "I didn't find anything when I dived."

Kenji Kira made a slow gesture of pity. "Tell me. Or she dies."

"What do you want it for? You have the ball. Just kill me."

"Oh, the ball," said Kira. He reached into his cloak, took it out. "It's an amusing trinket. But the sword? Kusanagi? It could give me the *throne*. The current shogun's line is protected by his possession of the three sacred objects. Only if a person were to prove that one of those was a fake—the most important one too—could they hope to break the succession." He tossed the ball from hand to hand, then put it away again.

Taro stared at him, appalled at the idea of Kenji Kira ruling Japan. He saw Hana shake her head again. He ignored her. "All right. I recovered the sword. But I honestly don't know where it is now," he said. "I had it and then—"

He was interrupted by Hana, who let out a piercing scream. He turned to look at her. She was gazing intently at Kenji Kira, naked anger in her eyes. To Taro, she had never looked so beautiful. She spat toward him. "You. You are *nothing*," she said. "A travesty. But I?" She emphasized the next three words, so that they came out as separate sentences.

"I. Am. Samurai. Come find me in death, if you must."

She grabbed the arm of the man holding the knife to her neck, and lunged suddenly, viciously forward, a war cry on her lips. Blood spurted.

The man tried to pull the knife away, only making things worse, sawing through her windpipe; Taro heard her cry turn to a whistling sound, as of air escaping a dead animal's stomach. The dead man dropped the knife—it clung for a moment to her ruined flesh, then fell to the deck with a clatter.

Hana put her hands to her throat.

She paled, never taking her eyes off Taro.

Then she fell to the ground.

CHAPTER 37

For a moment, Taro remained fixed to the deck, as if someone had nailed him to it. He could see Hana's blood spreading, pooling in the cracks between planks. The world swayed and throbbed, not just from the motion of the boat. He was about to step forward, to beg Kenji Kira to kill him also, when something he had heard echoed again in his mind, something the dragon had said.

I will remain in your mind forever, once you take the sword.

What flashed through his mind after that was shame. Surely he should die, now? He had nothing to live for, not with Shusaku and Hana dead. But there it was, still, this desire to survive that was like an unquenchable fire in him. Though it wasn't just that, he knew—there was something else, the seedling of an idea, but he barely dared to consider it fully, to give it voice in his thoughts, keeping it for now in the darkness lest the light burn it away to nothing, withering its leaves.

Kenji Kira stepped away from Hana's blood, moving almost with horror. "Why are you smiling?" he asked.

Taro hadn't known it. He was just thinking about the dragon, and about the Genji, and how Kira had been stupid enough to man his ship with the dead. He didn't know if this would work. But he knew it didn't matter. Either it worked or he died, and he could live with either of those. In a manner of speaking. He noticed that the ship's anchor was propped against the gunwale, just behind where Hana's body lay, its rope coiled beside it, like nothing so much as a tiny dragon, wrapped around itself.

Good.

Concentrating on the dragon, he said the same words again and again in his head.

The Genji have broken free from hell. They have come to take the sword. The Genji have broken free from hell. They have come to take the sword. The Genji have . . .

The Genji were traitors. They had risen up against the Heike, who were descended from the son of Amaterasu. They were offenders against the gods, against the dragons. They were the cursed dead. Taro could only imagine how the dragon of the sea would feel if he saw them come back to this place. He felt his smile widen, heard a growing rumbling coming from beneath the sea. "Stop that!" said Kenji Kira. "Stop whatever you're doing!"

Taro felt a sudden rocking, the noise from below intensifying, the sound like that of a tsunami, just before it hits. "Too late," he said.

The dragon burst into the air like spray from a whale's blowhole, only incomprehensibly bigger, the water falling like rain on those who stood on Kenji Kira's ship, pattering softly on the deck, on the blood of those who had died fighting, on the blood of Hana, who had died a samurai.

With a roar like thunder, like a thousand thunders, the dragon reared up above them, tall as a hill, its tail over the sea and its head close to the clouds. It belched blue fire, the heat of it scorching. Taro smelled his own eyebrows singeing. The men turned to look up at it, some dropping their weapons, some gaping, some screaming and running, crashing into one another. Kira himself was looking up, entirely still, his jaw hanging open.

Taro was injured, but he had just drunk blood—it coursed through him like molten iron, making him hard, making him strong. He was up and moving even as the dragon's head descended. He got an arm under Hana and cradled her as if she were an infant. He plunged his fangs into her neck, sucking her blood as he moved. Kenji Kira grabbed at him, but he was too quick; he was a vampire. Without even thinking about it, he pulled his mouth from her neck and pressed her face against his chest, her mouth against the wound where the stub of arrow still protruded, held her tight to him, a gruesome kind of suckling.

His fangs had entered her now, transmitting the infection. It needed his blood to enter her as well, to activate it.

He prayed for his blood to flow into her as, still embracing her, he grabbed the anchor—it was heavier than he expected, but he poured his *qi*, poured the blood he had licked from the deck into his arm and hauled it into the air, swung it over the side ahead of him—then jumped off the ship, and into the sea.

He wasn't prepared for the speed.

The anchor plunged down, the light not so much dimming as going out, like someone blowing out a candle at dusk. His ears popped, sending daggers of pain into his head from either side. Behind, an intense flaring of heat caught his feet and ankles, as an explosion of blue lit the darkness. The dragon. He held on as long as he could, then let the anchor go. It disappeared instantly into the murk, the rope trailing after it. He caught hold of the rope now, waiting for it to go taut when the anchor hit the bottom, or the end of the line, he didn't care which.

When it did, it snapped in his hand like a snake that had been playing dead coming back to life. Then he began to haul them up, one-handed, the other hand still holding Hana to him. He had no idea whether she would stir or not; he remembered turning Little Kawabata after dealing him a killing blow. But Little Kawabata had not been down for long before Taro dripped his blood into the other boy's life. Had it been too long, with Hana? Was the injury too great? He wasn't sure. It was remarkable, what vampire blood could heal—he thought of the sword that had transfixed his stomach before Shusaku turned him.

He remembered, though, that she didn't want to be a vampire.

But that was another thing he didn't want to think about.

Rising up along the rope, he could feel the heat, the sea like the heated water of the *onsen* springs in his village. A normal fire would be extinguished by water, but this was a dragon's fire. What if they came to the surface and the water was still burning? Would they be incinerated? He had to hope not—he had no real choice but to come up, he would drown otherwise. Already he could feel that fraying at the edges of his vision.

Breaking the surface, he gasped for air, pulling Hana up so that her face was clear too. Where the ship had been, there was nothing. No—some charred pieces of timber floated haphazardly, the debris of some devastating disaster. There was a smell of bonfires, and cooking flesh, on the air. Taro felt sick. Turning to look for the largest plank to cling to, he saw a spar that was still burning—as he watched, it tipped, sinking into the sea, hissing as the fire went out.

Nearby, there was a bigger fragment of boat, with a skeleton lying on it. Impossible to tell if it was Kenji Kira or one of the others. Anyway, when Taro reached the wooden raft, pulling Hana behind him, he caught hold of it and the skeleton collapsed into dust, into ashes.

He was pleased. It meant that Shusaku's skin, which Kenji Kira had pinned to his boat as a flag, would have been burned too, would be reduced as was the way of the Buddha, to particles on the breeze.

Taro was appalled, though, at the destruction he had wrought—appalled despite himself. He had been thinking of the dead that had attacked them so long ago now, of course, when they had been traveling to the inland sea. How fire destroyed them. But he had not imagined this—that there would be simply nothing left, that he could erase a ship from the world with a thought.

Unless some of the dead had dived, like him? Panicked, suddenly, he kicked with his feet—something grabbed them! No. It was a jellyfish or a dead man's hand; it slipped past his feet and was gone, into the depths. He had taken the anchor, had dived deep—nothing could have survived closer to the surface.

Cursing the pain in his chest and arm, he pushed Hana up, levered her and angled her until she was half on the makeshift raft. It was a laborious task. Eventually he managed to get her whole body onto it, then clung to the side, breathing hard. He could see boats setting out from the shore—no doubt they had seen the fire and would be coming to investigate. Hiro might even be with them.

Something touched him again, on his chest, where the air and water met. He twisted, hard—felt this round, smooth thing bob against him. He snorted when he saw it. Of course. It was the Buddha ball, entirely unharmed, as far as he could see. The clear glass showed mist and clouds, drifting over the surface of the Earth. He tucked it into his clothes, realizing that it had been foolish to try to get rid of it. Not wrong—he still feared the thing—but stupid. The ball was for him and of him. He could no more throw it away than he could remove his head and set it down.

Taro touched Hana's skin, stroked the back of her hand. It was cold. He treaded water, moving with his hands along the raft until he was level with her head. Her eyes were open. A bad sign. He lifted his head as much as he dared, without tipping her into the sea. Saw how pale she was, how her beautiful black eyes gazed up at nothing, seeing a different sky.

He felt a tear swell, hotly, in the corner of his eye. He was shivering with the cold of the water, now that the heat of the fire was gone from it, but he didn't care.

Hana.

Like the dragon, the word was in his mind. The word *was* his mind. It was a name and a prayer and a universe.

Gently he let go of the raft. He had one more thing to do, before he embraced oblivion, but he would have to die to do it. If Kenji Kira really was Enma, then being burned to nothing by the dragon was only half of killing him. For the second half, Taro had to—

Movement.

His name, spoken by a voice that he loved.

Hana rolled toward him, her eyes filled with red now, not bloodshot, but flooded with blood, where the whites should be. She spoke his name again, and he saw her canines, how they were lengthening even as she spoke.

"What did you do?" she said. "What did you do to me?"

"I had to," he said, the words coming out trembling and unsure, with the cold that was biting deep into his bones. "You were dying. You were dead. I don't know."

"My choice," she said, and he had never heard such fury in that voice he loved, such coldness and spite. "I'm samurai. I'm not a monster. I never wanted this."

He almost let go then, felt his hand slip. She thought he was a monster. This was the truth, this had always been the truth. "I couldn't live without you," he said. "I love you."

She spat blood at him; his blood. She rolled back and screamed. He knew what she was feeling—knew, from when Shusaku had turned him, the fire and boundless energy that was in her blood, the bloodlust racing through her. Then she turned to him again. "I want none of you."

As she said it, he knew she meant it. He had come to know her voice, its every tone and cadence. It was a voice he loved.

But now it didn't love him. He could hear it.

He let his head sink back until the sea was around his ears, touching his face, caressing it, mingling with his tears, carrying them away.

He understood.

He was paying the dragon's price.

CHAPTER 38

The lobster creel rose from the water like something appearing out of nothingness. It had taken them a while to find it. Only a small cork buoy bobbed on the surface, Hana having cut the line to the boat before she cast it adrift. So far, she had said nothing to Taro, except to tell him what she had done with the sword.

They were with the priest, on one of the boats that had set out from the shore to help them. The priest had asked questions to begin with, but had stopped when he saw that Taro had no intention of answering. The only thing Taro had said was that he was sorry about the man's boat—and that he would repay him one day.

When the dragon of the earth was dead. When he had the throne.

Hiro, meanwhile, was nowhere to be seen. He had not come on the boats. Taro realized that they really weren't friends anymore—it really was over.

Taro reached down and snagged the creel, pulling it from the water. Hana had pushed the sword through its bamboo bars before throwing it overboard. He unsheathed it and turned it in his hands, feeling its balance, its lightness. Amazing. He knew that there were swords of violence and swords of peace, but this was something different. It was a sword of power. He sensed that it would give you everything you wanted, even if it took away the one thing you might need.

"Is that . . . ," began the priest, before trailing off.

"Yes."

The priest said nothing. Just stared.

Hana was watching with empty eyes. Her throat wound had mostly healed over, and Taro had torn a strip from his cloak for her to wear as a scarf, covering her neck. Neither of them wanted awkward questions. As soon as Taro had the sword, she touched the priest's arm. "I'd like to go back to shore now," she said. "Is there a place in the village I can stay a few days?"

The priest looked from her to Taro. "You're not staying with—"

"No."

"Ah," said the priest, clearing his throat. His hair had gone a lot whiter since Taro had last seen him, and there were lines spidering from his eyes. He had a kindly but weary expression, as if he would have preferred a quieter life but was willing to make the best of what came along. "Well, there's always Taro's hut. . . . ," he said tentatively.

"Yes, fine," said Taro. He had no intention of letting her stay behind here, not really. He could feel the Buddha ball, cold and hard as an alien growth, pressing against his flesh, could hear—because he knew how to listen—the whispering of his blood in her body. But he was hardly going to tell her that.

"It will only be a short time, I think," said Hana. "Then I'll be gone."

"Where?" said Taro.

She didn't look at him. "I don't know. It depends on Hiro. If he wants to stay or not. Where he wants to go."

He felt that like a dagger blow. She would stay with Hiro, but not with him. He took a deep breath and sheathed Kusanagi. "Let's go, then," he said, his voice hollow as the empty, dripping lobster creel.

When they came to shore, he let Hana go with the others up to the village, telling them he would come to say good-bye before he left. For a long moment he just watched her walking up the hillside, the evolution of her stride as she went up from sand to scrub and then from there onto hard ground. She moved with a kind of lithe grace, her every step in tune with the world, a tribute to it.

Then, as was inevitable, she was gone.

He turned and walked along the dunes, his clothes still soaking, till he came to a rocky outcrop at the end of the beach, hidden from view by the huts of the villages. He climbed up and sat crosslegged, looking out to sea. He laid Kusanagi beside him. There was a risk of losing it, where he was going.

He could remember going into death from Mount Hiei. He knew how it was done—though he knew also that doing it again would be tricky. He focused, or rather didn't focus, trying to make the sighing of the sea, the rustle of the wind in the pine needles, the sharpness and cool scent of the rock beneath him disappear. He strove for the understanding that neither he nor the outer world existed, that all was one, and all was nothingness. He concentrated on the impossible trick of making his mind no longer aware of its own existence. He sought *mu*. The enlightenment of the Heart Sutra, the understanding of the emptiness of all creation, the illusion of life, the betrayal of all living things, which would always be nothingness, in the end.

The sun went down.

The scent of pine, of salt, gave way to the scent of cooking fires.

And then he found it.

CHAPTER 39

He opened his eyes—or rather, his eyes opened themselves for him, and he could see the glowing thread leading from him over the sea. He took hold of it, and walked beside it, onto thin air. Following it, he traveled the sea, vast and gray, then up and down mountains. He went through valleys and deserts, where time was short and infinite at the same time. He walked a journey that he would never be able to describe to anyone else, under strange moons and suns.

Finally he came to the bridge, and his ninja training took over. He made himself shadow-walk, a way Shusaku had taught him of walking in the margins of the world, making his profile as small as possible. He ducked behind the wall of the bridge, all inlaid with jewels, when he saw Horse-head on the other side of the Three Rivers. The demon was stalking the bank with a forked weapon in his vast, meaty hands.

Then he saw Kenji Kira. The man was sitting in Enma's seat, Ox-face beside him. Taro stared at the samurai general. He had been burned to ash, hadn't he? But . . . of course. This was death.

Kira was dead, whatever happened to him in the human realm. So there must always be a version of him in death.

Here in death, Kira was no longer a skeleton; his flesh hung on him a little loosely. Taro couldn't quite see from here, but he had an impression of . . . what? Wear and tear, he supposed, a sense of attrition. Taro crept closer. Yes. There were holes in Kira's face and arms—the man looked nibbled on, like he was a set of clothes, left in the darkness for moths or mice. Some of those holes—like the one that went right through his cheek—bore tooth marks.

This was why he had preferred to stay in the human realm, Taro realized, why he had killed Enma only to abandon Enma's duties, letting the dead roam the land with him. Taro remembered Yukiko's words to Kenji Kira when she killed him, which had seemed strange to him at the time. She had told him that he would be left to the flies and low creatures, for them to consume him, to carry him away in all directions in the air, and this had filled Kira with terror. Taro knew what Kira was afraid of now. He was afraid of being food, of rotting.

Taro thought further. This explained everything. Kenji Kira had made himself Enma so that he could go back and forth between life and death—because in death something had happened to him, some punishment for his many crimes that had left him frozen in this state of mid-decomposition, whereas in life he was clean, he was untrammeled bone. Kira had no interest in judging the dead, only in escaping the body death had given him. Probably he didn't even know that the dead were escaping, getting loose into the world, thanks to his dereliction. Either that, or he didn't care.

And now Taro had burned his bones in life, trapping him forever in this rotten death-body, down here in the world of shadows.

Taro couldn't imagine how angry Kira must be now, with his means of escape from hell turned to ash by the dragon.

A shout.

He had a horrible feeling he was about to find out.

Taro whipped his head around to see Horse-head running

toward him. He cursed himself. He'd stayed in one spot too long, staring at Kenji Kira and thinking. He was moving even as Kira stood liquidly from his throne, his face a torn mask of fury, pointing at him, sending Ox-face his way.

But Horse-head and Ox-face were demons, and they were big and unwieldy. He? He was a ninja.

He let Horse-head get close, as he crossed from the bridge to the cold ground of death. Taro ducked, and the forked staff went over his head as he rolled. Then he was on his feet again, having gone through Horse-head's legs, and was running, farther into Death. He heard both demons pounding after him, shaking the ground. They were twice as tall as men, twice as heavy. It made them fearsome fighters, but it made them slow. Their footfalls diminished behind him.

A voice drifted after him. Kenji Kira. "This is my kingdom, peasant! The deeper you go, the more I have you!"

Taro thought that was probably true. And that was why he reached into his cloak and took out the ball, thanking the gods that it had come with him into death. He knew that it would give him control over Little Kawabata, over Hana, would let him speak to his blood inside them, but would the opposite be true? Could he use it to call out, with Shusaku's blood that was inside him, to Shusaku? He didn't know, but he knew he had to try.

As he ran, through the endless mist and grayness of death, he kept his mind on Shusaku, picturing the ninja's blood running through his own veins, willing it to speak out, to find its progenitor. A part of him was Shusaku, forever. He just hoped that part could find the whole it had come from.

A tug, to his left—though it might as well have been his right; distance and space had no meaning here. He followed it and entered into a country of horrors. Looming out of the mist, there was a great pot on a fire, limbs sticking out. Demons were everywhere, stabbing, branding, chopping. Taro made the mistake of glancing to his right and saw a man being torn apart by four demonic horses. From then on he kept his eyes forward, dodging past the few demons who looked up from their tasks and tried to catch him.

One got hold of his cloak—he let it fall off him, just kept on running.

Another tug; he turned as he ran, powering off the ground, could feel some force inside him growing, something like excitement, or love.

Then, suddenly, there was Shusaku. He was tied to a tree, which seemed to have been put here for that purpose; there were no other trees that Taro could see. Two demons were flaying off his skin with whips. Shusaku's head was bent, his eyes closed. He looked as if he had given up—something Taro had never before seen.

Taro judged the distances, chose the demon with the dagger in its belt. He jumped even as he was running, closed the last *tan* in the air. He landed on the demon's back, unhooked the dagger from his belt, and climbed up, monkeylike. The demon was twisting toward him as he drew the blade across the thick-muscled neck. The demon seemed half bull, with horns growing on his head.

A gurgling noise; he jumped down to the ground, hearing the demon topple like a tree as he ducked to avoid the whip that swished over his head. Snapping his hand up, he caught the end of the whip, yanking hard. The demon was unbalanced only for a moment, but a moment was enough. As it stumbled, he lanced forward through space like a spear, the knife in two hands. It plunged into the demon's stomach, burying deep. He didn't stop there, though—he sawed it upward, gripping it with both hands, grunting with the effort. The demon screamed, high like a calling hawk.

Then it stopped screaming, and he didn't bother to watch it fall. Its black blood was hot on his skin.

Taro went to the tree and touched Shusaku's face. The ninja mumbled, half opening his eyes. He didn't seem to recognize Taro, or to want to free himself. Taro didn't give him the choice. He began cutting through the ropes that bound his mentor to the tree—he cut the upper ropes first, so that Shusaku slumped onto him, head lolling over his shoulder, like a drunk being helped home. Taro said a prayer over and over in his head, a mantra, asking for Shusaku to wake up.

"Please," he said aloud. "Please, Shusaku, you have to come back to me, you have to. You have to kill Kenji Kira, you're the only one who can." Shusaku had *told* him—he'd said that Enma could be defeated. Now he had to prove it.

A groan from behind—he turned and saw, to his horror, that the demon he had eviscerated was up on his knees, the flapping wound in its stomach knitting slowly shut. Taro turned back to the bonds, cut another.

He was on the last one, sweat pouring down his face, when he heard a voice behind him.

"Too late," said Kenji Kira.

He turned, Shusaku still draped over his shoulder. Then he felt a lightening of the load—Shusaku pulled away from him, coughing, agonized. Taro saw that the skin was fusing back to his body, and regrowing, in the places where it had gone. This was the punishment in this corner of hell, he realized. It wasn't that your skin was flayed, it was that your skin was flayed again and again.

Shusaku touched his arm. "Taro," he said. His eyes moved over Taro's face. "You look older. Sadder."

"I—you can see?"

"Of course," said Shusaku. "In death, we are remade. But what have you done? Why are you here?" His brow was furrowed.

"I came to find you. To remind you of what you said. About the Tibetan story. The Death-of-Enma."

Shusaku laughed a hollow laugh. "It can't be done. Certainly not by me. You've done nothing in coming here but doom yourself." His voice was harsh, twisted by the pain he had experienced.

Taro drew in a sharp breath, wounded. Shusaku closed his eyes, wincing, then put his arm around him.

"Sorry. I am grateful to you for coming. And I am sorry for making you leave me, back there in the passageway."

"I forgive you," said Taro.

Kenji Kira rubbed his hands. "Very touching, all this," he

said. "But I agree with your mentor, Taro. All you have done for Shusaku is to make him watch as I tear you to pieces."

The dagger was still in Taro's hand. He gripped it firmly. "You can try," he said.

"Ah, you are always so spirited!" said Kira. "I do so admire that. It reminds me of Mara."

Shusaku gave a sort of animal growl. "Don't speak that name," he said.

"She fought too, you know," said Kira casually, as if it were an aside; Taro knew it wasn't. "She was still struggling when I cut off her head." Taro could see the dull gray light of hell shining through Kira's open cheek, in his dead eyes.

Next to Taro, Shusaku fell back against the tree. "You . . . ," he said.

"Always. Didn't you know, deep down?"

Taro looked from one to the other. Kenji Kira had killed Shusaku's one love. Shusaku was clinging to the tree behind him for purchase; he looked as if he were afraid of falling off the realm of hell itself, into nothingness. Perhaps he was.

"Why?" said Shusaku eventually.

"Why?" Kenji Kira echoed mockingly. "A simple reason. I was to kill Lord Tokugawa, on Lord Oda's orders. She surprised me. She got in the way."

"She got in the way, so you killed her?"

Kira shrugged. "Can you think of a better reason?"

"You shouldn't have told me that," said Shusaku.

And then Taro was thrown violently to the ground, as Shusaku roared, spreading his hands, a predatory animal gone mad, before digging his fingernails into his own chest.

"Shusaku, what—," began Taro, but it was too late. His old friend and mentor was already tearing off a great sheet of his own skin. Blood misted in the air, spattering Taro's face, hot as lava.

CHAPTER 40

NEAR THE MONTO STRONGHOLD

MIKAWA PROVINCE

TWELVE YEARS EARLIER

The day Shusaku's true love died was also the day he was turned into a vampire. But even that morning when he woke, he had no reason to think either of those things would happen.

It began three days before, when Lord Tokugawa was struck down.

Shusaku and the rest of the Tokugawa army were in Mikawa province, fighting rebel monks. These troublesome men pledged loyalty to the Monto clan, and so were resisting Lord Tokugawa's attempts to unite the western part of the country. Lord Tokugawa had decided that they would be exterminated—and when Lord Tokugawa decided something, it usually came to pass.

That morning, before dawn, the Tokugawa samurai rode on the Monto positions. They were riding uphill, which was a disadvantage, but Lord Tokugawa had a thousand samurai at his disposal, including Shusaku—Lord Endo, in those times—who rode by his side. Also taking part in the attack were a hundred or so of Lord Oda's samurai, for the two daimyo had formed an alliance in the interest of suppressing the most violent resistance on their borders.

Leading these Oda samurai was a young general of whom Lord Oda spoke highly—a certain Kenji Kira. He had the left cavalry detachment, Shusaku had the right.

Shusaku pressed his heels into his horse's flank, breathing in the mingled smells of pine sap, morning dew, and broken ground. Beside him, Lord Tokugawa drew his sword. On his face he wore a tusked warrior's mask. Everywhere was the rhythmic boom of hooves. Shusaku felt the thrill of the imminent battle, as he fixed his eyes on the earthen barrier the Monto had erected ahead.

Then the hillside was lit, instantly and shockingly, by flashes of bright light, followed by a rolling thunder of explosions.

Guns, thought Shusaku dumbly. *No one said the Monto had guns.* The weapons had only just been introduced by the Portuguese, and only the richest could procure them—certainly the Monto could not hope to arm themselves in this fashion, unless . . . Unless they were willing to sell themselves to the Portuguese, or someone else. The question was who? No true samurai would approve the use of guns. They were weapons for those without honor, those willing to kill a man from afar. For a samurai, even a bow was a coward's weapon. If you had to kill a man, Shusaku thought, it was better to do it face-to-face. That way you gave him the dignity of seeing who ended his life.

It seemed, then, that the Monto must have some outside help, and from someone for whom honor was no consideration.

Lord Oda no Nobunaga, was Shusaku's first thought. He pushed it down, though. Lord Oda was his lord Tokugawa's ally. It was unthinkable—literally, he had to stop himself thinking it, or he would be disloyal to his daimyo.

Shusaku ducked down, clinging on to his horse. Beside him, he saw Lord Tokugawa thrown backward from his horse, turning over in the air to land facedown in the dirt. Shusaku pulled his horse to a stop and jumped down. He ran to where Lord Tokugawa lay, and knelt in the dirt by his lord.

Suddenly Mara was beside him. He couldn't understand what

she was doing here, in the heat of battle. She was Lord Tokugawa's serving maid, his most trusted assistant. Her place was in the camp—and by Shusaku's side, whenever circumstances allowed, because Shusaku loved her more than he had thought it was possible for a man of war to love a woman. She wore a simple gown with a large, deep hood. For a moment, he thought that was odd; then he forgot about it.

She pushed him aside, not bothering with rank or protocol. "Give us space!" she screamed. Men and horses were staggering all around them, though for now the Monto had stopped firing. Bleeding bodies lay everywhere. There was a dent in Lord Tokugawa's armor, where the bullet had hit, but it didn't look to Shusaku like it had penetrated the steel.

Please, Amida Buddha, let him live, he thought. Lord Tokugawa had taken Shusaku on as a samurai, even after his father disgraced himself by turning his cloak in the previous war. Lord Tokugawa had given him a choice other than ritual suicide, and for that, Shusaku would follow him anywhere. Even up this gods-forsaken mountain. Lord Tokugawa couldn't die. Shusaku wouldn't let it happen.

"I think there's internal bleeding," said Mara, examining the daimyo. She touched his eyes, and they fluttered open. Immediately she was shouting for help. "Pick him up!" she called. "Shusaku! Anyone! We have to get him back to camp."

To Shusaku's left, one of Lord Tokugawa's *hatamoto* pushed through the crowd and put a hand on Mara's arm, tried to drag her away.

"No women on the—," he began.

He didn't finish, though, because she snapped her elbow up gracefully, breaking his nose and dropping him on his back in the mud. Shusaku stared. She had never seemed so beautiful to him, her slender curves accentuated by the scene of battle, not overwhelmed by it. The strange thing was that the movement had been so loose, so casual . . . it was almost as if she knew how to fight. But that was ridiculous. Women didn't fight.

Mara bent down and picked up Lord Tokugawa herself, by the ankles. Shusaku could see that the other men were too shocked to do anything; he leaned down and grabbed the daimyo's shoulders, lifting him with her. Between them they carried him down the mountainside, through the mud and blood, through the melee of confused and injured men. The smell of blood was in Shusaku's nostrils.

"He'll live," said Mara. "He'll live."

Two days later, though, and Lord Tokugawa had still not recovered, and fever had set in. He rambled incoherently.

It was mysterious, because the bullet had not broken his skin. Still, a nasty bruise was spreading on his chest, the color of sunset. After one day, they had sent for a Taoist magician, the highest form of healer. The man was still there, trying to figure out what was keeping Lord Tokugawa's soul from fully inhabiting his body. Mara stood on the other side of the tent, quiet and subdued. Shusaku tried not to meet her eyes. The others didn't know of their relationship, and he wanted it to stay that way.

Shusaku watched as the magician chanted over the daimyo, who lay on his back in the large tent. The Taoist had determined that Lord Tokugawa was possessed by a *shiryo*, a dead spirit. This kind of possession could lead to death, if not treated correctly. As such he was chanting the sutras and spells designed to cast out the evil invader.

The problem was that it didn't appear to be working. Shusaku stayed for the space of two more incense sticks, before preparing to leave, his hand on the silk of the tent. Then he stopped when the magician addressed him—it was reasonable, he supposed. He was the highest-ranking man in the room.

"If it was a *shiryo* possession, the spirit should have gone," the magician said. "But see how he still sweats."

Shusaku came back into the tent and leaned over the body of his friend and lord. "You suspect a living soul?" he said. A person could be possessed by the spirit of a living person as easily as that of a dead one, though it was less common.

The magician shrugged. "An *ikiryo* possession by another living person is certainly possible," he said. "Of course, these things are usually romantic. When a man is possessed by a living soul . . . it's often that of a woman who loves him."

Suddenly Kenji Kira was at Shusaku's side. The man was the highest ranking of the Oda samurai here in the camp. Shusaku was wary of him—he was tall and thin, with limbs like a spider's, and had a predator's reputation. There were rumors about prostitutes, which Shusaku hoped were not true.

"There's only one woman here," Kira said. He gestured to Mara.

Shusaku saw her eyes—framed by those long eyelashes—snap wide open. She stared at Kira, startled.

"You think the serving girl might be doing this?" the magician said.

"I think nothing," said Kira. "It was you who said a woman is usually involved."

Shusaku narrowed his eyes. He wasn't sure what Kenji Kira was up to, but he knew it was nothing good—and he knew there was nothing romantic between Mara and Lord Tokugawa, because he was the one sharing her bed. Not that he could say that before all the other samurai. A man of his rank and stature carrying on with a serving girl—it was not done.

"Mara is just a serving girl," he said neutrally.

Kenji Kira, of course, smoothly denied that he had meant to imply anything else. His hands steepled, he spoke about curses and evil spirits and spiders—Shusaku was only half listening, concentrating with most of his mind on not blushing or looking too much at Mara.

Kira was still speaking when Mara cut him off, stepping forward. It was out of character—and dangerous—for her to assert herself like this, so Shusaku raised his eyebrows.

"I'm not poisoning him or possessing him," Mara said. "I'm just a serving girl. I've been with him for months."

Kenji Kira shrugged. "It was only an observation," he said. He let himself out of the tent.

The magician spread his hands. "I'll try the exorcism for a living spirit," he said. He began to take *majinai* charms and insert them into Lord Tokugawa's mouth.

Later Mara let herself into Shusaku's tent. She did it so quietly, he didn't hear her until she touched him—and he sat up, terrified. When he got over his shock, he kissed her—she tasted of strawberries, and sunshine. Whenever he looked into her eyes, he felt that he might fall into their depths and never come back to the surface again. He had not had any time alone with her since Lord Tokugawa was injured. In whispers, they spoke about the injury, about Lord Tokugawa's chances for survival, about Kenji Kira.

Shusaku was suspicious of Kira, but Mara seemed to think the man had some particular grudge against her—which Shusaku found hard to imagine. "He's a *hatamoto* and you're a serving girl," he said, with a flinch of embarrassment when he saw that his description had hurt her. He forged on, nevertheless. "What would he have to gain by hurting you?"

She shrugged. She didn't believe him, he could tell.

"Kenji Kira was only thinking aloud," said Shusaku. "Men always suspect women, when it comes to possessions and mysterious illness."

"It's not a mysterious illness. Our Lord Tokugawa was shot."

"He's recovered from worse injuries quicker."

Mara nodded. Good. Perhaps she was beginning to relax. He wanted her—he didn't want to be worrying about Kenji Kira right now, or Lord Tokugawa even. He just wanted to hold her in his arms, feel her body against his.

"Anyway," he said, "it's not unreasonable to think that you could render a man ill. You're beautiful."

She kissed him, and the world disappeared.

"Be my wife," he said without thinking.

Suddenly she was standing. "What?"

"My wife. I would like you to be her; I mean, you. I mean, I would like you to marry me," he said. "I'm sorry. I should have composed a poem, or something."

"I don't like poetry," she said. "Anyway," she added in a teasing voice, "I'm just a serving girl."

"So? You're a woman. I'm a lord, even if my estate is much smaller than that of our Lord Tokugawa. I can marry who I please."

"I'm not—that is—I'm not like other women."

Shusaku smiled. "I know. That's why I love you."

She opened the shoji door to leave. "You understand nothing," she said. Then she was gone.

Shusaku lay back on the bed and sighed. She was right.

He didn't understand.

The next day Mara died, and Shusaku was made a vampire.

He had been dreaming about Mara—a dream where she was his wife, and they were living in his father's castle together, the whole ten-thousand-*koku* territory theirs to do what they liked with. He had been holding her hand, looking out over the land, gleaming with paddy fields.

Now he was awake, and there were shouts all around. It sounded like they were preparing for battle.

No more than one incense stick later, he was mounted, Lord Tokugawa by his side. The daimyo was better, it seemed—perhaps it had been a living-spirit possession, after all. And Lord Tokugawa was not one to waste time, once he was back on his feet. He wanted the Monto wiped out, and he wanted it done that day. There was, too, the fact that it was raining. Rain prevented rifles from firing—the Monto would not be able to surprise them in the same way again.

On Lord Tokugawa's other side, Mara was sitting on a dappled mare, a woman's short-sword in her hand. Shusaku was surprised—when he first joined the others, he didn't recognize her, for she was wearing that same deep, cowled hood. But when she turned to him he did, and he asked Lord Tokugawa what he meant by bringing a woman into battle.

"She insists on it," said Lord Tokugawa. "Wants to protect me, she says."

Shusaku spoke quietly. "You have an honor guard for that," he said. "Me included." There were three samurai who rode with Lord Tokugawa, the brightest fighters of the army, and Shusaku was one of them. He wasn't proud of it—but he knew it was a true reflection of his skill with a sword. "She's a woman. She may get killed."

Lord Tokugawa gave him a hard look then. "Men get killed. Is it so different for a woman?"

Shusaku had no reply for that. He couldn't say that he loved her, that he lived for a smile from her lips. He just nodded, and lowered his helmet. Lord Tokugawa spurred his great stallion. His horned mask was already on, obscuring his features.

When they eventually charged, it was an uncompromising battle. Lord Tokugawa was fully back to strength—he cut down at least a dozen men, the Tokugawa *mon* fluttering in the rain-soaked wind as he slashed and parried, like a demon on horseback.

Shusaku, too, killed his share, finding as he always did that the world had shrunk to the ambit of his sword arm. Nothing else existed but that circle of steel.

Slowly, though, he and the rest of the honor guard, Lord Tokugawa also, found themselves forced to the side of the battlefield by arrows, which seemed almost to be fired at them for this very purpose, to herd them. It happened gradually, but before he knew it, Shusaku noticed that they were in the woods, below the Monto fortress.

He started to have a bad feeling. The stone walls of the fortress loomed over them.

"Ride at the wall," Lord Tokugawa said. His voice sounded oddly high. "Follow it round. We'll find a gate."

But just then a circle of Monto samurai came out from the trees, blades in their hands.

Gods, it's a trap, thought Shusaku.

He spurred his horse, wheeling. His first sword stroke took off the enemy's arm as it brought a blade swinging toward him—his second split a skull. He had the bloodlust rushing through him now, the *sakki*. It was battle-spirit, and he was infused with it, filled with it, as a drunk man is with wine.

Then he heard a crash. He turned to see that Lord Tokugawa's horse had been cut down, its forelegs severed by a sword. Lord Tokugawa stood unsteadily on the bare ground, sword in hand. Shusaku roared, leaping from his own horse.

Before he could reach Lord Tokugawa, though, he saw that Mara was already by his side. She raised her sword—Shusaku was struck by how quick the action was—and parried the blade of one of the Monto assassins. But there were two more behind her—she hadn't seen them, was still fighting the one who had attacked her—and time seemed to slow as Shusaku ran toward them, and they closed on Lord Tokugawa. Shusaku could see what was about to happen.

"Lord To—," he shouted—

Space stretched, so that the two *tan* or so that separated him from his lord became a thousand *ri*—

Mara planted her sword through the heart of her attacker, then turned, too slowly—

The two Monto samurai struck—

And Shusaku watched, helpless, as a blade cut through the mouth hole of Lord Tokugawa's helmet, like a dagger through a mound of rice, all the way to the hilt. The daimyo's blood spurted forth, a splash of red, a dragon breathing.

Inside Shusaku's mind was a white, meaningless noise, a kind of hush and susurration, like the sound of the tide on pebbles, or the wind in the leaves.

Apparently, something had snapped in Mara, too, because her sword whipped into movement as if animated by its own will, her hand and feet flying. The hood fell from her face; she was moving so fast that it seemed her very face was steaming. In a heartbeat, two at most, the three Monto closest to her were cut down. One's head had not hit the ground before she ran another through; all of it was happening too quickly for Shusaku really to take it in.

He stared. He could not move so quickly himself, and he was well on his way to becoming a sword saint.

It was his surprise at her speed and viciousness that was his undoing. He felt the sword come through his chest, heard the triumphant cry of the samurai behind him who had done it. He looked down, dumbfounded, at the metal growth sticking out of him. Another samurai was in front of him—it seemed that more had come from the trees. The Monto drew his sword back to deliver the final cut, to kill Shusaku dead.

I can't die here, he thought. *I was going to marry Mara and live in a castle.*

He went down on his knees. He saw, in the corner of his vision, Mara running toward him, a scream on her lips. She hurled her sword forward into the air, its blade turning over and over, catching what little remained of the light. Then her hands went to her sides and she was throwing things—he didn't understand, but he saw two of the remaining Monto fall, silver flowers blossoming in their flesh.

Throwing stars?

Without even looking up, Mara caught her sword again, which she had thrown into the air

(*to free her hands*, he realized)

and in the same movement as the catching, she brought the blade down, burying it in the forehead of the Monto in front of Shusaku. He saw that her face was red-raw, as if burnt. She pulled it out, snapped her sword hand back, and decapitated another who had come up behind her. Shusaku's mouth was open, and not just with pain. He had never seen fighting like this. Then the samurai behind him struck again, this time driving his short-sword through Shusaku's stomach.

Shusaku felt the world go dim, its sounds distant. He could smell the earth. It wanted to claim him.

From far away, he heard Mara scream again. He began to topple as she severed the sword hand of his killer—Shusaku saw it spin and then land on the mud, like a bloated, pale spider. She spun and slashed in a storm of steel, and the samurai around her died, and died, and died.

She's a demon, Shusaku realized. *She's a demon from hell, and she is sending them all there.* It was like she was dancing, and when she came to a stop, her head down, her blood- and rain-soaked hair hanging bedraggled over her face, breathing hard . . . she stood in a field of butchery. She looked up, and he saw her long eyelashes, and the pain in her eyes. He had never seen anything so beautiful.

He closed his eyes to die.

A lifetime later he felt a pressure on his face, and she was kneeling by him. There were tears on her cheeks.

"Mara," he said. "I wanted to marry you." He may have recited to her his death poem, which he had prepared for this moment. A samurai must always have a poem ready for his death. Either that or he just thought its words, without saying them out loud.

He looked into her eyes, and he fell into their depths.

He didn't come up again.

The next he was aware, he was on the back of a horse. Its motion was agony to him.

"Wait . . . ," he said. "My wound . . . I'll bleed out."

"What wound?" said a man's voice.

"The man's delirious," said another.

Soon afterward he found himself in Lord Tokugawa's camp. He managed to get himself off the horse . . . surprisingly easily, in fact. It was night, but everything seemed impossibly bright, the colors of the camp hissing and booming in his head. He could hear his own pulse, echoing. He could smell . . . he wasn't sure what he could smell.

But it was delicious.

He wondered if he was in heaven, and this was confirmed when Lord Tokugawa walked up to him, utterly unharmed, no sign of the sword that had been buried in his face.

"You're here, my old friend," said Lord Tokugawa.

"Yes," said Shusaku. "Have you seen Enma? Are we to be judged?"

A laugh—it resounded in Shusaku's skull. "You're not dead, man!"

"I'm not? But you died—I saw you. In the clearing. And then . . ."

"That wasn't me," said Lord Tokugawa. "You didn't really think I'd go back into battle, did you? The Monto aimed for me, with that gun. I have no intention of dying before I rule this sorry country."

Shusaku nodded slowly. Of course. He'd heard the high voice, hadn't he? The man riding with him and Mara had been an imposter, meant to draw the Monto out.

"Mara?" he said. Their relationship was a secret, but he seemed to have just died and come back to life, and the miracle made attempts at hiding his love for her seem irrelevant.

Lord Tokugawa's face contorted in pain. "I'm so sorry, Shusaku, my old friend," he said.

Shusaku swayed. "No. No. No . . ."

Lord Tokugawa put a hand on his shoulder. "You've been gone a whole day," he said. "My men only found you because they were recovering any swords that might have been lost on the battlefield. Last night . . . when you were lost . . . we found Mara outside my tent. Her throat had been slit."

"Her throat . . ." An image in his head: his lips, on the soft hollow at the base of her neck.

"Yes. All the way through, in fact. She'd been decapitated."

Shusaku had the feeling that someone had just told him he was standing on air, not the hard ground. He put out a hand, clung to Lord Tokugawa's arm. "Why?" he asked.

"I don't know," said Lord Tokugawa. "No one does."

Yet Shusaku did know—not then, but later. It was when he went back to his tent and examined himself in his silver mirror. His face was pale, and there were shadows under his eyes. He was so very, very thirsty.

And there were two puncture wounds on his neck. Dried blood

encrusted them. They were not so far apart. The width of a person's canine teeth, maybe.

He stared at them.

He thought of that deep hood, how it had come down, and her face had burned.

He thought of the throwing star she had used—a ninja weapon, and wasn't it said that all ninjas were vampires?

Now he had an idea why Mara had been killed. She must have been a vampire. And before someone killed her, she had made Shusaku a vampire too, had saved him by cursing him. He took off his kimono and ran his fingers lightly along the silver scars on his stomach and chest, the only trace of the swords that had cut him right through.

There were two things he had to do, one short-term and one long-term. In the short term he had to tell Lord Tokugawa what had happened to him. It would not be easy. The daimyo might choose to cast him out, or worse, require him to commit seppuku. Still, he was prepared for that. He was samurai. And what choice did he have? He couldn't go out in the sunlight anymore, he supposed. That wasn't so very easy a thing to conceal. Yes, in the short term he would have to tell Lord Tokugawa of his transformation, and be prepared for the consequences.

Also in the short term: He would need to find something to drink. Blood, he supposed. He noticed that the thought didn't disgust him.

Then there was the long term, assuming Lord Tokugawa let him live.

In the long term, he would find whoever had killed Mara. He had no idea who that might be. She'd seemed scared of Kenji Kira, but then how could Shusaku credit anything she said? She hadn't told him she was a vampire, a ninja presumably. He thought of the way she had fought in that clearing. It struck him that she might have been sent to assassinate Lord Tokugawa, and had been caught in the act. Only why had her interceptor not come forward, if that were the case? Anyone who could say that they had stopped a would-be assassin, saving the daimyo, would be a hero, could claim land and title.

It was a mystery. But Shusaku thought he might just have time to solve it, now that he was a vampire. He could be patient. He would keep Mara alive in his thoughts, remembering the darkness of her eyes, her long eyelashes, her slender form whirling with sword in hand; how beautiful she had been.

And then, when he found the person who had taken her from him, he would fix her in his mind and avenge her death, giving peace to her soul. It would be a *katakiuchi*, a vengeance killing. It would be an act of honor to kill the culprit, an act of cleansing.

Not that he would bother with killing him honorably, or cleanly. No. He would tear him to pieces. He touched his top teeth, and as his finger brushed them he felt his canines lengthening, sharpening.

Good. He would use them, when he did the tearing.

CHAPTER 41

THE REALM OF HELL

NOW

Mara.

Mara.

The name had been on his mind since he'd spoken about her with Taro on the boat. Then, suddenly, it had been on Kira's dead and decaying lips, a defilement, a travesty.

Shusaku opened his mouth to scream, but nothing came out. Inside him was a fire, consuming him. Hatred clouded his newly recovered vision in a haze of red. He felt that no water or ice could quench him, could put out the inferno raging in his flesh and his blood. He was a dragon, not a man. He could breathe this fire, if he wanted.

He had loved Mara, had wanted to marry her. He had never known a more beautiful woman; even Hana, to his eyes, was an imperfect carving, next to a masterpiece. But Mara had been kind, too, and quick, and humorous—and she had been the one to turn him. He had seen, when he used the ball, how his blood still flowed in Taro. He understood now that hers was still in him, that in some sense she would always live as long as he did.

But it didn't dim his rage. Kenji Kira had killed her. He had always suspected it, had always wondered, but now the hatamoto *had confirmed it. His mind was half on a mountainside, twelve years earlier, and half on the scene in hell before him, Kira standing there so smug, Horse-head and Ox-face beside him.*

The tearing of his skin came to him as an instinct. He simply knew that it was right. Maybe he had to get the Heart Sutra off him, to become what he needed to become—maybe, much as it stopped spirits and the gods from seeing him, it would stop, too, his own essence from bursting out, becoming more than itself.

His whole consciousness a scream, he tore the skin from his chest first; it was easy, because it had only just been flayed. Kenji Kira, he could dimly see through the red and the pain, was staring at him in horror. He dug his fingers into his waist, pulled a strip off his leg, the agony of it unbelievable, all-encompassing. It was as if his pain wasn't something inside him, an attribute or property of his, but was everywhere in the world, surrounding him, drowning him. He was drowning in blood and pain.

He understood that this was necessary, so that he could become the death that must come even to death, so that he could be the Death-of-Enma, but he had not been prepared for the pain, so much worse somehow than being flayed, because he was doing it to himself.

Taro had been right, it seemed, that he could do this, but he hated it all the same, was almost insane with the agony of it.

Yes, Taro had been right.

Curse the boy.

A ripping sound—the last of the skin on his leg came away, and he could see his own muscles and sinews, even the veins snaking around his naked soft tissue. He dropped the tattooed covering of flesh, saw it pool on the ground like bloody clothing, was conscious of putting behind him something he could never recover.

He didn't care.

As he tore, as he ripped, he was conscious of growing. The desire to kill Kenji Kira, to destroy him, was a kind of expanding feeling, like that of taking a deep breath into the lungs. He felt, too, though he couldn't explain it, that it wasn't just him who wanted Kira gone. That it was everything, the universe, the whole of dharma, *pouring into him, making him swell up, making him the vessel of Kira's annihilation. There was a sort of voice in his mind, a music, which he understood to be the harmony of all things, and it considered Kira an abomination.*

He wanted Kenji Kira dead.

The greatness of dharma *wanted Kira dead. It was filling him up like a drinking bladder, pushing him beyond the boundaries of the human, or the vampire.*

He was becoming the Death-of-Enma.

He looked down and was shocked to see how far below him Taro was, cowering, covered in a fine spray of blood. He wanted to tell the boy not to be afraid, but he couldn't find the words, or even the voice. He was just pain and anger, spreading to fill the vastness of hell's vaulted space. He reached behind his back and caught the last of his skin, ripped it off with a flourish. He felt the rushing sensation of air against him, shooting up—the height of the palace roof at Edo now, as his growing finally began to slow.

He took a step toward the three figures before him, heard it as an ordinary footstep, but saw Taro cover his ears, tiny Taro all that way below him, face screwed up. He was a giant, then; his step was painful to the ears of smaller creatures. He didn't want to think about that. He kept moving forward now, though softer, anxious not to hurt Taro—something he would never want to do.

Horse-head went down on one knee, head bent, and then Ox-face did the same. Shusaku smiled. This was good. As for their disloyalty to the order that should prevail in death, well, he would deal with them later.

Kenji Kira, to give the man his due, drew a sword like a toothpick and came at him, stabbed his weapon into Shusaku's leg. Shusaku bent down, caught the blade between finger and thumb, and tore it away, flicking it over the demons, far into the air of hell. He focused his qi *on his throat, on his voice. He spoke, and saw Kira close his eyes against the gale from his mouth, his hands up to his ears.*

"SAY HER NAME AGAIN," he said.

Kenji Kira was shaking, like an autumn leaf in the breeze. He mumbled something.

"LOUDER," said Shusaku.

"M-m-m-Mara," said the o-bangashira *of Lord Nobunaga no Oda's armies, the once-proud military leader, through lips that were green with mold, and he said the name as if he were begging for his life.*

In another life, in another time, Shusaku might have offered the man seppuku, as befitted a samurai of his rank. Not here. Not now. Not now that he knew what Kira had done. He picked the man up, lifted him till he was level with his own face, so high up. Kira was whimpering, or screaming, it was hard for Shusaku to tell—all sounds seemed small and far away.

"I WAS GOING TO USE MY TEETH FOR THIS," he said, as if Kenji Kira could possibly understand what he was saying, and then he tore the man—or whatever Kenji Kira was—in half.

He half flinched, expecting blood, but there was none, just a kind of black oozing. Kenji Kira's torso, head, and arms wriggled; like a worm, his legs did the same. Shusaku tore the legs apart, the head from the body, the arms, throwing pieces of the former hatamoto *to the ground. They squirmed; he stamped on them, picked them up, ripped them into smaller pieces. He was lost to himself for some time, whatever had poured into him taking over; he was just a force of destruction, in the shape of a giant person, stripped of skin.*

Eventually the bloodlust, the sakki, *faded, and he came to himself to see small parts of Kenji Kira all over the ground. He felt himself shrinking again.*

When he was almost Taro's size, he noticed that his skin was growing back, his tattoos creeping over his body to join at the chest and waist, as if writing themselves onto him. His burns, from when he'd almost been killed by the sun at Lord Oda's castle, were gone now, however—he was shining and new.

Taro was shaking his head in wonderment, in horror.

"I knew you could do it," the boy said.

Shusaku looked at the tatters and shreds that had been Kenji Kira, at the kneeling figures of the servants of Enma. "But what do I do now?" he asked.

Taro smiled. "You're Enma, aren't you? You rule death."

"I . . . do?"

"You do. Look at them." Taro pointed to the kneeling demons.

"But what about . . . us? If I stay here, I will not see you again."

"Yes, you will. One day."

He heard the catch in Taro's voice and understood. "Oh, Taro," he said.

"We all must die," said Taro. "Even death."

Shusaku looked around at the misty gray realm that was hell. He felt terrified, unequal to the task. "But ruling death, Taro . . . I wouldn't know where to start."

Taro, that incredible boy, walked calmly toward Horse-head and Ox-face, beckoning for Shusaku to follow. "I would start by getting back all those who escaped from here," he said. "Like the ones who attacked us that night. Gather them up, bring them back to death. Then you can worry about the rest."

Shusaku smiled.

The boy was right, of course. That was what he should do. He would go out into the human realm and take back all those who had gotten free when Kenji Kira was ruler here. He would set things back the way they should be. He would reverse the rot that had started in Kira's flesh, before spreading out through the world, through more than one world, through the realms of samsara.

Taro was right.

Bless the boy.

CHAPTER 42

Taro opened his eyes on a black world.

The sun was long gone, a sliver of moon hanging in its place. A few stars sparkled through the clouds. The sea was an expanse of rumpled cloth, darker than the sky. The horizon no longer looked very far away. Taro remembered when he and Hiro had been desperate to leave this place, to go and seek adventure in the wider world. Now he wished he had been able to stay. If he had never met Shusaku, he would not have to miss him, which hurt like the long ache after a gut punch.

He got up, his legs stiff, and made his way back over the dunes toward the village. The scents were those of home: salt air, pine needles, smoke. Under them all was the seaweed smell of the sea. He didn't just wish he had stayed two years earlier. He wished he could stay now. But Kusanagi was light and perfectly balanced at his side—now that he had it he could no more resist the call of Edo, of the dragon of the land, than he could unlearn the smell of cedar sap over salt water.

Arriving at the village, he made straight for his mother's hut. There was a flickering light glowing inside. He had the impression of being a ghost, come back to visit its relatives on *obon*, except that *obon* was still a month away or more. He opened the door. Inside, Hana sat by the fire. He was reminded of the night his father was killed, when he came home to see his mother sitting in much the same place. Only now it wasn't his mother. Now it was the woman he loved, who would never love him.

"Hiro is gone," she said, without looking up.

"Sorry?"

Her long eyelashes rose. "You were looking for him, I take it?"

"Ah . . . no. I was looking for you. Wait. He's gone? Gone where?"

"I don't know. He didn't say. Just talked about finding his own life."

"When did he leave?" Taro asked. He had a terrible sinking feeling. He had felt so betrayed—still did, a little. But since he had seen Kenji Kira finally die, after finding the Buddha ball floating in the ocean, unharmed, he had begun to feel that it was his destiny to hold it. Perhaps Hiro had been right to go after it. Perhaps he had been doing what he thought was best, for Taro.

Curses.

"Two days ago, I think," said Hana.

"Two . . . *days*?" He stepped toward her. This explained the stiffness in his limbs, the hunger inside him.

She stood, backing away from him.

"You don't have to be afraid of me," he said.

"I'm not. I'm afraid of me."

"You're . . . I don't understand."

She pulled up her hair and touched her neck, still covered by the makeshift scarf. He was overwhelmed by a rush of desire for her but pushed it down. He could see the delicate shadow of her collarbone and wanted nothing so much as to kiss it. He noticed that she had changed into a fresh, plain kimono. He wondered who had given it to her. She had such deep, dark eyes, in the firelight. He felt he could fall into them. That he already had. "I can feel my blood, singing out to yours," she said. "That's what makes me afraid."

"I love you, that's why," he said.

"No. You turned me. That's all."

His breath was shaky in his chest. She was looking at him like he was a thing to be despised, and he couldn't bear it. He wanted to turn around and go out the door, never come back, but he couldn't live without her, he knew that.

"Whose blood will I drink?" she asked, as he stared at her.

"Whose . . ."

"Blood. It's what I live on, now, isn't it? Tell me, Taro. Who should be my first victim? The priest? Or one of the children? I imagine they are easier to trap. To fool." The bitterness in her voice was like a blow.

"Hana, you know me," he said. "I'm not like that. If you come with me, I could show you how to hunt, how to take deer and—"

"I thought I knew you," she said. "Then you bit me. You turned me, after I asked you not to."

"You were dying."

"I would have been better dead."

He looked down, stung. "You'd rather be dead than be like me?"

She met his eyes. "Yes."

"Please. Please come with me." Shame was hot in his stomach. He was begging her not to leave him. It was pathetic. Shusaku would be disgusted. But he couldn't just lose her; it was unthinkable. He was dealing with the worst of all ironies: She was right there, two *tan* in front of him, but she might as well have been on the other side of the world. A week ago she would have married him. Now she was beyond him utterly, and he would never have her.

"I won't," she said. "I will never follow you again. You revolt me."

"You don't mean that."

"I do."

He touched his cloak. "I didn't want to do this," he said.

"Remember that. Remember I didn't want to do it." Then he took out the ball. He couldn't lose her. He wouldn't allow it to happen. He would not lose another person he loved. Not after his father, and his mother, and Shusaku, even Hiro. She would understand, maybe, one day. He hoped she would.

"Taro, no," she breathed.

He ignored her. Holding the ball, he allowed himself to drop through star-spangled sky, then to rush through blanketing mist and cloud. He roared down over the sea, the blackness racing upward to meet him, to embrace him.

He opened his eyes and was in the ball and in the world at the same time. He let his mind reach out, let his blood reach out. He could feel Hana, pulsing before him. He could hear the particular accent of his own blood inside her, speaking his soul, melding it with hers, making a rhythm of their two heartbeats inside her heart, a duet.

It wasn't enough.

Above it all, a high-pitched threnody: He could hear and taste and smell her hatred for him, spreading through her like a black cloud. He almost reeled, but he stayed firm. He could make her love him.

Reaching out to his blood, he commanded it. Hana stepped forward. He walked her toward the door, opened it, and made her go through. Outside on the path he stood behind her. It was easier that way; he didn't have to look at her face, the expression on it. He forced her up the path, toward the Edo road.

Her footsteps on the shingle of the path were a sigh, the soft sound of his soul dying. He felt a physical effort that was nothing to do with controlling her body. His teeth were gritted, his fists tensed. It was hurting him, doing this to her. But what choice did he have?

Then he heard it, above the sound of her footsteps. They had left the last of the village huts behind them and were almost in the forest.

She was sobbing.

Horrified, he stopped. What was he doing? This was madness. He sent out a message to his blood in her—made her stop also.

"You can make me go with you," she said. "But you can't make me love you. And as soon as you fall asleep, I'll be gone."

He knew she was telling the truth. He could feel it in her bones, in the beating of her heart. She could not lie to the vampire who had turned her, not when he was holding the Buddha ball.

The Buddha ball.

Closing his eyes, he dropped the ball to the ground, releasing her.

"I'm sorry," he said. "I just didn't want to lose you. It's like . . . like a hole, inside me."

"There is a hole inside me, too," she said. "It wants to be filled with blood."

He took a breath, steadied himself. "I'm sorry about that, too."

"I know you are. It's not enough."

He stooped and picked up the ball again, put it away inside his cloak. Kusanagi sat on his other side, warm against his hip. "What will you do?" he asked. "My mother's hut is yours, if you want it."

"Thank you." He could see what the words cost her, even without the ball that allowed him to know her inner workings, her heart's particular rhythm. "I think I'll stay in Shirahama a while. Where else do I have to go?"

"And blood?"

"I'll tell the priest what I am. Maybe he'll help me."

"Or he may throw you out. Or kill you."

She shrugged. "I'm prepared for that."

It was then that he understood, really understood, how much he had hurt her, how much he had failed her. He quailed. "Turn away," he said. "Turn away so I can't see your eyes."

She did, looking toward the forest. From the way her body tensed, he imagined that she must think he was going to kill her—maybe she even wanted it. He didn't look at her again, though.

He ran, pouring all his vampire strength into the action, and flowed past her to disappear into the forest. He heard her heartbeat fade, then disappear, behind him.

CHAPTER 43

SOME DISTANCE FROM SHIRAHAMA

LATER THAT EVENING

Hiro came down from the mountain pass into a high valley that was bathed in starlight. He was riding. He'd had money for a horse—Shusaku had made sure to distribute gold coins among the four of them, sewing them into clothing, hiding them in small pockets. It had been one of the ninja's mantras. You can never have enough hidden money, and you can never have enough hidden weapons.

So he'd traded a couple of the gold coins for the second-strongest horse in the village before leaving. Taro had gone out to sea and there had been some kind of battle, he'd heard. The sea burned, according to those who had seen it. After, he had half expected that his friend might seek him out, tell him about it. Show him Kusanagi. But when he asked, he was told that Taro was on a rock, meditating.

Meditating!

Hiro had always perceived emotions as colors, and right now his were a swirl of red and blue. He was ashamed and sorry, certainly, for betraying Taro. He had not meant to. He had only recovered the ball because he thought Taro might need it later, might have been acting too hastily, but of course Taro would never believe that. Or maybe he did believe it and he didn't care. He cared only that Hiro had lied to him. Taro could be inflexible like that, a harsh moral judge.

Which explained the red in Hiro's feelings—the anger toward Taro, who had cast him aside like a broken chopstick, and whose first act upon finding the legendary sword wielded by Susanoo himself was to go off on his own to meditate.

Well, let him stay on his own.

Alternately fuming and cringing with guilt, Hiro kept the horse to a steady trot, following a traders' path through a thin wood. From up here he could see the whole valley spreading out below him—the rice paddies, shelving down from the low flanks, the villages, quiet under the dark vault of heaven. Far on the horizon were the foothills, rising up, of the mountain range that would lead him eventually to Mount Hiei and the sweet oblivion of the monk's existence. The mountains themselves were lost in the blackness of the sky.

As he watched the hills, another emotion poured itself inkily into the palette of his feelings—a gray one, this. Sadness.

A tear threatened to form, and he rubbed his eyes angrily, a flash of red in his head. He had to fight away the sadness. It reminded him too much of the truth, which he was trying to avoid by riding away: He loved Taro. He owed him his life. Taro had saved him from a shark, when he was just a boy. He would lay down his life to save Taro, would do it over and over again if he were asked. This was why he had gone to get the ball that Taro had thrown away. He thought it might help his friend, in the long run. And now he was cast out because of it. Now Taro, who was the person he cared for most in the world, hated him.

Hiro spoke a curse word, loudly, into the shadows of the forest. He spurred the horse and speeded up to a canter. In this manner he rode down into the lower part of the valley. A couple of times, he thought perhaps he heard another horse; hoofbeats on the moss of the forest floor, over to the east. But when he stopped his horse, he heard nothing. Lost cattle, maybe, or wolves. The thought of wolves made him ride even faster.

He was riding through the second village, the path a little muddy underfoot now, when he saw the red lanterns of an inn. He slowed. He had been riding two days, and already one whole night had slipped by without sleep. He still had money, left over from the purchase of the horse. Maybe a room for what remained of the night . . .

As he considered, a figure stepped out from under the nearest lantern. Hiro's horse reared—he just clung on, whispering to it, stroking its neck, as it whinnied and stamped. When the horse was still, his hand went to the short-sword at his side.

"Is that how you greet an old companion?" said the figure.

Hiro peered into the gloom. The figure took another step forward, the light from the lantern illuminating its face. "Jun?" said Hiro, surprised.

"The same."

Hiro dismounted, holding on to the reins as he approached the inn. The last he had seen of Jun—who had been a constant, if distant, companion at Mount Hiei—was in Edo, before they saw the shogun. The boy was a little strange—quiet, not friendly but not unfriendly, either. They had spoken numerous times, while Taro and Hana were ahead together on the road, and despite that, Hiro had little idea of what Jun really thought about anything. Often Jun would startle Hiro by appearing behind him, when he hadn't heard the boy's footsteps. Or by firing an arrow straight into the center of a target even Taro would be proud to hit, when it had seemed at first to Hiro that he didn't have much in the way of muscles or fighting spirit. And then the next day Jun would be with the abbot, poring over ancient scrolls, reading Sanskrit with ease.

An enigma.

"What are you doing here?" asked Hiro. He began tying his horse to a post.

"I could ask you the same thing," said Jun. "Come inside. Let's talk."

Inside the inn, no one was to be seen. Jun seemed to know the place, though—he went confidently behind a simple wooden bar and came back with a bottle of sake. He lit a candle on a small, round table and motioned for Hiro to sit. From somewhere he produced two bowls of rice and stock, steaming. Like a magician.

Several glasses of sake later, and Hiro had told Jun most of what had happened since they'd left each other in Edo, a lifetime ago, leaving out certain key details. Jun knew already about Kusanagi—Hiro supposed the rumor must have spread in Edo that Taro was looking for it. Hiro added only that he and Taro had fallen out, without saying why, or mentioning that Taro had found the sword, and that as far as he knew his friend was going to Edo and the dragon alone. Jun was still a mystery, and Hiro didn't trust anyone, not anymore.

"Alone?" said Jun. "To face a dragon?" In the candlelight, it was hard to make out his age. He had black hair, fine eyebrows. No wrinkles on his skin. To all appearances a boy. Yet sometimes he sounded much older.

"Yes."

"And you're afraid for him," said Jun. "You would give anything to help him." It wasn't a question.

"Yes."

Jun poured another two glasses. "Well, in that case it is your lucky night," he said.

"It is?"

"It certainly is. What if I told you that you could *help Taro? That you could come to Edo with me, and help save his life?"*

Hiro narrowed his eyes. He was being offered a chance at redemption, he realized. To salvage his honor. To save his friend. Yet he was instinctively distrustful, too. "Why would you help me?" he asked.

Jun spread his hands and frowned in a gesture of humorous offense. "The abbot is very fond of Taro," he said. "Did you think he would just let him go, without making sure that friends were watching over him? There are people in Edo who are ready to assist him in killing that dragon. They want to see someone new on the throne of Japan. With Kusanagi, and with my powerful friends . . . Taro could have the throne. And you could be the one to give it to him."

Friends watching over him. That was what Hiro wanted to be. A friend who watched over. Who watched . . . who looked after Taro. Give him the throne. The one to do it. That was what he wanted. Yes.

"You want to help Taro become shogun?" Hiro asked Jun. He

remembered the prophecy that they had heard that night from the prophetess.

Jun nodded. "The current shogun is a disgrace," he said. "So, you'll come with me?"

"Yes," said Hiro. "Yes, I'll come with you. To save Taro."

Jun smiled and reached out his hand to shake Hiro's. "A good decision," he said.

Hiro leaned back. He was warm and full and there was sake in his belly. Upstairs there was a soft bed; Jun had said so.

His emotions were a still pool of calm and gentle amber, just like the flickering candlelight.

CHAPTER 44

NEAR EDO

ONE WEEK LATER

It wasn't hard to find the dragon. What Taro had done was to follow the burned villages, the piles of ash and scorched earth. As he climbed upward, the devastation increased, the heat, too. A red glow came from the mountaintop, a constant reminder of what waited up there.

That was what was hard—not finding the thing but climbing up toward it, knowing that every step brought him closer.

Taro stopped to rest on a large rock, warmer than the sun should have made it. His muscles were burning. He tried not to think that soon they might really be on fire. He was near the top now—could see the red-lit peak just above him. Where normally there would be snow, instead there were rivulets of molten fire, running in ravines and gullies. He had to tread carefully, even this far away. Twice he had nearly fallen into one of these cracks in the earth. He would melt like a candle if he did, he knew.

He thought about what it would be like to feel his own flesh burn. He really, really didn't want to find out. He tried to think about other things. He tried to concentrate on his surroundings.

There were no trees up here. No vegetation at all, actually—just bare rock, sweating and shimmering in the heat. When Taro turned, though, he could see forests extending out below him, a cool green blanket, uninterrupted until the great city of Edo. He wished he could take to the air like a bird, fly back out over that expanse of green, dive into it, and into Edo, too—he could see the canals and rivers of the capital, from this height looking like cool blue veins, spreading through the body of the city, filling him with a desperate thirst that confused the concepts of water and blood in his mind.

He thought of the deer he had brought down the previous day, and before that the pilgrim, who had been going to Edo on the way to Mount Hiei, and who Taro had knocked out with a branch, before drinking as much as he dared from the man's veins. Enough to give Taro strength. Hopefully not enough to have killed the man. Taro hadn't stuck around to find out.

Imagining the blood filling his mouth, his legs trembled and he nearly went down. He had not drunk nearly enough yesterday. He was meant to face the dragon, and instead he was gazing at distant cities and thinking of water and blood.

For strength, he touched Kusanagi, unsheathed at his side. He had traveled all this way—he wasn't going to turn around now.

He thought of Hiro, and Hana. Where were they now? Was Hana still in Shirahama? He had not stopped in Edo, so there was no way of receiving news of them. All he knew—because he had been careful to ask passing travelers—was that the dragon had not yet been defeated. Another ten young men had died in the attempt, though. Some said twenty.

In this way Taro stumbled on, thinking about his absent friends, craving blood. Craving water.

The mountainside got steeper and steeper. In places he was forced to use his hands as well as his feet, scrambling over scalding-hot rocks. He hadn't really thought through what he would do when he reached the dragon's lair. He did have a clear picture of afterward, though—he would walk into Edo over the Nihonbachi Bridge, the dragon's head in his hands. Or in a cart, if it was too big to carry. People would swarm out to thank him, to hail him as their savior. Then he supposed he would fight the shogun and take the throne. After that the details of his plan were sketchy. But he would make things better, he was sure of that. No one would starve, when he was in charge.

He came to a kind of channel in the rock, not dissimilar to the one in which Shusaku had died, only much steeper. It was when he followed this, turning sharply to the right, that he wished he had thought a little more about what he intended to do with the dragon.

In front of him was a vast, dark, deep cave, and at the back of the cave was a pair of red, glowing eyes. Black burn marks were everywhere on the walls. Some of them surrounded the outlines of human beings, their shadows fixed to the walls in attitudes of utter terror. Up above, a thin crack of afternoon sunlight showed through the broken rock.

Taro had encountered a similar voice in his head before, in a very different cave under the sea, but he was still not prepared for it.

"I used to ask questions," said the dragon. "But after a dozen or so I stopped. You all say the same things."

Taro drew Kusanagi. "I don't have anything to say," he said.

"Then you are different," said the dragon. It didn't speak further—just rolled up into the air, moving like an airborne snake, or a wave across a bay. It moved quicker than thought; one moment it was a pair of eyes, like great coals in the darkness, the next it was filling the space of the cave, scales and horns and teeth, enormous, a force beyond human comprehension that wanted Taro dead.

Roaring, blowing smoke, it descended on Taro. He noticed that the dragon had little legs on its underside, stunted ones. They would almost have been amusing, if the dragon wasn't bigger than four houses, with teeth the size of battle swords. Then Taro wasn't thinking anymore—he was ducking and rolling. He judged it almost right. He hit the ground hard, knocking the breath out of himself, turning to slash his sword at the leg that rushed past him, faster than a galloping horse.

The legs might have looked funny against the size of the dragon, but they were still big—and tipped with nasty talons. Even as he opened a wound in the one over his head, and dragon blood spattered him hotly, one of the talons struck his left shoulder, tearing a gouge in him a hand-span deep, ripping his shoulder blade from its socket. He screamed, crawling out of the way as fire scorched the earth beside him.

One leg—he'd wounded one of its legs and it had cost him his left arm. How many legs did it have? Dozens. He shouldn't have been so focused on its legs, though. Its head snapped on the air he had been occupying an instant before; he side-stepped, but his hip was caught. The sword-teeth went through his flesh like a rake through leaves, scraping against bone. He was spurting blood, from hip and shoulder. He staggered.

Stupid. Stupid.

He'd fought people before, with swords. Had thought that made him strong. He wasn't strong. Not next to a dragon. He was a mouse taunting a lion.

Images flashed in front of his disoriented eyes. Scaled skin. Red eyes. Flames, to either side of him, over his head, burning off his hair when he ducked. He could deal with human opponents—this dragon, though, was all around him, all over him. He thought it must be toying with him. He should be dead.

The dragon roared. A sentence with no words ached and throbbed in his head—it was the dragon's hatred, the dragon's fury that he had hurt it, had cut open its leg. He could see that wounded leg as the dragon flew around him, could see how it hung down limply. He could also feel, in his mind, how the dragon intended to punish him for it. He saw its jaws open, as the bearded head came at him fast and massive as a landslide.

I'm going to die here, he realized. *Even with Kusanagi, I'm going to die here.*

At the last moment, though, his muscles took over. Bringing the sword vertically upward, he flipped it in the air, and dropped his hand so that the sword went tip-first down the back of his shirt. It cut his back as it did so, but he didn't care. This was some survival instinct manipulating his limbs, some desire to live and fight that had seeped into his bones from all his training with Shusaku.

He flicked his eyes at the wall just to his right, measuring distance. As the head neared him, he feinted left, then shot to the right. A hot breeze on his skin, as the head went past him. His feet hit the wall; he ran up its sheer side for three steps, then pivoted off the ball of his foot, somersaulting backward.

For a moment, no gravity. He was floating in a world of heat and pain.

Then he crashed down, stomach-first, on the dragon's back. He twisted, getting his knees round it, riding it like a horse. He was just behind its head. He reached forward, seizing its horns. It twisted and bucked angrily—again that inferno of anger rushing through his thoughts. He reached round to his back and seized the pommel of Kusanagi. When he pulled it out of his shirt, he cut himself again. He didn't care this time either. His shoulder and hip and back throbbed; his clothes were soaked with blood.

"Have you heard of Kusanagi?" he shouted.

There was only one word of the dragon's in his head—it was *die*.

Die, die, die.

"No," Taro said.

He brought the sword down hard. It buried itself pommel-deep in the dragon's neck, and Taro withdrew it, with a meaty sliding sound. Blood erupted. Taro's head was filled with a sound like thunder, like a tsunami, like lava consuming a village. He clutched his hands to his ears, his knees weakening, and fell from the dragon's back. They were high up—he was weightless for several moments, longer than when he had somersaulted, and then the landing punched the air out of him, snapped his ribs, left him bleeding and whimpering on the ground. He spat out broken teeth, bloodstained grass filling his vision.

He braced for the dragon to fall on top of him.

It didn't.

Instead there was a deafening crash as its body slammed into the opposite wall, then slithered down it. The dragon tried to lift into the air again but fell to earth. It got onto its legs, one of them continuing to bleed profusely, the blood steaming in the air. Favoring its other legs, the dragon moved toward him. Its head hung heavy, bearded with blood, but it didn't stop.

All the time, it fixed Taro with its red eyes. Its voice sounded in his head again. "When a samurai acts as second for his friend's seppuku," it said, "he must try to sever the neck in one clean blow. It is a matter of honor. You should have done the same. In your case it is a matter of survival."

It took in a deep breath—Taro felt the cooling on his skin as air was sucked from around him, so hard that he was drawn forward, his feet skating over the dust of the ground. He flinched, tried to curl into a ball, tried to turn, but it was all too late. At the last moment he threw Kusanagi aside, so that it would not melt—he was about to die, but the sword was a legend, more than a sword, a key, a key that unlocked the country. It should not be destroyed.

Fire flowed forth from the dragon like a hurricane, like a demon wind. It rolled over him—his clothes burst into flame, as did the grass at his feet.

He found out, then, what it was like to feel his own flesh burn, to know the sensation of his melting eye running down his cheek.

It was unpleasant.

The merciful thing was: It didn't last for long.

CHAPTER 45

The dragon paced the cave, groaning, shuffling.

Taro opened his one, unruined eye. He was on his knees, near the wall of the cave. Against the rock was his own outline, his own silhouette—a crouching boy, surrounded by black. The grass around him was gone, everything burned to a thin, pale ash.

On his left side, his clothes had gone, or were fused with his flesh. His eye was destroyed. The left side of his face hurt like . . . well, like a dragon had burnt the flesh from the bone. He thought to himself that at least the wound in his shoulder had probably been cauterized, and he had to stifle a delirious giggle. Colossal, unbelievable pain surrounded him, like a beast that had swallowed him. It was total and all-encompassing. He was surprised he was even conscious.

Taro turned his head, felt every nerve on his left side call out in agony. His vision—his one-eyed vision—went black for a moment. The dragon was curled up on the other side of the cave now, licking its wounds, like a cat. It didn't see him looking. It occurred to Taro, then, that the dragon was used to killing *people*. It might never have fought a vampire, and so it would naturally assume he was dead. He should be dead. He had lost a lot of blood and had suffered appalling burns.

He wished he was dead.

He cursed Shusaku for turning him.

As Taro twisted back, something shifted at his side, then dropped heavily to the ground. He stared dumbly at the ground at his feet.

Lying there, unharmed, was the Buddha ball—it had fallen because the cloak that held it had burned away. He considered its cool, round surface. He glanced back at the dragon. Even through the red mist of pain he could see an idea forming.

Gods bless Hiro, he thought. He wondered where his friend was now. He'd cast Hiro out for retrieving the Buddha ball, but maybe the ball was the answer to everything. He wished Hiro could be here—he wished he wasn't alone with this staggering pain.

But he was alone. So he got on with it.

Leaning down, his whole back and side screaming out, he picked up the ball with his right hand—his left was a blackened, swollen lump, split in places, like a soft fruit left out to rot. Even if he survived, his injuries would be catastrophic. He would never move like a ninja again, swift and agile. But he could think like one. He could think like a ninja.

And it was possible that he could survive.

And if he survived, he would still possess Kusanagi.

He had come here to kill a dragon. He realized now that he had come for so much more. He had come to destroy everything that was holding the world in tyranny—not just the dragon, which was destroying people and villages, but also the shogun, who was starving them with his taxes, and the daimyo, who were taking their men to be fed into their great man-eating machine of war.

He put his hands on the ball, and immediately Sato's voice was threading through his mind, like blood in water. And somewhere far away, he thought he heard Lord Oda's voice, crackling abuse, but he tuned it out.

Looking down into the ball, he dropped into its sunlit sky. He fell through thin blue air, and then clouds, and then he was careering down toward a mountain that was rushing up at him, running with red fire like blood.

He snapped out of the ball, held himself inside and outside it. The dragon must have sensed something happening, because it looked up, weary, and its huge red eyes might even have been expressing surprise when it saw him struggle to his feet.

It lumbered up too, blood still dripping from its neck. It was badly wounded, Taro could tell. It came toward him, fixing him with those burning-coal eyes.

"You're brave," it said. "I will allow you that." Then it sucked in breath, and Taro felt that sensation again of air slipping past him, racing to fill the dragon's fiery lungs.

He spread his consciousness out, as he had that day in the shogun's province crippled by drought. He let himself become every droplet of moisture in the sky above, every wisp of every cloud. He was a dispersed entity now, something made up of billions of elements that were all one, and he understood that this was in fact the nature of all things. Everything was separate—and everything was one. Concentrating on that idea of oneness, he began to pull himself back together, to compress himself, make himself less spread out.

All of this, of course, happened in less than an instant.

Then the water in the sky was gathered into one enormous ball, a giant counterpart to the little Buddha ball in his hand, and he pushed it until it couldn't bear anymore to be pressed into so small a space.

The heavens opened.

Rain came down, not like rain, but like a stream or water running from a pipe, a continuous pouring of water. There was no spray, there were no droplets, just a river falling from the sky. Taro pulled himself back from the ball into the human realm.

As the water hit the dragon, there was a great hiss, as of a blacksmith's tool being plunged into water, or fat, and steam roiled out to fill the expanse of the cave—again, Taro felt what it was to be burned, but this was just a scalding, nothing compared to the agony he had endured earlier. He gritted his teeth, knowing that now he would have to do something that might kill him.

In his head was the constant boom of the dragon's anger, like waves on rocks.

Darkness wove in and out of his vision as he limped over to the wall where he had thrown Kusanagi. It was almost as if the world was breathing—he would see through a narrow aperture, ringed by black, then everything would expand, till his one eye perceived the cave in almost too much detail, and then the whole thing would start again, rhythmically. He felt sick.

He was slow to get to the sword, and already when he picked it up the dragon was following him, limping too, damp smoke rising from its nostrils now. Taro kept moving, not letting that great head with its teeth get near him. He stumbled and slipped toward the middle of the cave. He was heading for the pool of blood that had formed where he had plunged the sword into the dragon's neck. In his head was a picture of the past—himself, licking blood from the deck of Kenji Kira's ship. He had no idea what dragon blood would do to him, but he certainly couldn't fight the thing like this, his own melted flesh turned into a restrictive armor that hampered his movement.

The dragon was close when Taro got there—as he dropped to the ground, mouth open, one of its front legs came down on his foot, trapping it. He screamed into the blood, making it bubble and foam. He didn't stop, though. He put his lips to it, sucked down.

Fire caught inside him. There was nothing but him and the blood, spreading through him, sending its fingers of flame into his limbs, his face, his hands. He had never tasted anything like it. Raw power was what it tasted like. Just as the pain had swallowed him from the outside, so, as he swallowed, the blood of the dragon consumed him from the inside, transmuting his body, turning it from muscle and bone and ligament into something made of fire.

No.

Must stop—no time.

He wrenched himself away from the blood, which he could have drunk forever, and rolled clumsily. The dragon's teeth snapped closed on an unburned part of his cloak, or possibly some of his skin that had come away from his body. Either way, he didn't feel any pain. And the dragon had taken its leg from his foot in order to strike with its mouth—a foolish move. He jumped to his feet. His eye was still gone, of course; his flesh was still ruined. But he could feel the heat of the blood coursing through him, making him strong.

He was a ninja. He was vampire. He was made to kill.

Circling, he had to force himself to limp again, to make the dragon see him as slow and useless. He favored his unburned leg, made an effort to gaze around him stupidly, as if unable to see clearly. The dragon came at him, unguarded. It didn't bother to get around him, to come at him from his weak side—just charged right at him, jaws open.

There was a sword kata that involved skating fluidly to the side, letting the other's strike rush past you like a bull, before opening up his back with a slash on the turn. Taro did it now. Abandoning the pretense of the weaker leg, he slid finger-snap-quick to the right, sword already moving through the air. He noticed again its perfect weight, its perfect balance. It was a sword that wanted to strike out. It just needed a human hand on it to do it.

He wasn't quite quick enough—but then he hadn't expected to be. This was a dragon he was fighting, after all, big as a village. The teeth closed on his left hand, as his right brought the sword around and down.

The blade bit down next to the previous wound he had inflicted on that massive neck. He put all the strength that remained to him, and all the strength of the dragon's blood, into the blow. Flesh parted like rice below a chopstick, and the blade struck something hard. He realized it was the ground.

Pulling the sword out, he ignored the clamor in his head, ignored the dragon's struggles, its head-thrashing that severed his left hand and most of his forearm and sent it flying, a bloody starfish, across the cave. *Oh gods, my hand*, thought Taro. The idea that it could just be *gone* seemed too enormous and awful to grasp.

Shaking, he realized that shock had seized hold of him, threatening to unbalance his mind. He steeled himself. He had lost an eye; now he had lost a hand. He would lose nothing else.

Pouring all his *qi*, all his focus into what he was doing, he brought the sword down again, the dragon's blood covering him now, dripping on his face. He put out his tongue and caught it, like a child catching snowflakes.

The noise in his head was getting weaker now, quieter. He lost himself in a frenzy of sword work, hacking inelegantly at the neck, slashing like a farmer, not a samurai. Eventually he became aware that he was killing nothing but the blood-soaked earth of the cave.

Looking around him, he saw that the dragon's head was lying motionless on the ground, separated from its body. The ugly butchery of his sword work was plain to see. Taro lurched away and began to walk back down the mountainside, burned beyond recognition, stained with blood—some his own. He made it perhaps half a *ri* before he collapsed, and before he passed out, a single thought crossed his mind.

It had not been an execution a samurai would take pride in.

But it was good enough, for a ninja.

CHAPTER 46

Jun was higher up and saw the body first. Hiro broke into a run and caught up with the other boy as he knelt by Taro. Hiro saw him try to extract Kusanagi from Taro's hands. He was surprised by how plain the sword was, how little ornamented. It was just a two-edged blade with a leather pommel. But it kind of . . . pulsed. Or throbbed. It was like being close to a very dangerous animal.

"What are you doing?" said Hiro.

Jun let go of the sword's pommel like it was a snake. "Nothing," he said. "I wanted to make him comfortable." It was true that Taro was gripping the sword hard, his fingers wrapped partly around its blade. Blood trickled from them.

Hiro stopped thinking about Jun then, because he saw what had been done to Taro. He gasped. "Is he alive?" he asked. He felt that his stomach might drop out of his body; he was sickened, and he was horrified. This was his best friend, and Hiro was too late. He had not been able to save him. He had not been able to do anything. His best friend in the world was broken.

Dead.

"Breathing. Just." Jun held up a mirror to Taro's nose and showed Hiro the condensation that formed on it. Hiro let out all the breath he had been holding without realizing it. Tears were on his face. Alive! Taro was alive! He could smell blood, though, and charred meat. Emotions of black and red roiled in him like a whirlpool. Alive! But horribly, horribly injured.

Taro's one eye was closed. The other was gone from its socket, that whole side of his face a twisted mess of burned and blackened skin. His clothes had been roasted from his left-hand side, so that he was half-naked—though from a distance, such were his burns, Hiro had thought he was still attired all in black. His left hand was missing, along with a good length of his forearm. Blood soaked the ground on which he lay.

Beside him, shining in the grass, was the Buddha ball. Hiro stooped and picked it up. He tucked it into his cloak.

"Come," said Jun. "You can help me carry him."

Gently, ever so gently, Hiro took his friend's legs as Jun got his hands under Taro's shoulders, and they lifted him up.

"At the next village," said Jun, "we'll find a healer." Taro was still clinging to the sword; it rattled a little as they moved.

"What happened to him?" asked Hiro, his voice breaking. "What happened to my friend?"

Jun looked at Hiro and frowned. "A dragon happened to him."

By the time they reached the nearest village—those closest to the mountain had been burned from the map by the dragon—many of Taro's open wounds had healed over. Hiro doubted that his friend's eye or hand would ever regenerate, though.

Jun produced money from somewhere. Gold, Hiro noticed. Jun asked for directions to the healer and paid the old crone to take Taro, to cover him in poultices that Hiro suspected would be less effective than Taro's own vampire blood. Jun knew that Taro was a vampire, of course, but that didn't mean he knew what to do with an injured one.

Taro had still not woken up. Then, after finally managing to extricate the sword from Taro's grasp, so that the crone would not be tempted to steal it, Hiro and Jun returned to the mountain. Jun felt they needed proof of the dragon's death, so that Taro could claim the reward when he woke.

To begin with, Jun took Kusanagi, but Hiro just looked at it and shook his head. Jun shrugged, handing the sword over. Hiro strapped it to his side, noticing as he did so how light it was.

They climbed up into hell.

Coming into the cave, Hiro was appalled. Blood and scorch marks were everywhere, but these were nothing to the dragon curled dead in the center. Hiro had never seen a dragon before. He hoped, now, that he would never see a living one. It was huge—easily the size of a city street, with teeth as long as a man's arm. Its lifeless head lay close to its body.

"Gods," said Jun. "What a mess."

Hiro looked at it. Something struck him: This wasn't the aftermath of a fight for a title, for twenty thousand koku. *This was something else. He understood suddenly what Taro was doing. He was fulfilling what he thought was his destiny. Killing the dragon, taking Kusanagi back to Edo.*

He intended to become shogun. Even if he didn't know it consciously, it was what he was fighting for.

Jun and Hiro approached. Close up, it was obvious they would never be able to lift the head, much less carry it back to Edo. Jun took out a knife.

"We'll take a horn," he said.

Alternating, for it was arm-deadening work, they sawed one of the horns from the dragon's head. Even this was cumbersome and heavy. Hiro carried it, of course. Jun was a stripling next to him.

For what felt like hours, they traipsed down the mountainside, Hiro sweating under the weight of the horn. When they came back to the healer's hut, she was muttering incantations over Taro's body, waving mamoni *charms in the air. Hiro came and stood next to his friend.*

Just then Taro's eye opened.

"The spirit is expelled!" said the old woman. "The charms have worked their magic!"

Hiro smiled. Let her think so.

"Need . . . speak . . . alone," whispered Taro.

Hiro nodded to the old woman. She bowed and left them. Jun, too, left and closed the door behind him.

"What is it?" said Hiro. He thought perhaps Taro would apologize for cutting him off, for his reaction to Hiro's betrayal. He was prepared to tell him to forget about it. He would say that if Taro could forgive him for going behind his back, then he could forgive Taro his anger.

"Blood. Need . . . blood."

Hiro closed his eyes a moment. He understood—Taro was always a survivor. He didn't hesitate, however, just rolled up his sleeve. He cast around for a knife but didn't see one. Just Taoist charms, sutras, candles. He remembered Kusanagi at his waist. He took out the sword, unsheathed it. Drew it along his palm, biting his tongue. The sword was shockingly sharp—he cut much deeper than he had intended to.

Then he held his hand over Taro's mouth, the gesture almost like smothering, though he was giving life, not taking it away. Taro latched onto the wound, began to feed. Hiro stood, eyes closed. He could feel himself begin to sway, and the room began to rock like a ship on the sea.

When he couldn't stand it anymore, he pulled his hand away and tucked it under his other armpit, stanching the bleeding. Taro levered himself into a sitting position. Hiro imagined they had swapped skin tones—Taro's was ruddier now, more healthy. Hiro, on the other hand—he checked his reflection in the shining side of Kusanagi—yes, he was paler, some of the force leeched from him. But Taro was his best friend and had saved him once. He owed him more than a portion of his blood. He owed him it all.

"My eye?" said Taro. He was blinking with his good one, trying to assess the limits of his vision, it seemed.

"Gone. I'm sorry."

Taro looked down at his missing hand. "I am a little reduced," he said.

"But you killed the dragon," said Hiro softly. "You'll be the most famous man in Japan."

"Kusanagi?"

Hiro handed back the sword, still slick with his blood. Taro weighed it in his hands, nodding. Then he put it down beside him. "What about the ball?" he asked. His tone was neutral, but there was a charge in the air, and Hiro felt that this was a moment on which everything depended.

"It's here," said Hiro, withdrawing the ball from his cloak. "I can take it away if you like. Hide it. Throw it in one of the ravines, where the fires are still burning."

"No," said Taro. "You were right to save it." He reached out and took the ball. "It saved my life, actually."

"It . . ." Hiro felt a weight he hadn't known was there lift from his heart. He hardly dared to believe that his decision, when he pulled the ball from the sea, might have been right.

"Helped me to kill the dragon. Without it I would have died." Taro fixed his good eye on his friend. "Your debt is paid," he said, in a more solemn tone. "I saved your life. Now you have saved mine. You're free. You don't have to stay with me anymore." Taro turned away, and Hiro thought he saw the light catch on moisture in his one working eye.

Hiro paused.

"What if I wanted to stay with you?" he said finally.

Taro turned back to him. "You don't want to leave?"

"No."

"Well," said Taro, "if I wasn't a fearless, fearsome dragon slayer—"

"Which you are."

"Which I am . . . I would say that you're my best friend and that I love you, and that I'm sorry for how I treated you after the inland sea."

"It's a good job you are a fearless, fearsome dragon slayer," said Hiro.

"Why?"

"Because otherwise you'd be in danger of turning soft."

Taro laughed, and Hiro laughed with him. He touched Taro's shoulder. "I'm sorry too," he said. "And the other stuff you said. Now let's go and make you shogun."

"Did I say that was what I wanted?" said Taro, surprised.

"No," said Hiro. "You didn't have to."

CHAPTER 47

It was as they crossed the Nihonbachi bridge that they noticed, for the first time, the lack of guards.

Taro leaned on his stick. He had walked with it for the last five *ri*, having been carried before that by Hiro and Jun on a stretcher. After a while he had no longer been able to bear the humiliation. Now he hobbled along, using a staff Hiro had carved from an oak sapling. His eye had not grown back, of course, nor had his hand. But his skin, which had been a mess of bleeding and suppurating wounds, had healed to a silvery mass of scars. They had stopped at every inn they came to—not because they wanted to drag out the journey, but because Taro couldn't manage any more than a couple of *ri* a day. On the stretcher, the pain of his knitting skin was too great. With the stick, he grew too frustrated, hating his slow pace.

And tired. That too.

Hiro and Jun were a little way ahead, Hiro holding the cloth-wrapped package that contained the dragon's horn. The three of them had fallen into an easy companionship, though Taro didn't think Jun would ever be a friend. He was a strange boy, still quiet of disposition. Useful, though. He had money, and contacts, and had made the journey much easier than it could have been. What was nice for Taro was to speak to Hiro again, and the pair of them had spent much of the journey on their own while Jun scouted ahead, or hunted. They discussed Hana, her staying in Shirahama, what this meant for the future. Taro was no closer to a solution, but it was good to know he had a friend with whom to work on one.

The other thing Taro didn't know was what he was going to do when he got to the palace. Hold up Kusanagi and demand that the shogun step down? Challenge the boy to a duel? Both ideas seemed absurd—and no others seemed to be presenting themselves.

Now Jun peered over the bridge, discussing something with Hiro. Taro drew level with them. There was something odd about the way the people on the bridge were moving, and it took Taro a while to work out what it was.

Then he did.

They were all leaving Edo, not a single person going in their direction, into the city. And they were moving too quickly. Hurrying. The impression Taro had was of nervousness. Heads glancing back. Then he spotted that many of them were carrying belongings with them.

"Where are the guards?" asked Hiro.

"I don't know," said Jun. Usually there were samurai of the shogunate on the bridge, watching over the flow of traffic. Now they were nowhere to be seen.

Taro stepped in front of one of the people leaving the city. A harried-looking woman, a child at her hip. "What's going on?" he said.

"We don't know. There's fighting in the streets."

"People say the shogun is dead," said a man who was passing.

"Dead?" said Taro. He remembered the young boy on horseback, shooting dogs. He had just been thinking about how to challenge

him, how to claim his destiny, and now it seemed like the decision no longer mattered.

"He's gone mad, I heard," said an old woman. "Ordered all his men to commit seppuku. Best to turn around and go back where you came from."

Taro looked at Jun and Hiro. They both shrugged. "We've come this far," said Hiro. So they forged on over the bridge, against the current of the people and carts. From the city, several plumes of smoke rose, but it was impossible to say if they were ordinary cooking fires, or something more sinister.

They crossed more bridges, drawing closer to the Palace of Long Life. This time there were no street peddlers, no performing monkeys, no street magicians, no purveyors of vegetables and fish. Instead there was chaos. Everywhere they were assailed by the sounds of shouting, crying, and fighting. Some of the people they passed were leaving—others were breaking into houses, or carrying objects they had obviously stolen or looted. They ignored Taro and his companions, for the most part.

At least, they did until Hiro dropped the dragon's horn.

They were deep into the pleasure quarter at this point, the cheaper end of it, anyway. Not the floating world of the island where the best geisha worked, but the narrow streets where last time they had seen the *tsujigimi* with their mats. As soon as the package hit the ground, it rolled—there hadn't been rain here for months, with the dragon drying the air with its fires. The horn came out, stopped against a stone in the road.

It seemed like in an instant, every man on the street was looking at them—and Taro realized for the first time the fear and greed that was in their eyes. "What's that?" said the closest man, a wiry character with a bald head.

"It's nothing," said Hiro unconvincingly.

"Doesn't look like nothing."

Taro saw another man peering at him. This one had a tattoo on his arm. Not a good sign. It meant he was *yakuza*, a member of the criminal fraternity who ran gambling houses and the lower class of brothel. His eyes ran down Taro's face, his left arm. Right down to where his hand should have been.

He's seeing my burns, thought Taro. You didn't get to be in the *yakuza*—no, you didn't get to be in the *yakuza* and survive—if you were an idiot. Taro could almost see the calculation taking place in the man's brains. If anyone were to know he had killed the dragon and was on his way to claim the prize, it would not bode well for him. Not when everyone knew that if they could take his place, they'd win land and a title—an income for life, that amounted to. After all, how was he going to prove it? By turning up with the dragon horn. Anyone taking it off him could do the same. . . .

"It's a dragon horn!" the *yakuza* shouted. "He's only killed the bloody dragon!"

Sure enough.

Taro didn't think. Some part of him that wasn't his conscious mind counted the men in the little street. No more than ten. Easy. He whipped up the stick he used for walking, smashing it into the man's face, feeling the nose break under the impact, maybe some of the teeth, too. Immediately he whirled, stick spinning to—

No. He tried to whirl—

His leg gave way beneath him. He went down on his other knee, hard, cursing. The blow he had intended for the next man's head connected with his stomach, winding him, but not severely. The *yakuza* bent over for a moment, then came up with a knife in his hand, making for Taro.

Taro glanced over at Hiro. He was flipping a man who had made the mistake of running at him, using all that energy and momentum to catapult the moving body into the wall behind him. Jun, meanwhile, had produced a nasty-looking knife from somewhere. Full of surprises, that boy. Taro watched as Jun let a thrust from a short-sword go harmlessly past him, then impaled the heart of his attacker.

All that, of course, in a moment.

Taro turned his eye back to his own opponent and got the stick up just in time to deflect a stab. He turned the stick, brought the other side down on the man's wrist, and had the satisfaction of hearing it snap. This was what he lived for, he might have realized, if he was capable of thought in this moment. Losing himself in the fight, in the kill-time.

It was a kind of meditation.

He jammed the stick into the ground, pulled himself up to standing. He roared as he swung the stick to knock the man out—

And he stopped, seeing Hiro and Jun lower their weapons too, backing toward him.

There were more *yakuza* entering the street, all armed with unpleasant-looking weapons. More *yakuza*. And he was crippled, not capable of fighting at his usual strength. He turned around. More behind, too.

Dozens more.

A club caught Taro on the back of the head. He staggered, still swinging wildly with his stick; more by luck than anything else, he struck his attacker's jaw. The man's head snapped sideways, and he dropped to the ground, unconscious. A moment later Taro heard Jun call out as a dagger tore his arm. Blood spattered on the cobbles. Hiro was grappling with a burly *yakuza* who was trying to make off with the dragon's horn. Giving Hiro an advantage was the fact that another *yakuza* was attempting to get his hands on it too, whacking his supposed companion on the back with what looked like a whip.

Taro cast his eye around desperately, looking for an exit from the alleyway. Nothing—just houses on either side, a walled passage, like the one in which Shusaku died. Taro had faced death so many times now that he was surprised it still scared him. He wasn't ready to meet Shusaku again; there were things he wanted to do. If he died now, he would never have the chance to apologize to Hana. He would never have the chance to fulfill his destiny.

One of the men came at him, a dragon tattooed on his neck. Taro ducked, tripped him with the stick—he felt the Buddha ball press into his side as he bent down. The man's head collided with the wooden door of the house behind Taro. He slumped to the cobbles.

That was when Taro noticed the door.

There was a red lantern hanging by it, not lit right now. But where normally there would have been *o-fuda* charms, or red monkey carvings, to ward off evil spirits, there was nothing at all. Hope flared in Taro, like a torch lighting in the darkness. He knew only one street where the businesses along it would not need, or want, such protection.

He turned to the others. "In here," he said. He didn't wait for any response—he just lifted his good leg and kicked out, straight forward from a bent knee, a kick Shusaku had shown him that was usually used to force an opponent backward, buying time. The door shattered inward, the top hinge breaking, the remaining boards hanging crazily from the bottom hinge. Taro was moving in already.

There was a woman in front of him. He wasn't sure if it was the same woman, the same house, as before.

"What are you—," she began, but he pushed her aside, plunging farther into the candlelit gloom. He heard footsteps behind him and hoped it was Hiro and Jun. He spun on the spot, stick up. Hiro came skidding to a halt.

"Hold them as long as you can," he said. Hiro nodded. The narrow corridor would force the *yakuza* to come one by one.

Taro carried on, going through the open door at the end of the corridor. The space inside the ground floor of the house was made up of a single room, like a warehouse, but it was subdivided by silk screens, painted in the Chinese style with peacocks, carp, cranes, and mountains. A dull red light glowed through the screens. As Taro went deeper into the room, he began to make out the customers, lying on beds. Smoke was rising from just off to his left, and for a moment he panicked, thinking it might just be an opium den. But then, resolving out of the penumbra, he saw an incense stick smoldering. The woman lying on the bed beside it had two circular holes in her neck, trickling blood.

Yes.

In Taro's head, a vague plan had been forming. He could hear sounds of fighting behind him. *Let Hiro hold them a little longer*, he thought. Taro didn't have a blade on him, apart from Kusanagi, and he didn't want to take that out from its hiding place under his clothes. He sank his teeth into his wrist instead, tearing as he bit, like a dog feeding. Blood swelled, then poured. He started with the woman below him. Her eyes were wide and staring; there was no way of telling if she saw him or not.

He gently opened her jaw, let the blood trickle into her mouth. Guilt gnawed at him, more painful than the wound in his wrist. But he reminded himself of what the woman vampire had said, last time he found himself on this street—most of these people would die anyway, growing sicker and weaker the more they were fed on. At least this way—if he turned them—some of them would survive.

Without waiting to see if the blood had worked, he moved on to the next addict. A young man this time. This one's mouth was open; he let his blood fall in. Then the next, and the next, and the next. He moved around the room, between and around the screens, absorbed in his task. He realized he must have gone all the way round when he saw the woman he had started with crouching on her bed, alert, blood filling the whites of her eyes.

Just then Hiro burst into the room, bleeding and panting. Taro couldn't see the dragon horn. He tried to remember if Hiro had been holding it when he saw him in the corridor.

"Coming," was all Hiro said. Jun was just behind him, holding his arm to his side as if it was broken. The woman Taro had turned didn't hesitate—she leaped right at Jun, obviously seeing him as the weaker target. Her pounce was like a cat's, hands stretched out in front of her like claws, mouth open, teeth long and sharp. Jun didn't even get his weapon up in time—she flew toward him and—

Taro's stick formed a blurred arc in the air, then connected heavily with her head, sending her sprawling into a screen, knocking it over. She had just been turned and she was strong, but he was more than that. He was trained. He glanced at her crumpled body, a little ashamed, but he didn't have any time for that. The Buddha ball was in his hands. And besides, she would soon recover—his blood was in her veins.

As the first of the *yakuza* poured into the room, he was already falling through clear skies toward the islands of Japan below him, droplets of steel in water. He allowed himself to be in the Buddha ball and the human realm at the same time, pouring all his *qi* into a single call, the call of his blood to his blood, spread among the lost people in this room.

They had been fed on, again and again, and now they had fed.

It was a feeling like the harmony of different instruments, like a chorus, when his blood spoke back to him. All these vampires he had just made were uncontrolled, untrained, but he had turned them, and they recognized him as master. The room echoed with the sound of his own heartbeat in fifty chests, a rhythmic percussion that resembled an enormous, collective *yes*. He funneled his life essence into a silent voice, shouting the words in his head.

I am your master.

Leave these two. Leave my friends. A picture of Hiro and Jun formed in his head, and his one eye focused on them too.

Kill these. Feed on them. He focused now on the *yakuza*—even as he brought up his stick to parry a blow from a short-sword, even as Hiro ducked under a punch and swept a man's legs out from under him.

With a colossal effort, he unbound the new vampires, threw them forward. They surged forth like water, around him, over him. They were fresh, all of them, and Taro remembered that feeling. They moved, men and women, of all ages, so fast and fluid that the *yakuza* were taken off guard, the only ones in a fighting stance those who had been clashing with Hiro and Jun. Some were lifted from their feet even as they came through the door, slammed backward to the ground.

Then the beat of Taro's own blood, echoing back at him, was drowned out, as the room resounded with the sound of screaming.

CHAPTER 48

There was a sickness in Taro's soul as he looked around the room. Some of the *yakuza* had actually survived—he had commanded the vampires to leave them, then had told those *yakuza* to run. They had complied, more than willingly, whimpering as they lurched from the slaughterhouse. Most, though, were dead or dying. He chose an already dead one who looked strong, thick banded muscles below his tattoos, and knelt to drink deeply himself. He needed the strength, after turning his little army.

"What have you done?" said Hiro, glancing warily at the new recruits.

"Saved our lives," said Taro. He gestured at the corpses. "Find the horn," he said.

Hiro wandered off, head down.

Jun, on the other hand, seemed impressed. He was watching the vampires as they came to stand behind Taro, obeying his silent order. "They are like slaves," he said.

Taro frowned, uncomfortable. "Yes."

A little while later, Hiro—who had disappeared down the corridor—came back with the horn in his hands. It was stained with fresh, red blood. He jerked his head back toward the door. "Come on then," he said, without meeting Taro's eye. "Let's get this to the shogun. If he's still alive."

Jun nodded. "We should hurry," he said. "Before more come."

Taro squeezed the ball. He sent out a thought. *Guard us. Half in front. Half behind.* Then he headed to the exit.

"You're bringing them with you?" asked Hiro.

"What else do you want me to do with them? Anyway, the streets could be teeming with *yakuza*, for all we know. Better that we should be protected."

Out on the street, the new vampires fanned before them and after them, sniffing the air, moving silkily along the ground. Taro could understand, suddenly, why people were afraid of vampires. Why they were seen as evil spirits. These he had just turned would drain babies, he thought, if they came across them. He wasn't sure why he had been so different—perhaps because he'd been running from ninjas at the time. Anyway, he was glad he *had* been different, when he was turned—but for the first time he could see, really see, why Shusaku had considered it such a bad idea to confess to Lord Tokugawa that he had turned his son.

Or maybe the minds of these ones had simply been weakened by all the blood they had given up, in return for the bliss of being bitten.

He hoped it was that.

Negotiating the complex maze of streets and bridges, they drew ever nearer to the palace, the vampires flanking them. The journey was relatively uneventful now—those who did want to make trouble were soon discouraged by the sight of the vampires or, in a couple of unfortunate incidents, their teeth. The city was still a mess, though, with looters and semi-uniformed soldiers running amok everywhere. They passed quite a few corpses, many of them wearing the shogun's *mon*.

When they came to the gates, they were halfway through before a nervous-looking guard peered out from the gatehouse. It looked to Taro like he had torn the *mon* from his chest, so as not to show his allegiance, which struck Taro as strange and worrying.

"Halt," the guard said, his voice not as confident as the word suggested. "You can't go in there."

Taro indicated the men and women he had brought with him. "These are vampires," he said. "*Kyuuketsuki*. I can order them to tear you apart."

The guard hesitated still, so Taro sent out a thought.

Show him your teeth.

An instant later the guard was shut behind the door of the gatehouse, and they were going deeper into the palace, through the corridors and gardens.

Here, inside the shogun's palace, which had once been the palace of emperors, it was quiet. Dead quiet. It made Taro anxious. Not a single person greeted them, or even walked past them—no one was to be seen in any of the paper windows. Most disconcertingly, there were bloodstains at odd intervals on the ground, as if a great running battle had been fought, but there were no bodies anywhere.

"I don't like this," said Hiro.

"You always say that," said Taro.

"I know. Because you're always dragging me into dangerous situations."

Taro smiled. His friend almost sounded like his old self. "Well," he said, "I have to try to get rid of you *somehow*. I kept thinking you'd get the message, but—"

Hiro punched him in the arm—the sound was loud in the courtyard they were passing through, uncomfortably loud. They both shut up after that, their smiles fading. They went through a door, and then Taro could see the way they had gone when they'd found the shogun shooting dogs. He began to follow the path.

"Where are you going?" said Jun. He had stopped by an ornate door.

"This is the way we went last time," said Taro.

"I know. But that time the shogun was practicing his *inu-oi*.

This is the most direct route to the throne room."

"It is?"

"It is."

Taro stopped. "How do you know that?" he asked. He didn't mean for it to come out sounding pointed, but it did.

Jun didn't seem to notice, though. He shrugged. "Shusaku showed me the floor plans of many castles when I was assisting him. He thought I would make a good ninja one day." A touch of pride had entered his voice.

"Lead the way, then," said Taro. If Jun had gotten angry, or defensive, he might have been more suspicious. But he didn't seem to notice the accusation beneath Taro's words, and if he did, he didn't seem to care about it.

Taro went over to the door, which Jun was holding open. He sent a message to the vampires, asking them to follow, but not too close. *If I call you*, he said to them, *come to my aid*. Jun went ahead, down a corridor lined with tapestries. Beautifully decorated *katana* swords were attached to the walls too, in between the fabric hangings. A red silk carpet that looked to be of ancient Chinese manufacture covered the floor.

As they walked, Hiro hung back, then drew close to Taro to whisper something. Taro didn't catch it. "What was that?" he said.

Hiro grimaced at him, putting a finger to his lips. He glanced ahead at Jun, who was following the curve of the hallway out of view. "We never told him about the first time we came here," he said, under his breath. "About the dogs."

Cold fingers stroked Taro's spine. "We must have," he said. "Or how would he know?"

Hiro shrugged. "I don't know. But I don't—"

"Like it?"

"No."

Taro closed his eye, scrubbing his face with his hands. "No. Nor do I," he said. "But we can't go back now." He reached under his cloak, taking out Kusanagi, swathed in cloth. He unwrapped the legendary sword, then let it hang easily in his hand. He pointed to where Jun had vanished around the corner. He could hear the shuffle of the vampires behind them. "Let's get into a dangerous situation."

On the other side of the corner, they almost bumped into Jun. He was standing in front of a door carved of oak, and inlaid with ivory. He nodded, then opened it with a flourish.

Jun stepped in first; Taro followed him. His blood froze in his veins.

He recognized the throne room, only this time they were entering it from the side, not from the back. It was in shadow—the shutters being closed, and no candles lit. The Three Treasures hung from the wall behind the throne—no, not the Three Treasures, but two treasures and a fake.

This, though, was not what had made his blood freeze.

Sitting on the throne was the shogun—or more accurately, what had been the shogun. His own head was cradled in his lap, his neck cut clean through, as if by a diamond-sharp samurai sword. He was drenched in blood, which even now pulsed slowly from his neck. He had been killed only minutes before. His young man's face looked balefully, accusingly, at Taro from his waist, the whole effect sickening and horrifying.

"Quite the scene, isn't it?" said a voice that Taro knew, from behind the throne. A figure stepped forward—his face for the moment obscured by the gloom of the unlit room.

Oh, no, no, no, thought Taro. *Let me be mistaken. . . .*

He was not.

Lord Tokugawa Ieyasu walked into a narrow beam of light shafting from a closed shutter. He held a *katana* in his hand, dripping with blood, the noise tapping like a heartbeat, like a beetle behind a wall.

"Taro," he said. "I see you've brought the sword."

Taro opened his mouth, but no words came forth to his mind.

"Speechless, I see," said Lord Tokugawa. "That is all right. We do not need your words. You are most welcome here, Taro."

Lord Tokugawa paused. And then he spoke a sentence that stopped Taro's breath in his lungs.

"You are *truly* welcome . . . my son."

CHAPTER 49

Taro looked to Hiro, who was staring too.

"You—you know who I am?"

"I have always known it," said Lord Tokugawa. "I know, too, that you are a vampire."

"But—if you knew—"

"Why did I let you labor in the darkness? Why did I leave you to the mercy of Lord Oda?"

Taro nodded. It was all he could manage.

"Did you not *kill* Lord Oda?" said Lord Tokugawa. "*That* is why I didn't reveal what I knew."

"B-but—when we were here, before . . . Why didn't you say anything?"

Lord Tokugawa pointed to the sword in Taro's hand. "I needed you to bring me that," he said. "I didn't want you distracted by a family reunion. Speaking of which . . ." He made a show of peering around the room. "Did you not bring the charming Hana, daughter of my greatest enemy? When I heard you had killed Lord Oda,

I was overjoyed. When I heard you had fallen in love with his daughter . . . I asked myself if you had quite lost your senses."

"She left me," said Taro.

Lord Tokugawa nodded. "Good." Then he pushed the body in the throne. The shogun pitched forward onto the wooden floor. The head rolled away from it, drawing a high-pitched squeaking sound from the boards. Taro guessed they had been calibrated to sing when an assassin tried to creep over them, to protect the shogun.

In this case it had not worked. The killer had been behind him—all the time.

"Why did you do it?" said Taro.

Lord Tokugawa laughed, as if it was a stupid question. "He was a little in the way of the throne," he said. He sat down on it, ignoring the blood. "Of course, I couldn't just kill him and expect the people to welcome me with open arms. But when I heard you were on your way, with Kusanagi, and with the dragon's horn . . . I knew the moment had come at last."

"You heard?" said Hiro. "How?"

Jun walked away from them then, toward the throne. Taro had known it in the heartbeat before the boy's feet moved. "I sent a pigeon," Jun said. "From the road." He went to stand beside Lord Tokugawa, and a little behind. Just as Lord Tokugawa had stood behind the shogun. He said nothing to the daimyo, though—just stood with his hands folded. Taro thought Jun might mention the vampires outside, but he didn't. Maybe they had already been dealt with.

"Traitor," said Hiro.

Lord Tokugawa waved the word away, as if it were an irritating insignificance. "Now," he said to Taro. "If you could give me Kusanagi, the dragon horn, and the Buddha ball, I will ask for no more of your time."

"Give you . . ."

"All of it, yes." Lord Tokugawa had a thin, hard smile on his lips.

"You knew about the Buddha ball too?" said Taro. He was holding it under his robe.

"My dear boy," said Lord Tokugawa. "My dear boy, I planted the very *idea* of it in your mind. You didn't really think you had a destiny, did you?" He laughed that hollow laugh again.

"What do you mean?" asked Hiro. His voice was rough with anger.

Lord Tokugawa sighed. "I hate having to explain myself. Now, guards, if you could just—"

"I'm your son," said Taro, and Lord Tokugawa turned back to look at him again, the expression on his face one of irritation more than anything else, as if he had dismissed Taro from his attention and had not expected to have to return him to it. "I think you owe it to me." Inside his mind was the water underneath the waves, in a windy bay—tumultuous, turbulent, turning and turning, whipping up sand and foam.

A strange expression passed over Lord Tokugawa's face—halfway between a smile and a grimace. "Very well," he said. "Many years ago I first heard the story that only the son of an ama could claim the Buddha ball. I knew the ball was essential, the first object I would require in order to claim the empire. It would give me control over rice production, and with that, over all the money in the land."

Taro closed his eye. He had known it himself—from the beginning. The clue was in the prize, even. Twenty thousand *koku* for killing the dragon . . . and what was a *koku* but a unit of wealth, made out of rice. One koku—one samurai fed—one year.

The ground began to fade beneath his feet.

"So, I found and seduced an ama woman." The voice was like a pestle, like a mill wheel, grinding Taro's existence down to nothing. "It took a year of my life, but I have always been patient. I waited till she gave me a son, then I left one of my bows with you as a mark of your provenance. Eventually, when you were the right age, I leaked your existence to one of Lord Oda's spies. That man always thought he had one up on me—but in reality I had several thousand up on him.

“He sent ninjas to kill you, of course. So predictable. But I sent one to save you—the best of them all. I sent Shusaku. He knew everything, of course. All along.” There was a cruel barb in Lord Tokugawa’s voice as he said this, and it caught in Taro’s mind like a hook in the mouth of a fish, made him collapse to his knees.

“Not Shusaku . . . ,” he implored. He thought he had felt betrayal after Hiro recovered the ball, after Hana left him. He had not felt betrayal at all. He wanted to die at that moment. He wanted to die so that it wouldn’t be true that Shusaku betrayed him, that his friend and mentor could have treated him in this way.

“Oh, very much Shusaku,” said Lord Tokugawa. “He has always been a key element in my plans. It is a shame he is not here today, to witness my final victory. I believe he would be pleased.”

“You’re crazy,” said Hiro slowly.

“No,” said Lord Tokugawa. “Just very, very clever.” He put his hand down on the arm of the throne, then lifted it, making a moue of disgust, his fingers slippery with blood. He wiped them on his silk robe.

“The next part,” he continued, “was to arrange for the prophetess to tell you about the ball. I added in the part about you being destined to be shogun, of course. A touch of genius, in my opinion.”

The whole room swayed. Jun was grinning; it made Taro feel sick. “You . . .”

Lord Tokugawa paid him no attention. “It may surprise you to learn,” he said, “that the majority of people are good, not bad. I had an idea—which proved to be correct, by the way—that you *might* try to find the ball because you wanted power, but that you would be practically guaranteed to try to find it if you felt it was your *destiny*. People will do all sorts of things if they believe it is fate.”

“So . . . ,” said Taro hesitantly, “the story the prophetess told us . . . it wasn’t true?”

“Some of it was. The bit about the ball being lost at sea, and only the son of an ama being able to find it. But the bit about you being shogun? Pure invention, I’m afraid.”

"Why would she lie?" asked Taro.

"Oh, love, of course. She loved me. The poor fool."

Taro felt a presence beside him; Hiro took him by the arm, steadying him, and then lifted him to his feet. "None of this changes who you are," he said in a low voice.

"Yes," said Taro. "Yes, it does."

"What are you two muttering about?" asked Lord Tokugawa. He didn't wait for an answer. "The next part, I have to confess I didn't plan. Originally I felt that you would go to get the ball. But I had underestimated your desire to avenge your foster father, the pathetic fisherman your mother married. When it became obvious you weren't going to rest until you had faced Lord Oda, I contrived to send Shusaku to kill Hana."

Taro frowned at that. "I thought we were going to kill Lord Oda."

"No. Always Hana. In revenge for the attempt on you. It was part of my plan, and I couldn't let it go. It would have made Lord Oda see me as weak."

"And Shusaku knew . . ."

"That your mission was to kill Hana, not her father? Yes. Of course he knew."

Taro felt his knees buckling again. Hiro held him up.

"Of course," went on Lord Tokugawa, "you didn't kill her, and once again my plans went awry. But you were still desperate to take your revenge—even more so after that hothead Kenji Kira attacked you on Mount Hiei. I used Shusaku to deliver new guns to the Ikko-ikki, guns capable of firing in the rain. I knew that once you had the Buddha ball, you would be able to render Lord Oda's guns useless. I waited—I thought it might take years for you to find the ball. But it didn't. Within half a year you had it, and Lord Oda was attacking you on that mountainside, and everything I had planned came together in his death. After that?" He pointed to Kusanagi. "After that I needed only the lost sword of the emperors."

Taro held Kusanagi in his hands. "You could have just found it yourself," he said.

"I don't do things myself," said Lord Tokugawa with contempt. "Besides, I really did think it was at Miyajima. A daimyo cannot simply attack a monastery. Especially not such a rich one."

"So the dragon . . ."

"Was never important. I woke it myself." Taro had not realized he could feel worse than he already did, but it turned out he could. It was his father's fault that he had lost his eye, his hand. He had faced two dragons, real monsters, and neither of them was as monstrous as Lord Tokugawa appeared now, in his eyes.

Taro pointed to his stump. "All this," he said. "And for what? Why would you wake a dragon, of your own free will?"

"It was only a means to an end," continued Lord Tokugawa. "A way to make you get the sword. Of course I wrote to the abbot at Mount Hiei too, to ensure that you would take up the challenge." Lord Tokugawa saw the expression on Taro's face. "Yes. I am afraid he is one of my agents too. But now all my scheming has come to a head. You have brought me the ball and the sword. I have the power to starve or feed my peasants, and so the poor are in my grasp. I have the sword Amaterasu gave to her descendants, and so the educated rich and the religious must bow to me. I have it all."

"You did all this," said Taro, "so you could be shogun?"

"No," said Lord Tokugawa. "I did all this so I could be emperor." He made a broad gesture with his two hands. "Now," he said, "I have talked enough. Bring me the sword and the ball. The horn, too. I will say that the dragon sacrificed itself, to bring about an end to the rule of the pretenders. I will say the age of emperors is come again."

Taro glanced back at the open door behind him. "No," he said, edging toward it.

"I very much feared you would say that," said Lord Tokugawa. He clapped his hands, and samurai came pouring into the room—from the end, from behind the throne, from the door Taro had just looked at. They were all armed, and they all wore the hollyhock *mon* of house Tokugawa. "Kill them," said Lord Tokugawa. "Both of them."

Taro stared at him in horror. Last time he had seen his father, he hadn't noticed the hardness in his eyes, the wiry frame that bespoke a lifetime of sword practice and riding. This was someone with not a single soft surface about him. "But I'm your son," Taro said, as the samurai closed in.

"No," said Lord Tokugawa. "You are a means to an end."

Then the first blade met Taro's skin.

CHAPTER 50

THE HOME OF THE PROPHETESS,

FOSTER MOTHER TO HEIKO AND YUKIKO

TWO YEARS EARLIER

Kenji Kira swept one of the bowls off the table and onto the floor, where it smashed into pieces. It was a gesture meant to intimidate, and it worked—despite herself the prophetess was startled, and then she was angered to see the gratification in his eyes when he perceived her fear.

She knew she was going to die here—not because she could see it in the future, but because she knew how samurai operated. Right now she was a prophetess, but once she had been a woman in love with a samurai, and she had seen men opened up with swords, from throat to belly. She was familiar with their code, with their honor. She had seen those they killed with their honor, those they forced to kill themselves.

She still saw them, sometimes, when she slept.

Kenji Kira—she knew his name, had witnessed his barbarities on other battlefields than this one, which was her home—was sucking on something, staring at her with a look that told her he wasn't just angry, he was mad. She hoped that Heiko and Yukiko were far away already. She hoped that Shusaku would guard them, as he had guarded her before, even if he didn't know how she was betraying him and his young charge.

Betrayal.

The word stuck in her mind. Why was it that loyalty to one person always had to mean hurting others? She told herself it might not do too much harm, the lie she had told.

But she knew it would. It had to. It was for the purpose of doing harm that Lord Tokugawa, who had once been a young samurai—who had once loved her, she was sure of it, as she loved him—had asked her to do it. And she owed him, didn't she? He had saved her, again and again.

From death. From her parents. From prostitution.

She owed him everything, including her life. Lying to the boy was nothing, spinning him that ridiculous tale about having a destiny, that preposterous prophecy.

And yet, why did it lodge in her mind, sharp and shining? Why did she feel she had helped to put into motion something very bad indeed, something that would cause nearly as much damage in the world as the stupid honor of the samurai, rippling out from this moment like water from a stone?

Perhaps, though, just perhaps, she could atone a little for what she had done to that poor boy Taro. By dying at Kenji Kira's hand, and giving him more time to escape. Of course, he might escape from Lord Oda, but he would never escape from his own father, who had planned his life from the very beginning.

This—the way that Lord Tokugawa had planned everything from the very beginning—was the secret the prophetess knew, and Shusaku and Taro didn't. It was a secret she intended to take to the grave.

"You laid out food," Kenji Kira said. "Yet you feed on blood, do you not?" He poked the empty bowl. "Who was eating with you, when we arrived?"

"The bowls are for the spirits," she said. "I am a prophetess. I must set out food for them."

Kira sighed. He made a hand signal to one of his samurai, and the man went to stand behind her, the blade of his *katana* resting cold and sharp against her neck. "I know about your kind," he went on. "You can only be killed by decapitation, or a blade to the heart. Don't think I won't kill you if you fail to give me the information I need."

"And what information is that?"

"I want to know where the boy went. And the ninja with him, and his fat friend."

"No one like that has been here," she said, lying. It was something she knew how to do.

"Yes, they have. They were seen entering the door in your garden."

"Then perhaps they broke in for supplies."

"What about the girls?" he asked. "We are informed that two girls live with you."

Despite herself, she felt her chest constrict, and she was sure he noticed it. Heiko and Yukiko. She loved them, she was surprised to realize. At first she had taken them in because Shusaku asked it, and Shusaku was an old favorite of Lord Tokugawa's. A friend of hers, too. But she had grown fond of them over the years. Even Yukiko, who had a cold heart under that pretty exterior of hers. Cold as the snow she was named for. She was concerned about what Yukiko might become, saw violence in those shiny eyes of hers—and it didn't diminish her love for the girl by a single particle.

"They . . . are playing . . . in the woods," she said.

"Then we shall wait here for their return," said Kira. "It will be such a pleasure to meet them."

"No . . . please . . ." She cursed herself. Pathetic. If Lord Tokugawa could see her now, she who had fought by his side in battles far bloodier than this one, he would be repulsed.

She noticed that Kira was trying to grin—the effect was ghastly, as if the spirit of an animal, a fox maybe, had gotten into his body and was trying out human expressions. She noticed that he did not look well. He was too thin, too white. And she had observed the way he grimaced on seeing the fish stew on the table. He had disguised his distaste by smashing the bowl onto the floor as if to frighten her, but she thought that was only half the reason.

Much of seeing the future was just reading people from their expressions, movements, and words—no more magical than reading words on a page—and the prophetess was good at that. The best she had ever known, and she knew that without arrogance.

"Are you all right?" she asked. "You look very pale."

He blinked, then nodded to the man holding the sword to the woman's neck. "Tell me where they went. Or I give him the order."

She ignored him. "There's more fish, if you want it," she said. "I'm sure the spirits won't begrudge you it."

Kira gagged, turning from white to a pale green.

Interesting.

Time passed. She stretched out her mind—though much of being a prophetess was being able to read people, some of it was just magic, which required less skill. She closed her eyes and imagined herself into his mind.

She saw him on a battlefield, trapped by a fallen horse. He sucked dew from the ground, and moisture from the cold swords of the dead. As time passed, the bodies around him started to fill with living things, to crawl with them. Rats emerged from the stomach of the horse, chittering. Worms crawled from men's eyes and nostrils, quivering in the air. And there were flies, too. Endless flies, feasting on flesh.

She felt his horror. She felt his terror. She felt the need in him not to die like that, not to be consumed by the ravages of decomposition, of the low creatures that infest the dead.

Crack. Kira's hand struck the side of her face, snapping her head round. Her cheek stung. Kira leaned back from the table. "Now, old woman. You had better tell us where the boy has gone."

"I've seen the future," she said. "If you know anything about me, you know that I can do that. I've seen the future, and that means I know that I will never answer your questions, no matter what you do to me."

“Perhaps not. But you’ll have to endure the pain of the questioning, nevertheless.”

She smiled. “Questioning is always painful. That’s what people don’t understand about fortune-telling. But, as much agony as I feel, I will tell you nothing.” She paused. “No. Wait. I will tell you two things that you don’t know.”

“Go on,” said Kira, his voice neutral.

“The boy is going to get the Buddha ball, and he’s going to use it to kill Lord Oda.”

Kira sneered. “The Buddha ball is a silly story.”

Perhaps—perhaps not. She didn’t know if the Buddha ball was real or not, and she didn’t particularly care. What she did know was that Taro would never be shogun, as she had told him he would.

She knew this because Lord Tokugawa had come to her and asked her to do one last thing for him, for the love she had once borne him. She still did love him, in fact, but she didn’t tell him that as he stood in her garden, still slim and strong, after all those years. Then he had explained what he wanted. A boy named Taro would be coming to her—he had been seen, with his guardian Shusaku, nearby. It was important that she tell this boy the old legend, about the ama and the Buddha ball, but Lord Tokugawa wished her to add a new ending to the story.

He wished her to include a prophecy, spoken by the ama before she ascended to the Pure Land, saying that the descendant of an ama would be shogun one day—and he wished her to tell the boy that the prophecy applied to him.

“Why?” she had asked. “Why do you want me to lie to the boy?” She could see that this boy Taro was Lord Tokugawa’s son—it was clear from the daimyo’s eyes, even without going into his mind. And she did not mind lying to his son. She should have been the one to give Lord Tokugawa sons, anyway. But she was curious, nevertheless.

“I need him to recover the Buddha ball,” he had said, that old glint in his eyes that she had always liked. “Only the son of an ama can claim it. That part of the story, at least, is true. I think so, anyway."

"Then ask him to. Wouldn't that be easier?"

He sighed. "Of course not. He must feel he has a *destiny*. That way he is sure to do what I need. People will do all sorts of things, if they believe it is fate's will."

"But why do you want the ball so much, even assuming it exists?"

He looked at her with an expression mingling mild surprise and disappointment.

She thought for a moment. "Of course. You want to be shogun yourself."

This time he actually laughed. "No," he said. "Being shogun is nothing. I want to be *emperor*."

She might have laughed too—there had been no emperor in Japan for a hundred years—but something about his eyes told her not to. When Lord Tokugawa wanted a thing, he tended to get it—herself included—and, as was always said of him, he planned in years, not days. If he said he wanted to be emperor, the chances were he had worked out exactly how to do it.

"Give me one good reason I should do this," she had said.

"Because you loved me, once upon a time, and because I loved you, too," he said simply. "You are the bravest woman I know." After that it was only a distance of a few steps, a few tender words, to her bed.

And that was enough.

Now, back in her modest house, where she had brought up the ninja girls for Shusaku, who also loved Lord Tokugawa, she concentrated on the man in front of her, wanting him to suffer before he had the pleasure of killing her.

"You may think what you like about the Buddha ball," she said. "But Oda believes in it. Why do you think he wants the boy so badly? Merely because he's Tokugawa's son? Tokugawa can sire as many sons as there are leaves in a tree; he has only to find women of child-bearing age, and there are enough of those in his province."

Kira flinched, and she saw she had guessed correctly. Taro really was Tokugawa's son. What had the wily lord done—impregnated an ama so that he could make sure his own flesh and blood claimed the Buddha ball? She marveled at a man who would create a life and let it grow for fifteen years, just to achieve his ambitions.

"I really think you should take some fish," she said to Kira, who was holding on to the table now. "You do look very weak."

"I don't eat fish!" he screamed.

"No, of course," she murmured. She smiled in genuine amusement. If she couldn't smile now, when she was about to die, then when could she?

"What?" he demanded, petulant. "Something amuses you?"

"I said I would tell you two things."

Kira thought for a moment. "You did. You said the boy would get the Buddha ball, and that he would kill Lord Oda."

"That's one thing. I will tell you another, if you wish to hear it."

Kira nodded. "Very well."

"It is this," she said. She lowered her voice to a whisper. "When you die, your body will languish for many moons, consumed slowly by the creatures of the night. Worms will eat your eyes. The eggs of flies will hatch among your sinews." She paused, feeling her smile grow wider. "You cannot escape it."

He looked at her through bloodshot eyes. "You can see the future, yes?"

She nodded.

"Then you must have seen what I am about to do." He looked at the samurai behind her and made a cutting gesture with his fingers. The man swung back his sword.

"Yes," she said. "Yes, I have."

She had seen her own death, yes, she had.

But she had also seen his—she hadn't been lying about that. And in the moment before the sword struck her neck, she saw everything else, too, saw how it would all go, how it was good and all of it was good.

She was glad. She was a prophetess, and she didn't want to die with a lie in her mouth. She wanted to die knowing what would happen, and knowing it was good.

Lord Tokugawa *would* be emperor, she knew that now. He would get everything he ever wanted, and it would never be enough, and he would die miserable and alone, never having the love of a wife or children, reviled even by his own son.

She was glad about that, too.

If she couldn't have him—if she couldn't make him happy, bear him his son, then she didn't want him to be happy.

She loved him, but she was selfish, too. She had lied for him, given his son a false destiny, but he couldn't make her think kindly of him, couldn't get into her mind the way she could get into his, no matter what she owed him.

She saw it all and she smiled.

Then the blade met her skin.

CHAPTER 51

Help me.

The words echoed in Taro's head as he unsheathed Kusanagi, parried, pushed the closest samurai's sword off to the right and then sprang forward, running him through. Then he stumbled, unbalanced—he had tried to splay out his left arm, to steady himself, and had discovered again that it wasn't there.

Hiro, off to the side, caught the wrist of another samurai, pulled him past as he snapped the thin bones of the forearm, relieving the man of his sword in a smooth motion. Hiro stepped back, sword raised.

Taro could see Lord Tokugawa, sitting on the throne, smiling. Taro wanted nothing more than to reach the daimyo and wipe that smile off his face with a blow of his sword. But there were too many samurai—pressing in on him, swords flashing. Worse, he had a blind spot on one side, where his missing eye had been, and this was making it difficult to perceive how far away the opponents were. The samurai were cautious, though, harrying rather than going in boldly for a killing strike—and this was the only reason Taro was still alive. Worried about damaging Kusanagi, perhaps? Taro was not so proud as to think that they might fear him.

Sword moving nimbly to counter the various strikes, he moved backward, coordinating with Hiro through glances. They ended up back to back, each protecting the other's blind side. Their swords stood firm in their hands. For the moment, the soldiers didn't move, just surrounded them. Only two samurai were down—the one whose wrist Hiro had broken, who was cradling his arm, whimpering, and the one Taro had killed. As Taro watched, one of the other samurai sighed, and then brought his sword tip down on the fallen man's chest, stabbing it through, ending his murmurs of pain.

"It's been a privilege to have you as a friend," said Taro.

"I know," said Hiro.

Taro laughed—a short, hollow sound.

"Get on with it," said Lord Tokugawa, from the other end of the room. And with that, the samurai were on them for real, fighting in earnest now. Taro cursed. Where were those vampires? Just as he thought it, there was a clamor from the direction of the door they had come through earlier. The vampires burst in, catching the samurai off guard.

If it has the Tokugawa mon *on it*, thought Taro at the vampires, *kill it.*

After that, everything was chaos.

Some of the samurai broke off to head for the throne, to protect Lord Tokugawa.

Other samurai continued to harass Taro and Hiro. That was a mistake. Taking advantage of the general confusion, Taro flicked the sword from the hand of the man in front of him, then opened his chest. A thrill shot through him, something like the feeling of his first kiss with Hana.

It was Kusanagi. The sword was sweet as honey in his hand—its weight and balance and perfection like the touch of a loved one, like the smell of home.

As the samurai fell, Taro ducked to the side, severing the foot of his nearest companion. The sword was an extension of his hand, a feeling of clarity, sunshine on an autumn day. With it, he could not be defeated. The man toppled sideways. Taro jumped over him, bringing his sword up and down even as he flew through the air, and almost cut the next samurai in half diagonally, the sword entering at the shoulder and lodging in the hip. The man's legs gave way and his weight dropped, twisting the sword and catching it further. Taro's wrists sang out. Annoyed, he tugged hard on—

A blade bit into his left side. He hadn't seen it coming, his missing left eye cutting off a swath of his vision. With a yell, he finally got Kusanagi free from the dead man, who dropped to the ground. Taro reached out to snatch the sword from his hand, so he would have two, before remembering that he had lost his left hand to the dragon.

Spinning, he got his blade up before the killing blow severed his head. The samurai who had wounded his side was big, with a blotched face and a broken, swollen nose. He looked unwieldy—but Taro could see from the way his sword moved that he was not clumsy or slow. In fact, Taro struggled to hold off his blows, all the while glancing behind him to try to join up with Hiro again.

Hiro was holding his own against two samurai, his sword a blur. Most of the others were engaged with the vampires—the men and women were falling on them hungrily, viciously, and several samurai were on the ground, twitching as the vampires fed. But the samurai were trained killers, and they were armed. To Taro's horror, he saw that the vampires were being pressed back, and some were already dead, their heads separated from their bodies.

Clash.

The stocky samurai's sword rang against Kusanagi. He pressed forward, his own blade rasping down its length, unstoppable, coming to rest deep in Taro's knuckles, for Kusanagi had no pommel guard. Taro cried out. The *katana* scraped against the bone of his fingers. He could smell blood in the air; the room gave a little wobble.

He felt pressure against his back and flicked his one good eye to see that Hiro was with him again, still standing. Most of the vampires were not. The samurai were winning, inexorable, their swords and their years of kata drills more than a match for the newly turned vampires' strength and speed.

Remembering the door of the brothel, how he had shattered it with his leg, Taro raised his knee and kicked out. The samurai fell back, winded, his sword leaving the flesh of Taro's hand with a spurt of blood. Taro had a thought. He whipped his sword round, missing the samurai's head by a good margin. But that had been his intention. Following the arc of his strike, drops of his blood fanned out into the air. The samurai staggered backward, eyes closed, as the blood blinded him.

Taro didn't want to move too far from Hiro—he took just one step forward and effected a shallow slash that opened a horizontal wound in the big samurai's belly. The man fell, groaning.

On either side, samurai pressed in. Taro's head turned from side to side, like a crow's. He could take the left one first, since that was his weak side—then turn and—

"Taro."

It was Hiro's voice. Taro turned to look at his friend. His hands were empty, his sword on the ground. Two samurai held *katanas* pointing right at his throat. In his eyes was a wordless apology.

"It's all right," said Taro. He noticed that the samurai in front of him had stood down, their swords still up but not trying to strike him. He lowered Kusanagi. All around him were dead or dying vampires. Grief flooded him, like bile.

They would have died anyway, he told himself. *They would have died anyway.*

Footsteps creaked on the nightingale floor. The samurai in front of Taro parted, and there was Lord Tokugawa, still stained with the shogun's blood. He held his own sword in his hand—a masterpiece, Taro noticed, with the hollyhock *mon* engraved on its shaft. A cool blue wave of steel shone down its length.

"Give me Kusanagi," said the daimyo.

"You'll have to take it from my dead hand."

Lord Tokugawa nodded. "All right." He waved the samurai aside. "Kill the other one," he said. "I don't want any more complications." Taro felt Hiro backing away quickly behind him.

What happened next was a blur of movement—like a bat flitting in front of Taro's face, in semidarkness—and then a ringing in his arms, as Lord Tokugawa's blade smashed against his own. Taro's sword had only just gone up in time. He staggered backward.

He's a kensei, he thought. *Lord Tokugawa is a sword saint, and no one ever knew*. It wasn't surprising. There was a lot people didn't know about Lord Tokugawa.

Clash.

Taro parried the next two strokes, then felt a stinging, hot pain in his face—he had stopped a strike, only for Lord Tokugawa to flick his wrist up, bringing his sword raking across Taro's cheek. If he hadn't already lost his eye, he would have lost it then. Blood ran hotly down his face to his neck.

Lord Tokugawa grinned, sword balancing casually in his hand. He moved around Taro, keeping his distance now, showing Taro that he was in control of the fight. "Lord Oda liked to advertise his skill," he said. "People loved to challenge him, once it was known that he was a sword saint. And he loved being challenged. He loved the theater of it."

He drove forward suddenly, again the impression that of a pigeon surprised in a tree you're passing, a bat there in front of you and then gone. Taro just got a clumsy parry in the way, then stumbled, his ankle twisting. He scrabbled away, on his back, as Lord Tokugawa walked calmly toward him. He just got up to his feet and brought up his blade as the daimyo's whistled toward his neck. The blow resounded down his arms, right to his shoulders. Taro felt tired. So very tired.

"But this is the thing about the theater," said Lord Tokugawa, his breath not even straining. "It's the people behind the scenes who control everything. I am a better swordsman than Lord Oda. I say this not to brag. All those I have defeated were killed, and disposed of quietly. I didn't want anyone to know how good I was. That is the difference between me and Lord Oda."

"There is no difference between you and Lord Oda," Taro spat bitterly. He had thought his father would be a better man, not motivated in the same way by power. In the end, it seemed his father wanted power more than anyone.

Lord Tokugawa flickered forward. His blade met Taro's, upstretched from an awkward sitting position, and like the big samurai before him he scraped Taro's sword down to the pommel. Only he didn't cut Taro's fingers again—he twisted, and Kusanagi fell to the floor.

"You would never have beaten me," Lord Tokugawa said. "A fighter who fights because of *sakki*, because of bloodlust, can never defeat an opponent who is at one with *naige dajo*, the totality of things, who has come to see that object and subject are mere facets of the great everything. I know the secret of the sword. You do not. This is why I was always going to destroy you."

This was not, in fact, true, thought Taro. He *did* know the secret of the sword—the abbot had taught it to him, the previous year. He knew that he and the sword were one, or that neither he nor the sword existed, which amounts to the same thing, because all existence is an illusion. It was one thing to know it, though, another thing to truly understand it—and enlightenment is a hard thing to come by when you have lost an eye and a hand, when you are injured in the side and the face and the fingers, when you are a ninja spilling blood all over a ninja-proof floor.

But as Lord Tokugawa raised his sword for a final time, Taro lifted his hand. "Wait," he said. Lord Tokugawa stayed his blade, curious.

Taro was in no position, in this time and this place, to clear the anger and betrayal from his mind, to make himself at one with Kusanagi, even if the sword had been still in his hand. But there was one way in which he had achieved oneness, again and again, in the last few months. There was a shortcut to enlightenment. Smiling, he thought of how he had traveled into death to look for his mother, and again to rescue Hana, and wandered there forever, and when he came out he had not been gone a moment.

"You can kill me," he said. "But give me one moment. As a favor to your son."

Curtly, Lord Tokugawa nodded.

Taro reached his hand into his cloak and seized the ball.

And then, for the last time, he was no longer in the realm of humans and beasts but was falling through the infinite sky.

CHAPTER 52

When he came over the bridge, he saw Shusaku immediately, sitting on the seat of Enma, Horse-head and Ox-face beside him. The ninja seemed at ease, comfortable in his new role. When Taro stepped off the jewel-sparkling bridge, though, Shusaku leaped to his feet.

"No . . . Taro . . . It's too soon. . . ."

Taro waved a hand. "I'm not dead," he said, and the bitterness must have been apparent in his voice, because Shusaku took a step back.

"What's wrong?"

Taro let his eye rest on the gray expanse of death, colorless sky, and leaden ground, and he felt that this landscape was only an extension of the one inside him. "You betrayed me," he said. "Lord Tokugawa told me. You knew that he'd planned everything, from the start."

"I don't know what you're talking about," said Shusaku.

Taro snorted. "I'm talking about him conceiving me deliberately, because he needed the son of an ama to get the Buddha ball. I'm talking about him getting the prophetess to lie to me, to tell me I was destined to be shogun, so that I would be sure to go after the ball. I'm talking about him sending me to find Kusanagi, so that he could use it to claim the throne."

Shusaku raised his hands. *"What?"* he said.

Taro shook his head. "You don't have to lie anymore. It doesn't matter. Back in the other realm, my father is about to cut off my head."

"N-no," stammered Shusaku. "No, it cannot be." Oddly, he seemed genuinely upset. "No, I have served him all my life. He welcomed me when my own father pledged to another lord, he kept me on even when he knew I was tainted, I was turned. . . ."

The terrible possibility that Lord Tokugawa had lied to him, again, blossomed in Taro like a malignant flower opening. "If you're telling the truth," Taro said, "then Lord Tokugawa did not do those things out of kindness. He did them because you were useful to him."

Shusaku rubbed his eyes. Because of Lord Tokugawa he had lost his sight, he had been burned nearly to death, he had been slaughtered and skinned by Kenji Kira. Taro could only imagine what he was feeling. "I'm so sorry, Taro," he said eventually. "You deserved better from your own father."

"Yes," said Taro simply.

A cast of determination came over Shusaku's face then. He pointed into death. "Come with me," he said. "There is someone we should talk to. At the least, she can confirm that I knew nothing of Lord Tokugawa's plans."

Taro followed. Horse-head and Ox-face turned their heads, silent, to watch ninja and pupil stride deeper into death.

Though Taro had been to death several times now, he could never get used to it—they walked for a period of time that could have been vast, or short, and they crossed landscapes that could have been mountains or deserts or even seas. The experience was of being in a trance, or a dream only half remembered. When finally they stood in the hell realm of *meifumado*, he was not even sure if they had walked at all.

They passed demons and the dead, locked in eternal cycles of awful punishment. Taro tried to keep his good eye ahead, not to look to the side, but he did, of course he did, and he knew that the images would stay with him forever. Finally they came to a place where a demon was dragging the fingernails from a woman. Shusaku turned to Taro. "This is the part of hell reserved for traitors," he said. Then he gestured for the demon to stop.

"Shusaku," said the woman, looking up. Her eyes were black and endless with pain.

"Prophetess," said Shusaku.

The woman turned to look at Taro.

"Ah. And Taro. Has he killed you, then?"

Taro already knew his father was a monster. Somehow, though, this casual confirmation of it struck him like a blow. "No. He's about to."

"So how—"

"The Buddha ball."

She nodded. "You did well to recover it."

"I thought it was my destiny," said Taro, putting an accent on the word "destiny."

"Indeed," she replied. Her voice was cracked with agony, like a cup shot through with barely visible, jagged lines of stress. Taro noticed, however, that her nails had already grown back. She would suffer this punishment again and again, and before each time she would be made new. "My fault, of course."

"What about Shusaku?" said Taro, trying to ignore the ninja—now the judge of death—standing beside him. "Did he know it was a lie?"

She looked genuinely surprised. "No. Of course not. He always loved Lord Tokugawa, like I did. But we were different. He loved what he *believed* Lord Tokugawa to be. I knew what he really was, and I loved him anyway."

“And what is he really?”

“Evil. Brilliant. Cold. A man who loves nothing but his own mind.”

“So you loved him, but you knew he could never love you back?”

She looked at him, infinite tenderness in her eyes. “Yes. I think you know how that feels.”

Taro turned away, uncomfortable. In his mind, Hana was always turned half away from him, light falling on her eye, part of her cheek, her hair obscuring the rest. He heard her voice sometimes, indistinguishable from his own thoughts. The sun on rice paddies, the sea at dawn, the dew in the mountains, all carried her scent. “Why would he tell me Shusaku betrayed me?” he asked, turning the subject back to Shusaku.

She shrugged. “To hurt you, I suppose. He enjoys that. No—that’s not quite right. He is not a *cruel* man. He is curious. He likes to see how people react to things. He likes to manipulate. Were you armed when he told you this, were you trying to fight?”

“Yes.”

“Then I imagine he told you to break your equilibrium. To make you angry. To fill you with *sakki*, instead of calmness. To blind you with bloodlust.”

Taro looked at her. He could see, from her expression, that she had known Lord Tokugawa a long time, that she had seen him do terrible things, many of them, no doubt. All of a sudden he knew she was telling the truth.

“Thank you,” he said. He touched Shusaku’s shoulder. “Must she stay here?” he asked. “Can’t you forgive her?”

Shusaku sighed sadly. “It is not so simple, I’m afraid. She lied for Lord Tokugawa. She is therefore condemned to *meifumado*. It is a thing I cannot change. There are forces more powerful than me.”

“He’s right,” said the woman. “Leave me. I will beg forgiveness. It’s all I can do now. And besides—even the lowest can rise again through the wheel of samsara, if they accumulate good karma.”

"Then I wish you luck," said Taro. He realized that he was crying.

"And I thank you."

They turned to leave, and Taro linked his arm with that of Shusaku, the man who, along with Hiro, was the closest thing he possessed to family, and behind them they heard her begin to scream.

CHAPTER 53

When Taro snapped into the ordinary realm again, Lord Tokugawa's sword was still raised. Stupid. How long did the daimyo think it would take to swing that blade through all that dead, slow, treacly air?

There was no anger in Taro anymore, no bloodlust. The realm of *meifumado* still lingered all around him, wisps of gray mist. He had been served an undeniable reminder of the transience of all things.

Thought and action separated by nothing at all, he rolled to the side, over wooden floor that didn't really exist, through air that wasn't really there. He snatched up the illusory sword and jumped to his feet—or perhaps it would be more accurate to say that the sword entered his hand and he was standing, all at once, because a person observing would have seen no movement.

Lord Tokugawa's blade moved painfully slowly through the air. Taro watched it with something like contempt. He imagined himself behind the daimyo, and then that was where he was; he allowed Kusanagi to strike out, snakelike, shallow. Lord Tokugawa's strike was still arcing down in front of him; Taro was not even sure he was yet aware that his target had moved. Kusanagi cut through the ligaments at the back of Lord Tokugawa's knee. The older man pitched forward, stopping himself from landing on his face by putting out his left hand. Taro heard his wrist snap.

There was a clatter like the sound of enormous drums, as the sword in Lord Tokugawa's hand fell to the wood. Taro kicked it, and it went spinning off across the floor. A samurai moved toward him. He raised Kusanagi and glared a warning. The man stopped.

He thought himself next to Lord Tokugawa's sprawling form. He hauled the daimyo to his knees and rested the blade of Kusanagi against the back of his neck.

"You told me the abbot was one of your agents," he said. "In that case, why do you suppose he taught me the secret of the sword?"

Lord Tokugawa sucked in breath, surprised. Taro had guessed right. He didn't know what the abbot's motivation had been—perhaps he was hedging his bets, uncomfortable with the idea of all the country's power being in one man's hands. The monks had always resisted the samurai. Or perhaps it had simply amused him to give Taro the same weapon he'd given to his father.

"If you knew it," said Lord Tokugawa, "why did you let me unarm you?"

"You made me angry," said Taro. "That was good. It nearly made you win."

"Nearly?"

"But you also lied to me. That was stupid. You don't really know what the Buddha ball can do, do you?"

Lord Tokugawa looked at him, uncomprehending. It was pathetic, really.

"I'm going to kill you now," said Taro.

"Please," said Lord Tokugawa. "Allow me seppuku."

Taro thought of Kawabata Senior, who had asked the same thing after betraying him to Lord Oda. "No," he said.

Lord Tokugawa took a long, ratcheting breath.

Taro raised Kusanagi—

—and stopped.

He looked for Hiro; saw him being held by two samurai. "Release my friend," he said. He beckoned Hiro to come forward. What felt like an eternity later, his best friend was standing beside him.

"Kill him," said Hiro. There was no forgiveness in his voice.

Taro wavered. He still had that image of Hana in his head from when he had been in hell, or that impression of her, because it was an image made of light and sound and smell. He felt almost as if she were trying to tell him something. It was as if there was a word, right there at the front of his mind, on the tip of his tongue, that he couldn't quite recall.

Just get on with it, he thought. *Kill Lord Tokugawa. Run. Get out of here with Hiro. If you're lucky, you'll get past all those samurai. . . .*

But *would* they get past them all, even now, even now that he had regained the secret of the sword?

Perhaps not. And even then, if they did escape, or if he laid claim to the throne, what then? A thought that had been lurking at the back of Taro's mind, in the dark, stepped forward into the light. It was hideous, a grotesque thought, upsetting to him, and that was why he had locked it in the darkness.

The thought was: *I took those people from the brothel and made them my slaves. They were addicts, yes, they would have died eventually, but I took away their choice.*

Was that what being shogun would be like? Only instead of a brothel where people were fed on by vampires, it would be the whole country. . . . Everyone in his power, everyone forced to do his bidding. Of course, he'd set out to do the right thing, everyone did. But what about the times when circumstances arrayed themselves against him? All it had taken was an attack by *yakuza* to make him steal the lives from those poor vampire addicts, to turn them into a private corps of bodyguards, totally subject to his will. One little threat to his life, and he had taken away theirs.

His skin crawled with revulsion.

It struck him then that power might not be a good thing, not a good thing at all.

Then, suddenly, and for no reason he could think of, the image of Kenji Kira flashed in front of his eyes. And a voice, echoing in his head.

Anyone who claims the sword pays with the thing they love.

I will remain in your mind forever.

An idea began to form. Could he do this? Would it work? It was worth a try.

He let the blade rest, ever so lightly, on the daimyo's skin. He could only imagine how cold and hard it felt, how final. "Send your samurai away," he said. "Tell them we are not to be harmed. If you do that, I may let you live."

Lord Tokugawa didn't look up, but a shaky breath escaped his lips, the breath of one who has lived by a code of honor, of bravery, all his life, and who has just realized that survival makes honor an object of ridicule, an irrelevance. Taro knew that feeling well. Knew that any living thing will give up all his honor for one more day of life. Lord Tokugawa was no different.

"You heard him," said Lord Tokugawa loudly. "Get out of here. Don't come back." Taro watched as the samurai backed away toward the door, vacating the room.

Taro raised Kusanagi a fraction, so that it was hovering above the daimyo's neck. "I am thinking of giving you this sword," he said. "So that you can be emperor."

"What?" said Hiro. "Taro, I—"

Taro raised a hand. He gave Hiro a look they had used all their lives, when they were in difficult situations and could not speak freely. It was a look that said, *Trust me*.

Hiro shut up.

"Why—why would you do that?" said Lord Tokugawa. All the arrogance had gone from his voice.

"You're my father," said Taro. "Despite everything you have done." He was surprised to see, then, that a tear was rolling down Lord Tokugawa's cheek. It hit the wooden floor with a boom. Thin beams of light shafted in through the closed shutters, motes of dust dancing within them, like living things. Silence spread in a thick pool from where the three of them stood.

“You have conditions,” said Lord Tokugawa. It wasn’t a question.

“Yes. First, you will leave the Buddha ball with me. I have tried to use it, to give rain to the rice crops. It only flooded those in the lower valley, spreading death and destruction. If you attempt to use it for gain, to increase your rice yields, it will end in disaster. Also, you will waive the rice tax for all peasants affected by the drought. Your agents will conduct a survey: Any who are starving will be allowed to keep their own rice. You will treat the peasants fairly. You will have to, because I will be watching you.”

“Agreed,” said Lord Tokugawa, his voice strained.

“There are only two more conditions.”

“Yes?”

“I defeated the dragon. You will give me the rank of daimyo, and a province of my own.”

“Very well.”

“I haven’t finished yet. I have a particular province in mind.”

“Go on.” Through gritted teeth.

“Shirahama. It was Lord Oda’s, so you own it now. You will give me the land, the title, and all the wealth associated with it. When I have left here, you will draw up the paperwork. You can send it to me care of the abbot, at Mount Hiei.”

Lord Tokugawa nodded fractionally. “Done. And your final condition?”

“It’s not so much a condition,” said Taro. “More a necessity. You see, I cannot give you the sword. You must *claim* it.”

“I must . . .”

“Claim it. You must speak the words.” Somehow, Taro knew this to be true. “You must say, ‘*I, Lord Tokugawa, claim Kusanagi from Taro.*’ Say it.”

Taro’s true father hesitated, almost as if he feared the trick, knew that there must be one. He was the master manipulator, Taro supposed. After all, he planned in years, not weeks or months. He must know that this was foolish, and yet he didn’t want to die, and Taro understood that, too. The urge for survival was stronger than all other things, stronger than honor, stronger than pride, stronger than bravery.

He pictured Hana again.

But not stronger than love.

Only—and this was the key—

Only . . .

Lord Tokugawa did not understand love.

The kneeling daimyo looked over to the throne. Blood was pooling under his severed knee. The shogun's blood still dripped from the ornate chair—*tap, tap, tap*. "Very well," he said. "I, Lord Tokugawa, claim Kusanagi from Taro."

Taro wasn't sure if it was his imagination—no, that was a lie, he *knew* it wasn't, knew this was real—but there was a sudden sensation of weight lifting, the room suddenly growing brighter. He felt rather than heard the dragon of the sea chuckling in his mind.

"Good," he said. "Take it then." He dropped the sword beside the miserable figure of his kneeling father, and then he turned, Hiro behind him, and walked out of the room, never to return.

CHAPTER 54

SHIRAHAMA

TWO WEEKS LATER

Taro and Hiro walked round the headland, the scent of pine in their nostrils. Any moment now and there would come a break in the trees, and they would see Shirahama bay laid out before them, the sea sparkling, like a promise. Taro remembered the other times he had come back—when he was looking for the ball, when he was looking for Kusanagi. Both those times he had been desperate, afraid, following another path that he knew would take him away again.

This time was different.

This time he was coming home.

A rabbit, startled, shot off into the undergrowth. Taro thought of the day the ninjas came to Shirahama, when all of this had started—how he had killed a rabbit that afternoon, was looking forward to eating it with his mother. Two years later and his mother was dead, and he had done little killing since that day, apart from men.

Just then the trees thinned, and a moment later they were on the bluff, looking down at the beach and the huts. The fishing boats were bobbing at anchor in the bay, unused. Well, that was the first thing Taro would change.

Hiro put his arm around his shoulders. "I can't believe we wanted to leave so much," he said.

"We wanted adventure," said Taro.

"And now?"

"Now I would be happy never to have another adventure in my life." He had come to know that adventure was not as it was described in stories: It was cruel, and bloody, and not everyone made it to the end. He felt that it wasn't just him and Hiro standing here, among the roots of the cedars, with the land falling away in front of them to sunlit sea—there were the shades of his mother, too, Shusaku, Heiko, Yukiko, the prophetess. All of them sharing this moment, this homecoming, this end to the horror of a real-life adventure.

The priest must have seen them up there on the high headland, because as they made their way through the dunes to the outskirts of the village, passing the shrine to the Princess of the Hidden Waters, he came to greet them.

"Taro!" he said, coming forward. Taro was surprised by how pleased he was to see the old man. "You did come back," the priest continued.

"Yes. Is Hana still here?"

The priest winced. "Yes."

"She is not well?"

"She's well. For a vampire." The priest smiled at Taro's discomfort. "It's all right; she told me everything. I don't have the same views as some on the subject, and I don't blame you for what you did. You did it to save her. I just don't know if she will want to see you—I don't know if she can forgive you for it."

"He saved her life!" said Hiro, indignant.

"She's a samurai," said the priest, shrugging. "They spend half their lives training to die. She probably thought that was the honorable thing."

Sadness and loneliness—a feeling like standing outside in the cold—spread over Taro. He fought the feeling away. He had to believe that what he had done with Lord Tokugawa, his attempt to pass on the curse, had worked. He had to cling to that idea, as he had clung to the wreckage of Kenji Kira's ship, in this very bay.

He reached into his cloak and took out a drawstring bag, which he threw to the priest. The priest caught it—he might have been a temple official, but he was a fisherman and a farmer, too. "What's this?"

"That's payment for your lost boat. I did promise."

The priest shook his head, embarrassed. "I can't take—I mean—" No, that wasn't just embarrassment. That was pain. As if he didn't want to give offense, but . . .

Suddenly Taro understood. "You think it's stolen," he said. The priest always listened more than he talked, and observed even more than he listened. He knew Taro was a vampire, that he had turned Hana. No doubt, despite the priest's kindness, Taro would need to work to prove the kind of man he truly was, despite his *kyuuketsuki* nature.

"It isn't?" The priest's tone wasn't judgmental, just interested.

"No."

"Taro has rather a lot of money now," said Hiro.

"Ah! You defeated the dragon!" said the priest. Taro had not mentioned it to him, but he supposed the rumor of the reward must have reached Shirahama, too.

"I did," said Taro. "And the new emperor gave me a province. I will be living there from now on. But not in a palace. In a village, as an ordinary person."

The priest smiled a wan smile. "So," he said. "Another flying visit? Hana is still living in your mother's hut, if you want to visit her. How long will you stay this time?" There was a tinge of disappointment in his voice.

"Forever," said Taro.

"For—"

"Ever," said Hiro. "See, Taro is daimyo of *this* province."

The priest stared for a moment, eyes wide open. Then, instinctively, he began to bow, but Taro put his hand on the man's arm, stopping him. "Don't bow to me," he said. "I should be bowing to you. You're my elder, and a priest."

"But you're a lord. . . ."

"Only in name. Actually, I plan to live in my mother's hut. I may fish, a little. Occasionally I will need to go to the castle, to settle disputes and so forth. But I'm hoping"—he was hoping Hana would be by his side, would give him the benefit of her wisdom and humor, her experience as the daughter of a daimyo—"I'm hoping someone will help me."

The priest was smiling now. He clapped his hands together. "This is wonderful!" he said. "But I'm holding you up. You will want to go to your hut now." He pointed toward the shrine of the Princess. "I was heading that way. I will see you later. Perhaps you'll eat with me tonight, both of you?"

"It would be our pleasure," said Hiro.

After that they carried on, until the scrubland of the dunes gave way to hard sand, and then to the rocky path that led up into the heart of the village. Taro's heart was beating a tattoo in his chest. He didn't notice Hiro falling back, but suddenly he realized that he was walking on his own. He turned—Hiro was facing out to sea, arms crossed. When he saw Taro looking back, he waved him on.

He's always been my best friend, thought Taro. *He knows what to do without even asking.*

Alone, he followed the path up to his mother's hut, where he had spent all his early life. He thought of the last time he had done this, at night that time, when the light had been on inside and he had imagined that he was a ghost at *obon*, come back to haunt the living. That time, Hana had thrown him out. Had told him she hated him. And then he had tried to force her to come with him.

Would she forgive him that?

There was another question, which he could hardly bear to acknowledge, and which went beyond forgiveness. Could she ever love him again, now that he had turned her, made her into a monster, as she saw it?

There was only one way to find out.

He raised his hand to knock on the door, and his hand fell into empty space because the door was already opening, and Hana was standing there. She was more beautiful than he had remembered, than he could have possibly imagined. Her eyes were gray in the afternoon light, clear, framed by soft, dark eyelashes. Her skin, which had been pale, was a little tanned by the sun and sea air. She had been turned by him and so, like him, she could go out in the light, even if she was a vampire. She wore her hair pinned up loosely, in the peasant fashion.

"Taro," she said. Her tone was neutral, giving nothing away. She glanced at his missing eye, raked her eyes down him, taking in his scars, the hand he'd lost to the dragon. "You killed the dragon?"

"Yes."

"You won the prize?"

"Not exactly."

"Ah. Poor Taro. And you paid dearly." There was some accusation in her voice—but did he detect a little tenderness, too? He wasn't sure whether he was imagining it. He wasn't sure what was real and what was not.

He closed his eye for a moment, gathering his strength. "I'm sorry for everything," he said. When he opened his eye again, she was looking at him steadily, though a muscle twitched by her eye.

"Is that it?" she said.

He took a deep breath. "No. I also wanted to say . . ." He remembered her walking toward him after she'd wrestled that peasant who had tried to rob them to the ground. "I wanted to say, I think you're amazing."

She rolled her eyes. "Didn't I tell you, when we first left Edo, I would drop you in the mud if you carried on?" she said.

"You did."

"And yet here you are. You brought me back from the dead, made me a vampire, just to tell me I'm amazing?"

"No," said Taro. "I did it so that I could tell you I love you."

There was a dreadful, silent pause. She was still gazing at him steadily, without expression. Then she gave a very slight smile. "You know," she said, "blood is not so bad, once you get used to it."

"No," he said. "No, it's not." Hope was a driftwood fire in his chest, holding back the night, holding back the black.

"But what about you?" she asked. "I mean to stay here—I've come to love the sea and the people. You wouldn't like it. You need adventure."

He touched his left eye socket, raised his stump of an arm. "I don't think I could survive any more adventure," he said.

She looked again at his injuries. "Perhaps you're right," she said. "You're happy, though, to be a poor peasant, for the rest of your life? With a poor peasant wife, who used to be a samurai?"

"Well," said Taro. "Not exactly. I need to talk to you about that."

"About what?"

"It can wait a moment. First things first. Didn't you just propose to me?"

She frowned. "What? No."

"You did. You called yourself my poor peasant wife."

"Oh no—I was talking about someone else—some other woman—"

"I *was* surprised to hear your proposal," he said. "Because you did tell me that you never wanted to marry a daimyo. You were very specific about it."

"Well, yes. But that was my father's dream. It's not likely to come about now."

He smiled. "You might be surprised," he said. He handed her a scroll, which she unrolled. He watched as she scanned the kanji characters.

"You're—but you said you didn't win the prize. . . . I mean, this is just unbelievable, it's—"

He cut her off by kissing her. He thought she might push him away, or punch him playfully.

She didn't.

She melted into his arms, and he knew he really was home.

She pulled away finally.

"It's strange," she said. "I was so angry with you. I really hated you. But then, two weeks ago, it just went. And all that was left was the memory of you saving me, the thought of our time together. If the dragon had killed you, it would have broken my heart."

Taro smiled. The curse really was lifted. He had passed it on, to his father. For an instant he wondered if he should feel guilty about that. No. If anyone deserved to lose the one thing that made them happy, it was Lord Tokugawa Ieyasu.

"Just to be clear," he said. "You will marry me?"

She did punch him playfully then. "Of course I will."

They went into his mother's hut, and before the door was even closed their hands found each other. They performed a trick, then, a sort of meditation or accomplishment of enlightenment; they made the rest of the world fall away from around them, Shirahama, the sea, the cedar trees and the wind, all disintegrating to leave nothing at all in all the realms of samsara but these three things: them, their bodies, their love.

And he bit her, yes, he bit her.

But she bit him, too.

CHAPTER 55

THE PALACE OF LONG LIFE, EDO

TEN YEARS LATER

Emperor Tokugawa Ieyasu leaned back and closed his eyes. Another interminable session on the throne, listening to the petty grievances and pointless disputes of the peasantry. He got up and beckoned for Jun to come with him, for a private conferral. Good old Jun. The boy was loyal, he had to give him that. Well, loyal in that he would stay with Emperor Tokugawa until someone more powerful came along, and Emperor Tokugawa could understand that. He respected it, even.

He longed for a battle, but by now the whole country had been subdued, all its daimyo brought under his control. Taro among them, of course—and in this way Emperor Tokugawa saw his son relatively frequently, the boy coming to Edo for ceremonial events, discussions of outside threats, what to do about Christianity, whether to let it spread or cut it out like a canker; that kind of thing.

Not that Taro appeared to consider himself still Lord Tokugawa's son, and really, who could blame him? He never stayed, after a recital of the sutras, or whatever it was he had come to the capital to attend. He and Hana, his wife, would bow just as low as convention required, to an emperor, and they would smile, but there was nothing behind those smiles. They paid the exact amount of respect that was required—just as they paid the rice taxes for their provinces—and then they left.

Well.

Emperor Tokugawa had ordered the boy killed, after all. He could hardly blame Taro for not loving him as a father.

And he had Jun. He would always have Jun. Not a son, maybe, not even a friend, when it came to it—but an ally, a confidant.

Until someone more powerful came along.

Cursing, he drew his katana *and slashed the tapestry hanging in the corridor he was walking down. Curse it all. He had tamed the wild monks of Monto; he had orchestrated the death of Lord Oda and the absorption of all his land and men; he had engineered, in a plan that took nearly twenty years to come to fruition, the seizure of the entire country.*

But he had lost his son in the process.

Not only that, he was slowly starting to realize, but he had lost the plotting *in the process. The problem with scheming for years to take power was that once you had taken power, there was no more scheming to be done, not really. There was low-level stuff, of course—the kind of thing he was soon to speak to Jun about. Intrigues and manipulations that were necessary to keep his grip on the daimyo. Occasionally some jumped-up lord would decide that it was wise to conceal a gold mine on his land, or divert taxes to the building of an unlicensed castle. One of the first things Emperor Tokugawa had done was to demolish any castles that could be used for military purposes. That, and force the eldest son of every samurai family to come into his service.*

Yes, there were things to be done. But none of them gave him the satisfaction, the thrill, of the plan that had brought him here in the first place.

And then, apart from those rare games, the rest of the time was spent in the terribly dull business of making the country work better. In Edo he was celebrated not as the hero who had rid the country of illicit rule by pretenders, the bearer of the legendary sword Kusanagi, but as the man who had introduced bell towers, regularly spaced around the city, to warn in case of fire. Five times in as many years Edo had been leveled by fire before Lord Tokugawa's time—now it had not burned at all in ten.

In this way, his reputation had slowly become that of a sensible, intelligent, just ruler, if a little prone to extravagant displays of his own power. It was enough to make him sick. Had he tortured and executed his peasants, for no real reason other than pleasure, as Oda had? Had he made them starve, as the shogun had, by raising exorbitant taxes on rice?

No.

And yet they would never love him.

He thought of Taro. Lord Shirahama no Taro, as he was now called. Somehow—though Taro swore he had never spoken of it—rumors had spread quickly that it was Taro who'd killed the dragon, Taro who had recovered Kusanagi from the sea, where it had been lost with the last Heike emperor.

And so in this way, at the same time, Taro's reputation had grown to be that of a hero, pride of the nation, young and humble—a symbol, with his cursed insistence on living in that fishing hut with his beautiful wife and their beautiful children, of the resilience and simplicity and tranquility that the Japanese seemed to think was their national character, despite it having been Emperor Tokugawa's experience that they needed only the faintest of pretexts to slaughter one another in the name of grasping a little more land, a little more influence.

Taro?

He, they loved. He who had given up everything—he had been rewarded with the love of Lady Hana, the love of the country. Emperor Tokugawa had never even spoken to the children, his grandchildren—usually Taro and Hana left them in Shirahama, and when they were brought to Edo, they were kept away from him. As if he might infect them with his coldness. Which was probably true, now he came to think of it. Hadn't he turned away everyone who had ever loved him? The prophetess, Taro? Even Shusaku, in the end—he had betrayed the man's memory by lying to Taro about him, just so that Taro would be unbalanced, just so that the fight would go out of the boy.

Curse them. Curse Taro. Curse everyone.

He came to a wooden door, opened it. His vision was a little blurred, and he had to blink to clear it.

Inside, Jun was already sitting at a map that was spread out on the desk, drawn in the Dutch style. Emperor Tokugawa had confined the Dutch to an island just off the coast at Nagasaki, not allowing them onto the hallowed soil of Japan. Not because he particularly cared about that hallowed soil, or its supposed defilement by the foreigners—he thought their diet disgusting, but in most respects they were just as base and greedy and weak as the Japanese, no more so—but because he didn't want any of the daimyo learning of their advances in war, medicine, or science, lest they use them against him.

He, of course, made use of them all the time.

"We think the illegal gold mine is—" Jun broke off, staring up at him. His finger wavered above the map.

"What is it?" said Emperor Tokugawa. His voice sounded croaky to his ears.

"It's . . . your face," said Jun. He touched his cheeks, as if trying to show Lord Tokugawa where he had some dirt that he should rub off.

Emperor Tokugawa raised his hands to his face and gasped. It was wet! Then he understood. The difficulty seeing; the blurred quality to the room.

He was crying.

CHAPTER 56

TWO HUNDRED YEARS LATER, OR TWO THOUSAND

Shusaku turned his back on the new Enma. He had known, somehow, when he judged this one, that the man was good, that he was the right candidate to replace him—and the voice in his head, which he increasingly recognized as that of *dharma* itself, the harmony of all things, had agreed. That same voice had answered when he asked where he should go now, what he should do; saying that he should walk on into the grayness, and he would know soon where he was going.

He walked over deserts; he walked over seas.

Before long, though—or perhaps after long, it was difficult to tell—Shusaku found himself on a mountainside he recognized. There was a castle, farther up. There were cedar trees, wreathed in mist. Far below, thin rivers stretched like jewels, like silver chains, through valleys of startling green.

He was in Monto territory, once again. It was exactly as he remembered, only there were no people, no Tokugawa samurai milling around, no cook fires pluming into the sky from the Monto stronghold above. There was only the singing of nightingales in the trees, the heart-soothing and continual creaking of the crickets in the grass.

He wasn't sure where he was going. He walked to Lord Tokugawa's tent, found nothing but the daimyo's belongings laid out—weapons, writing brushes; both of which, in Lord Tokugawa's case, amounted to the same thing, for he had used both to kill and subdue, to effect his conquest of the country. Shusaku had experienced the pleasure, some decades or hundreds of years before, of personally leading Emperor Tokugawa to hell.

Emperor Tokugawa plans in years, was a thing had people said about him. Well, now he would have an eternity to enjoy the fruits of his plans. To discuss them with the demons who tormented him. Shusaku smiled at the thought, though there was a little sadness there too. He was not so naive as not to recognize that a part of him still loved Lord Tokugawa, despite what he had done to betray him, to betray Taro.

He turned his back on the daimyo's tent, on the scene of all that plotting and scheming, and went out again into the late summer day. Maybe that was the worst punishment for Lord Tokugawa—here was Shusaku, a vampire, walking in sunlight touched with the smells of the forest, enjoying the sounds of birds and insects, while his old protector and employer roasted in *meifumado*.

Shusaku bent down to touch a blade of dew-kissed grass. He had been so long in the all-pervading gray of death that he had forgotten what grass looked like, what it felt like. He plucked a flower, raised it to his lips, let a drop of dew fall into his mouth. The joy of the world exploded there, on his tongue.

This is heaven, he allowed himself to think. He had known it, from the moment he came onto the mountaintop. Admitting it was a different thing, though. Only . . . if it was heaven . . .

If it was heaven, then where were the people?

He let the flower fall to the ground, imagined that he heard it booming in its impact. No—he couldn't have come this far, only to find that he had gone no distance at all. Could he?

Then, from the east, came the soft sound of singing—a sad ballad, of the kind the ninja clans sing, for they know that life for them is cruel, and must take place in darkness.

He knew at that moment where he had to go. He walked past the tents of the army, all empty, and the unoccupied stables where the horses had been rested before battle. Flowers were growing everywhere—poppies, daisies.

Eventually he reached his own tent. He recognized it by the Endo *mon* flying on a flag over the top—he recognized it because it had been the scene of his dreams, all his life. His heart fluttered in his chest—free and tied, at the same time, just like the flag.

He drew closer.

He saw the outline of a woman, waiting by the tent.

He walked toward her, and the sun caught the trees at that moment, came slanting down, that buttery afternoon light in late summer that would sometimes make his breath stop in his chest, filling him with a sensation that was neither happiness nor sadness but just the deep and all-encompassing recognition of the holiness of the world, the oneness of all things. Some of that buttery light fell on her face, too, half-obscured by her long black hair, and she was lost to him in a blaze of gold that came down from the perfectly clear sky, blinding him, making a flared corona around her, bathing her in glory.

She was in sunshine, and it was not hurting her.

And then she stepped forward and resolved out of the glare, fully illuminated now, so beautiful that for a moment he forgot how to speak. She had been in his mind for so long, and now she was in front of him, and he was tongue-tied, useless.

He remembered how she would come to him at night, through his shoji door, how she would lie in the dark beside him, and he would feel that nothing could harm him. He saw her—this beautiful woman—and at the same time he knew her bravery, knew that she had saved his life in a forest clearing, turning him into a vampire, and that she'd saved Lord Tokugawa, too, and had been killed for it by Kenji Kira.

She was a marvel.

"How long have you been here?" he asked eventually.

Mara smiled. She wore a chain of flowers around her neck, he noticed—she had pinned up her hair with pine needles.

"Forever," she said. She took him by the hand, led him through the shoji door into his old tent; it was exactly as he remembered it.

"And how long can we stay?" he asked her.

She smiled again. He thought he would never get used to the sight of that smile, the small miracle of it.

"Forever," she said.

Acknowledgments

As always, I'd like to thank the people who helped this book through its various drafts. Caradoc King, Elinor Cooper, Louise Lamont, Alexandra Cooper and Amy Rosenbaum all made excellent suggestions, and are in no way responsible for any mistakes that I made. A special shout-out too, to Liam Curren, who helped me research the rice harvesting songs of feudal Japanese peasants.